P9-CDT-126

BEYOND THE
BLACK
DOOR

FIFTY EIGHT

BEYOND THE BLACK DOOR

A.M. STRICKLAND

[Imprint]
MAKE YOUR MARK
NEW YORK

[Imprint]
MAKE YOUR MARK

A part of Macmillan Publishing Group, LLC
120 Broadway, New York, NY 10271

Library of Congress Cataloging-in-Publication Data is available.

ISBN 978-1-250-19874-7 (hardcover) / ISBN 978-1-250-19875-4 (ebook)

Our books may be purchased in bulk for promotional, educational, or business use. Please contact
your local bookseller or the Macmillan Corporate and Premium Sales Department at
(800) 221-7945 ext. 5442 or by email at MacmillanSpecialMarkets@macmillan.com.

Book design by Elynn Cohen

Soul chart art © 2019 by AdriAnne Strickland

Imprint logo designed by Amanda Spielman

First edition, 2019

1   3   5   7   9   10   8   6   4   2

fiercereads.com

Steal not this book, dearest reader,
By hands, piracy, or other means foul,
Elsewise face the wrath of the gods,
Or, worse yet, set Darkness on the prowl.

*To Terran, knight in shining armor, for opening many
doors with me, but also for walking through a few
big ones on your own. You're an inspiration.*

1

BURNING CURIOSITY

I was five the first time I asked my mother about the black door. The moment seared itself into my memory.

We were walking together through her soul, my hand in hers, the deep blue tiles of the place that was both hers and *her* as cool as water beneath my silk-slippered feet.

We'd done this for as long as I could remember, exploring her soul while our bodies slumbered, our spirits free to traverse the sleeping realm to which souls belonged. My mother would explain how people such as us—soulwalkers—could wander souls by night, and she would describe the gods. And yet she never mentioned the black door I always found in her soul.

On this particular night, I finally gathered my courage and stopped in the wide hallway, pointing. "Mama, what is that door?"

In my mother's soul, the sandstone halls were rosy, lit as if a fireplace burned merrily next to every stretch of wall. There was no fire; it was my mother's warmth, *her* light. The walls were pale and smooth, perforated with airy latticework that revealed the glow of rooms beyond, as if there were nothing to hide here, while the long hallways with deep azure tiles beckoned like fingers, hinting at wonders just out of sight.

But the black door was closed tight. Its sleek black surface parted the creamy sandstone of the wall like a slick dark stone in bright water, the sinuous lines of its frame meeting in a point at the apex. It gleamed like midnight fire. Despite seeming to draw in the light around it, it lured me like a candle's flame.

By then I'd learned that fire would burn me . . . but only through touching it several times already. I'd never touched the black door, and I wanted to.

This dark, tantalizing danger didn't seem to belong in my mother's bright, inviting soul. My mother, her eyes narrowing, stared at the door for a moment, her jaw clenched, a look on her beautiful face like I'd never seen. There was resolve, anger, and yes, fear. I'd never before seen my mother afraid.

Turning away, she knelt before me, took both my hands, and said very seriously, "Kamai, you can never open that door. It's best if you just forget about it."

"But, Mama, you said I could go anywhere in your sleep house."

A smile tugged at her mouth. "My soul house, not my 'sleep house.' It's about time you started using the proper name: nehym." The word actually meant "soul house" in the old tongue. "And that door isn't a part of my nehym. It belongs to somewhere else. You must understand how these things work, Kamai, because someday you'll be able to walk anyone's soul at your whim and find what you will inside. But you must never"—

she leaned closer, holding my eyes with the liquid brown of her gaze—"open that door."

Trepidation overrode my curiosity. "Is it hiding something bad?"

She leaned forward to brush her lips over my forehead— lips, I would one day learn, that were the envy of both men and women. *Marin Nuala's lips*, I'd later hear someone say, *could unlock anyone's.* "Something very bad. Something evil. You won't be safe from what's behind it. It *wants* the door to open."

I was both intrigued and disturbed that the evil thing behind the black door could *want*, that it had desires . . . and that it was lurking in my mother's nehym. "What is it?"

She stared at me for a long moment. "I pray you'll never know." She stood and strolled the hall, away from the black door. Even here, where only I could see her, she dressed like a queen, her pale skin accented by a silk blue gown that swirled about her hips as she walked, her belt of fine gold links glimmering in the warm light. "Now, come, tell me what else I've taught you this evening. If you repeat it true, I'll give you a surprise."

I couldn't keep the excitement from my voice. "Will it be my own sleep hou—nehym?" I could learn quickly, when I had an incentive.

My mother glanced down, rare sadness in her gaze. "You don't have one, my dearest."

My feet ground to a halt. Everyone's soul was a house. It could be as dark, primitive, and dank as a cave, or as vast, ornate, and mazelike as a palace. My mother's nehym was as warm and welcoming as a sprawling country villa, but with so many halls and wings and doors, no walls in the waking world could have contained it. To not have my own made me want to cry until I got one.

"Do I not have a soul?" I asked.

"Of course you do, sweetness," she said, swiping away my brimming tears with her thumbs. "It's only that sometimes these things are hidden from us, kept secret, even from within." She placed two warm fingertips over my heart. "You don't have a nehym because your soul is so deeply asleep that no one can find it. No one can walk your halls and discover your secrets that way."

Something flickered across her face, like a shadow, and I knew she wasn't telling me the entire truth. Even then I had a decent sense of such things.

"It is good that it stays hidden," she added, smoothing down my hair, a tousled mirror of her own cascade of dark curls. "For it stays safe."

"Like from the evil creature behind the black door?"

She drew in a breath. "You're safe from it. But I don't want you to speak of the door or what's behind it anymore."

"Did *you* open the door?" I asked, glancing over my shoulder. "Is that why it's here?"

She shook her head. "No, my darling. It's here because you are. It follows you, because it knows that only you can open the door. But that's why I'm safe too, because I know you won't. Now, tell me what else you've learned this evening. No more talk of the other thing. Who can walk the halls of souls and discover the sleeper's deepest secrets?"

"People like you. And me," I added, with some satisfaction. "And priests and priestesses. But we're different from them, because we're soulwalkers." That was what my mother called us. At five years old, I didn't understand everything by far, but I at least knew for sure we weren't priestesses, since I found going to temples dreadfully dull, and this wasn't dull. And besides,

4

everyone knew that priests and priestesses could explore souls. No one knew we could.

"And what *is* a soulwalker, when we're asleep like we are now?"

"A spirit." Which was a layman's term for our cerebral, conscious aspect—just like the soul was our subconscious, but I didn't yet know any of those words.

"And who can know what we do?"

"No one," I said quickly.

"Not even Hallan and Razim, remember?"

I nodded with proper solemnity. Hallan and Razim were the closest thing I had to family after my mother, close to a stepfather and stepbrother, though not quite. It had been difficult not to brag about my secret soulwalking ability to Razim, older than me by a couple of years, but I'd managed.

And now it seemed like there was a new rule that was just as serious, if not more so, than never betraying the secret of our soulwalking:

Never open the black door.

I didn't press her about it, because I wanted to believe it was as simple as that: I wouldn't open the door, and my mother and I would be safe. And maybe, if I learned enough about soulwalking, practiced hard enough, not only would I make my mother proud, but someday I would find my own soul.

"Now tell me the gods' story," my mother said.

I drew myself up as tall as possible. "In the very beginning of time, there was a husband and a wife, and they were surrounded by darkness."

"*The* Darkness," my mother corrected.

"That's what I meant. Darkness kept following them, trying to swallow them, so they always had to move. But one day, they

5

were going to have a baby, so they stopped running. They fought the Darkness back to make a home for the baby, and then circled her every night after she was born to keep the Darkness away. They're our sun and moon, and their daughter is the earth."

It was a highly distilled version of the gods' history, but it was easy enough to remember. Simple stories for a simple age, and yet it was a story we all on some level believed. It comforted me to think of bright parents hovering over a sleeping girl's bed, keeping her safe from danger.

Despite that, I was already drawn to dark mysteries. And my question about the door had only left me with the burn of unassuaged curiosity. Later, I couldn't even recall what my mother's promised surprise had been, but I could remember the way my eyes drifted back, seeking one last glimpse of the black door.

I was nine when I first touched the door.

Razim drove me to do it. A guest was staying at our villa— well, my "stepfather's" villa, where my mother and I lived with him and Razim. My mother and Hallan weren't actually married, though they pretended they were, presiding together over Hallan's home of pale tile floors, arching doorways, mosaic-patterned ceilings, and fountained courtyards, buried in the coastal forest near the capital. It was a mask, my mother said, for who they really were, what they really did. But what it masked, I didn't yet know.

Early that evening, after our parents had gone upstairs with the guest, Razim and I stayed downstairs under the watchful eye of our tutor. A nighttime breeze wafted the sheer white curtains in front of the open shutters, letting in the coolness and the scent of flowers growing outside the windows. I was practicing my letters, but Razim was only pretending to read a book, *actually* practicing a look of haughty adult boredom, the very picture of a young lordling in his new silk shirt embroidered in shades of deep red like his father often wore. When our tutor left the study to relieve himself, Razim's boredom vanished, revealing the boy of eleven. He grinned at me, white teeth and bronze cheeks glowing in the candlelight, and whispered, "I know what our parents are doing up there."

My mother had told me only that she and Hallan secreted themselves away with their guests for business.

"I do too," I said, glancing down at my paper and betraying the lie.

Razim smirked. "What are they doing, then?"

"*Work*," I said.

"I know *exactly* how they work," Razim said slyly. "My father told me."

I knew my mother would often walk in the souls of various guests, but I was never to tell Hallan and Razim, just as I was never, ever supposed to mention the black door. Not that I had much *to* tell about the latter. Whatever secrets my mother whispered about soulwalking, about the cities and people of Eopia, about the gods and half-forgotten myths, she wouldn't tell me anything more about *it*. As if it didn't tug at my attention whenever I soulwalked with her—and only her so far, never alone—despite my trying to ignore it. It was like a secret I had to keep even from myself.

But now Razim knew something else about the nature of their work.

"How, then?" I asked.

He leaned over the polished inlay of the wooden table, his black hair glinting, and whispered, "They have sex. I'll bet you don't know what that is."

"I do too," I said, even though I didn't exactly. My mother had explained the basics, and that I wasn't to do any of it until I was older. Which was fine by me, because it sounded like a supremely awkward thing I never wanted to do. I'd had no clue that was what she was doing upstairs with the guests.

"What is it, then?" Razim pressed.

I looked down, feeling suddenly uncomfortable. "You get naked, and you, you know, *do* it. Down there."

Razim seemed disappointed that I knew even that much, and he leaned back. "Yeah, well, they do it with all sorts of people. My father has even done it with the queen consort."

I gave him a skeptical look. We didn't have a queen like we had a king, because the official queen, at least in absentia, was Ranta, the earth goddess, daughter of Tain and Heshara, the sun god and moon goddess. Just as Tain was the guardian of spirits and all things cerebral, as fiery and exacting as the sun, and Heshara was guardian of souls and the sleeping realm, as cool and mysterious as the changing, shadowy faces of the moon, Ranta was the beautiful guardian of physical bodies, and thus had married the first king of the land both to better protect the earth and to gain further protection herself from the encroachment of Darkness. No one had ever seen Ranta, of course, not even her husband, but every time a new king rose to power and took the sacred oath to the earth goddess, people swore they could feel her blessing settle over them like a warm blanket.

The king still had to produce heirs, and so he needed to marry a *human* woman as well, one who actually slept in his bed and stood beside him at royal functions. This was his queen consort, never equal to him in power but a powerful figure nonetheless. And so I found Razim's claim that his father had some relationship with the queen consort a little dubious. Important-looking people often came to the villa to visit, but never anyone *that* important, as far as I could tell. I told him as much.

"That's because it's a secret!" Razim hissed. "She wouldn't come when someone like *you* could see her."

"Then someone like *you* wouldn't know for sure, either. I don't believe you."

I didn't want to, really. I loved Hallan, and we were all supposed to revere the king nearly as much as the gods. The king protected the land and Ranta, just as she protected us. Even if the queen consort wasn't his official queen, it seemed a poor way for Hallan to pay the king respect.

Razim shrugged and made a show of going back to reading. "Fine. You'll see. Maybe your mother will tell you the truth. And maybe she'll even let you in on a bigger secret. *Why* they're doing it with people."

My curiosity always got the better of me. "Why?"

Razim shot me one last grin before the study door opened and our tutor returned. "I can't tell."

I scowled at him and got scolded for failing to finish my letters. But it was too much for me. Everyone had their secrets—Hallan, Razim, my mother—and the black door hid the biggest one of them all. Except I could hardly even glance at it, let alone ask about it, with my mother always by my side in the sleeping realm. But perhaps if she wasn't near . . .

Later that night, I sneaked down the stairs and out the servants' door. The trek to the neighbors' wasn't difficult. I'd already learned that while my mother was occupied late into the evening, it was easy to slip away. As long as it didn't rain, which it rarely did outside of the wet season, or I didn't soil my dress too badly, no one ever noticed. Usually, I would just wander nearby, listening to the songs of insects and the soft snorts of the horses dozing in the stable, or lie on a rock staring at the stars. But this night I walked.

The surrounding countryside, while blanketed in a scrubby, palm-filled forest canopy, was threaded with sturdy roads and further interwoven with sandy paths. We were close to the king's court, just a couple of hours by carriage outside of the royal capital, Shalain. Our king had shepherded in a new age of trade with other lands and thus prosperity for our island kingdom, and the orderliness of the countryside reflected that. I certainly appreciated the quick ease with which I found my way to what I sought.

Soon, I stood by myself in a neighbor's soul that was as rustic as a farmhouse, the rough-hewn stone walls and splintery wooden ceiling enclosing a space not much bigger than our entryway. My body lay in the sand under a bedroom window of their villa, napping behind a screen of palm fronds, close enough to allow my spirit to reach the sleeper. The body was the outer walls of a nehym, inside of which the soul unfolded like a maze, unguarded while the spirit slumbered.

The difference between the elaborate villa in the waking world and this farmhouse of a soul were stark enough to make me smirk. Our neighbor was definitely compensating with much bigger walls in the waking world. Not that they *knew* their nehym was tiny, and not that I should have laughed at it, since I didn't have one at all.

Solar, Lunar, Earthen. Cerebral, subconscious, physical. Spirit, soul, body. Those were the three aspects of the gods that made up a person, and I was missing one of them—or at least a nehym. But I could walk *other* people's souls.

And with access to everyone else's, I tried to tell myself I didn't need my own. I also told myself I didn't need Razim's stupid secrets. Whatever Razim was hiding felt like nothing next to the black door.

Although I usually preferred darker, more mysterious souls, I wasn't disappointed by the simplicity of my surroundings. I wasn't even sure which of the neighbors this nehym belonged to. Since they weren't soulwalkers, as most people were not, their spirits weren't allowed in Heshara's sleeping realm while their bodies rested. And I didn't care to figure out whose it was.

I was only there for the door. I'd seen it, at least once, in every soul I had ever walked. It was always in a different place, even within the same nehym. I poked about on the lower level, but there wasn't much to see, no room for anything to hide, and so I started up the rickety staircase.

Nothing, not even my mother's dire warnings, could smother the curiosity that burned within me. Only *it* held the answers to its dark mystery.

Nevertheless, I was careful as I searched the nehym, following my mother's rules: I didn't shout or run, so as not to disturb the sleeper's peace. I didn't touch or move anything. I was *never* to do that if I could help it. Small adjustments would soon return to the way they had been, but if you moved too much, a soul could be irreparably changed . . . and thus, so could the person. Meddling like that, my mother said, was what had gotten soulwalkers branded as witches in the old days and burned alive. Priests or priestesses of Heshara, who had years of training built upon centuries of knowledge and wisdom, were the only ones openly sanctioned by the king to affect another's soul—or even to walk in one.

And of course I still planned on following the most important rule of all: to never open the door. But that didn't mean I couldn't touch it.

I found it upstairs. I froze at first, and then stood, arms folded, frowning at it in challenge across the rough floorboards of a hallway. It was like a massive, fine-cut gem nestled in the crude stone. The black surface flickered in the dim candlelight, but the door itself gleamed, large, dark, and oppressive. It was like the glint of a glaring eye, a ruthless, crystalline, *intelligent* stare.

The impressiveness of it distantly reminded me of something, and it took me a moment to figure out what.

In human form, the god Tain was depicted as a towering, imperious man with dark skin and hair of bright orange flame, or simply portrayed as a giant eye of fire glaring out of the center of the burning sun. The goddess Heshara, when she wasn't the white-pale woman with her face half-shadowed, her midnight hair speckled with stars and her smile an untold secret, appeared as one of the phases of the moon, usually the quarter moon, equal parts dark and light. Less often she was the full moon, and even less the new moon, completely dark. But the darkness that stood before me was different even from that: Tain's opposite, as if an unseen eye were peering from the deepest part of the night sky.

I should have been afraid. But I wasn't.

I rubbed my fingers together, took a breath, and darted across the hallway. The merest brush of my fingertips was all I allowed. I expected the door to be hot, or even cold. Anything but what it was.

It was as warm as flesh and felt alive, even though it was the texture of glass. It thrummed like blood under skin. Clutching my hand to my chest as if burned, I fled back to my body, where I awoke with a gasp.

2

HARD LESSONS

I was twelve when I put my ear to the door.

Guests were staying at the villa again. Dinner had been long and lovely, with multiple courses of succulent seafood, coconut shrimp and spicy squid steaks with avocado, followed by a dessert of papaya pudding and cashew cake, all of it basking in abundant candlelight. My mother and Hallan laughed and drank deeply, their eyes and pearly teeth shining. They were equally beautiful: my mother with her creamy coloring and tumble of curly brown hair, and Hallan with his bronze skin and muscle tone, his black hair cropped short and sleek. When they smiled at each other, it was easy to imagine them married and in love. I was jealous of the picture they painted.

But Razim had been right. In the simplest form, they were courtiers, entertaining the upper classes to gain favor. Less simply, to my mind, they used their bodies to do so, elevating pleasure to an art. It didn't bother me, but I also didn't understand it, as if my mother were off upstairs speaking a language I couldn't comprehend and didn't care to learn. What I *did* care to learn was more about souls, and my mother had said we would practice our secret talent on our guests tonight.

When everyone retired, the couples split—my mother with the woman, Hallan with the man. My mother got the better end of that deal, I thought. The woman was at least a little pretty, with her tan skin and long, dark hair, but the lines in her face were deeper than in my mother's, and her nose was too sharp. The man, however, was sickly pale and balding. Hallan didn't seem bothered, putting a strong arm around him before they slipped out of the dining room.

Razim made a face of distaste behind their backs. I had been suppressing one a moment before, rinsing my sticky hands in a ceramic bowl floating with water lilies, but his reaction left me nervous. Two years older than me at fourteen, he had a much better idea of what was happening between our parents and the guests, and if *he* didn't find it appealing . . . how would I ever?

"Gods, I hope I never have to do that," he muttered, and then he became aware of my attention and his face went still. Focused.

"How are you progressing on the lyre?" I asked with false sweetness. I knew he practiced playing so that, when he debuted in court, he would have a different means of entertaining people from his father. He acted determined to follow in Hallan's foot-steps, but despite his eagerness those few years ago to brag about what our parents did with their guests, I could tell he wasn't too excited to do the same.

And neither was I. But while Razim seemed unenthusiastic about the *particular* people at hand, I was uninterested in . . . any of it. With *anyone*.

14

"The lyre's going well enough," Razim said, his voice deepening, trying to sound more adult as servants began to clear the table. "Enough that I don't need to practice this evening. So, Kamai, what should *we* do?"

I had some time before my mother needed me, so I grinned and said, "We could play Gods and Kings, if you're ready to be beaten again." It was the one card game everyone played, the game of royalty and peasants alike, but it was especially prized by courtiers competing for status and recognition. It took strategy, wit, and storytelling, and I didn't find any other activity as much fun. Even at twelve, I was already a deft player, better than Razim.

"Or we could play a different game." Razim's dark eyes held me like hands around a moth. I couldn't move.

Somewhere in the past year, this had started happening. Before then, I was someone underfoot, someone taking the last honey fritter at dinner, someone who left a puddle of water in Razim's chair, someone who told on him when he pulled my hair in retaliation. Someone, like my mother, who occasionally stole Hallan's attention. I was all the annoyance of a little sister without actually being one. It didn't help that my mother seemed to dislike Razim. She wasn't cruel to him—I didn't think my mother *could* be cruel—just cool, distant, when she was rarely anything but warm with everyone else.

But now it seemed to mean something different to Razim that I lived in the same house and yet wasn't his sister. Something tempting, even forbidden. He looked at me in the waking hours like I tried not to look at the door while asleep. As if something enticing lay underneath my outer layers. Like I held answers to questions he didn't even know yet.

Before I could reply, one of the serving women, Zadhi,

gently put a hand on my shoulder. "The young lady must study tonight and then go to bed early, Madam Nuala said."

That was often how it was, if both my mother and Hallan were occupied and left Razim and me alone without a tutor. Zadhi became our minder, or at least mine, at my mother's direction. And my mother seemed to want me directed *away* from Razim.

Razim looked at Zadhi darkly. "*Madam* Nuala isn't here right now."

"Hey," I snapped. It was no secret in the household that our parents weren't married, but everyone usually kept up the pretense. I didn't appreciate his disrespectful tone besides.

Zadhi glared at him, her hands on her hips. "Watch yourself, young man, or else I'll speak with Mr. Lizier. Last I checked, it was still your father's house."

Razim stood abruptly and stalked away from the table. "Not always, it won't be. Someday it will be mine, so maybe you should watch *yourself*."

Zadhi pursed her lips at his back as he left. "That boy has darkness in him. You'd better get to studying, hm?"

I didn't know if Razim had darkness in him. I hadn't walked in his nehym yet, because my mother had expressly forbidden it. I was not to intrude upon the souls of anyone in the house. I wasn't sure if that was out of respect for their privacy, or because she didn't want me discovering something I wasn't supposed to know. There were a lot of secrets under this roof. And the more I tried to discover them, the more secrets I found.

My mother had also made it clear that she didn't want Razim and me sleeping anywhere near each other. Our rooms were at opposite ends of the villa, where we both headed after he shot me one last look in the turquoise-tiled hall outside the

16

dining room. Candlelight glowed on his bronze skin, and his eyes were liquid pools. He still looked hungry, even though we had just eaten. Growing up, I'd thought our living arrangement meant my mother didn't want me to wander into Razim's soul, but now, with the way Razim was acting, I understood there might be other reasons. I was oddly grateful for her precautions—oddly because maybe I *should* have wanted more than just to walk Razim's soul. I was getting older, after all, when I was supposed to begin wanting other things . . . things that Razim seemed to want at least some of the time from me.

"Good night, Kamai," he murmured.

"Good night." I stared after him, mostly at his shoulders, broader and higher by the day. I frowned, caught between wanting to say something more adult and to childishly stick my tongue out at his back. As always, I dragged my feet in the other direction, upstairs to my room.

This night, my mother had given me strict instructions to wait three hours before sneaking into the guest bedroom and slipping under the bed. This trick only worked with guests who wished her to sleep beside them. If I got caught inside the room, or if Razim or one of the servants spotted me going in, I could use the excuse that I needed my mother.

Like hiding under bedroom windows, this ploy wouldn't work forever. At twelve, it was already a stretch. But I was willing to take the risk, because tonight, she said, she had something important to tell me. So important we needed to meet in the sleeping realm for me to hear it, which I hoped meant it was going to be a critical lesson in soulwalking.

I studied to pass the time, as Zadhi had suggested, lying on my bed behind the gauzy swath of mosquito netting with my chin perched in my palm, reading history and poring over an atlas of Eopia. My room was my haven, the intricately tiled floor covered in an even more intricate rug of teal and black spirals, my dark-posted bed with its embroidered silk sheets and cushions like a cradling hand at the center of it all. Heavy wooden shutters kept out the night, though I could hear insects singing in the dark. On my bedside stand stood a small statue of pale Heshara with her secret smile and cloak-like black hair, watching over me, alongside a bronze censer burning spicy incense to keep the air smelling pleasant. I felt safe here.

I never minded studying. When my hands weren't holding a spread of Gods and Kings cards, they were turning the pages of a book. Myths, histories, maps—it was all a type of magic, transporting me somewhere else, even if it was only to other places in Eopia. Books were doors I was allowed to open with the flick of my wrist . . . unlike the black door. Tracing the jagged contours of our sandy island continent and the rocky volcanoes crisscrossing it always made me feel small with how little I knew of them and breathless with the potential they held. The land was made up of familiar pieces—sandy deserts and dense forests, palm-lined beaches and sunbaked, rocky peaks—but they were used to build something bigger, just like the halls and rooms of a nehym.

I was so engrossed I lost track of time, glancing up to realize the candle had already burned past the mark my mother had made for me. I leapt up.

My slippers were silent over the tile of the upstairs hallways, and I knew every obstacle to avoid tripping over in the darkness. And my mother and Hallan kept every knob and hinge welloiled, so the door to this particular guest bedroom didn't make a sound as I cracked it open and slid inside.

The orange light of dying candles made my mother's pale skin glow like coals. She lay on her stomach, her back bare above the covers of the bed. The woman, more careful of her nudity, wore a satin robe, her arm draped comfortably across my mother's shoulders as they slept. The sight didn't bother me or inspire me . . . until I tried imagining myself in my mother's place. *That* made me want to run.

Shaking my head, I refocused on the task at hand. I tiptoed inside and quietly laid myself out on my mother's side, under the bed, a thick rug keeping me cushioned from the tile. She'd be the only one to accidentally step on a stray arm of mine then, and she could warn me if her patron awoke.

I used to be unable to fall asleep like this. Just in case, my mother always made sure I had a couple of vials of sleeping tonic, distilled from the herb mohol, to knock me out in a hurry. But it was late enough, and I'd been staring at the atlas for long enough, I didn't need one.

I was standing in the familiar dark glade almost immediately. This was where my spirit usually ended up if I stopped halfway between wakefulness and dreams to soulwalk—where my own nehym should have perhaps been, but wasn't. There wasn't much to explore in the clearing. The edges faded away into blackness, like a line of trees that I couldn't distinctly make out. Whenever I tried to step into it, I couldn't. If this was the only place I could have gone, being a soulwalker would have been dreadfully dull. Fortunately, it wasn't.

If there was someone nearby when I fell asleep, I would often end up directly inside their soul. This time, I had a choice. Two doors stood before me—only the doors, free of walls— one of rich, warm wood that I recognized as my mother's, and a high, narrow, stately one. My mother had told me to meet her in our guest's, so I turned its knob, slowly out of habit from the waking world, trying not to make a noise.

Where one might have expected to see the clearing on the other side, a hallway as high and narrow as the door greeted me, made of the same dark wood. The place wasn't what I would have called bright or cozy—the air was stuffy, smelling slightly of must, the lighting dim. It could have been unpleasantly oppressive, but the silent hallways felt heavy with potential, filled with mysteries and secrets, leaning claustrophobically in on me as if to murmur them in my ear.

"Kamai." I heard my mother's soft voice. I followed it into a sitting room that was as stuffy as the hallway. Even the chairs seemed stretched thin, with high backs and narrow seats. My mother was seated in one, her beaded silk gown in airy blue contrast to the walls around her, and she patted the cushion of the chair next to her. "Sit, dearest. It's time we spoke on a certain matter."

Despite her seeming casualness, I knew this was important. She'd said so herself. I sat, alert, without leaning back.

My mother laughed. "This isn't a test, I promise." She pursed her lips. "More of an interview, in a sense."

My eyebrows furrowed. "We're not going to explore?"

"Not right now." She sat back in her chair, studying me. "What do I do for a living, Kamai?"

"You're a courtesan," I answered promptly. It was easy enough to say. A pretty word for a confusing thing.

"That's a position at court, yes, but how do I make my living?"

I swallowed. "You sleep with people."

She smiled at my inevitable blush. "Close, but not quite. Hallan and I, we are pleasure artists. Much like actors, we use

20

certain masks: our smiles, our words, and yes, our bodies to please others. But we are different from common pleasure workers, and not just because of the particular mask of our *marriage*. The distinction is silly, but to maintain our reputation—and our patrons' misplaced sense of pride—we receive no money in return for our art. We can accept gifts, of course, and favors, and influence, but . . ."

"But that's not how you make your living," I finished slowly, realizing the puzzle for the first time, one that had been right under my nose for my entire life. I was embarrassed I'd never thought to question it.

But my mother beamed, satisfied I'd figured it out now, at least. "Precisely. And while Hallan and I are considered members of the upper class—some might even call us famous—we are not nobility. We don't have extensive lands or holdings beyond Hallan's villa, or income from investments. Patron gifts would not pay our taxes to the king, or keep us in fine clothes and jewels, able to host lavish dinners such as tonight's. With that alone, we would not be able to maintain an appearance worthy of the court and its nobility—our very important patrons."

Razim had been hinting at some other purpose behind their actions for some time, but I'd never realized that while their supposed marriage was a mask for their art, their art might be *another* mask for something else entirely. "So what do you do?"

She leaned forward, her eyes intense. "We deal in secrets, Kamai. The intimacy we share with others affords us a certain vantage. It exposes vulnerabilities. People let slip things they wouldn't otherwise. And because these people are often powerful, their secrets are worth the most."

My heart was thundering in my chest—not from fear or nervousness, but excitement. "Who do you sell them to?"

Her face grew oddly still. "A secret organization called the Twilight Guild. They're a broker of secrets, in a sense, and they pay their members well. They resell the information to interested parties who will pay even more for it."

Maybe it was her tone, but my mouth suddenly felt dry. "Are they good people or . . . are they bad?"

My mother didn't brush the question aside; instead she considered it for a moment. "They are neither. The information they sell could be used to do good things: to expose lies, to reveal who paid an assassin to murder someone at court, or to uncover a plot to steal money from, say, one of Tain's temples." I shuddered at the thought of the sun god's fiery eyes narrowed in displeasure under the burning pyre of his hair. Who would want to steal from *him*? "Or it could be used for what we might call evil. The secrets we sell might engender lies, or lead to someone's assassination, or betray how *best* to steal from a temple. We don't decide what people do with the secrets. We merely sell them to the guild, and they sell them to the highest bidder. It's the same as a crafter of swords. Steel in someone's hand can be used for good or ill; it is not for the blacksmith to decide. He creates the weapon, not what is done with it."

It was strange to think that my mother's actions could lead to someone's death, though it didn't scare me as much as it should have. It made her business even more fascinating, like dark things often were to me. Of course that death wouldn't be her fault, but the Twilight Guild could certainly choose whom they sold information to and try to avoid it. They sounded shadowier in purpose than a mere blacksmith, and not only because of their name. "The guild would never hurt you or force you to do anything you didn't want to do, right?"

"I joined them of my own free will, and they have never hurt me. But one would be wise to never cross them." She paused, smiling ruefully. "And to remain valuable."

"So they're not dangerous?"

"That depends. They have been around for centuries, with hundreds if not thousands of members. No one except their leader—whose identity is always a secret—knows how many, or how deeply they are seeded in this land, but I know they have members in the lowest levels of society up to the highest. No such organization could have clean hands. Take the clergy, another ancient organization. Are Heshara's priests and priestesses danger-ous? To some people, yes, others no. They reveal a soul's deepest secrets for the king, for better or worse. They've brought both fortune and death down on people's heads with that knowledge. They've hunted down unlicensed soulwalkers and allowed them to be burned at the stake in years past, but they've also healed people's souls and long served the moon goddess. I love Heshara and her worship, and yet her servants are a danger to me."

It wasn't only the sun god and his searing gaze that seemed frightening now. As a soulwalker, I'd always prayed to Heshara first, most comforted by the thought not only of the goddess of night and souls but of a mother figure watching over me. And yet, just as there were many faces to the moon, Heshara, with her pale visage half-shadowed by her curtain of starlit black hair, seemed to have other, darker sides as well.

As did my mother.

"So you're saying the Twilight Guild isn't dangerous to *you*?" I asked.

My mother smiled, though it didn't quite reach her eyes.

"They need me. I'm one of their best harvesters of secrets. They—even Hallan—think it's because of my skill as a pleasure artist, but as you might have guessed, it's also because I can soulwalk."

I could hardly breathe. To make a living off curiosity, exploration, and *soulwalking*, turning a dangerous liability into a profitable blessing . . . it seemed like a dream.

My dream now. And maybe not mine alone.

"Is Razim planning to join the guild?" I asked, already knowing the answer.

"He already has," my mother said with a slight frown. "He's young but determined. And Hallan allowed it." She sounded as if *she* wouldn't have.

"Can . . . can I?" I stammered.

She hesitated. "Someday, perhaps, which is why I wanted to speak to you about this now. It would affect the course of your studies both in the waking *and* sleeping realms. There are tricks in both worlds to sussing out secrets. But . . ."

My forehead furrowed. "But what?"

"You realize, Kamai, that either Hallan's path into the Twilight Guild as a courtier, or mine as a courtesan *and* a soulwalker, would require you to sleep with people."

I opened my mouth and then closed it. And opened it again. "But what about Razim? He doesn't want to sleep with people, either. He's just pretending if he says he does. That's why—"

"He's studying music to perform as a courtier, I know, hoping it will stir up emotions and trust and perhaps secrets on its own. That *is* another path, but only time will tell if he can make it worthwhile to the guild. Perhaps they see something else of value in him," she muttered half to herself, staring off in thought for a moment before blinking back at me. "But for you, as a soulwalker, there really is only one way."

She was right. I'd just been thinking myself that the time for sleeping under windows and beds was drawing to a close. I would have to start sleeping *in* beds.

"But I don't want to force you down this path," my mother said quickly, earnestly. "While you are still young, I want you to think long and hard about it. Especially since I haven't seen you noticing boys, or girls, very much. That might come later, but I want this to be *your* decision. Until then and, needless to say, until you're older, I won't begin any of your training."

I wanted to say yes immediately, but . . . she was right. I hadn't noticed anyone in *that* way. Sure, Razim was handsome and I wanted to explore his soul, but I didn't feel the desire that he had in his eyes when he looked at me. And yet maybe that would come later, as my mother had said.

But I was beginning to doubt.

She sensed my hesitation. "If you don't want to answer now, it's okay. And if you never want to do this at all, I understand completely. Maybe it's even best . . ." She trailed off, glancing to the side, as if keeping a lookout for something.

The black door.

I didn't want to stay away from souls. I didn't want to miss out on the opportunity to do something so exciting as *spying* to learn people's secrets. And I wouldn't let myself admit that I didn't want to stay away from the black door, either.

And if sleeping with people was the path . . .

My mother patted my knee. "I'll leave you to think on it." She stifled a yawn. "I'm going to get some sleep. Feel free to explore, just remember—"

"No touching or moving anything, I know."

She smiled, stood up, and vanished.

There would be no touching souls, probably not until I was

okay with touching bodies, I guessed. My studies in the sleeping realm had likely come to a halt until my mother was sure I could go down this path.

I grimaced and stood, turning angrily away from the room that I couldn't *really* explore. But the walls leaned in close . . .

And I couldn't help that my arm brushed against the black door. It had appeared right next to me this time. Almost as if it wanted me to bump into it.

When I did, something tickled my skin, like an exhalation. A whisper. Without thinking, I put my ear to the smooth surface, since I could have sworn I'd heard something.

It was like putting my cheek to someone's chest. There was the same warmth, the *aliveness*, thrumming through it like a heartbeat. My scalp prickled, my hair stirring with what felt like a breath.

"*. . . Kamai.*"

If the night wind could whisper, this would have been its voice. There was no doubt about what I'd heard. I threw myself back, crashing into the opposite wall and banging my head. I stared at the door, wild-eyed, and it once again seemed to stare back at me. For a moment, my face was reflected in the sheen of the gleaming surface.

It *knew* me. But I didn't know it. For once, the part of me that wanted to was overwhelmed by fear.

I didn't care about the secrets held by this darker soul, or what my mother would think about me leaving so soon. I tore open the other door, to the outside, to my body, to safe familiarity, and hurtled through it.

I was sixteen when I yelled at the door.

I was in my bed, and a girl, Ciari, was propped on her

26

elbows above me, her long dark hair curtaining our faces. She was kissing me.

And I was . . . trying . . . to kiss her back. I couldn't silence the buzzing in my head. Not a pleasurable buzz, but more like an agitated hive of bees. I couldn't think. There was only the hum of wrongness. It wasn't helping my technique.

Not that I'd been taught much, either by my mother or Razim or anyone else. To be fair, I hadn't asked.

I told myself again that I wanted this, but I couldn't silence the rising scream inside of me. The *no*. I'd long thought Ciari was beautiful, and I even had the urge to be near her, but as soon as she'd started kissing me, as soon as I started even *imagining* going beyond kissing with her, I lost interest. More than that: I wanted to run the other way. The solid posts and silk sheets of my bed, glowing softly in the spicy candlelit air, no longer felt like a hand cradling me in safety, but one offering me up, exposing me, and Heshara's statue with its secret smile, gracing my bedside stand, seemed to know something I didn't.

Ciari pulled away, her lips glistening. "Are you okay?"

"Yes, fine," I said, a little breathlessly, following her gaze down along my body to my fists, which were crumpling the satin skirt of my lace-trimmed nightgown.

I want this.

No, I don't. But I want to soulwalk, to join the Twilight Guild, and this is how I do it. Be brave.

Ciari took one of my hands. I managed to unclench it.

"Have you never done this before? With a girl?" she asked, tracing my fingers with a lovely gentleness that made me shiver.

She thought I feared something new. She didn't know I feared something I didn't want, had never wanted, and might never want.

27

"No. Not with a boy or girl," I admitted, a blush flaring up in my face. "But I like both."

I liked the *look* of both. Both had the potential to make me want to draw nearer. But when I did . . . there was nothing. I had a complete lack of that desire to get even closer—and less clothed—which everyone around me seemed to have. *That* was more embarrassing to me, a much deeper secret, than my lack of experience.

Ciari grinned, and it was an evil, beautiful thing. "I can teach you how."

It was as if she were talking about how to feel what she felt, rather than how to have sex, and I wanted to believe she could. "Okay," I whispered.

She leaned in to kiss me again. This time, her hand reached down and started gliding up my leg, lifting my nightgown, seeking . . .

My hand shot out before I could help it. "*Don't*," I gasped, panicked, against her lips, and I tore my own lips away and flung my head to the side. Horror at what I had done flooded me, and I glanced back at her with wide eyes. "Sorry, I . . ."

Ciari rolled off me. "It's okay," she said, though she was clearly disappointed. She sat up and smoothed the front of her nightgown over a lovely pair of breasts. Not lovely enough, apparently, for me. Nothing was ever enough. "We are just supposed to be playing cards anyway, and then going to bed, while our mothers and Hallan have their fun."

She sounded very much like she wanted to be having that sort of fun too. We'd been playing cards downstairs earlier, whiling away the time as Razim made eyes at the both of us, but Ciari only had eyes for me. We'd gone upstairs early, giggling, leaving Razim flushed and frustrated, but I had ruined it.

28

I felt ruined. Broken. And for the life of me, I couldn't figure out why. At least, I knew what made me a disappointment to Ciari and my mother—and myself. My lack of sexual desire was all too obvious. But I didn't know why *I* was this way.

Afterward, Ciari and I hardly spoke, beyond what was required for another uninspired round of Gods and Kings. It didn't help my mood or hers that I beat her. Afterward, she rolled over on my silken bed cover and snuffed out the candle.

I wanted to soulwalk, but it took me a while to fall asleep lying next to Ciari. Being in bed with another person was supposed to make it easier to use my talent, not harder. Yet another thing I was failing at this night.

I eventually ended up in Ciari's nehym. It was a stone house, small but nice enough, tidy with rich wood accents. I didn't pause to look around, because the black door stood across from me, and it drew all my suddenly furious attention.

"What do you *want*?" I shouted at it before I really knew what I was saying. Before I realized what I actually wanted to say:

What do I *want?*

No one was apparently the answer.

I knew what *it* wanted anyway. My mother had warned me long ago, and I had felt it every time I had seen it since.

It was my evening for thwarting desires. I didn't open it, and, strangely, I felt nearly as regretful in denying the black door as I had Ciari.

———

I was seventeen when the door gave me a gift.

One late afternoon, my mother called me into the sitting room. She'd been pacing there all day, and laughing less and less for months while the faint lines in her lovely face deepened.

"Kamai," she said, taking my shoulders, which were no longer lower than hers. I was expecting her to comment, like usual, on the fact that my dress was too dark for the sunny, dry season, making me look morbid instead of appealing, but it was far more serious than that. "I can't explain everything, but you must listen to me. If something happens before I can get you away from here, go to your father, in the capital. His name is Jidras Numa, and he won't like it, but he'll take you in. You may not like it either, but it's the only place that will be safe."

"Wait, *what*?" I wanted to reel back, but my mother's grip kept me rooted. She'd never told me anything about my father. I hadn't even known that *she* knew who he was. "Why now?"

For a second I thought it was because I was failing her so badly. There had been no awakening of my desire, which was making it harder and harder for me to get near enough to anyone to soulwalk—harder and harder to follow my mother into the Twilight Guild. If I could have made myself more like her—so beautiful and beguiling and knowing—not only would I discover the world's dark secrets for myself, but maybe I wouldn't feel broken anymore. Maybe I could make her proud.

But desire wasn't something I could study and learn to feel, just like my soul wasn't something I could search for and discover.

All I had was the black door, and I could never open it. I couldn't feel the proper things I should have felt, and the one forbidden thing I *shouldn't* have wanted was what I craved most.

Maybe she was casting me away because I truly *was* broken.

Reading my face, she said, "Kamai, my sweetness, it's not you. *I've* done something I might regret."

"What have you done?"

She smiled faintly. "I fell in love." The smile vanished,

replaced by steel. "Forget everything I've told you about the Twilight Guild. Forgive me—I wasn't entirely honest with you, for reasons I can't explain right now. They *are* bad. They *are* dangerous to you and me. Very. And whatever you do, *don't* trust any of their members. Not even Razim. Stay away from him. If anything terrible happens, they're all responsible."

I could have laughed, if not for how grave and urgent she sounded. At nineteen, Razim was moody and withdrawn, but not *dangerous*. Then again, I didn't know quite what role he had played for the guild in recent years, since I hadn't been able to join them and learn for myself. "What about Hallan?" I asked, breathless.

Her softer smile returned, and suddenly I knew whom she had fallen in love with after all these years. "He won't be the problem, in any case. But *stay away* from Razim. Now go, pack only what you might need!"

"Wait, *right* this moment? What about you?"

"I have places I can hide, if . . ." She didn't finish, and I got the sick suspicion her sentence would have ended with *if I make it.*

"Come with me!" I said. "I'm sure my father will hide you as well!"

She shook her head ruefully. "I doubt that very much. In any case, I can't follow you right now, Kamai, because I'll only put you in greater danger."

My mother no longer held me in place—in fact, she was trying to steer me away from her—but I kept my feet planted. "I'm not leaving without you!"

The steel returned to my mother's voice and I flinched away from it. "You will do as I say. Go pack. And don't panic; we have some time before they make their move."

As it happened, she was wrong.

A short while later, a little after sunset, someone pounded on the front doors of our villa. I'd been gathering my things in my bedroom in a haze of disbelief, unsure this was actually happening. When I heard the noise, I leapt up to peer downstairs through the crack of my door.

My mother glanced up in my direction. "Don't let them in!" she shouted at the servants hurrying toward the commotion.

The pounding turned to hammering. The doors shuddered on their hinges.

"Stay hidden, Kamai . . . and run!" Those were the only words my mother had time to spare for me. I didn't run. I couldn't. "You there," she continued to the servants, "bar the doors! Arm yourselves with whatever you can!"

She herself seized an ornate ax from a plaque on the wall. It was nearly too heavy for her, the tip gouging the floor, but she managed to heave it upright. I cast about for some weapon of my own, but my room held only soft things. In the meantime, Zadhi and another servant were dragging a heavy chair to block the entrance.

None of our efforts mattered. A group of men wearing soldiers' uniforms kicked in the doors. Before my mother could do more than clumsily swing her ax, which they deflected easily, they slit the servants' throats in the candlelit entryway, faster than I could follow the line of their daggers. Zadhi, who I'd known most of my life, fell gurgling and choking on her own blood.

And then, there, in the front room, without any ceremony, one of them ran my mother through with a sword.

The blade entered underneath the front of her rib cage and came out, red, from between her shoulders. Her eyes widened, beautiful lips parting, and she made a sound like a strangled cough. But when her attacker lowered his sword, she was silent as she slid off and fell to the ground, her own weapon slipping from limp fingers.

My knees hit my bedroom floor at the same time. I choked on a scream, my agony silent, just like my mother's. She wouldn't have wanted me to draw attention to myself, but my silence was less for survival's sake and more because I was paralyzed by the sight below me. All I could see was her blood, soaking into a pale blue rug and pooling on the white tile beneath her. Her limbs jerked, and yet her eyes were sightless. A piercing keen rose in my ears, but only in my head—the scream I hadn't released.

One of the soldiers, his blade gleaming red, called out, "Kamai Nuala?"

I dropped all the way to the floor, fist in my mouth to keep even my ragged breathing from reaching him. *Why me?* was all I could think. Why not Hallan or Razim as well?

The soldier tried to move for the stairs, but another caught his arm, pulling him back, shaking his head. "If the girl was in the house, she's not now. She wouldn't have kept quiet through all that. Let's go."

He gestured at a third soldier, who poured a clear liquid all over the floor, including the base of the stairs, flinging it on the curtains and furniture while he was at it.

They weren't going to leave anything behind.

They knocked over a standing candelabra, and all the guards backed out the front doors and into the evening as everything went up in flames.

3

STRANGE COMFORTS

I dashed to the top landing to go down to my mother, but the heat was sudden, immense, like running into a wall. I leapt back involuntarily, away from the fire, my skirts snagging as I scrambled back down the upstairs hall on hands and knees. Thick black smoke was already pouring up after me, churning across the ceiling's bright mosaics like river rapids over stones, swallowing them. I didn't make the decision to run from it. I just did.

There was a second staircase the servants used—*had* used. They were all dead now. When I wrenched on the handle at the base of it, the door didn't budge. It was supposed to open into a back entryway, with a door just beyond it that I'd often used to sneak out. But the soldiers must have blockaded it.

I ran back up the stairs and had to drop into a crouch to breathe. Coughing, I crawled into my room and kicked the door shut.

Other than the haze in the air, it was peaceful, candles casting a soft glow over the teal and black spirals of the rug, the heap of silk pillows on the bed, and the statue of smiling, serene Heshara. Like my entire life wasn't burning down around me. I flung open the window shutters.

The grounds below were quiet in the deepening twilight. The air still hung heavy and hot from the day, but it was only the weakest whisper of the heat behind me. A horse whinnied shrilly somewhere far away. Perhaps the men were gone, but it didn't matter; I'd still break my ankle if I jumped. I couldn't even see my landing. I spun back to the room, looking for anything I could use to climb down, but froze when I saw the smoke flooding in under the crack of my bedroom door, forcing its way in.

There wasn't time. I had nowhere to go. If the black door had suddenly appeared in the waking world, I would have thrown it open and dashed inside to escape.

"*Kamai!*" came a hoarse shout.

I turned back to the window, squinting and coughing. It was too dark to see clearly, but a shape slipped out of the shadows of our garden.

"Jump, Kamai, and I'll catch you!"

I wasn't sure who it was, but I didn't think twice. I tossed my legs over the sill, only making sure my skirts were clear, and then shoved myself out into the night.

It wasn't like in the stories, where the brave rescuer catches his lady and sets her on her feet in the same smooth motion. I may have been slight, but I hit hard. My cheek smashed into a shoulder, my skin tore against the studs of leather bracers, and my delicate silk dress ripped at the waist. My weight dragged both of us to the ground, knocking the breath from my lungs.

So I couldn't scream when I saw it was Razim who'd caught me.

He sat me upright, his arm firm and steady around my back despite our collision. "Are you hurt? Can you move?"

I opened my mouth, but only to gasp and cough. My mother's words echoed in my mind. *Dangerous. Stay away from him.*

"Come on," he said, lifting me to my shaky feet, while he stood tall and strong from the years he'd grown and trained since boyhood. "I'm not sure what Marin did to bring this down on our heads, but you'll be safe if we hurry. The Twilighters will still take you in, even if you're not one of us."

The Twilighters. My mother said they were behind this. And Razim was one of them. That was why my mother's killers hadn't called his name, at least, along with mine: he was already with them. And now he was likely trying to finish what they'd started, to lure me closer in order to kill me, or else this rescue attempt was some other sort of trick to betray me to them.

My mother had also told me to run. So even though it shamed me later, I did.

Razim caught my arm before I'd made it five steps and hauled me back. "Where are you going? The wagon is this way!"

"Let me go!" I screeched, trying to wrench my arm out of his grip.

He held me tight, lifting his other hand in the darkness to his lips. "Quiet, idiot! Are you trying to get yourself killed?"

All at once, I quit pulling away and turned on him, like I should have from the beginning. "Why do you care? You want me dead anyway. This is all your fault!"

"What? No, those were the *king's* soldiers—"

"Anyone can hire soldiers or even dress like them, especially the Twilighters!" I spat. "I'm *not* an idiot, but I would be one to believe they're not responsible!"

Razim squinted. "Why do you have reason to fear the guild? What did your fool mother do to—?" He cut off when one of my hands caught him on the cheek, and the other clawed for his eyes. "Kamai, stop!"

I didn't stop. I shrieked like a wild animal and threw myself upon him, hitting, scratching, and kicking. Somewhere in there were sobs, and a grief that was eating me alive. I would tear Razim to pieces with my bare hands if it meant I could somehow escape it, reverse what had happened. Bring my mother back to life.

Razim seized my wrists, pinning them together, and tried to drag me with him. I bent and bit his hand as hard as I could.

He shouted a curse and let me go.

I took off in a blind sprint in the opposite direction. I didn't know where I was going, only that I couldn't go with him. He was one of *them*—the men who'd killed my mother and set fire to the villa. I wasn't sure why he wanted me to follow, but the reason couldn't be good for me.

As if to prove me right, Razim slammed into me, bringing me to the ground. His weight crushed my ribs, twisting my wrist underneath me.

His hand gripped the back of my neck, holding me down, and he leaned over and growled in my ear, "Gods, Kamai, you stupid girl! Fighting me now will get you nothing. Come with me, and *be quiet.*"

I screamed into the dirt as loudly as I'd wanted to when my mother had been stabbed through the heart.

He clamped a hand over my mouth, pinching my lip hard against my teeth. I tried to twist away and claw at him, but he swung his leg over me, sitting on my lower back and pinning my arms between us. He kept hold of my mouth with one hand while fumbling with the other. I gasped and tried to bite him again, without success. In seconds, he tossed a handkerchief next to my face and then let me go only long enough to block my shouts with the cloth instead. He cinched it brutally behind my head. I sobbed and gagged, vaguely hoping I wouldn't vomit into the handkerchief.

"Kamai, you're making me do this," he whispered, his voice furious. His weight shifted again, and something whipped the warm air—his belt as he yanked it off. Hot, it was so hot with him on top of me, and I could barely breathe to fight. I felt suffocated by his proximity, but it was too late—his hands found mine in the darkness, and he bound my wrists tightly behind my back with the leather strap.

He rolled off me then and heaved me to my feet, seizing my elbow like a vise. That didn't stop me from struggling, so much he practically had to carry me under his arm.

The blow to the back of my head stopped me, finally, as we made it into a dense stand of palms. I'd been bent forward, kicking and writhing, so I didn't see where it came from. It wasn't Razim, since both of his hands were occupied. I didn't have a chance to look around as the pain blinded me. I only saw the back of a covered wagon.

Razim let go of me, and I fell to my knees, and then on my face since I couldn't catch myself on my hands. I rolled onto my side, blinking away the sweat and dirt, to see Razim seize a man by the shirt . . . only to shove him away.

"Don't touch her," Razim snarled.

I heard the smirk in the other man's voice even if I couldn't see it. "It looked like you needed help. Ranta's tits, what a match!

I would have rescued you from your fierce little assailant earlier, but I didn't want to draw any more attention to our position than she already has."

"Gods." Razim wiped sweat, and maybe blood, from his brow, and looked down at me. "She must be mad with grief."

"Doesn't she know who her friends are? Stupid girl."

"Don't call her that," Razim said. "Whatever her fool mother did to get herself killed, Kamai must have watched her die. It can't have been easy."

"Your father is dead too, and yet you're holding it together."

My breath caught. They'd killed Hallan as well? Horror rose with the bile in my throat.

Razim raised a hand, his voice tight. "Don't, Nyaren. I . . . it's too new."

"Have it your way. Just know that every one of us have sacrificed a lot for the guild. We've all lost someone, but that's just the price we have to pay. She'd best learn the same lesson too."

Hallan . . . Hallan might have been only pretending to be married to my mother, but I'd known him all my life and he was the closest thing I had to a father. A sob lodged in my chest, a terrible whine escaping from behind my gag.

In contrast, Razim was just standing there, when the men who'd murdered his father were nearby—maybe even right in front of him, in the form of this Nyaren. It didn't matter if the Twilighters would spare my life in exchange for my compliance, if their offer wasn't just a trick to discover what I knew before they killed me. That wasn't a trade that I, or anyone, should be willing to make.

And yet Razim must have made such a bargain for himself, if he wasn't already their creature through and through. In either case, he wasn't just dangerous. He was inhuman. I thought I'd known him, but I'd been so very wrong. How could I know anyone? That was a lesson my mother had tried to teach me; I'd just learned it too late.

But perhaps I'd learned a final lesson, even if it was too late for her: Never fall in love. Because this was apparently what happened when you did.

Nyaren turned my way. "Still making noise, is she? Is she even worth all this trouble? Although she is a pretty thing, I'll give you that."

Razim was in his face again. "She's *mine*. I told you not to touch her. *Never* touch her."

A pretty thing. *His*. Maybe that was the only reason I wasn't dead. He'd finally managed to claim me.

I'd always viewed my lack of desire like a stone in the path of becoming like my mother. Now it would be a stone that I would use to build a wall between me and people like this, so they could never touch me. I would refit my brokenness to be my armor.

If I ever escaped.

Half rolling, half inching along the ground like a caterpillar, I tried to drag myself away from them both.

"Get control of yourself." Nyaren shoved Razim back. "So she's yours. Understood. Now do you want to get her in the wagon or let her crawl away?"

They both came for me. Razim took my shoulders, his fingers digging into my arms as he climbed into the back of the wagon with me, while Nyaren took my legs. I thrashed, trying to kick Nyaren in the face, without success. At least he let go of me once I was inside. I kicked the side of the wagon instead, over and over, my feet pounding against the wooden slats like a giant's knock. I bruised my heels through my thin slippers, but I didn't care.

"She *is* a wild one," Nyaren said. "I didn't think you'd need it for your lady love, but there's some mohol in the satchel there."

Razim drew me to his chest to hold me still, trapping my legs with his and leaning against the front wall of the wagon. His skin was hot, sticky, touching too much of mine. "Shh," he said in my ear—gently, somehow, after all the violence. Comforting. I wanted to vomit more than ever. He leaned, reaching with one arm, and pulled a small bottle from a leather bag.

I couldn't see clearly in the darkness, but I knew well what mohol was. I struggled harder, sobbing, but it was no use. He slipped part of the soggy handkerchief up over my nose, uncapped the bottle with his teeth, and poured some in his palm. Then he pressed his hand over my nose and mouth.

I had time to thrash once more before the dizziness hit me in a wave.

"I've got you, Kamai" was the last thing I heard in the waking world.

For a while, I couldn't open my eyes, not even in the sleeping realm. Unlike the diluted tonics my mother had occasionally given me, straight essence of mohol kept me too far under at first. I didn't know how much time was passing, but I had the vague, drugged sense of it slipping by in my muddled nightmares.

When I next opened my eyes, there was no covered wagon around me, only walls. They were the thick gray stone of an impenetrable keep. Torches burned in sconces every few feet to keep the shadows at bay. I was alone, standing in a surprisingly warm hallway, and wearing a clean black dress, darker than ever,

no stains or rips. This wasn't the waking world, then. But
isn't my clearing. The air had a familiar clean, woody scent—
Razim's soap.

Razim had held me as I'd passed out, and he must have gone
to sleep next to me in the wagon. That would mean this was his
soul, his nehym. I wasn't dizzy here, or sweaty and battered and
bound. But I was just as afraid, and the weight of my grief was
enough to crush me. Despite the rich tapestries lining the hall,
the lush burgundy rug under my feet, the warmth in the air, this
place felt like a prison. I spun a full circle, hugging myself and
quaking like a palm frond in the wind.

I tried to wake up, but I couldn't. The mohol had relaxed its
grip on me, but not enough for my spirit to come fully back to
my body. The mind was always less affected by sleep than the
flesh, which was how soulwalkers could do what we did.

For so long, I'd wondered what Razim's soul looked like.
Now I only wanted to close my eyes again. Anything but explore,
which would feel like drawing closer to him than I already was.
But there was no way I could let myself slip back into dreams; I
was too vulnerable, too afraid to just let go and drift. And yet,
without my own nehym or the ability to wake up, I had nowhere
else to go. I could have found the door out to my clearing, but I
didn't think my legs would carry me that far. They were already
threatening to buckle.

I wanted to curl up in a corner and hide, but I couldn't
stomach letting the walls of Razim's soul touch me. I would have
rather stood in one spot and not moved.

It was then that the black door appeared.

I hurtled straight for it, as if running into its embrace.
Somehow, for the first time in my life, it was a source of comfort. It was familiar—something I'd seen my entire life, no mat-

ter the soul. It was something I'd so long associated with my mother, even if it was only through her prohibition of it.

I wasn't stupid enough to open it. Not yet. But I threw myself against it and slid down its length, pressure building in my throat and behind my eyes.

Hallan . . . Zadhi . . . oh, gods, Mama. Mama, Mama . . . There, with my shoulder pressed against the smooth, warm surface and my knees hugged to my chest, a cry ripped through me. I sobbed until I couldn't anymore.

Eventually, I grew calm enough to see straight. I was every bit in the same place—alone, in danger, and with no one I could trust—but I felt empty, at least, if not at peace. Blinking swollen eyes, I looked down past my arms, to where something rested on the dark stone next to my foot:

A single red rose petal. Just thin enough to have been slipped under the black door.

4

CREEPING THINGS

The sight of the rose petal jarred me so much that I jumped awake. When I opened my eyes in the waking world, the air was cool with deep night and I was alone under a blanket—but not alone in the wagon. Across from me, Razim leaned against the sideboard, broad shoulders slumped, arms resting on his knees, head hanging forward. He was definitely asleep.

No one else was with us. We weren't moving. I turned my head, cushioned on empty feed sacks, and heard logs snapping and saw the soft glow of a campfire through the wagon's hide covering. Nyaren was probably right outside. I had no idea where we were, but we'd traveled far enough that there was no evidence of the inferno that had been my home.

Nyaren was likely keeping watch out there and Razim in here. The bottle of mohol sat at his side, his handkerchief folded by it. It was too dangerous to give mohol to a person already under its influence—they might never awaken—so he was probably supposed to watch for signs that I was coming around.

Razim had retied my wrists with proper rope, probably for my comfort—a kindness I would make sure he regretted—though he'd also bound my ankles. Even with my hands before me, it would have been impossible to free myself without my mother's gift.

I had to go through quiet contortions, but I was able to reach into my bodice and pull out the slim, wooden-handled pocketknife she'd given me for my tenth birthday. It was made for a man's pocket, of course, not my makeshift one, but my mother had always insisted I carry it nestled between my breasts.

My mother had trained me well, if not for this *exact* scenario. I knew how to move silently, how to trick people in darkness, and how to free myself without looking. My hands contorted again to pop open the blade. I slipped it between my wrists and sawed at my bindings. With the tension and the sharpness of the blade, the rope parted like string. Carefully drawing my knees to my chest, I made short work of the ties around my ankles too.

My skirt went next. The silk was lightweight, meant for the heat of the day, but voluminous, and it would only snag or slow me down. It was barely attached in the front, where it had ripped at the waist as I'd fallen into Razim's arms. I finished it off, leaving only the thin lining beneath, which was fortunately as dark as the rest of the dress—the better to move unseen. Slowly, barely breathing, I slid out of the skirt and out from under the blanket.

Razim hadn't moved. Using my arms for support, I pulled myself into a crouch in front of him. I kept my eyes on his face as I picked up the bottle of mohol, glancing down only long enough to pour a good deal of it into the handkerchief. Then, in the same motion I would use to smash a fly between my palms, I clapped one hand behind his head and the cloth over his nose and mouth, holding tight.

I wasn't sure if he ever awoke. He jerked once as if trying to respond but then slumped more heavily than before. I let his head down slowly, so as not to make a thump.

For half a second, I considered cutting his throat with the knife. But I didn't know if mohol would keep him under for that, and if I fumbled it he might wake up screaming, or simply thrash in his sleep, and then I would be discovered. Besides, I'd already seen too much blood tonight. I'd never killed anyone or anything, never mind someone I'd tried to pretend was my brother for my entire life. Someone whom I'd both played tricks on and laughed with, who'd both pulled my hair and once held my hand all the way back to the villa when I'd skinned my knee running through the jungle. I almost couldn't recognize this hardened, vicious side of myself. She was new, born just hours before from fire and blood.

Moving quietly and carefully, I heaped my skirt and some feed sacks under the blanket in the approximate shape of a body. If anyone peeked in, I hoped the scene would look as before: both of us asleep, me under the blanket. Then I crept to the front corner of the wagon, farthest from the light of the fire and the laced-up exit at the back.

Slicing the hide covering was slower, but also quieter than I expected. It was under tension too, fitted tightly to the arching frame over the wagon bed. It parted with only a whisper but required a lot of pressure. If my hands weren't already in agony, they would have been by the time I cut a slit big enough for my shoulders to slip through.

The night air was fresh, cool, and alive, insects buzzing loud enough to mask any sound I made. My arms shook as I used all my strength to silently lower myself to the ground alongside one of the front wheels. Thank the gods we were still in the coastal forest, not exposed among the frequent expanses of sandy hills that were farther north and inland. It took all I had of a different kind of strength not to bolt through the shadows and into the surrounding trees, where I would find cover but no doubt crash around loud enough to rouse someone.

Not that I could even hope for Nyaren to be asleep. Someone had been feeding the fire.

No, I needed to move without dead twigs snapping underfoot or rustling underbrush, and that meant following the narrow road we were traveling. The way we'd been heading was the easiest route, since the fire was behind the wagon.

I sent a silent prayer to Heshara to keep me hidden, touched the horse's neck as I passed so as not to startle it, and then began to move faster. My heart was beating so loudly I could hear it against my eardrums. Once the wagon and the fire were a torch's glow behind me, I broke into a loping run, landing on the balls of my feet first, so my steps wouldn't pound.

I ran like that for as long as my lungs held out, until the arches of my feet cramped, my calves burned, my tongue was parched, and I was gasping too noisily for comfort. Only then did I duck off the road and make my way into the trees, the firelight long swallowed by the darkness of the woods behind me. The air grew heavier and humid under the canopy, muffling any noise I made and singing with life. Unfortunately, my surroundings also *felt* alive. I groped my way forward with each step, one arm stretched out and down to gently part the ferns and other undergrowth, the other held up in front of my face to part the vines and spiderwebs.

So many spiderwebs. I hated spiders. Several times something crawled along my arms or shoulders, and I hastily batted it away.

And there were creeping things other than spiders. Something large danced across my ankle once, maybe a snake or a giant centipede.

I took deep breaths and focused on stepping carefully, not on my skin crawling. Besides, how could I let insects affect me, after what I'd just been through? *No, don't think about that.* But it was too late. My eyes started to swim, blurring the looming shapes of the forest around me, as if it wasn't hard enough to see already. I gritted my teeth and dashed away my tears. *You can cry later. Right now you have to move.* That was what my mother would tell me to do. I could practically hear her voice in my head:

Move, Kamai.

Eventually, it wasn't tears that made my eyes blur. And nothing could keep my eyelids from drooping, not creeping things or even fear of pursuit. It was the lingering effect of the mohol, or likely that I was dead exhausted. I had to stop. Through the shadows up ahead, I spotted a downed tree, covered in moss. I could lie on the other side of the trunk, tuck myself out of view of anyone coming this way, and sleep. I wished I could lie on top to keep off the ground, but then I might as well serve myself up on a platter for whoever came along. Better the bugs found me.

Or so I thought.

Low to the ground, my foot kicked into something without much resistance, like a spiderweb. But unlike a spiderweb, it came alive and attacked me as soon as it broke apart. Within seconds, whatever I'd disturbed swarmed up my foot, and then my legs.

Ants. I'd kicked a tunnel.

It wasn't a tunnel made of dirt. I'd seen them moving at dusk through the forest ringing our villa, creating walls out of their own warriors' bodies to move their unhatched young safely within. The whole colony would form a miniature black river winding over the sand and through the trees, often farther than my eye could trace. The warriors linked with their jaws outward, so every bit of the living structure literally had teeth. I'd once poked one with a stick just for fun, and had to drop the stick when the warriors latched on, breaking formation to funnel up it in a ferocious storm.

Now my body was the stick, and in seconds I was covered in ants. Pinching, biting, stinging ants. My skin burned like fire.

I couldn't help it: I screamed. It didn't make me feel any better. Nor did running in circles and beating at my skin. I screamed again as the ants began savaging my neck and face.

If a light hadn't flared in the trees behind me, I may have just collapsed right there and succumbed to death. Instead, I ran for the light, not caring who it was. It was toward the road, but in the opposite direction of the wagon, at least. Even so, it could have been Razim with a torch and I still would have run to him and pleaded for help, such was the pain.

It wasn't Razim or Nyaren. But the sight of half a dozen men carrying lanterns and swords, bare steel glinting in the darkness, was enough to make me pause.

I dropped to the sandy ground behind some bushes, ignoring the pain as best I could, trying not to make any noise, even though I wanted to keep screaming. If I had managed the agony of seeing my mother killed in silence, I could do this. I stuffed my fist in my mouth and bit down on it hard enough to draw blood, while I used my other hand to swipe at my face and neck. Nothing helped. I was burning to death, like I almost had in the villa. And yet these men might complete the job if I didn't keep quiet.

"Over there!" said a voice. "I heard rustling."

"Could be an ambush by whoever started the fire. That lad had a strange look about him; he could have been lying."

"No, a girl was screaming." A feminine voice. They weren't all men. I almost cried out and gave myself away then, though I wasn't sure why. A woman was just as capable of deceit as a man. Maybe it was that I wanted to hear a different woman's voice—my mother's—so very badly. This voice sounded younger, rising to call, "Whoever it is, don't be afraid. We're only looking for someone—a girl, to help her. Jidras Numa sent us from the capital to find his daughter, Kamai Nuala. We're here to bring her to him."

Go to your father . . . it's the only place that will be safe. Between my mother's urgent instructions and the use of my father's name, I doubted this was a trick. It was enough for me, at least, to leap up and fling myself right into the middle of them.

All my pain and fear came pouring out of me in the form of wailing and waving arms. "Ants, ants, get them off me!"

For a second, they looked startled, like I was a ghost who had come winging out of the night. Then they all plunged into action. In a matter of seconds, swords were dropped, several men were batting at my arms and legs and hair, and the woman was tearing at the ties on my bodice to loosen it. Normally, I would have shied away in horror, but at the moment I was happy to help her undo them.

"Ranta's tits, they're all over her," one man exclaimed. "Ouch! One bit me."

"Think how bad it must be for her! Now, watch your language, give me your canteens—and don't look," the woman barked at the others. Awkwardly, a couple of men sidled forward with their eyes averted, holding out their offerings, as she dropped my bodice down around my shoulders.

The woman took the canteens from them and unceremoniously dumped them over my head, splashing water over my face, neck, and chest, washing most of the ants away. The rest she carefully picked away as she spotted them, crushing them between her fingers. I helped as best I could. My usually pale skin, wet in the warm glow of lantern light, was angry red and covered in welts.

"You must be Kamai?" the woman murmured. All I could do was give her a shuddering nod. "You have his nose," she said.

Once the top half of me was clear, the woman tugged my bodice up to cover me, passed the ties into my hands, and hoisted my slip. "Let me get your legs." More splashing of water, more light pinches of her fingertips against my thighs and calves. I didn't feel the slightest bit awkward, not even when I noticed one of the men grinning at the sight of the woman down on her knees in front of me, half under my dark shift with a lantern lighting it up from within. I just thought he was an idiot.

"Need any help?" he asked, his tone innocent. I glared, but my watery eyes probably ruined the effect.

"Shut it," the woman snapped, and his grin turned sheepish.

When she finally pulled away, she had to smooth down her short brown hair—mussed by my skirt. She looked to be in her early twenties, and while her jaw was square, her nose slightly crooked, and her brown cheeks chapped by the sun, she suddenly looked like the loveliest person in the whole of Eopia to me. "All right?" she asked.

I almost wanted to laugh and say, *No, I'm not all right, but at least ants are no longer eating me alive.* Instead, I started crying huge, breathless sobs. They shook my entire body.

"There, there, come on, then." The young woman patted me awkwardly. The men were suddenly scouting the trees, shuffling their feet, or checking their swords, happy to leave the crying girl to a woman. Not that she looked or acted a whole lot like any woman I'd ever met—tall, no curves or softness to speak of, all lean muscle and martial movements. I'd heard of women, even seen a few, who were guards or soldiers and acted more like men, but never one who seemed to be *giving* the orders. "Let's get you to the carriage and to your father," she said.

"Carriage? Where——?"

She pointed through the trees. "It's right over there, in the road. I'm Nikha, head of your father's household guard, and he sent us when he got word of . . . well . . ."

Never mind the fact that she was a woman, she seemed remarkably *young* to be in charge, especially of a bunch of older men, but I didn't have long to consider it. My eyes were swimming again. "My mother," I said, my voice breaking.

Nikha's eyes grew grim. "We're not sure what happened, only that your father received a missive that his daughter, one Kamai Nuala, was in danger. Never mind that none of us were aware he *had* a daughter. When we arrived at the location he gave us, the place was embers. You're some ways away from there, in the opposite direction of the capital, so we're lucky we found you. We were about to turn around. We only thought you might have gone this way by accident, if you hadn't . . . if you weren't . . ."

If I weren't embers like everything else.

I suddenly remembered Razim, the danger that was still out there. "Did you see a covered wagon?"

She must have heard the fear in my voice because her gaze sharpened. The others were looking my way now too. "Yes, we passed one, with a man dead drunk in the back and another dousing his fire. He seemed suspicious but said he'd seen no sign of a lone girl, or even a rider. We carried on a bit farther because we didn't like the look of him, and that's when we heard your scream."

"He's lying. I think they helped start the fire, though there were lots of other . . . men . . . too"—I didn't want to say soldiers—"and then the two of them kidnapped me. I was in the wagon, but I ran."

Swords were immediately in hand again. "Maybe a few of us should go look for them," one of the men said darkly.

Nikha frowned. "No. They're probably long gone, and we need to get her back. They're not our business." She turned to me. "Do you know who they were?"

I shook my head. I couldn't tell them that Razim was supposedly my stepbrother, because I would have had to explain why he was kidnapping me, and that would lead to the Twilight Guild—and too many dangerous secrets. "My mother might have known, but she . . . she didn't make it out of the house." Luckily, my choked voice disguised the rage and disgust in what I said next. "I don't think my *stepbrother* did, either." Which was true, in a sense. He was no longer my stepbrother, in pretend or practice or otherwise. "And Hallan, my stepfather . . . I heard one of the attackers say he was dead."

Nikha put her hand on my shoulder. "A carriage was ambushed between your villa and the capital, both the driver and passenger pulled to the side of the road and beheaded. I think the passenger was Hallan Lizier. I'm sorry."

Beheaded. Hallan's deep voice, his sharp eyes, witty mouth—all severed from the rest of him. I knew he was dead, but to hear how made bile rise in my throat. "Why?" I cried, even though I probably knew more than she did—at least *who* had done it. The Twilight Guild.

"I think your father will be able to explain better than I can," she said hesitantly. "Let's get you home."

Home. My home was ash, but I nodded anyway.

"They don't"—I had to swallow—"those two men in the wagon, they don't know where we're going, right?"

"No. The man asked who we worked for, but I told him it was none of his business. You'll be safe."

That wouldn't necessarily stop Razim or the Twilight Guild from figuring out where I'd gone. My mother said the guild had members tucked everywhere, from the poorest alleyways up to the king's court. *Safe.* The word felt as hollow as *home.*

Sleep came despite my burning skin and the nickering of the horses, and most especially despite the worry that, even though Razim's wagon was indeed gone, he would somehow come after me. My head tipped slowly, dropping onto Nikha's arm. I couldn't help it, and she was already asleep anyway, so I didn't think she would mind.

Nikha's soul was surprisingly expansive. I already knew that a person's nehym didn't often match their body in the waking world, but the difference here was more drastic than usual. Nikha wasn't what I would have called beautiful, but her soul

54

was. It was like a tree house, wooden floors winding through different levels and passages, smooth branches twining the walls in intricate patterns. The entirety of it glowed like polished furniture in firelight.

I should have just left it and drifted into dreams. Instead, I looked around, my anger and despair building.

It was beautiful, but it was not my mother's. My mother should have been the one to tend my wounds. Hers should have been the shoulder I leaned upon. This should have been her soul. Her nehym was the closest thing I had to a nehym of my own, and now I would never see it again. Those sandstone walls were a greater loss to me than those we had shared in the waking world. It felt like a physical pain in my chest, enough to nearly double me over. I truly was no better than an empty shell— what I had always feared.

I had lost everything. I only had a father's name. My mother had said neither of us would likely be pleased to meet each other, so why go to him? I wasn't even sure why I'd bothered escaping, other than to spite Razim. Spite was all I had left to fill me.

The black door appeared then, as if summoned by my dark mood, drawing the color and warmth and gleam from the wooden wall. I laughed at the perfect timing.

And why not? I thought. What did I have to lose? My mother had told me never to open it, but now she was dead, and I had nothing else. A small, petty part of me was furious at *her* for dying and wanted to get back at her, even if it killed me. Maybe especially if it killed me.

Besides, how could something that had given me a rose petal be *that* dangerous?

Perhaps if I'd had my own nehym to give me somewhere

to go as I slept . . . Perhaps if my mother weren't dead . . .
Perhaps if she had told me what was hidden behind the door . . .

Perhaps then I wouldn't have opened it.

But I took the sleek, warm doorknob in my hand and turned
it. So much hinging on something so small. The door opened
soundlessly, though I could feel the density of its heavy black
material—was it wood or stone or something else?—pushing
against me, as if it had been waiting for my touch.

My mother's voice came back to me: *It* wants *the door to open.*
It.

Like a large animal's head nudging against the hand of a
child, the power was startling, unbalancing, its friendliness
dubious. Uncertainty and fear flickered through me like a candle
flame sparking back to life, but it was too late. The door swung
wide, and the way stood open.

5

OPEN DOORS

Beyond the black door was a dark hallway, darker than even the dimmest soul I'd ever visited. The way ahead vanished into blackness after only a few feet. The walls leaned in to meet at a point above; they and the floor were made from the same flawless material as the door—at least insofar as I could see, which wasn't far at all.

Hairs rose on the back of my neck. This didn't seem . . . *right*. The darkness almost looked tangible, like my reaching hand could disappear into it as if into black water.

I slammed the door without hesitating. Oddly, it didn't resist, its weight gliding back into place with as little sound as when it had opened.

Maybe because it didn't have to resist. The door no longer latched. As soon as I let go, it began to swing inexorably open again. Panicking, I cast around for something to barricade it and saw a lovely wooden table, made of entwined branches, lining the wall nearby. I wasn't supposed to move anything in a nehym. That was one of my mother's rules, but I'd broken so many of those already. Pinning the door closed with my foot, I grabbed the end of the table and dragged it in front of the frame.

It held. But even at my most hopeful, I knew the solution wasn't permanent. After all, my mother hadn't told me *Never open the door, Kamai—but, oh, if you do, just block it with a table.*

But all I could do, beyond hope, was pretend this would be enough. And then, since I didn't want to think about what I had done, I fled.

Nikha startled awake when I did. The first thing to occur to me, as I flushed with embarrassment, was that I'd practically shifted my legs onto her lap to avoid bumping the man who was sleeping across from me in the carriage.

The next thing was: Nikha. The fire. The black door. This was all real. My mother was dead, and I'd opened the door.

"Nightmare?" she murmured sympathetically. She gave me a traditional blessing, using three fingers to touch the crown of her head, between her eyes, and her lips—symbolizing Tain, Heshara, and Ranta—and then my lips. A kiss, of sorts. Father and mother, protecting their daughter from the evil behind the stars. "We'll arrive in the capital in another hour. Sleep a bit longer, if you want."

I was too stunned by her kindness to respond. The last person to bless me like that had been my mother. Her absence felt like a hole straight through me, gutting me, while the memory of the darkness behind the door refilled me with something sickening and awful . . . and somehow a morbid anticipation of what might lie beyond it. Shame followed quickly on those heels, and nothing could keep my eyes from tearing.

Central Library - Circulation
12/19/2019   2:10:08 PM

- PATRON RECEIPT -
- CHARGES -

1: Item Number: 37244242505544
Title: Beyond the black door /
Due Date: 1/9/2020

2: Item Number: 37244244276011
Title: The Guinevere deception /
Due Date: 1/9/2020

3: Item Number: 37244243413789
Title: The starless sea /
Due Date: 1/9/2020

To Renew: www.lapl.org or 888-577-5275

Looking for something special to do this
holiday season? Check out our calendar!
https://www.lapl.org/holiday-events

--Please retain this slip as your receipt--

Nikha reached for me in a heartbeat, cradling my head against her chest. It was hard and mostly flattened under her leather tunic, the opposite of my mother's soft curves, but it was still a caring gesture. I had guessed that she was awkward with such things, but maybe she wasn't now that her men weren't watching her.

The kindness flayed me, worse than the ant bites. She thought I cried because I missed my mother and my home, or maybe even because my skin burned. Not because I had done something awful—maybe even to her.

The act was what kept me going. If I hadn't needed to pretend I was only a grieving girl, I would have lain down and never moved again. If spite had filled and animated me before, now it was lies.

Through my tears, I searched Nikha's eyes for a sign that something was amiss, that I'd unleashed something dark and horrible in her soul—or that even moving the table had upset her in some way. She *did* seem slightly off-balance, shaking her head and blinking a few times, as if to clear a fog or knock something back into place—but then all she did was grimace over my ant bites anew and encourage me to go back to sleep.

I shouldn't have been able to sleep. I didn't *want* to sleep ever again. But I had to know.

I ducked into the soul of the man across from me, because I didn't want to risk hurting Nikha further. It was a creepy place, cramped like a cellar with ropes and chains hanging from the low ceiling, each dangling strange items—I saw a crudely stitched doll and a red-stained, lumpy satchel before I spun away. I was glad I hadn't let my knees touch his.

When I turned, I found myself facing the door. It was open again.

The blackness bored into the rough stone of the nehym's wall, like I was looking down into a deep pit in the floor. For a second I was disoriented, dizzy. But then my eyes locked on to something that hadn't been there before, and I froze.

On the smooth floor, just beyond the black threshold and before the thick darkness, lay a single red rose. An offering.

Or maybe bait.

I waited, watching and listening for anything else in the murky gloom beyond the doorway. Nothing came. I wanted to close the door and block it again, but I didn't want to touch a single thing in this man's soul, and not out of respect for the rules. Besides, I couldn't spot any object heavy enough or that I could easily drag.

Backing away without taking my eyes off the door, I slipped away into dreams.

When we arrived in the capital, the sun was just peeking over the mountains and setting rooftops alight. I'd been to Shalain only a couple of times, even though we lived a mere few hours away. *Had* lived.

I supposed I lived in the capital now. My mother had often made appearances with Hallan at court, the two of them on display like jewels for coveting. They had frequently stayed with others in the city or even at the palace, though on rarer occasions, they'd allowed guests of their own to come out to the villa, which was when I'd practice soulwalking on strangers. Truly though, my mother had kept me away from the court's eyes.

And now I was here, while Marin and Hallan were dead. Despite the horrific circumstances, I couldn't help staring out the window in wonder.

The city was made of sandstone and coral like many of the villas outside of it, but it was built narrowly upward rather than sprawling outward. Bronze domes gleamed against the white stone in every shape and size, wavering in the air like coins at the bottom of a fountain. Most of the buildings hid private central courtyards within their tall pale walls and colorful tiled roofs, rising in a neat slope toward the mountains like pearly rows of teeth. The capital was in an easily defended position, in a niche where the central mountain range, Ranta's Fingers, bisected Eopia and met the sea at the southern tip of the island continent. The port lay shimmering deep blue to the south, while rocky, forest-veined mountains rose jaggedly behind the city to the northeast. The only easy access was from the west, the direction from which we'd come. The sun fully crested the peaks as we wove our way into the city, making the buildings glow in pink and orange, the bronze domes flare like torches, and the ocean glitter aquamarine. For a second, the view made me forget that everything about my arrival here was miserable.

Just like the roads threading the countryside, the city was impeccably well kept and organized. It was no wonder to me that the king was loved and respected, especially by city folk. They were cared for by their king, and perhaps by the goddess who was bound to him. I could almost imagine the sensation of Ranta's presence that people had reported at the king's coronation. The very streets and its inhabitants seemed blessed.

City folk were out and about, walking or riding horses, some in plain attire, others in rich finery, and still others hidden away in carriages as richly decorated as desserts. Even several horses had their manes and tails braided with silk, their harnesses hanging with chiming disks of bronze, glinting in the morning light. The sun shortly grew strong and hot, which explained the white and pastel silks and linens that dominated the streets, matching the city walls. I was used to the shade of the forest and the cool tile halls of the villa, but in this baking heat, even I would have been tempted to forgo the dark colors I preferred.

Despite the warmth, many heads were covered. Women wore scarves for a number of reasons: to keep the beating sun off, and, if they were devout, out of respect for Heshara, who hid her bright self during the day. Although the moon goddess was often partially shrouded in the night sky as well, many argued it was her loose black hair that curtained her pale face, so it was far more common for women to go without scarves in the evening, unless they *really* didn't want a breeze to disturb their hair. I'd never bothered with them, at the villa.

Skin color varied like clothes—the bronze like Hallan's from the original inhabitants of the island, said to have been Ranta's first children; the darker brown like Nikha's that may have come from once-nomadic sailors of the distant east; the deep black of our nearest neighbors from the green continent to the west; and the pale tones of the traders from far across the sea who'd stayed and since multiplied, resulting in the likes of me. Many peoples had, throughout time, arrived here to mingle and create Eopians. Historically, such intermixing was seen as particularly blessed, since Tain had dark brown skin, Heshara improbable white, and Ranta, whether depicted as a babe in her parents' arms or a voluptuous woman, was somewhere in between, her hair and skin a rich light brown. Statues of all three, from human-size to building height, stood among the population as reminders of their favor. Most recently, the foreign trade that the king had encouraged had resulted in the city's latest wave of prosperity, a blessing that felt much more tangible.

So many bright people, so many new fashions. I felt pride for my homeland rise within me, and I turned from the carriage window to exclaim something to Nikha. Suddenly, as if cold water were splashed in my face, I remembered who I was with and why I was here. I sat back in my seat and looked at my hands, ignoring the eyes of the sickly souled man across from me, which flickered in my direction far too often. I tried glaring, and then a staring contest to get him to stop, but neither worked. I wished I had something to discreetly throw at him.

Finally, the carriage rolled to a halt. We were on a quieter, cobbled lane, the stones pale cream and smooth under the wheels. A town house sat elegantly alongside a cluster of equally large, lavish buildings. This was no doubt a neighborhood of business and culture, the homes of the wealthiest merchants and maybe even minor nobility. For the first time, it occurred to me that my father might be higher in society than Marin and Hallan.

The two men inside with us piled out. I caught Nikha's arm when she shifted and jerked my head at the man who'd been sitting across from me, now stretching his back in the morning light.

"He's a foul man," I muttered to her.

"Gerresh?" she asked in surprise. She frowned but kept her voice as low as mine, her tone turning hard and deadly. "Did he say something to you? *Do* something?"

"No . . ." Of course, I couldn't explain what I'd seen in his soul. "It's just . . . his eyes. A feeling I have. Be careful around him. He's sick."

She blinked, looking at me oddly, a ragged girl she barely

knew, warning her, a grown and heavily armed woman, to be careful of one of her own men. For a second, I thought she might laugh at me. But then she nodded and slid out of the carriage, extending a hand afterward to help me down.

The men headed through a narrow alley that ran along one side of the house, toward a back service entrance. But Nikha escorted me up the main walkway.

I found myself standing in front of a new door, sky blue to match the lacquered roof tiles several stories above us, trimmed in gilded wood set in the white sandstone walls. It should have been far less intimidating than the black door, but it wasn't.

Nikha took a deep breath and shot me an uncharacteristically nervous glance. "Just be patient with him and remember that he *did* send us to find you last night, the very moment a message arrived from your mother. He cares."

Which definitely didn't make me feel better. I wanted to hold back, assess, slip in quietly instead of march right in the front, sneak around like I would in a nehym, but she didn't wait, opening the door for me to step inside.

6

SURPRISING MONSTERS

The interior of the town house was cool and dim, with sunlight filtering through thick shuttered windows and gauzy curtains. The floors were polished dark hardwood, accented with pale, intricately woven rugs. The upholstery of the furniture was equally rich, but reserved, with creams and dark browns set against each other in constrained geometric patterns. A golden statue of Tain lorded over a small alcove, his hair like sunbeams and his gaze stern. The whole place was dark and light, buoyant and heavy, opposites holding each other in check with strict, refined order. Every surface was impeccably clean.

A man appeared at the top of a sweeping set of dark stairs. He was dressed in a fine linen suit in shades of cream trimmed with white, a pale blue silk sash at the waist, his airy attire in contrast to his severe expression. He stared at us—at me, rather. Indeed, he had my nose.

"Sir," Nikha said, bowing. "This is Kamai Nuala. Kamai, this is Sir Jidras Numa, His Royal Majesty's esteemed head of tax collection and lord of the Numa family estates in the Risha province."

Risha was well north of us. Inland, up against the mountains, even more arid without as much of a wet season, and cooler. They made wine up there—red grape wine, not white palm wine, like down south. *Superior* wine, supposedly. I preferred palm wine. It was sweeter.

Tax collector told me the rest. I suddenly remembered Hallan's rich tone of amusement at dinner a couple of years ago. *The only thing tax collectors are good for is pinching their rear ends together and pennies out of the populace; tight asses, is what they are.*

I suddenly wondered if Hallan had known who my father was and had been needling my mother. Based on the way she had laughed and shot him an exasperated glance, it was probable.

As if Jidras could sense my thoughts, he looked down at me like I were some ragged piece of junk Nikha was trying to hawk. I probably appeared no better than that, with my gown half-torn away and my still-red skin. I stared back at him, too overwhelmed for any real defiance. I did what I always did when unsure of my footing: I studied him.

Jidras Numa's skin was a touch darker than mine, a creamy tan. His eyes were an odd shade of blue, very unlike the brown of my mother's and mine. His hair was straighter too, and tied tightly behind his head with a ribbon. I could see why my mother might have liked the look of him; he was handsome, aside from the scowl on his face.

All my mother's careful training in decorum and manners evaporated like a spray of water under the beating sun. "Um," I said.

He wasn't bothering with niceties, either. He stepped the rest of the way down the stairs and stood in front of me, his shiny leather shoes clicking on the hardwood floor.

"Sweet Heshara, she looks like her." Jidras's eyes narrowed farther. "And like me." He said the latter like it might be a bad thing.

"Trust me, the feeling is mutual," I murmured. My voice was faint, so it took him a second to realize I might have been insulting him.

Nikha cleared her throat in the awkward silence that followed. "Sir, if I may be so bold, Kamai had a rough night. This *is* your daughter," she said as if reminding him.

"And Marin's daughter," I interjected, anger rising quickly.

"Good gods, she even *sounds* like her." This was definitely a bad thing.

He wasn't much taller than me, and yet he was speaking over my head as if I weren't there. I tried to stand straighter, throw back my shoulders, but my ant bites chafed under my bodice. Even so, I was about to say something in the haughtiest voice I could muster when his next words hit me like a punch to the stomach.

"Just so we're clear, Kamai is *not* my daughter," he said with a hard glance at Nikha. Then he brushed me aside and headed for the interior of the house.

Still without saying a word to me.

As my breath whooshed out, Nikha's hissed in like she wanted to say something. When I glanced at her, her jaw was clenched so hard a muscle twitched. Even as the head of his guard, she probably couldn't completely speak her mind.

Well, he couldn't fire *me*. If he didn't like whatever I said, I would be no worse off than I already was: homeless and hungry.

"Hey," I snapped as I followed Jidras. "You can't just walk away like that. My mo—Marin said—"

He spun on me in a wide hallway, his eyes angry again. "I can do whatever I wish in my own house. As for your mother's *claims*," he sneered, "I may have been the one to help put the bulge in her belly, but I've had nothing to do with you, no part in your upbringing. And that was how she wanted it, so blame her if you feel like blaming someone."

The vitriol in his words made me take a step back. At least he was speaking directly to me now.

"But . . . if you *are* my father . . ." It was like he was insisting that something was both true and false.

"As far as you or I are concerned, I'm *not*. You might look something like me, but don't go calling me Father, or anything of the sort. You're your own person, and I'm my own, separate. And let's keep it that way." He resumed his march toward a set of double doors with golden knobs. Their inset glass windows revealed a leafy green courtyard of white stone, drenched in delicious-looking shade.

So he didn't want me. This wasn't a safe place. It probably should have been obvious as soon as I'd stepped inside. And yet he was my last hope. "But I have nowhere else to go," I nearly shouted. "My mother is *dead*."

He paused with his hand on the golden knob. His fingernails were trim and clean. I looked down at mine, which had dirt crammed under the pale half-moons. They blurred in my vision. I could feel Nikha at my back, like a shadow.

Jidras's words were suddenly much softer. "I thought she might be, if you were here. Her letter said . . ." I desperately wanted to know what her letter had said, but he shook his head and changed the subject. "Anyway, that would be the only reason she'd allow me to see you." He opened the door and stepped into the cool, shady courtyard. He glanced back at me. "Well? I'm very busy. Do you need something from me?"

Only everything. Food, a home, a family. Was he really going to make me beg to stay even as an awkward houseguest?

No. I almost said it out loud. He couldn't take away my pride. I would leave before I would beg.

But he continued before I had to. "If not, then Nikha can show you to your room and a bath—and then take one herself so she can stop tracking dirt all over the floor. Afterward, Nikha, report to me outside. Oh, and call for some coffee to be brought out to me." He cast another glance of distaste at me over his shoulder. "Call for a tailor, as well. We can't have her looking like that."

I almost couldn't believe it, despite the arrogance and implied insults. "I can stay?" I whispered.

"I'm not going to throw you out on the street." He gestured at himself, his fine clothes. "What do you take me for, a monster?"

Close, I nearly said, and then he shut the courtyard door in my face.

Nikha showed me to my room—rooms, actually: a guest suite on the second floor—and even helped me fill the large tiled bath and slip carefully out of my tattered gown. I gathered this wasn't her usual job, but she must have sensed I needed a friendly face. Though the servants dutifully brought copper buckets of hot water, they were staring at me like I was dirt.

"Just give him time," she muttered, bent over the bath, testing the temperature of the water. "And them," she added, with a flick of her wrist at the servants who'd left. "This is new.

They'll adjust." She spoke with more hope than certainty, adding a dollop of cool-smelling oil to the water. For my skin, no doubt.

She was so considerate, and I was undeserving. Even so, I needed one more favor. While curls of fragrant steam and the leaves of potted plants on the bath's edge surrounded me as I sat down in the water, my mind was still wholly on what I'd left behind in the ashes. "Nikha, thank you, but I need to know what happened with Hallan, or even at the villa, if you know something I don't. You told me to ask Jidras, but I . . ." I swallowed. "I don't want to."

She stared at me a moment and then nodded. "He probably wouldn't tell you anyway. He doesn't want any of us talking about it because, from what I can gather, Hallan Lizier was quietly killed—executed—by the king's troops." Her voice grew even gentler. "I imagine the fire at his estate . . . your mother's death . . . had something to do with the king's soldiers as well."

Despite the steam, my throat was suddenly so dry it felt like the bottom of a desiccated riverbed, the cracks reaching down into my chest. "No, I don't believe it." It was the Twilight Guild, but I didn't say that. This was exactly what the Twilighters would want people to think, using such a disguise. "What could Hallan have possibly done to anger the king?"

Unless . . . Something told to me a long time ago niggled at my thoughts. Something about Hallan and the queen consort. But it was so unlikely I hadn't even believed it at the time, when I'd been a far more gullible child.

Nikha shrugged. "I'm sorry, but I don't know. Whatever it is, *you're* not at fault, and your fa—Sir Jidras—has sworn to protect you. He's solidly in the king's favor, and he can quietly change your name to his and introduce you at court as his daughter, sent from Risha to live with him just before you came of age."

In a little over two months, I would turn eighteen, the age of adulthood. Time enough for my past life to vanish, for people to believe I was only ever his daughter. Never mind that he couldn't even acknowledge me as such to my face, or to his household. But then, some things were easier to do in public than in front of those closest to you.

His daughter. His name attached to mine—Kamai Numa, not Nuala. His protection. His home. None of it my mother's any longer.

My mother was well and truly dead. All because of secrets I didn't know. Secrets I desperately wanted to find out.

Just then, a servant came bursting into the room, kicking over a bottle of oil and sending it clattering on the tiles. But she only looked to Nikha, her eyes wide. "News from the court," she gasped. "The queen consort, she died this morning—only thirty-eight, and yet *still* without giving the king a proper heir. They say it was a sudden seizure, natural, but already there's talk of poison. Can you believe it?"

Nikha and I stared at each other. I couldn't say anything, and not only because I was speechless with disbelief. But it didn't matter—already, I could see the connections forming in her eyes.

Most knew that Hallan was not only a courtier, but also a well-known pleasure artist. Nikha didn't need much more to conclude that Hallan must have had an affair with the queen consort, and the king had punished them both.

But then the Twilighters would have had no reason to get involved. His death wouldn't have been their fault, like my mother had said it was—at least she'd said they'd be responsible for anything terrible that happened. And there would have been no reason to kill *her* as well and burn down the villa.

Maybe Hallan—the thought was like a cold knife in my chest, the pain spreading—maybe he had somehow poisoned the queen consort for the Twilight Guild. My mother might have known of such a plan. Everything that had befallen us *could* still have been the king's retribution, but Hallan had always been so careful; how had the king traced it to him?

There were too many secrets. Too many mysteries: the deaths, my missing soul, the black door. And now that my mother was dead, I might never discover the truth about any of them.

Perhaps that was for the best. Some secrets weren't meant to be discovered. Some doors not meant to be opened. I'd already made that mistake once, and I shouldn't be tempted to do it again. I flinched as I settled deeper into the bath, tears stinging my eyes.

7

HEAVY SILENCE

If I'd found something resembling a monster behind one door,
I had yet to find anything more than a rose behind the other.
Not that I looked at the black door . . . much. Part of me didn't
want to look at all, but part of me had to. I needed to make sure
it wasn't *doing* anything, at least nothing horrible.

It was my responsibility, after all. And maybe I just needed
to satisfy my own undying curiosity. But the black door didn't
reveal much. It remained open in the nehyms I managed to visit,
and yet the lone offering inside wasn't enough to overcome the
terrifying quality of the darkness behind it. It didn't help that
the rose never withered, seemingly frozen outside of time. The
whole picture made me shiver, so I never drew closer for anything more than an occasional glimpse inside.

Jidras's home turned out to be equally frustrating in its own
way. Everyone continued to effectively ignore me in the weeks
that followed my arrival. My appearance in the town house was

far less remarked upon than the death of the queen consort and all the theories surrounding it.

Hallan's death, and my mother's, weren't remarked upon at all. It was as if they had never existed. And, just as strangely, the Twilight Guild hadn't yet found me—to finish the job of killing me, to interrogate me, to recruit me, or to do anything else. There wasn't a breath of them or Razim. I didn't want there to be, but it made my entire life feel imagined. I felt as if *I* hardly existed.

Servants who wouldn't meet my eyes and barely responded to my questions fed and clothed me. My father employed a chef who turned out papaya and pineapple slices on silver platters, avocado and tomato salads, prawn and peanut soups, coconut and cashew rice with spice-glazed chicken, and honey fritters that melted in the mouth. My father's tailor made fine dresses and scarves and shawls for me out of the highest-quality silks and linens, embroidered or beaded or lace-trimmed in the latest fashion. I had no grievances with any of them, except the silence.

Only Nikha talked to me. She truly listened too—she let Gerresh go as a household guard within a week. Shortly after that, she began regularly playing Gods and Kings with me.

"Tain's eye, you have a martial mind-set," Nikha said as my hand beat hers for the fifth time in a row. The two of us were alone at a small table in the courtyard, playing the version that didn't require a third person as judge. Ties in this case were resolved by a complex subset of rules about the order cards were played—rules I'd mastered—instead of each player making an argument one way or another for a nonbiased observer to decide.

Nikha was humble, unlike me, and usually won or lost without more than a shrug. Not that she was used to losing, which made her attitude all the more admirable. She regularly beat others at the game, and I'd seen enough in the previous weeks to know that she also almost always won her duels during her regular training sessions with the household guards under her command.

"I've been wondering," I said. "You're only a handful of years older than me. How did you come to be the head of Jidras's guard? You're good, but . . ."

"But he would only want the best?" She smiled, as if to tell me she wasn't offended. "Well, I am one of the best. I was the second woman to pass the royal test to become a licensed bodyguard."

The test was incredibly rigorous, from what I'd gathered. I'd never even heard of a woman being allowed to take it, let alone passing.

"Of course, once they realized there was a woman's body under all my armor," Nikha added, somewhat reluctantly, "they disqualified me from truly becoming a royal bodyguard, never mind how well I'd done."

My mouth fell open. "But if you have the skill, that's unfair! It shouldn't matter what you are."

Nikha shrugged awkwardly. "Those are the rules. But at least I gained a reputation, despite . . . how I look. Enough of one for someone of Sir Jidras's standing to hire me."

I'd heard several of the servants, both men and women, alternately scoff at her—behind her back, of course—for either being a female guard or being "mannish." It was another area, it seemed, like the royal test, where she couldn't win no matter what she did.

"So the first woman to pass the test must have been disqualified too," I said. Nikha nodded, and I couldn't help but ask, "Who was she?"

"My mother," she responded shortly, going back to scrutinizing our card game. I let my bubbling questions subside, since she didn't seem to want to talk about her mother—something I could understand. She leaned forward on a leather-braced forearm and rubbed her chin. "You know, I wonder what you might do with an actual weapon."

I grimaced. "Not much—Wait, Nikha, please, no!"

But she was already leaping up, going for a pair of practice blades.

After that, she regularly trained with me in the interior courtyard, the draping vines and canopy of leaves shielding us from the beating sun. I was no good with a sword—I hadn't been falsely modest. I could barely lift one. My attempts only triggered the memory of my mother trying to heft the ax in the entryway before she was murdered, further distracting me. Once Nikha realized I was hopeless, she helped me build on my existing skill in self-defense with a knife and bare hands. Things every woman should know, she insisted.

Jidras didn't mind the lessons, or at least he did nothing to stop them. He hired a tutor as well, to continue my other studies of subjects like geography, theology, and law. My tutor only spoke to me in a lecturing tone that didn't welcome any sort of response. I vastly preferred learning from books, which I continued to do on my own time. At least books didn't have a nasal voice.

My tutor asked me only one personal question, on a rainy day just shy of a month after I'd arrived in Shalain, nearly six weeks before my eighteenth birthday. "You must decide which realm to enter, of course. Which shall you choose?"

"What?" I'd been staring out the second-story window of the library, tracing the tracks of rain on the bubbly glass and wondering if I could resist checking the black door again that night. It was about all I was good at. Over the weeks, I'd cautiously ventured into the nehyms of Jidras's household to ascertain that no one here was a soulwalker. I'd also tried to glean any information I could about my mother's death, or the Twilight Guild, but I couldn't find anything. I didn't even know what to look for, nor even how to fully search a nehym, beyond wandering around and squinting for the answers my mother had always seemed able to extract. Jidras's soul might have held more clues, but I hadn't been able to walk in his nehym yet.

"The topic of discussion is which artistic realm you will decide upon as your means of employment in six weeks' time," my tutor said stiffly. "You will be a woman at eighteen. This is your *future*, so you might pay attention."

Of course *now* he wanted my opinion, when it was the last thing I wanted to consider. Facing my future meant entirely leaving my past, my mother, behind me. I put my pen down with a sharp click. "I wasn't aware we had discussions."

He went on as if I hadn't spoken. "Sir Jidras works in finance, and that would be an admirable pursuit within the Solar Arts, blessed by brilliant Tain." He touched the top of his head with three fingers. "You might also consider a career in law, medicine, astronomy, or other such cerebral paths." In response to my obvious distaste, my tutor continued, "Or perhaps in the Lunar Arts, blessed by wise Heshara." He used the same fingers to tap between his eyes. "You could be a diviner or poet or musician." He knew I had only the faintest aptitude for music, but then he brightened as much as he was capable. "Or perhaps a priestess of Heshara. It's never too late to be tested for the ability to peer into one's soul, since you may not even realize you possess the talent. Usually, only candidates with likely bloodlines are investigated since the gift is extremely rare, but an exception might be made for you because of Sir Jidras's prestigious reputation, and, at the very least, you could serve as an acolyte and then perhaps become a theologian."

He acted as if being tested were an honor and not a requirement if one came under suspicion of unsanctioned soulwalking. Besides, I already knew I had the ability and had no desire for anyone to find out. Priests and priestesses spent their days locked in temples, searching souls for some fault the owners might perceive or for mistruths when suspects were put to the question by lawful authorities. I couldn't imagine a duller future, so of course my tutor would favor that option for me.

Even if I wanted to go that path for some twisted reason, I would face bigger obstacles than tedium and isolation. Aside from the fact that I was fully aware I'd been illegally soulwalking for years, in testing to become a priestess of Heshara, it would take little time for someone to discover I had no soul—or at least one nobody could find. Would they think me a monster? Would they find the black door—open, no less? Imagining how it would feel to burn alive was all I needed to forever board up *that* door in my mind.

"What about the Earthen Arts?" I asked in my sweetest voice.

My tutor's tawny cheeks pinkened in embarrassment. "Those are not for you."

"Is Ranta not due her respect?" I threw his own words back at him. He liked to say we all owed Ranta reverence equal to that of her two parent-gods—fiery, exacting Tain and cool, mysterious Heshara; sun and moon; spirit and soul.

"The Earthen Arts do not befit your status as Sir Jidras's dau—ah, responsibility," he corrected himself. Even as a lover of pure fact, my tutor knew well by now not to call Jidras my father, or me his daughter. "That is the realm of the body—of soldiers, herbalists, farmers, *dancers* . . ." His voice grew more scandalized as he went on.

"Whores?" I said, arching my eyebrow for maximum effect. "Like my mother?"

I'd heard the servants whisper it: *the whore's daughter.* The proper name for my mother's calling was *pleasure artist*, since Marin and Hallan had accepted only gifts in exchange for their talents, never money, and they'd always had a choice of who they slept with. But it was a silly distinction, since even common pleasure workers deserved respect for the trade of their choosing, and getting paid shouldn't have made them any less artists. I balled my hands into tight fists every time I heard the servants' disrespect, wanting to hit something.

Nikha *had* hit one of them, early on, a male servant, when he'd whispered too loudly in her hearing. As a guard, she was herself an adept of the Earthen Arts. And maybe she'd done it because, for some reason, she cared about me when no one else here did.

"Sir Jidras would prefer you to follow his path, or at the least find a new one—not *hers*," my tutor continued.

He hadn't called my mother a whore, but he was certainly thinking it. My anger erupted before I could contain it—at him, at my father, at this new life that I didn't want. "Then he should godsdamned tell me that himself! And I'll tell *him* how much of a hypocrite he is since he took full advantage of her artistry when it suited him. In fact, you can both take your slimy opinions and choke on them!"

My tutor sat up even straighter, if that were possible, huffing as if I'd slapped him. "Language, young lady! Shall I inform Sir Jidras of how you are speaking to me?"

I stood and curtsied in the highest courtly form my mother had taught me, and my tutor's eyes widened in surprise. Marin would have been proud. "Since he won't hear it from me, by all means," I said icily. Then I touched my lips in benediction to Ranta, and I stalked out of the library.

It wasn't that I even wanted to work in the Earthen Arts, I reflected as I stormed through Jidras's town house up to my room. Not at all. Marin had worked in *all* three realms anyway: Solar as a spy, Lunar as a soulwalker, and Earthen as a pleasure artist, but of course I couldn't explain that to the idiot man. I just didn't want him to think he could insult my mother, or tell me which path I should choose.

I didn't know what I wanted to do. I felt lost, directionless without her.

I didn't want to be a tax collector for the crown like Jidras, or a priestess, or really anything other than what my mother had brought me up to be. Not that I entirely knew what that was, in her absence. I never wanted to make love, so that would make things a little difficult as a pleasure artist. *Soulwalker* wasn't exactly a viable profession, especially since it could get me locked away and perhaps executed. *Spy* was also unlikely, despite all the secrets I wished to discover, since the only people I knew who could employ me belonged to the Twilight Guild. I would rather die than work for my mother's murderers.

No, I'd rather kill them all. Starting with *him*.

I wondered if *assassin* was a possible profession.

———————

Jidras didn't reprimand me later that evening, despite my hope that my behavior would force a confrontation. He only sent a servant up to my third-floor room with my supper, to tell me I

80

was to eat alone and go to bed early if I couldn't keep a civil tongue.

I'd wanted to yell a message back to him, but what I was about to do would be more satisfying than that. And so I sat on my bed and waited.

My room was bearable. I had a comfortable four-poster bed, with white gauze netting strung between the carved columns to block insects. It was the pink that I minded: pink silk bedding, pink-painted walls, a pink floral rug leading to a pink-curtained window.

This hadn't been my room at the start. In those first couple of weeks, I'd stayed in a guest room in tones of brown and dark blue on the second floor, next to the library, which I much preferred. Meanwhile, Jidras had this room decorated for me—or rather, for someone he imagined was me. I felt spoiled because I could have had nothing—or could've been dead—but he'd designed it for the most prim and proper sort of girl, proving that he had no idea who I really was, and that he didn't care to know. Perhaps he thought he could eventually make me into the young lady he thought I should be.

Despite the pink, I had no problem retiring early in my room. I was going to do what my *mother* had taught me to do.

I was going to soulwalk.

All I had to do was wait until the servants went to bed and the house was quiet before tiptoeing to their doors. Their rooms were small enough that if I fell asleep leaning up against the wall nearby, I would next open my eyes inside their nehyms. I couldn't reach Jidras's soul like this—his master bedroom was too large—but despite the fact that I might have learned something from him, I didn't really want to be in his nehym anyway.

I was going to go back into the servants' nehyms and try *practicing* this time. Prying out secrets, even if they weren't those I wished to learn. I didn't quite know how to do it, but the day would soon come—at least I hoped it would—when I would need to know.

I flopped back on my bed to pass the time, closing my eyes so I didn't have to stare at the candlelit pink of my room.

And the next thing I knew, I was standing in the dark clearing, my halfway point between the waking world and dreams. I had fallen asleep, faster than if I had downed a vial of sleeping tonic. I glanced around in surprise, but then my eyes locked on to something. My entire body tensed, ready to run.

The black door was there, darker than anything else in my shadowy surroundings. I didn't need much light to see it was open.

I spun in a circle, actually checking that this was the same clearing. It was. This shouldn't have been possible. And yet the door had followed me *here*—to nowhere, really. All this time I'd thought I had to be in someone's nehym to see it.

It had never appeared here before. So why now?

Probably, because I'd opened it. I'd let whatever was in there into *me*. My mother said my soul was hidden, and so maybe this clearing was the closest thing I had to a nehym, the nearest the door could get to finding my deepest self.

When I looked at the door again, my breath caught.

There was more than one rose. They were identical and evenly spaced, leading away from the threshold, vanishing into the yawning darkness within.

Whatever was in there seemed to want me to follow.

My fingers dug into my thighs through my skirt. I was wearing one of my dresses that had burned with the villa: black and beige silk panels, with wide, embroidered sleeves and a scooping neckline. Wearing clothes that were mine, even if they didn't really exist anymore, gave me courage. This clearing was *my* place, as empty as it was. The black door was *my* mistake. And I was going to find out, once and for all, what I had done. I would follow the roses to their end, to whatever was waiting.

I tried to ignore the part of myself that *wanted* to follow. That wanted to see the dark end of this, if only to know what it held.

My feet carried me hesitantly over the murky ground. My clearing may have been dim, but at least there was some light. Behind the door was only darkness so complete, it was like its own substance, swallowing the trail of roses.

When my thin slipper touched down on the perfectly smooth material of the threshold, I almost jerked away. Just like every other time I had felt the door, the black stone there wasn't cold, but warm through my slipper. Alive, somehow. I almost expected the floor to shift underfoot, to stir at my touch, as if I were treading on the back of a sleeping beast.

I took another step, bringing myself fully inside the door for the first time. The air felt different—neither chilly nor warm, but thicker, like I was slipping behind a veil. Without taking my eyes off the darkness, I bent to pick up the first rose. It felt normal against my fingers. Cool, smooth stem, skin-soft petals. Like a rose in the waking world.

Nothing moved in the black ahead. I straightened and exhaled a breath I hadn't realized I was holding.

That was when the door slammed shut behind me, plunging me into total darkness.

8

IMMOVABLE NIGHTMARES

I froze. I should have been looking behind, not forward. I should have tried to prop open the door beforehand. I should have—

Kamai . . .

The darkness spoke to me in that night-breeze voice I'd tried so hard to forget. My thoughts fell still. And then all I could hear were my own panicked breaths and something nearly like a whimper escaping my lips. A whisper of air tickled over my skin, prickling my neck and scalp. I squeezed the rose so hard a thorn pierced my finger. With a gasp, I let it go.

I almost gasped again, because as soon as I dropped the rose, light flared overhead. I spun around and shielded my eyes. The light wasn't intense, but it was powerful in contrast to what had come before.

A long dark hallway stretched before me, lit by dangling, ornately patterned black orbs glowing in red and indigo. I couldn't tell what the lamps were made of, or even what held them suspended. When I stared, their silhouetted patterns—different for each orb—changed. Some recalled thorny rose branches shifting in front of an illuminated window at night, others swirling clouds across a strange moon. The colorful luminosity blended down the hallway, neither cold nor warm, simply unearthly, and cast detailed shadows on otherwise bare, smooth black surfaces. The walls and floor seemed to writhe slowly. Or breathe.

I couldn't help thinking it was beautiful, if eerie. More roses led the way down the hall.

I glanced behind me at the door. The way out. It was shut so tightly I could barely see the seams. I knew it wouldn't open, even though I tried anyway.

I wondered what would happen if I never escaped, never awoke. Would my body simply waste away, unable to nourish itself? Would Jidras think some mysterious illness had befallen me, since he didn't know I was a soulwalker? Would he send for a priest or priestess of Heshara? Would he even care?

I squared my shoulders and took a deep breath. I didn't care if he didn't care. And if a priest or priestess found out what I was and what I had done, I might be better off trapped here. Besides, I'd entered this place of my own free will, to discover what was behind the door. And I had to admit . . . a part of me had always wanted this. To learn what dark secrets the door hid. I took a slow, shaky step down the hall, then another. And another. The strength in my legs grew with each stride, and my breath evened out.

But when the way forward suddenly opened up around me, my jaw dropped and I stumbled to a halt. I stood in a cavernous entry hall bigger than any palace's. It was bigger than imagination. Bigger than dreams or nightmares.

The entry hall alone was wider and longer than any ball-room I had ever seen in the waking or sleeping world. Everything was black, and the lamps simply floated high overhead, with no pretense of hanging from anything. Staircases leapt off in all directions: three arching sets on either side of the hall in increasing size, rising like black waves before the final two at the end that curved in a mirror image of each other. There was no indication of where the last pair went. They disappeared into huge vault-arched hallways that reminded me of depthless eyes.

But none of those architectural wonders held my attention for long next to the one right before me. A massive spiral staircase rose right out of the center of the hall, wider than three carriages abreast, and it continued rising . . . into nothing. As far as I could see, there was no ceiling above my head, only darkness. More disturbing, the stairs twisted into the floor in an equally endless fashion. When I gathered enough courage to sidle over to the banister and glance down the central shaft, it seemed to fall forever.

I pulled a pin out of my hair and dropped it, forgetting the rules about not altering anything in the sleeping world. Maybe it was because this place felt immovable. Unchangeable. The oppressive, towering walls almost seemed amused at the thought that I would even try to affect them. I was as insubstantial as a gnat buzzing alongside.

I didn't hear the pin land. The darkness swallowed it as if it had never been.

If this was a nehym, it was the grandest, darkest, and most imposing I had ever seen. I was no longer sure I wanted to meet whomever it belonged to.

And yet part of me was in complete awe. The roses were still trying to guide me, as if they understood my fascination. My twisted desire to see *more*. One rested at the base of the second staircase on the left side of the hall, another at the top of those arching black steps.

My heart leapt in my chest almost hard enough for me to hear it, and that almost-sound was the loudest noise in the place. Silence, there was so much silence. It was almost a presence itself, like the darkness. I stepped back from the banister dizzily. The brush of my slipper over the smooth floor was like a heavy boot scraping over gravel, echoing all over the hall. I flinched, but there was no one to hear me.

Every surface was as frozen as a mask. But almost as soon as I thought that, the light shifted to create a checkered pattern on the floor in shades of black and red, and vines made of cast shadows seemed to grow up the wall, creating the illusion of something living. The floating lamps seemed to shine a deeper crimson over the roses.

I'd never had a soul respond to my thoughts before, if that was what it had done. I felt a thrill, but caution struggled to replace it.

It wants *the door to open*, my mother's voice murmured in my mind.

Maybe, unlike other nehyms, this place had desires of its own. And maybe this wasn't a soul at all. There were tales of monsters and lands beyond our understanding. Not the stories of the gods, which everyone knew to be true, but legends and myths that may have had kernels of truth. This might be some vast, forgotten place on the fringes of the sleeping realm, waiting to swallow the unwary. Or the utterly foolhardy, in my case. *Here there be monsters,* like the old maps said along the edges of the known world.

But then, why the roses?

Bait, I thought again. Or maybe they were a sign of something alive, something sweet and soft in here. As I saw it, there wasn't much else for me to do except continue down the path I had chosen.

That didn't stop me from taking my mother's knife out of my bodice and nestling it in my palm, the solidity of its smooth wooden handle reassuring. I was surprised I even had it in the sleeping realm. I'd never noticed it here before. But then, I'd never needed it until now.

Not that I imagined it would do me much good in a place like this.

Despite my wariness, my steps weren't as hard to take, this time, across the checkered floor of the entry hall. The stairs weren't difficult to ascend. There wasn't even a door to open when I reached the top, only another yawning hallway.

I followed the roses on the ground like a trail of crumbs, almost eagerly, taking twists and turns, passing by many other hallways that vanished into darkness. The lamps above my head kept the checkered pattern under my feet and the shadows of foliage around me. I hoped that either they or the roses would be able to show me the way back in a hurry, if need be. I had a disturbing hunch that the paths through this place wouldn't stay the same for long.

Finally, the hallway ended, but not at a door. I hadn't seen a single one since *the* door that had brought me here. The archway opened onto a small room—small, at least, relative to everything else.

It was a dining room bigger than the king's, most likely, and contained the first furniture I had noticed so far. A glinting black table and chairs stretched the length of it, underneath windows that looked out into complete and utter darkness. I shuddered to think what was behind them, and yet they kept drawing my eyes, even as I studied the rest of the room. The table and chairs were all the space held, other than a vase of bloodred roses as a centerpiece and a silver coffeepot with a single cup resting next to it. They were easily the brightest things in the room, glowing in the lamplight.

I shuffled up to the table in a heady daze, the swishing of my silken skirts susurrant and loud. *This* was why the roses had led me here, through this impossible place? For a cup of coffee? I couldn't help it; a laugh, shattering the heavy silence, burst from me as I gripped the back of a chair.

"Why, hello."

I spun. Someone was leaning in the archway, arms folded. A man—a young man—was blocking the only way out. I couldn't help the startled cry that tore out of me either, piercing the thick air.

He smiled at me. For some reason it made me back away from him, into the table, and nearly tip over the chair. I would have toppled myself if I hadn't been clinging to it.

"I figured if you were laughing it would be okay to introduce myself," he said. "But now I'm confused."

I was beyond confused. I hadn't seen another soulwalker since my mother had died, and she was the only one before that. The young man's hair was the same thick black as Hallan's but longer, falling to his shoulders. That was where any resemblance ended. Hallan had been handsome, but the person before me was far more beautiful, almost too beautiful to be a man, yet with features too sharp to be a woman's—too much for either sex. He was something else, his hair a sheath for a face that cut like a knife. His skin was even paler than mine, white as bone, as if he'd never seen the sun. His jaw was beardless, his eyes dark, lined in heavy black lashes and maybe kohl. He looked to be about my age, or a few years older at most, though something in his gaze looked far older.

I realized I was staring. I didn't care. He was one of the most fascinating people I'd ever seen. Maybe it was in the way he held himself, but I also understood he was dangerous. And yet he wasn't speaking in the hair-raising voice I'd heard long ago beyond the black door, the one like an endless night's whisper, but in tones like coffee: rich, smooth, and with a sharp bite. I wanted to hear more.

"Who . . . who are you?" I stammered. "Where did you come from?" I couldn't tell anything from his manner of dress. He wore no clothes I'd ever seen before—a sweeping midnight robe, belted at the waist in copper. The sleeves were pinned at his shoulders, parting like curtains to reveal muscular arms cuffed with matching gold and silver armbands.

He arched a sleek black eyebrow. "Shouldn't I be asking you that? This is my house."

This was his soul, his nehym. This unimaginable place was an expression of his internal self. His subconscious creation. I tried to take another step back and forgot I was already against the table, jostling and nearly knocking over its vase of roses.

After waiting for the rattle to quiet, he added, "Though I suppose there's no need for me to ask, since I already know about you."

"What?" My throat felt parched.

"You're Kamai Nuala . . . pardon me, *Numa* . . . from just outside of Shalain. Or, wait, are you *in* the capital now?" He shrugged, armbands glinting. "You are ever so difficult to keep up with these days. Have some coffee. You sound thirsty."

I ignored him, asking again in a whisper, "Who are you?" He

had to be a soulwalker, perhaps working for the Twilight Guild . . . and maybe tracking me.

His eyes narrowed for a split second. "You may call me Vehyn." He almost sounded unsure.

Vehyn. It was a name as strange as his clothing, one I'd never heard before. The only word I knew that sounded anything like it was *nehym*, "soul house" in the old tongue. I tried it out silently, and his eyes shot to my lips when my mouth moved. He smiled again.

"No family name?" I asked, grasping for whatever I could learn. His own mouth was distracting me for some reason.

"I don't have a family."

"No other names?"

"I don't need others."

I wasn't quite sure what that meant—if he actually didn't have any, or if he didn't want to give them to me. Whatever the case, he deemed his single name enough, and yet it told me nothing. My teeth clenched to keep me from growling in frustration.

I straightened, pushing off from the table, channeling the feeling. Anger was better than timidity. My mother's advice for this type of situation rang through my head: *Don't show fear; it will only encourage a man.* My voice came out stronger, louder. "Have you been following me?"

He threw back his head and laughed, flashing perfectly white teeth between lips that were sensual enough to be a match for my mother's. His canines were sharper than usual. "Oh, Kamai. It's amusing to hear you ask questions about what you don't understand in the slightest."

I didn't like how he kept repeating my name, as if it were familiar to him. He didn't know me—or at least we'd barely

91

met—and he was already insulting my intelligence? *Bastard.* "So help me understand. Tell me about the door, about this place, about *you*, so I don't have to be afraid."

If all else fails, act like you need their protection . . . for a time.

His amusement diminished. "Not right now. Have some coffee."

"What if I told you to take your coffee and kindly shove it where Tain's light doesn't shine?" So much for following my mother's advice . . . as usual. "Hypothetically, of course," I added with too much sweetness to be genuine. "I'm just trying to understand how things work here."

"Tain's light doesn't shine *anywhere* here. That aside, your suggestion still gives offense. Hypothetically, of course," he echoed with equally false politeness that didn't reach his eyes. His gaze flicked down. "As does threatening someone with a knife. I would advise against both courses of action."

My hand froze where it had been slowly working open my mother's knife in the shelter of my palm.

"Who's threatening whom?" I whispered, my throat tight.

He sighed and unfolded his arms. "I fear we've gotten off on the wrong foot. Let's try this again." Swooping forward too fast for me to recoil, he took my hand—the one with the knife. He raised my fingers to his lips, staring at me with eyes that looked liquid black in the lamplight. When his head bent and his mouth pressed against the back of my hand, I could have sworn I felt the tip of his tongue brush my skin. "It's truly a pleasure to meet you face-to-face, Kamai."

I shivered. It wasn't a bad feeling at all, and almost entirely new. Why my body chose to respond to him, despite any good sense I might possess or any danger I might be in, was beyond me. But I couldn't help it.

That didn't mean I wanted to kiss *him*, or for him to even kiss my hand again, let alone anything else.

I came to my senses and ripped my hand away. Vehyn let it slip through his fingers, but he kept my knife.

"That's *mine*," I said, shaking myself. He'd used his touch like an attack in disguise and then disarmed me. I should have known better, especially since someone touching me didn't usually throw me off balance like that. *Double bastard.* I held out my hand. "Give it back."

"Mm, I think not. For my own protection, of course."

Somehow, I didn't think I could hurt him with a knife anyway. One soulwalker *could* harm another, even kill them, and the effect would echo in the real world. My mother had hinted of assassins, abhorrent to her, who killed other soulwalkers. While wandering the sleeping realm, a spirit was still tethered to the body—which was why *other* sensations here affected us, as if in the flesh—and if the spirit was cut down, a body couldn't live. The victims simply appeared to die in their sleep. But that happened mostly in the old days, before a previous Eopian king put strictures upon soulwalking—as rare as the gift was—limiting its powers to only priests and priestesses of Heshara and requiring known bloodlines to be tested. As my mother told me, soulwalkers like us were breaking that law and risking everything.

"Wait," I said. "You're not a priest of Heshara, are you?" It sounded absurd, but my mother had warned me against both the clergy and the black door my entire young life, so maybe the two were somehow connected.

Vehyn threw back his head again and laughed. And kept laughing.

My cheeks grew hot. "Fine, so you're not a priest."

"No," he said, swallowing his laughter. It had made him look

93

younger, almost certainly my age, but then that strange look returned to his eyes that hinted at something deeper, older. "No, I'm not a priest."

"Then what are you?"

"Ah." He raised a single, elegant finger. "Now, *that* is the question, isn't it?"

He was suddenly looming over me, again moving too fast for me to anticipate, forcing me to lean back against the table. He was a lot taller than me, taller than Hallan or even Razim, I realized. My elbow bumped the coffeepot, and I gasped, but couldn't spare it a glance. His gaze was locked on mine.

"*What*. Am. I?" he murmured, tipping a fraction closer with each word. His face was inches from mine, lips close enough to kiss. But kissing was even further from my thoughts than it usually was. His eyes were bottomless pits like the windows. Like a skull's.

A realization struck me, suddenly, for no particular reason. Maybe it was those strangely ageless eyes—the unsettling wrongness of them. Maybe it was this place, like no nehym I'd ever seen. Fear returned full force, then doubled, quadrupled, hitting me like a barrel of cold water. It swallowed me. I couldn't breathe, and my knees almost buckled. Vehyn caught my arms in a cool grip that felt as immovable as the black walls.

"Take a breath, Kamai."

I did, ragged and gasping. "You're not . . ." I couldn't say it. But it was repeating, over and over again, in my head:

You're not human.

He seemed to know what I meant to say. "No." Without adjusting his hold, he lifted me, seating me on top of the table so I wouldn't fall. "I'm not. You're perceptive." I couldn't tell if he was mocking me. He kept leaning forward, bracing his arms on either side of my legs, both a predatory and possessive stance. Despite a certain feminine grace, his arms were muscled, masculine. Far stronger than mine.

Did arms even have anything to do with strength, in this place? Or if he wasn't human? I had no idea of the ways he might be stronger than me. The ways he might be able to hurt me.

What did that even mean, that he wasn't human? Aside from his eyes, he didn't look particularly monstrous, unlike the stories that haunted children's nightmares. There were legends of beings from before the gods' time, some subjects of fables to tell over the dinner table and some that faded into ancient myth, only found in dusty crumbling texts or whispered about near campfires. But *none* of those stories were believed to be as real as the gods. And yet here he was, this strange, impossible being, standing before me. Cornering me.

"Where did you come from?" I asked again, leaning back on my hands, away from him.

"I live here," he said simply, still looming over me.

It wasn't exactly an answer, but it was a clue. This place wasn't really a nehym, at least not like a human's, not if he stayed here and never woke up—if he was even asleep and didn't simply exist here. There were myths of strange places other than the waking and sleeping realms, not just strange beings. I hadn't even seen the sleeping realm outside of my clearing and a few other sleepers' souls. I had no idea what else might be out there.

Vehyn was out there.

I swallowed loudly. "How long have you been here?"

He smiled. "A while."

I had to get out of here. Now. A good, healthy part of me no longer wanted to know who or what Vehyn was. But that other part of me wouldn't shut up. "Can you leave?"

95

His smile flickered. "It wouldn't be wise, at the moment, but I stay by choice. A choice I now have, thanks to you opening the door."

Holy Heshara, what have I done? Instead, I asked, "What do you want?"

He reached toward my face, and I flinched. But he only tucked a lock of my hair behind my ear. "A lot."

I forced the words out. "What do you want with *me?*"

Abruptly, he withdrew, pacing back toward the arching hallway. "I was *trying* to have coffee with you."

I took a deeper, slower breath, relieved that he'd moved away, but a voice of alarm was still screaming inside of me: *Gods, he's not human. He's not human. He's not human.* My heart was a galloping horse in my chest. "And now?"

"I'll let you go, if you'd like." He leaned in the threshold again. But instead of the long, stretching hallway behind him, now there was the black door.

If I could have been sure my legs would stay under me, I would have shoved off the table and run for it. As it was, I slid onto my feet and held the back of a chair for support.

"But under one condition." His words were enough to stop my forward momentum.

"And what's that?" I asked.

His eyes held me in place as surely as his hands had. "You must come back to see me."

One part of me filled with dread, and the other with taut anticipation. However unsettling this place was, I didn't think I could just leave it—and someone like Vehyn—and never look back. And if swearing to return was the only way to escape, I would do it. "Just once?"

"Frequently. Or else, fine, once, and we can have this same conversation the next time you try to leave."

A regular schedule wasn't exactly what I'd had in mind. My jaw clenched and my fingers tightened on the back of the chair. "*How* frequently?"

"I don't know, what's a good amount of time? Soon, but not *too* soon. I don't wish to tire of you," he added with a smirk.

"Every year?" I suggested, too quickly.

He clicked his tongue, guessing my game. "Sooner than that."

"Every month?"

"Mm, still sooner, I think."

"Every . . . week?"

That sounded like far too often to me, but he said, "Perfect. The last day of every week, as soon as the sun sinks fully from your sky."

Your sky, he'd said, not his, because he didn't belong to the waking world. I repressed a shudder—a bad one, this time.

"But that would make my next visit in four days." That was *much* too soon.

He shrugged. "At least, that's when you are *required* to visit," he clarified. "I won't forbid it if you want to come back more often."

"Not likely." I hesitated. "And if I say yes to this, but I break my word . . . ?"

His already black eyes seemed to darken, the air thicken. "You'll wish you hadn't." He shrugged, and the sudden pressure in the air—the power—lifted as if he were shucking it off. "And besides, then you won't learn the answers to your questions."

My breath caught. "You'll tell me who you are? And explain the black door?"

"Eventually, yes . . . and so much more than that."

Curiosity got the better of me, even now when I should have been running for my life. "Like what?"

He stared at me for a moment, considering. "I know who killed your mother. And why."

I stared right back, holding his eyes without fear, the thought of revenge burning everything else away, so hot in my throat I didn't know if I wanted to cry or scream. The words were out of my mouth before I could stop them. "Tell me."

"Only when you return. And now that I'm sure you will . . ." He stepped aside and held the door open for me, a sly grin on his eerily beautiful face.

9

BETTER QUESTIONS

Vehyn was right. I did come back to the dark fortress—if *fortress* could even encompass its sheer size—that lay beyond the black door, and not only because of the vague, looming threat of some terrible consequence if I didn't. I wanted my answers. I needed them. More than knowing what I had done by opening the black door, I wanted to know why my mother had died, and who had killed her. Then I wanted to kill them.

And maybe I couldn't resist taking another peek behind the black door.

Not that I forgot about the danger, especially as I stepped over the threshold for a second time, on the prearranged evening. It was nearly all I had thought about in the past days. Nikha, as well as my tutor—and even Jidras, who actively *tried* not to notice me—had commented on my distraction. While my thoughts roamed, a chorus of anxious questions rose constantly in the background: What would my mother think of all this? Who *was* Vehyn? *What* was he?

This time, Vehyn was waiting for me in the immense entrance hall. Although he appeared otherwise occupied, gazing down the center shaft of the great spiral staircase. I didn't approach too closely, in case he decided to hurl me into it.

"Kamai," he said, turning and smiling, shocking me once again with his youthful face and strange eyes, his otherworldly beauty. "You came."

"Yes." I shifted on my feet, breathless and ready to run for my life. "So . . . I'm here. Now what?"

He cocked his head. "Impatient, are we?"

"I upheld my end of the deal. I want answers."

"And you'll get them. But first, I want to show you something."

He headed right for me and held out his hand, which looked especially pale against the stretch of midnight floor between us.

Feeling like I was once again opening the door, trying not to think about what it meant, I took his hand. Despite his skin being warm and silk-smooth, I could feel the strength underneath it.

We climbed—not the spiral staircase, but dozens of others, taking twists and turns I never could have remembered. I tried not to dwell upon the endless hallways stacking behind me, walls upon walls, trapping me here. Even so, my eyes hungrily ate up every step into this strange, dark labyrinth. And they traced Vehyn's outline, over and over again, in wary curiosity.

Not human.

And yet he wasn't turning around and lunging at me, or sprouting claws or fangs. The longer he didn't, the less wary and the more curious I became.

We eventually emerged onto a tower rooftop shrouded in

blackness, looking out over a seemingly endless rise and fall of the spires and bridges of the fortress. There, in the center of the rooftop, stood a round black table, small—intimate—by the usual proportions of this place, dwarfed by its surroundings. Red roses blossomed in a vase, and a spread of shining silver plates and gleaming wineglasses awaited us on the table. Who had laid it out, I had no idea. I highly doubted Vehyn had. Which meant it might have been the fortress itself, since no one else was here.

Vehyn pulled out one of two tall-backed black chairs for me. I hesitated.

He grinned, flashing those sharper-than-usual canines. "I'm not going to bite." His voice was rich with amusement.

"There are a lot of other ways you could hurt me," I said quickly, trying not to look at his teeth.

His dark eyes grew more serious. "I promise I will let no harm befall you, Kamai."

The words were so certain, so absolute, that I found my feet carrying me forward. I tried to ignore him as I sat down and he scooted my chair in. But he was warm behind me, like a fire. When he moved away, I breathed a sigh of relief. Or maybe simply of *release* from the tension.

Before long, we were facing each other over the table.

"Wine?" he asked.

"Who killed my mother?"

Vehyn pursed his lips and made a chiding noise, but his eyes were alight with mirth. "So soon? If we eat dessert before the meal, you won't be hungry for the rest."

"And what exactly is that supposed to mean?"

"There were many steps to get up to this tower, no? Take it slow, enjoy the journey."

"You mean you won't tell me right away, because I won't keep coming back."

"If you want to look at it in such a harsh light."

"Did *you* kill my mother?" I didn't think he had—I didn't know *how* he could have, being trapped in here without a body in the waking world—but I wanted to shock him into giving me at least some sort of answer.

All he said, infuriatingly, was, "That's not how this works. You don't get to ask a question until you've answered *mine*."

I blinked. "What question?"

He lifted the bottle. "Would you like any wine?"

I couldn't help the sharp, short laugh that guffawed out of me.

"I take that as a yes." He reached to pour, gracefully holding the sleeve of his black robe away from the silver platters. The liquid splashing into my glass was dark as blood at night.

I eyed it suspiciously and then reminded myself that he could have killed me well before now. Why go to the trouble of poisoning me?

I took a mouthful—heavy, rich, and sweet, just how I liked it, except better than anything I had ever tasted in the waking realm. I couldn't resist taking another sip, and then regretted it when my head began to buzz almost instantly. It was strong.

I made my voice firm, steady. "I answered your question. Now you should answer mine."

"No," he said. I thought he was refusing me until he added, "I didn't kill your mother."

"But then—"

"My turn," he interrupted. "What is your favorite dish?"

My favorite dish? That was what he wanted to know? I even thought he might already know, since he seemed to have intuited my preferences with the wine.

"Garlic-and-coconut-crusted octopus with papaya and peppe—"

Before I could finish, Vehyn whipped away the silver lid of one of the platters, and there it was, papaya and pepper sauce and all. I didn't know if he'd anticipated what I would say or if this place had conjured it upon my word. Whatever the case, I couldn't help but be a little impressed, despite myself.

I doubted the meal would nourish me in any measurable way, but it tasted divine as I took a bite. I didn't allow eating to stop my flow of questions, though. "Where are we?"

"Where I live," Vehyn answered patiently, not sampling the food, only taking small sips of wine.

"That's not an answer. Are we even in the sleeping realm?"

"No. Somewhere just outside of it."

"But *where?*"

"Elsewhere." Before I could groan, he said, "Kamai, you might consider that you would get better answers if you asked better questions."

I glared at him. "Okay, then—"

"No, my turn again," he said, making me grit my teeth. "What do you like to do in your leisure time?"

"Read. Play Gods and Kings. Explore souls. *Receive answers to my questions.*"

He leaned back in his chair and steepled his fingers, studying me as if I were a puzzle box. "You will. I promise."

"When?"

"When it's time."

I nearly bent my silver utensil as my hand clenched around it. "But—"

"Do you like living at your father's?"

My irritation ebbed like a wave, leaving me feeling bare and grittily raw. "No."

"Why?" That was two questions from him, but I barely noticed.

"I . . . miss my mother." It wasn't the real explanation. Or maybe it was, at the heart of it.

Vehyn's sharp, dark eyes seemed to soften. "Kamai, just know if ever you need a place, an escape . . . you'll always be welcome here."

My throat squeezed down tight against my will and I focused on the red of the roses, the shine of the silver, the residue of sweet wine on my tongue. I would *not* cry in front of Vehyn. Not at the first bit of kindness he showed me. Quickly, more harshly than I intended, I asked, "Why? Why do you want my company?"

"Why is that surprising to you?" Vehyn responded, unruffled. "Do you not hold yourself in high regard?"

Now my cheeks threatened to flush. Because *not always* was the answer, and it shamed me. I knew I should honor and take pride in myself like my mother had always taught me, and yet I could too easily recall my shortcomings. Instead of indulging him with an honest reply, I said, "Receiving only more questions in response to my own doesn't inspire me to answer."

He smiled. "I appreciate your company because you are the most interesting person I've ever met."

I sputtered over my wine. Even allowing for self-honor and pride, I found that hard to believe. "I'm not the *only* person you've met, am I?"

His eyes gleamed, and he laughed. "No, Kamai, you're not."

"That still doesn't make sense," I snapped. "You don't know a thing about me."

He arched a dark eyebrow. "I don't?"

His regard was making me feel warm and strange. Or maybe that was the wine. "At least you *shouldn't*," I grumbled. "I don't know anything about you."

"Someday," he said, his words heavy as a promise. It sounded both enticing and foreboding, and that, more than anything else, made me stop questioning him for the moment.

For the rest of the night, Vehyn indulged me by playing the tour guide, leading me to new places I could have never imagined behind the black door. We ventured through vast arches and vaults, stretching galleries lined with windows opening onto nothing, and always stairs, endless twisting and twining stairs.

The tour ended with Vehyn leading me into the bowels of the fortress. The place he took me didn't seem as unfathomably deep as the well of the great spiral staircase, but it hinted at such depth just the same. The underground cavern had an arching bridge spanning a wide crevasse. As we stood on the bridge, I leaned over the railing and looked down. The world seemed to end beneath my feet, in a vast chasm of nothing.

When I shuddered, Vehyn put his strong hands on my shoulders. For a brief, fearful second, I thought he might shove me over the railing and off into oblivion, but instead, he steadied me.

I didn't shrug his hands off. I should have been alarmed at his touch, but I wasn't. *Why* I wasn't was beyond me. Maybe his hands even felt . . . good. But that was as far as it went. I certainly didn't want him to try anything *else*, deadly or otherwise. And somehow, I trusted he wouldn't.

He sighed, almost in pleasure. "This is one of my favorite places here."

"Is the bottom of that spiral staircase another one?" I asked, unable to tear my eyes away from the void. "Because they're both equally terrifying."

Which wasn't true. The stairs were *more* terrifying, since they invited one down into the darkness, making it a place I could actually try to go.

His hands slid away, and I turned to face him, almost . . . *almost* . . . missing the feel of him. He gave an answer to a question I *hadn't* asked: "That spiral staircase has no bottom."

I'd guessed as much, but it still made me shiver to hear the impossible truth spoken so plainly.

Despite my fear, my guilt, my impatience, I found the black fortress utterly fascinating. Looking around, I was consumed by the same awe as when I looked at a map of Eopia and tried to imagine everything the island contained. Except this place felt bigger than an entire continent, while being somehow more accessible. That made it even more intriguing.

And yet, like the fortress itself, my fascination was rooted in something darker than in the waking world . . . as was Vehyn himself, and perhaps my growing fascination with *him*.

———

Vehyn apparently had a different concept of time than I did, because those "eventual" answers to my questions never seemed to arrive. Another four weeks passed in Jidras's house, punctuated by four more trips behind the black door—the required number of visits. My eighteenth birthday approached. I never forgot that Vehyn wasn't human, but he didn't seem to want to hurt me—if torturing me with impatience didn't count—and so, gradually, I began to relax in his presence. In all that time, he never answered a single question in a way that didn't leave me with more.

For one visit, to vex him because he was vexing me with his vagueness and arrogance, I only stayed for a short while. Since I'd stuck to the terms of our agreement, he couldn't do anything about it—or at least he didn't try to. This latest visit, I'd felt deprived of the world behind the black door—not *of Vehyn*, though, I told myself—and so I wandered the black fortress with him for what felt like hours in the sleeping realm. A mind was conscious while soulwalking, so even though my body rested, I never felt as rejuvenated after nights like these.

As soon as my mind was alert enough to think the next morning, I was disgusted with myself. My mother had been dead for two months, and I was no closer to figuring out why, despite opening the black door. That wasn't why I'd opened it in the first place, but now I desperately hoped something could be gained from doing the one thing my mother had forbidden me.

If Vehyn wouldn't give me answers, I would find them on my own. But I knew only one group who might have them: the Twilight Guild. I told myself that I didn't have to join them to spy on them.

I bided my time until Nikha and a few guards were readying to accompany Jidras's steward on a trip to the port-side market. Household servants went out into the city daily on trifling, smaller errands, and I was never allowed to come along, but picking up a bulk load of dry goods required an armed escort.

Nikha frowned when I asked her if I could come as well. "I'm not sure Sir Jidras will grant you permission. He wants everyone to forget you exist, as least until he presents you at court."

"*I'm* in danger of forgetting I exist," I muttered.

My self-pity seemed to help my case, because Nikha's gaze softened. "I'll ask." She pursed her lips. "As much as I hate to say it, wearing a scarf would help. If you stay covered—"

"Of course!" I said. I had no problem keeping the sun off my head and paying respect to Heshara at the same time, especially if it would encourage Jidras to allow me to leave.

Miraculously, Jidras wasn't out on business, and even more miraculously, he agreed to the excursion, as long as I promised to stick close to Nikha and keep my head down and covered. Maybe he felt bad about the fact that I'd been cooped up indoors the past couple of months. Or maybe he just wanted me out of his way, where I could go be a bother to someone else. He even gave each of us a small purse of coins.

I cringed inwardly as Nikha helped me into the carriage and took a seat next to me. I hoped I wouldn't cause her too much trouble or worry, but there was nothing else for it. The carriage was departing. Jidras's steward sat up front with the driver, while another couple of guards followed on horseback.

White rows of beautiful town houses fell away as we rode down the hill, away from the palace at the highest point of the city under the mountains, and the wealthier neighborhoods nestled beneath its walls. Toward the center of town, the city's architecture had room to flourish.

Beautiful promenades lined the streets. White stone columns arched into balconies that overflowed with greenery, providing cool, fresh shade in the heat. Coral fountains and gazebos bloomed on street corners and in busy intersections, their rounded tops echoing the white and bronze domes that defined the bright skyline—pointed like onions; scalloped like melons; or simple, smooth hemispheres that glowed like rising suns against the sky.

At the fountains' centers, surrounded by the glittering flow of water and mosaics, stood stunning statues of the gods: Tain with solid gold eyes and hair flaring in the sunlight against his dark visage, Heshara with her serenely smiling face of white marble draped in onyx locks, warm-skinned Ranta proffering bushels of wheat and bouquets of flowers so artfully rendered they looked real. I'd heard that in other lands, they had rules against depicting the gods outside of temples or at all, and the gods even went by different names, though they still represented the sun, the moon, and the earth—the father, the mother, the daughter— the holy trio that had risen to replace the more multitudinous gods and mythical beings from a forgotten age. Still, the entire world acknowledged Shalain as a holy city, the birthplace of the oldest, most traditional form of the gods' worship. Here, it was only the king who forbade his own likeness in public, supposedly to pay respect to the gods by not attempting to imitate them.

As we neared the port market, most of the grandeur dropped away, but what remained was no less exciting. More organic and chaotic buildings sprouted up around us, jumbles of stone and wood like crooked teeth in a smile, with colorful awnings and jutting stalls. Only clay statues of voluptuous Ranta could be seen here in small, rough-hewn alcoves. Racks of beautiful cloth and woven rugs, along with tables of fruit and fresh fish, spilled out into the street, making traffic impossible. Soon we had to park the carriage and continue on foot.

I spotted all manner of people buying, selling, and trading, from nobles to wealthy merchants to harried servants to those barely better than beggars—and quite a few actual beggars. Jidras's steward immediately embarked into the fray, attended by several guards, while Nikha stayed with me.

"We don't need to go with them?" I asked.

"They'll be fine without me." Nikha grinned and stretched. "Besides, I wouldn't mind a break from bargaining for flour, beans, and nuts for the next two hours. I'd prefer fresh air instead . . . though I wouldn't mind some of *these*."

She dropped a coin into a passing vendor's hand and scooped up a handful of cashews from his cart, ignoring his look of astonishment—perhaps at her armor or the brashness with which she conducted herself, both usually reserved for men. The nuts were roasted with a mix of cinnamon and spicy pepper. She passed me half, and they were still warm as I ate one, thinking.

Nikha and I being on our own would make my plan easier, but I couldn't lose focus in all the excitement. There was nothing I'd rather do than wander the market with her, taking in the sights and smells and flavors, but I'd indulged myself enough behind the black door.

I tossed back my cashews quickly and dusted off my palms, already sticky in the heat. "I'd really like to go to a wine shop— I've heard Esva's is a good one."

Nikha blinked at me. "Why? Sir Jidras has plenty of wine, down in the cellar. You remember he's from the Risha province, right?"

"There's a particular kind he doesn't have that my mother liked—an import." That much was true. "I just . . . I thought the taste of it might remind me of her."

I had actually never cared much for the flavor—too dry— but such an excuse would prevent Nikha from questioning me much.

She didn't, only frowned, as if she didn't like the thought of me drinking. It didn't matter that we weren't many years apart in age, and that I was only a week away from turning eighteen. I still wasn't a legal adult yet, and she was my guardian, which made her a touch parental at times, not just protective. I kept my face free of impatience.

"Well," she said finally, "if anywhere would have it, Esva's would."

Esva. The wealthiest, most successful wine merchant in

Shalain. Her shop was near the port, as was the market. I had never been there, but the woman had been both a patron and a peer of my mother and Hallan—and a member of the Twilight Guild. Ciari was her daughter. It was she who ran her mother's shop and absorbed all the drink-loosened secrets of the world's wine enthusiasts and reported them as a member-in-training of the guild.

And it was she I wanted to speak to. But Nikha couldn't know that I knew Ciari from my previous life.

Nikha started off into the crowd, pointing out her favorite food vendors on the way. She bought us each grilled shrimp and pineapple on a stick, dusted in salt and chili powder, and ate hers like a child with a pilfered piece of candy. At least someone was enjoying themselves.

Despite my mission, the sight of the port opening up before me made me gasp. Towering masts, furled sails, and rigging spread out like a leafless forest of tall trunks and taut vines, with the wide blue ocean glittering beyond. So many dhows, huge and small, from the king's largest warships to sleek trading vessels to the tiniest fishing craft, and many different boats from other lands all floated in the harbor, while sailors with equally myriad styles of dress and skin tones populated them. The whole world lay beyond this port.

Nikha and I soon reached the store, a flush stone building with layers of alcove-style windows, arching to points and peering down on the bustling street like spying eyes. The building also commanded a fantastic view of the comings and goings of the port and was the perfect place to stop in for a bottle—or a shipment—of wine. Esva and Ciari would be sure to take your secrets with your money.

The shop was cool and dim like a cave, low lamps in bronze

sconces lending a soft gleam to the hundreds and hundreds of bottles racked on dozens of shelves. And this was only the first floor. There were no doubt more prized wines on the upper floors and in the packed cellars down below.

I recognized Ciari immediately—tall, with her smooth fall of black hair that went nearly to her waist now. Her features were too angular to be truly gorgeous, but she was still a striking, handsome figure. I suddenly and uncomfortably remembered her eyes, hovering just above mine as we lay in bed together, peering down at me with mischief and lust.

She certainly recognized me too. She turned away from a customer—a wealthy merchant by the looks of him—and nearly dropped her stylus and paper-lined tablet.

I had to quickly signal to her—a subtle swipe of my hand, palm down—to not recognize me. I was using the Twilight Guild's secret sign language, which both my mother and Hallan had begun teaching me. And then I held my breath. I had no idea if she would respect my wishes, but I had reason to hope.

Her face immediately smoothed, and she excused herself from the merchant to approach me. I made another gesture toward an oblivious Nikha. *She can't know.*

"May I help you?" Ciari asked politely, no trace of familiarity in her voice.

I asked after the bottle of wine I was looking for, all the while making low hand gestures. *Need to talk. Alone. Need a distraction.* I patted my purse of coins absently and glanced at Nikha, all the while striking up a conversation with Ciari about how she'd gotten into the wine trade at such a young age.

"Let me have one of my employees check for that vintage," she said after a suitable amount of friendly chatter. "It might take some time to find it, especially if we have to send a runner to one of our other cellars. Feel free to browse, or take in the sights of the port." *Go outside*, she signed. *Wait a half hour. Distraction.* "I'll send him to find you, wherever you are."

Even if I managed to get Ciari alone, I could only ask her what she knew in vague terms and perhaps hint at an interest in joining the Twilight Guild. I had no intention of doing so, but if I could kindle enough of a friendship, perhaps I could entice her to visit me at the town house. I had no intention of sleeping with her, of course, but she might take a nap, or I could slip some mohol into her coffee or wine, or something, *anything*, and then search her soul for answers.

A start.

Nikha and I wandered outside. "Are you sure you want to wait?" she asked, squinting into the bright sun, her spiky brown hair uncovered by a scarf, unlike my voluminous curls that were trapped under a deep blue silk I was beginning to regret in this heat, despite my love of dark colors. "We can always have them deliver the bottle to the house."

"No," I said hurriedly. "I mean, I don't want Jidras or anyone to ask about it, because I don't want to explain why I wanted it. They don't need an excuse to talk about my mother more than they already do."

She nodded immediately, so ready to trust me, and my heart twinged at my deception—and the fact that there was more to come. To pass the minutes, I ordered a grilled fish wrapped in palm leaves from a street vendor, which would take a while to cook. I timed it as well as I could, purposefully moving a short way off to wait, in the shade of the fish market's awning.

When I saw the grubby-looking boy lurking in the shadow of the wine shop, trying to catch my eye, I gave him the slightest nod and then turned to Nikha. "Oh, I think the fish is ready. Do you want to go check? I'm feeling a little faint. Must be the heat."

She shot me a concerned glance, gave the area a cursory scan, and then strode toward the street vendor with the grilled fish. I had to give the boy credit; I didn't see or hear him sneak up behind me. He waited until Nikha was as far away as she would get and then snatched the coin purse from my hip. I'd loosened the ties for him.

"Nikha, my purse!" I cried.

She spun, hand on her sword, to see the boy duck through the fish market. Still, she hesitated to go after him.

"That's how I was going to pay for the wine!" I whined in my most pathetic voice. "Don't worry, I'll wait right inside the shop."

Her eyes narrowed in a flash, as if she didn't like the idea of chasing him, but then she was on the move, dashing around the side of the fish market, trying to head him off. Even though I'd seen her in action, she was still shockingly quick on her feet. I worried she might catch him—and fast.

I didn't have time to waste. Turning toward the wine shop, I bumped right into someone.

"Oof!"

For a split second, I thought it might be Ciari, but the chest I'd hit was hard and flat, the shoulders much broader and higher than mine. A man's. When I raised my hand to brace myself, strong fingers caught my wrist in a manacle-like grip. I gasped, and my gaze shot up to a shrouded face, wrapped in a light gray scarf. Familiar eyes stared down into mine.

It was *him*, behind the shroud. Ciari had told him I was here, and now he had found me.

Razim.

10

PETTY SECRETS

That Razim had arrived so quickly meant he was living in Shalain now too, and that he was likely looking for me. Perhaps he had even asked Ciari to keep an eye out, since she was a mutual acquaintance in the Twilight Guild and knew my face.

My plan had been a stupid one.

Ciari, to be fair, probably had no idea Razim, my supposed stepbrother, was the last person I wanted to find me.

Everyone was about their own business around us, bustling by too quickly to notice anything strange. His skin was hot against mine, his chest rising rapidly as if he'd run to get here.

I would scream if I had to, but I knew how quickly he could cover my mouth and haul me away. I had to stall him, but already he began pulling me toward the alley alongside the wine shop, likely where a horse was waiting.

"Let me go," I rasped, trying to jerk my hand away, my slippers skidding over the rough cobbles.

He held tight, his tug insistent. "No, you're coming with me."

"Is that so?" said a hard voice nearby. Nikha, a dagger in her hand. "Thought I would fall for that, did you? That a small coin purse would be worth dropping my guard?" She'd obviously only circled around the fish market and come up behind us. The dagger now threatened those dark eyes I knew so well. "Now how about you tell me what you want with her, and this will be less painful."

Razim let me go and, at the same moment, muttered to me, "Get back."

He didn't need to tell me twice, and I stumbled away. Before I could figure out why he was warning me, he was moving, lightning fast, ducking Nikha's darting blade and drawing his sword in the same fluid motion—one that might have gutted me had I been closer. In a scuff of boots on stone, Nikha's dagger was now in her left hand, her own sword out and in her right, only half a second after his.

They stood, facing each other, blades perfectly still and glinting in the sunlight, while people jumped back with cries of alarm.

"A woman, huh?" Razim said.

"A dead man, huh? Besides, you're the one wearing the scarf." Nikha's grin didn't reach her eyes. "Don't want anyone to see your face?"

And then she lunged. Razim danced back, parrying, but barely in time. His eyes widened in surprise at her skill but immediately narrowed in focus as she got past his guard and almost skewered him a second time.

I'd seen Razim train at the villa. He'd had a private tutor, a sword master, giving him lessons every other day. But Nikha trained twice as often. And if Razim was stronger, she was better.

The fight was as ferocious as the burning sun, their blades gleaming and licking at each other. Razim kept trying to circle my way, but Nikha kept beating him back with her sword, her dagger nipping at him. So he circled the other way until he reached one of the street vendor's fish grills, kicked it over, and flicked burning coals at Nikha with a sweep of his sword. She couldn't help flinching, and Razim lunged.

Nikha pivoted fast enough to dodge his blow, but still I screeched, "Don't!"

Razim paused at the frantic sound of my voice, long enough to nearly lose his head, but he threw himself onto his back, rolling to his feet a moment later.

A shout rose from the nearby street. Soldiers were coming. Nikha didn't turn to look or take her eyes off her target. Razim, however, turned—*away* from the commotion. He ran, with only one backward glance at me. His eyes were like coals themselves, burning right through me.

Nikha didn't chase him—she left that to the soldiers, after she hurriedly explained and pointed them in the right direction. Then she dragged me against the wall of the wine shop, into shade and relative safety, her back to me, sword still raised in my defense.

"Who," she said, panting over her shoulder, "was that?"

"I don't know," I whispered.

In a way, I truly didn't. What had he wanted with me? Why had he directed me out of harm's way, after he'd tried to abduct me? And he'd listened to me when I told him to stop.

It didn't mean I wanted to kill him any less. I would just have more questions for him beforehand.

Despite my efforts, I still only ever had questions, and never the answers.

I sagged against the wall. The experience felt like old wounds being reopened. But none of that compared to the shame of putting Nikha in so much danger. I felt gutted as I stared at her strong, heaving shoulders.

She could have been killed. Defending me. In a situation I had arranged by lying to her.

"And why," she said, sounding angrier, "didn't you break his grip? You know how to get out of a hold like that—I taught you!"

Heat rose to my cheeks, because she was right, on top of everything. Not only had she drilled me on self-defense, my mother had taught me basics before her. I should have put up more of a fight, but I'd been so surprised to see Razim that I'd frozen.

"Oh gods, Nikha, I'm so sorry," I gasped, holding my stomach, tears stinging my eyes. I felt like vomiting.

"It's okay," she said, softer now. She was still on her guard, not facing me. "None of this is your fault, but I know that *you* know how to play your hand better than that." I caught her reference to Gods and Kings—what had led her to start teaching me self-defense in the first place. So much for my "martial mind-set."

"You can't hold me to your standard. You're *really good*." Somehow I managed to hurl the compliment like an insult, and it made us both choke on a laugh, probably from nerves. "Seriously. You should be a royal bodyguard, not here with me."

"Good thing I *was* here," she said, not letting me off so easily. "It's not like you to hesitate. You're *sure* you don't recognize him from somewhere?"

Even if it felt like shame was devouring me from the inside

out, I still had to lie. Or else she would never relax around me again. I would never be free enough to hunt for my answers, at least not in the waking world. "No," I said. "I only saw his eyes. He just said I looked like a rich girl. He must have wanted to kidnap me, ransom me, or——"

"Or worse." Nikha spat on the stones beneath her feet and finally turned to me, sheathing her sword. "A pity I couldn't kill the bastard. But at least you're safe. Do you want to fetch your wine before we go?"

"No," I said quickly. The less contact with Ciari, the better. She would want to know why I hadn't gone with Razim. "I'm not in the mood for it anymore. Besides, you didn't get my purse back," I added, in an attempt to tease her.

She arched an eyebrow at me but smiled. "I'm glad I didn't. Let's get you home, then."

I caught her arm as she moved toward the street. "Nikha, please don't tell Jidras about this."

Her forehead creased. "Why not?"

"Because he'll never let me leave the house again!"

Nikha grimaced. "I don't know if you *should*," she said. "At least not like this. Not until you've trained with me more."

"But I come of age in a week!" I cried. "Even as an adult, am I supposed to leave only to go to an apprenticeship, or palace functions, or a temple, only seeing the inside of a carriage in between?"

Nikha sighed, running a hand through her hair, making it even spikier. "I don't know, Kamai, but you have to admit, this was strange. I'm still not convinced he didn't know who you were, and he was particularly well trained—not your average cutpurse. If I hadn't been suspicious of the whole situation . . ." The unspoken words were *And you were no help*. "This isn't safe."

No, it wasn't. And Nikha had been in the most danger, yet all she cared about was me.

Tears threatened my eyes again. "I'm sorry, Nikha. I promise not to leave the house without you, if I leave at all, to have as much protection as you think I need, and to train with you as much as you wish, but please, *please* don't tell Jidras." If he grew suspicious that my past life was trying to catch up to me, he might lock me away forever. Even if all I had to look forward to was a life indoors after my eighteenth birthday, at least the walls would change. And better Nikha's overbearing protectiveness than Jidras's.

She stared at me for a long time. "You promise? You swear to me that you'll let me guard you as necessary, and you'll practice even more with me?"

"I swear," I said, even as my stomach sank. "You have my word."

And she did. So much for a new course of action. But even I had to admit, after seeing Razim, that my plan hadn't been the wisest. What if he told the Twilight Guild he'd seen me? I still had a hard time believing they didn't know where I was, but now they definitely had a trail to follow. And Nikha wasn't exactly inconspicuous. They could easily find out who employed her.

Or they could just follow us home now. Nikha seemed to have the same thought, glancing at rooftops and down alleys, eyes darting warily. But we made it to the carriage without incident. And without catching sight of anyone else watching.

But I couldn't shake the image of Razim's fierce, dark eyes from my mind. For the next few days, at least, they distracted me from *another* pair—one that didn't exist in the waking world.

My birthday actually fell on the date I was scheduled to visit Vehyn, and I wondered if he'd somehow planned it that way. I didn't know if the thought made me apprehensive or secretly thrilled. In any case, I tried not to count down the hours.

As the night of my eighteenth birthday approached, I wondered what Vehyn had planned. I couldn't believe I'd known him for almost a month and a half. Known *of* him, at least. I doubted I would ever really know who, or what, he was, especially at the rate he was doling out information.

The day I became a legal adult had a night that held a new moon. It was either fitting or ominous: a new beginning, but one shrouded in darkness. And rain. My birthday frequently marked the beginning of the wet season, and rain pounded the pale stone of the city outside, drenching everything in heavy gray shadow.

I almost expected to receive an appointment at an accounting firm as a present from Jidras, or maybe a carriage ride to a temple of Heshara to test as a priestess. No matter how much he or my tutor had pushed, I hadn't given either of them a clear answer on what I wanted to do with myself. Maybe because I didn't know, and they'd granted me less than six weeks to decide the course of the rest of my life.

Or maybe because what I truly wanted, they couldn't give me: Answers. Retribution. Only Vehyn could give me that.

The ribbon-wrapped boxes that Jidras's servants passed to me ended up containing half a dozen luxurious new dresses.

"Such that a woman would wear," Jidras said without meeting my eyes, staring at his folded hands. He sat in his armchair in the parlor, while I sat on a divan, opening my presents with Nikha and several servants looking on. I was about to thank him. The gowns were a much less torturous present than I'd been expecting, even if most of the colors were a touch bright

121

for my taste. "Or a wife," he added, and the words froze in my mouth.

A wife? What sort of wife could I be to anyone? I simply couldn't imagine it. I had no desire to run a household, to have children, or to even participate in the act that led to children.

Perhaps he was only letting me know that he didn't mind the possibility, if I wished to find someone suitable. I let the remark slide without comment, hoping both he and I would forget that he'd mentioned it.

But I couldn't forget.

Nikha gave me a beautiful dagger that I could wear at my hip if I ever found myself outside again. It was a less discreet version of the pocketknife I still carried between my breasts—in the waking world, at least, since Vehyn had taken it in the sleeping realm—the gift my mother had given me on my birthday eight years ago. Oddly, it was a more hopeful present than Jidras's, despite the potential danger it implied. Better a fight than marriage.

That night, the black door opened into a parlor that was a dark mockery of the bright one I'd sat in earlier with Jidras, the floating lamps making a red-and-indigo-striped pattern on the black walls and furniture. Vehyn was facing away from me when I entered, standing perfectly still and silent. I drew up short at the eerie sight of him, but then he turned.

"What has upset you?" he asked. He always seemed to know when I was distraught, even when I tried to hide it. I found his youthful face and old eyes both oddly comforting and unsettling, and as beautiful as always.

I sighed, half wanting to vent over what Jidras had said and half wanting to never speak of it. "Now that I'm a woman grown,

Jidras mentioned the possibility of my becoming a wife." I didn't mention the trip to the market, which was still weighing heavily on my mind. It was too shameful, how badly it had gone. And I didn't want him to know how much more I needed his answers now.

"And you didn't appreciate the idea of marriage."

"No."

He was suddenly in front of me, in that sinuous, instantaneous way he had of moving sometimes. He leaned forward and brushed my cheek with a cool kiss. It was the first time he'd done such a thing, and for a second, I forgot how to breathe. It wasn't a good or bad feeling. It was the jolt of taking a step and missing it—something startling, a little exhilarating, and potentially dangerous.

"That is a lovely dress," he said.

I glanced down to remember what I was wearing. I'd arrived in the sleeping realm in one of my new gowns—a lacy midnight-blue creation with a plunging neckline and sleeves like spiderwebs. The darkest of the lot.

The corner of his mouth—of which I was oddly aware, after his kiss—twitched in a half smile. "I prefer black, of course, but the color suits you."

I'd never seen Vehyn appear in anything but his strange black robe with its copper belt and his gold-and-silver-cuffed arms.

"It's not my favorite," I said in a dismissive tone. Secretly, I was pleased. He often complimented me, though more and more, I'd been sensing something . . . hungry . . . in his dark eyes. When he looked at me like that, I had to admit it wasn't altogether unpleasant, like his kiss.

But I was an idiot. I was playing with fire, and I knew it. This wasn't anything beyond a strange fascination for me, a curiosity that never, ever ended in the same place as the other person was imagining. Vehyn caused my body to react in ways that no one else had, but even those sensations didn't lead to a desire to end up naked together, let alone *doing* anything.

And yet, was that what Vehyn was imagining? Did he even experience desire in the same way others did? I found the idea of him wanting me, even if I didn't want him, perversely intriguing.

You're doubly an idiot, playing with fire twice over. He's not human, I hissed at myself. *You don't even know if he's dangerous. No, you do know he's dangerous. What you don't know is if he's* deadly.

The thought was almost too frightening to contemplate. His hunger, for all I understood it, might be much too literal.

He abruptly turned away. "Come, I have a present for you."

I couldn't help looking around, as if some strange, new gift or unearthly vista was about to be revealed.

"Nothing like that," he said, back to watching my face closely. I reminded myself—again—to be more guarded. He could guess what I was thinking too easily. "Here."

With a gesture, a blue door appeared.

It was a shockingly familiar shade of blue, nearly the color of Jidras's front door in the waking world. Except this one wasn't gilt-framed, but lined with white-painted wood that was flaking. It looked like the entrance to a child's room. An *old* room, one that hadn't been used in ages.

"What is this?" I asked, apprehension roiling in my stomach.

"You wanted secrets. This isn't everything you want by any means—only petty secrets—but it's something."

Vehyn was making no move for the door, so I stepped forward and touched its brass knob, which was another strange, tarnished reflection of the gold-plated one in the waking world. "This isn't quite what I was expecting. I was picturing something rather more romantic."

I wasn't sure why I said it. Of course I wanted secrets, more than anything, but he'd already admitted they were *petty*. And yet romance might not be what I wanted, either. I didn't know what I wanted, only that I most assuredly didn't want what romance usually *led* to. Vehyn, for his part, blinked at me in mild surprise.

I opened the door before I could regret my words or confuse us both further. The room beyond was coated in the same flaking blue paint. The floors were scuffed wood that needed both a dusting and a refinishing. There was a white dresser and a brass bed without blankets, both child-size. But as soon as I stepped inside, I understood what this was.

"This is Jidras's nehym." I knew without a doubt, just by the feel. Vehyn didn't bother confirming it. "How . . . ?"

I'd thought I had to be near someone to gain access to their sleeping soul. What was this? Did Vehyn have some power I didn't know, to call forth other souls at his command?

"I want to teach you something," he said, without answering my unfinished question. "Open one of those drawers." He nodded toward the dresser, and I stepped carefully up to it, unavoidably making tracks in the dust.

"I don't want to disturb anything," I said, my voice smaller than I expected. "I don't want to hurt him."

"You won't." Vehyn's tone was softer, gentler than usual, and it made me want to trust him. He hadn't left the doorway, or even set a toe inside the room. He was a dark shadow against the black fortress behind him, framed by flaking white, his pale face like sheet music in a gloomy parlor, shaded and inscrutable.

Somehow, the sight was heartbreaking—both the room I was in and the darkness beyond. However lonely Jidras's soul struck me as, it was nothing like Vehyn's. I'd managed to forget how *wrong* that place was until I saw it side by side with something so pathetically human. The darkness was lonely too, no doubt, but it was loneliness raised to an ungodly intensity—a cavernous emptiness, a bottomless craving.

I didn't want to be here anymore, standing between these two places that together struck such a chord of sadness and longing through my own hollow core. Definitely not how I thought I'd spend my eighteenth birthday. But Vehyn wouldn't let me leave until he was satisfied, I was sure. And maybe I didn't want to disappoint him.

I opened the drawer. I had to tug hard, and it gave with an unpleasant, woody screech.

"There's nothing inside," I said.

"Try again," he urged.

I turned, shooting him a glare. Curiosity could only carry me so far.

"Close your eyes and concentrate." He was as patient as I was impatient. "Focus on how you want this place to talk to you, to divulge its secrets. Souls can hide themselves, even when you walk through them. I'll help you do it, but it's a skill you might find useful on your own someday. This *is* a gift, Kamai."

This was what I had been needing to learn. I took a deep breath and closed my eyes. I thought of my father—yes, he *was* my father, wasn't he?—and how I wished I could understand him better.

Why do you hate me? was the thought that flashed, unbidden, to my mind.

When I opened my eyes, I had to swallow a gasp. There was

a ratty woven blanket on the once-naked bed, blue and yellow, with matching stained pillows. There was an old figurine of a soldier on the desk, chipped and worn, its hand empty where it might have once held a sword. There was also a brass picture frame, tarnished like everything else, encircling a painting of my mother. The portrait was beautiful, and yet the paint was flaking, her skin seeming to fall away in decay. I flinched from it.

"Look in the drawer again," Vehyn said. "The hidden places hold the deeper secrets. This is how you truly soulwalk."

It sounded more like soul-searching, but I didn't say that. So many nehyms that had looked so empty—what more could they have shown me? Had my mother known how to do this?

I looked at her wise smile in the painting. Of course she had, and I simply hadn't been ready to learn such things. I knew she hadn't completed my training, that she hadn't taught me everything—she'd told me as much. And now Vehyn was teaching me in her place. As with mostly everything to do with him, I felt a churning mixture of giddiness and trepidation.

I looked in the drawer. There was a stained brown leather journal.

"And that, my dear, is the prize," he said.

I held my breath as I touched the cover. Did this mean souls could simply be read like books, if one had the knowledge and power to figure out how? The thought of my having such access to a person's inner world was dizzying.

"Read it."

I followed his command, cracking the cover as if I had no control over my hands.

I loved her so much. I thought . . . I thought if she perhaps had greater reason to stay . . . I swapped out the herbs she was taking,

127

*put something in their place that tasted identical but that had
no effect.*

*I was wrong. Not even a child made her stay. That is the type
of woman she is.*

I slammed the journal shut. My hands trembled on the cover. My breathing came in sudden gasps. I almost couldn't believe the words—the meaning behind them. But no, I'd read enough to understand.

"Kamai?" Vehyn's voice, behind me, giving nothing away, unlike the book.

"Don't," I rasped.

It was clear enough what had happened. My mother hadn't wanted me. Jidras—I would never call him my father again— had used my conception to try to tie her to him. I knew it was true, just as I'd known this was his soul. It simply fit.

His own words, spoken the day I'd met him, floated up like an echo: *I've had nothing to do with you, no part in your upbringing. And that was how she wanted it, so blame her if you feel like blaming someone.*

I hated him . . . and I realized with burning clarity that I *didn't* blame my mother. Not at all. Maybe she hadn't planned for me, but there were ways to rid oneself of a child. It would have been her right, especially after her body had been so used against her. Instead, she must have left with me, found her way to Hallan somehow, and raised me, for the most part, without a father.

That was why Jidras had hated her—and why he hated me now. But *I* was fiercely proud of her, the person she had been. She *would* take a child from someone who would use a child to get what he wanted. And even if she hadn't planned to have me, she'd loved me as if she had. *That* was the type of woman she had been.

And now I knew for sure what type of man Jidras was.

It made me wonder, all the more, what type of man Vehyn was to show such a thing to me, on this of all days. No, not a man. Maybe I *had* forgotten what he was:

Inhuman.

"Why?" I asked quietly, my eyes still closed.

"What do you mean?" he asked, sounding innocent.

"Why now? You must want me to hate him bitterly. You must hate *me*."

"I simply wanted you to have the truth. Isn't that what you want?"

"You haven't given me the truth about *anything* yet," I spat, rounding on him. "Until now. So it must be only for your purposes, your own gain. Is it because I said Jidras wants me to marry? You want me to despise him so much that I would do anything to thwart his wishes? You want me to feel unwanted, not just by him, but my mother too? Only wanted by you?"

I'd felt it in occasional flashes—Vehyn's possessiveness.

"I can't believe you would do this to me," I continued, "so callously, so cruelly, so *selfishly*—and on my birthday!"

His eyes narrowed. "What did you expect? *Romance?*" His voice was mocking, sharp. A knife's edge. But then it gentled. "Kamai—"

"Don't!" I cried, throwing the journal back in the drawer and slamming it closed. "Don't talk to me. Don't come *near* me."

I expected him to be mad, but a slow smile spread across his face. "I'm afraid you can't escape me."

"Is that so? You can't leave your dark hole. And I don't think I'll be coming back."

He kept smiling, unconcerned at my outburst. "I can wait for you to get bored in there and come back here. I've waited for you long enough. A little longer won't hurt."

A shiver crawled down my spine. I wasn't sure what he meant, and I didn't want to know. "Don't bother waiting." I closed my eyes, pushing myself to wake.

Vehyn's voice sharpened. "Kamai, wait." He spoke in anger, in threat, and yet there was something else in his tone too, but I was sick of listening to him. "I said *wait*."

By then it was too late to realize he was warning me. Because when I opened my eyes in the waking world, I wasn't in my bed.

I wasn't even inside.

I was slipping on rain-drenched tiles under the heavy darkness of the night sky, instinctively scrambling for purchase before I even realized what was happening. But my wet grip wouldn't hold, and then I was falling—off the roof and down to the courtyard four stories below.

11

HIDDEN STRENGTH

My hand caught the gutter at the last possible second. The clay fixture cracked and gave slightly under my weight. I was hanging, for the moment, right alongside Jidras's master bedroom window on the fourth floor. Rain pounded down around me.

I had wondered how I was in his nehym. Now I knew. I'd been as close to him as I'd always needed to be, right outside his window. Vehyn didn't have some hidden power to open up souls for himself. But he had a hidden power to make me sleepwalk. I must have crawled out the attic's dormer window.

Some vague part of my mind registered that I was soaked to the skin—I must have been outside for a while. The air wasn't too chilly, but the rain was. Wet like this, asleep on a cool clay roof while drenched, my fingers had gone numb. And now they were slipping.

"Please," I whimpered, to no one in particular. I wouldn't have minded if Jidras had thrown open his window and reached for me. It was amazing how quickly hatred shied away in the face of death.

But the window didn't open. I slipped some more.

Then I felt the shove. It was like someone bumping into you in a hall. Except this was in my head. I wanted to push back, but something told me that the effort would distract me, I would fall, and I would die.

And then I heard the voice: *Kamai, reach up with your other hand and reinforce your hold. Now.*

It was a very familiar voice. Apparently, Vehyn could not only make me sleepwalk, but speak directly into my mind when he felt like it.

Stop complaining and do it.

I tried to inch my other hand up, but my grip slipped more and I let loose a scream that was lost in the drumming rain. "I can't, I'm going to fall, I'm going to—"

My arm suddenly tingled, flushing with warmth. It was almost the same living-stone sensation I had when touching the black door, except it was *in* my flesh. My hand flew up by its own accord.

So this was how he'd done it. How he'd made me move.

But he wasn't fast enough. Or he was too fast. The gutter snapped out of my grip, and I was dropping, too startled to even scream. The white sandstone passed in a blur—and stopped. My breath hitched out of me.

My extended hand, the one that felt like stone, gripped the bottom edge of a third-floor balcony. The force of my arrested fall should have yanked my arm out of its socket. Or, at the very least, my fingers shouldn't have been strong enough to catch my weight. But my grip held.

His grip held.

I squinted up at my arm through the rain and then wished I hadn't. Deep black marks limned my wet skin from my bunched shoulder to the tips of my fingers, curling and spiraling as if the patterns were cast by the lanterns in the black fortress.

It almost scared me more than the thought of dying. "Oh gods. Oh gods."

Your gods aren't helping you, Kamai. I am. Now grab the edge with your other hand and actually keep hold this time. Without giving me any time to react, he continued: *In case you were wondering, it's much harder to manipulate you when you're awake. Do please hurry. I might get tired.*

I lifted my other hand. My normal hand. It felt like a numb weight at the end of my arm in comparison to the warm strength in its twin. But it didn't have to be inhumanly strong. It just had to brace my weight while the other hauled me up on its own.

It shouldn't have been possible—none of this should have been possible—but, one-armed, that was exactly what happened: I pulled myself up the balcony rails. Rather, Vehyn pulled me up. Once bent over the railing, my feet perched precariously on the slippery outer edge, I gave up any pretense of coordination and simply tumbled headfirst onto the balcony.

My strange arm caught me, preventing me from breaking a wrist, or my face. For a few moments, I just lay there on the tiles, breathing, as the rain pattered on my skull. I watched the black marks fade from my skin. The warmth seeped out of my flesh as well, leaving me cold and utterly drained.

"You still in my head?" I asked. I sounded drunk.

Get inside, Kamai. You're in shock. This is your *balcony, by the way.*

So it was. I hadn't even noticed.

You're welcome. But I expect your thanks in person.

I ignored him, lurching to my feet and fumbling at the door

handle. Luckily, I'd left it unlocked. I toppled inside, managing only a few more stumbling steps before I collapsed on my bed and dragged the blankets over me.

I fell asleep instantly. Maybe he helped with that too.

I soon turned up in the clearing. I might have meandered through dreams first, scraping together some real rest, but eventually the currents of sleep took me in the clearing's direction. Or Vehyn did.

The black door was there and open. He was standing at the threshold, his muscular arms folded.

"You bastard." I didn't know what else to say. There were too many places to start.

"I never intended for you to discover this." He sounded like it was merely unfortunate, not that he was at fault.

We could start there, then. "You *never intended*? All this time, you've been able to manipulate me like that?"

"Not before you opened the door, of course, and it's much easier when you're asleep, especially when you're in here with me." He gestured over his shoulder. He was being remarkably forthright, for once.

I figured I'd return the favor. "Then I *really* won't be coming in again."

He didn't even bother responding. "Kamai, do you realize . . ." His jaw hardened. "You could have died. Forcing my hand like that—"

A barking laugh tore out of me. "You mean *you* literally forcing *my* hand? And in the process, I accidentally made you admit that you have a terrifying amount of control over me? Oh, *I'm sorry*."

"I saved you. You thanked Nikha for something much less impressive."

So he *had* known about the market and just let me pretend I could keep it from him. And now he was trying to belittle Nikha on top of that. "If you want thanks, you can choke on it. You could have just let me die instead."

"But I didn't want that."

I opened my mouth to argue, to spit more curses at him, but nothing came out as his words sank in.

He didn't want me to die. It wasn't the highest form of regard for a human life, but it was hard not to feel grateful after he'd just saved mine—even though it had been in danger because of him.

I really, *really* hadn't wanted to die. Tears welled in my eyes at the memory, raw in my mind. I should have been angrier. I should have hurled more accusations and insults, more questions at the very least, about this power he'd revealed. But right that second, I was bone-tired and shaken. I just wanted to hold on to the thought that he hadn't wanted me to die, that he'd saved me. That someone still valued my life.

I was hugging myself before I even realized it, simply for something to hold.

Vehyn must have seen the look in my eyes. The door's frame disappeared and reappeared right in front of me. It should have been frightening. It would have been if I hadn't wanted him close, but at that moment I did. I sprang onto my tiptoes and threw my arms around his neck, burying my face in his shoulder. Vehyn obviously wasn't accustomed to me taking the initiative, because his entire body registered the surprise—he stiffened like stone. Then his arms relaxed, and his hands came to my cheeks. He tipped my head back, but only by a few inches so he could peer into my eyes, curiosity written all over his face. The upper half of my body was still leaning through the doorway. I leaned closer.

I didn't know what I was doing.

"Is it romance you truly want?" he asked, his eyes both hungry and searching.

"I . . .," I stammered. "I don't know."

Before I knew what *he* was doing, he'd bent his head. His lips touched mine. Now it was my turn to freeze.

His mouth didn't claim mine. He moved tentatively, testing out my top lip, and then the bottom, biting each one with a featherlight nibble. Briefly, his tongue tasted mine.

I didn't reciprocate. Logical thought had stuttered to a halt. Did I want this? I didn't think so. Did I want him to stop? Not necessarily.

He pulled back, a slight smile on his face, his lips flushed and shining. "So much for romance. This really doesn't do it for you, does it?"

I would have thought he sounded the slightest bit insecure, if not for the fact that he'd stabbed right to the heart of *my* insecurities. I jerked away, stung.

"I thought you knew everything about me," I said, trying for haughtiness and failing.

"I do, for the most part, but such matters of both flesh and soul run deep." As if to illustrate, he braced one hand on my lower back and flattened the other on my belly, spreading his fingers, digging lightly into my dress. It was both intimate and alarming, because I could feel his immense strength even as he held it perfectly in check. He likely could have ripped my guts out if he'd wanted to. "Case in point," he said, squinting, as if seeing something I couldn't. "I'm not sure if you like this. It's hard to tell. I sense both a thrill and a pulling back. When I try to dig deeper, find some hidden desire, there's nothing there."

Nothing there. That was what lurked beneath the surface,

when he tried to reach for my depths. Nothing. He thought I was broken, just like everyone else would if they knew my secret. If romance was only a prelude to everything that was supposed to come after, then to indulge it would be feasting on appetizers when all anyone wanted was dinner. I would be fooling myself and other people that I was something *more*.

"Perhaps romance isn't for me." I tried to make my tone light, but instead it came out bright and brittle. Shame washed over me in a sudden flood. I tried to pull away from him, but his hands shifted around my waist and held me still.

"Kamai, stop. I don't mind at all how you feel. It's . . . interesting, honestly." He sounded almost surprised, and *that* utterly surprised me—until doubt came raging in with my shame.

"Yes, interesting. Like I'm some freak of nature. I'm all wrong. I don't feel things like . . . like . . ." *Normal people.*

"You're more like me."

His admission took my breath away. In the following silence, he gave me time to probe the idea. This mysterious being who'd so fascinated me felt the same as I did, at least insofar as it came to sex. I wasn't alone.

And then Vehyn spoiled it. "How you feel isn't unheard of among humans. It's entirely normal, if a superior way to be, in my opinion. Since I'm a superior *being*, how I feel is both different and similar."

I squinted at him. "What do you mean?"

"I can't imagine ever degrading myself to such a base mortal activity as *that*. But whereas you don't feel the hunger for such things, I feel hunger of a different sort."

I didn't want to know about his hunger, in case what I discovered was too terrifying. And maybe because I *did* have a

137

hunger of my own, for what I'd thought of as appetizers. For romance. And I didn't want him to laugh at me. Because if Vehyn thought sex was too base and mortal, how would he feel about something as silly as kissing? But then, he *had* kissed me. He had given me roses. Maybe he was interested in romance in his own way, just as I was. And yet, he lacked something else that was bothering me, and it certainly wasn't a desire for sex.

There was something missing in his eyes—within that empty, ageless darkness—that had told me he wasn't human. Something missing in *him* that I didn't want to think about too much.

If not broken, then at the very least I was something different. And maybe it was good to be different from Vehyn.

"Gods forbid you have to stoop to a mortal level like mine," I said finally, attempting to cover my surprise, my wonder, with anger. I tried to pull away again. "I guess we're not alike after all."

He held on to me, giving me a little shake that was almost affectionate. "Kamai, Kamai, I don't wish to antagonize you. I merely want to know you. To understand you. So I can give you what you want."

What did I want? I flushed to my ears with embarrassment this time, and I couldn't look him in the face for fear he would read my thoughts.

Vehyn's liquid dark eyes were on me, waiting, calculating, and hungry at once. *Predatory.* "What are you thinking?"

"Nothing." Which was a flagrant lie. A thought occurred to me, one I couldn't halt: Was this, was *I*, somehow what he actually wanted? And could I give *something* to him in a way that might satisfy his hunger, whatever it was? My breathing increased in spite of myself, and a smile flickered across Vehyn's face, as if he *did* know what I was thinking.

I mentally berated myself. How did I know he wasn't lying

about how he felt? And why in all three hells did I want to give him what he wanted?

"What do you want, Kamai?" he whispered, leaning closer to me, his breath a warm caress against my cheek.

It was hard to focus, but I managed. I had to know if he was only toying with me. And maybe that meant toying with him. I needed to ask for something small, almost inconsequential . . . but something I knew for sure he wouldn't want to give, just to see what he would do. But first, to throw him off the scent . . . "I want you to tell me who killed my mother."

"Not yet."

Of course. It was the bait that kept me coming back to him. "Fine." I took a deep breath. "Then I'll settle for an apology."

His eyes narrowed. "An apology?" He repeated it as if unfamiliar with the word.

"Yes. That's what I want. Apologize for your cruelty in Jidras's nehym. And for not telling me about what you could do with me."

"I won't say I'm sorry for the latter," he said, cupping my face in his palms, "because you'll know I don't mean it. I will say this: take more care with yourself. I would hate to lose you."

It took me a second to realize he hadn't apologized for the first thing, either. *Crafty bastard.* "Then don't drive me off by being cruel," I murmured into his hands, trying to remind him of what I'd asked. His fingers were gravitating to my mouth. I didn't mind him touching me, not at all. His hands felt like they were exploring, studying me, like my own fingers had traced over maps of Eopia to learn its geography. But I would have liked them even more if they came with an apology.

"My intention wasn't cruelty," he said gently, almost contritely.

139

Almost. "I didn't want your father to be able to hurt you anymore. It was a gift."

I snorted, a very unladylike noise, but I didn't care. "Some gift. *You* hurt me in the process, so why would you care if he does?"

Just apologize, I thought, *so I can enjoy your hands.*

"Because no one should be able to hurt you." He brushed my cheek with his index finger, tracing the line of my jaw. His thumb caught my lower lip. My heart began to beat faster. "No one but me."

My blood abruptly turned to ice, and my scalp prickled in warning. "You had me until that last bit."

"You would do well to remember, now that you're no longer a child," he said softly, as if still speaking tender words, "I'm the only one who can hurt you, and so I'm the only one you need fear."

I hadn't known it was possible to fail a test so badly, but he had. "Apology not given, not accepted, but lesson learned." I took a step back into the clearing, finally withdrawing from his touch. "I'm definitely afraid."

The doorway hovered closer, bringing him with it, and prickles raced over my arms and legs. The trick wasn't charming anymore. He'd let me go only to chase me, a predator toying with its prey. "But you don't have to fear me, so long as you listen to me," he said as he drew nearer. "Come here."

I backed away. "No."

"I said come here."

"And I said no! I'm not a dog." I breathed the words in nearly a gasp, but at least I said them. And I retreated farther into my bare, sad little clearing. At least he couldn't leap right through the doorway.

"No, but you are mine."

Mine. That was what Razim had said too. Apparently, I belonged to all sorts of people—men, or at least strange inhuman creatures that kind of looked like men—without even knowing it. The memory of the pattern that had burst all over my skin—*his* marks, *his* strength in my limbs, *his* voice in my head—didn't help my temper. Anger flared again, making my voice ring clear. "I am not!"

He cocked his head at me. His next words almost seemed like a change in topic, but I knew better. "What do you think happened, when you opened this door?"

Oh, holy Heshara, what have I done? The question echoed in my mind, not for the first time and probably not the last. "You can't get out."

"Is that so? Are you forgetting this evening, how I affected you?"

"But you can't get beyond . . . beyond me." At least I hoped with every scrap of my being that he couldn't.

"You opened the world to me, but the way is through *you.* You are my door, Kamai. It's only that I haven't fully opened it yet."

Who are you? I wanted to ask. But I knew he wouldn't tell me, and I knew where he was going with this. "That doesn't make me yours."

"But you *gave* yourself to me, Kamai. That means you are *mine.*"

My words only grew louder. "So why not just kill me, then? Kick me down like a door and be free in the world?"

"Because, as I've already told you, that wouldn't please me."

"What *does* please you?" I nearly shouted. "What do you want from me?"

He only smiled at me.

I took yet another step back.

. His smile slipped and, surprisingly, he gave me a real answer. Or real enough. "For the immediate present, I want you to stop running from me, accept your fate, and . . . why, maybe even enjoy yourself in my company."

I couldn't help a strangled laugh. "You pretty much ruined any chance of that with the whole 'Fear me, I own you' part of your speech. You forgot to add 'happy birthday.'"

"But I also protected you and gave you gifts of knowledge and strength. I take care of what's mine."

"There you go again, assuming you have what you don't. You could really work on your courtship skills." My voice should have blistered him with its sarcasm. "Have you been getting tips from Jidras?"

I mostly hoped he would scoff at the idea of courting me, but when he didn't, my stomach clenched in a way that was both horribly good and bad. If this was courtship, I was in trouble.

"I would rather learn from you," he said, entirely unperturbed. "So you tell me, what can I do to make you feel better?"

"Take it back. Say it isn't true, that I'm not yours." I paused. "And then godsdamned apologize."

He only stared at me again. Yet this time he pursed his lips. "But then I would be lying," he said eventually.

"As if you don't do that already!"

"I often withhold the truth from you, but I rarely speak falsehoods."

"You're lying now!" My voice rose to nearly a screech. I took a deep breath and said more steadily through gritted teeth, "I am mine, and mine alone."

The slight smile returned, but it didn't touch his eyes. "As you wish. You are yours, and I am sorry."

Now he was lying. It was plain as his smirk. And he knew I would be able to tell.

"I hate you," I spat.

"I know. But I also know that's not all you feel for me. Besides, where is the fun in absolutes?"

I wanted to scream. Instead, I closed my eyes to wake up.

He didn't try to stop me. Not because he couldn't—he probably could—but because he was once again letting me go. And he knew I knew it, which only made me more furious.

I hesitated, reopened my eyes in the clearing, and slammed the black door in his face. Oddly, it stayed shut for the second I lingered to see if it would. But maybe that was also only because he allowed it. I kicked the door before I left, only bruising my toe, and I knew there was a lesson in there somewhere.

But none of those lessons mattered anymore, because I'd ignored the most important one of all: The *first* thing my mother had tried to teach me about the black door. Not to open it.

There was another lesson that mattered almost as much: *Never fall in love.*

I wasn't too worried about that. I figured I could maintain a pretty strong hatred for Vehyn, if tonight had been any indication. Still, his sly, insinuating voice echoed in my mind even after I woke up stiff and sore and mildly damp. Not his actual voice, just the memory of it:

That's not all you feel for me.

I spent the rest of the night tossing and turning and wondering if there was the possibility that he might be right. Which was probably the exact effect he'd intended.

You bastard.

12

BLOOMING
SHADOWS

Staring into my own reflection in the vanity mirror the next morning, I realized my eyes had dark circles underneath. The deep shadows even seemed to reach my irises, making the brown look nearly black. Almost like Vehyn's. Perhaps it was the result of only a bad night of sleep, compounded by the gray light filtering in from outside.

But I couldn't shake the memory of the black patterns surfacing on my skin, taking control of me, lending me unnatural strength. Maybe something inside me had changed, and my time in Vehyn's realm was lending shadows to my eyes from more than simple sleeplessness. I shuddered to imagine him peering out through my own face, speaking in my head, moving my body. He was silent now, but I knew that wasn't permanent.

How had it come this far?

Something was wrong. With Vehyn. With the fortress behind the black door. With me. But I didn't know what to do about any of it, and it was easier to focus on the wrongness outside of me, under *this* roof.

I put on a lot of powder before heading downstairs. I even tried on a creamy peach gown to lend me some warm, bright color, but it only made me look worse, and I hated peach besides. I settled on the midnight-blue affair that I had worn last night. The one Vehyn had complimented.

Stop thinking about Vehyn.

As I fitted a pair of glimmering earrings that would hopefully distract from my face, a knock at the door made me startle. It was only Nikha.

She took one look at me and said, "Sweet Heshara, did Moholos breathe too hard on you last night?"

Moholos was a folk figure, sometimes described as an old man, sometimes a mischievous imp, who purportedly carried out tasks for Heshara and also occasionally got up to no good. He put people and especially children to sleep by exhaling on them. He wasn't in any religious texts, and at an early age my mother had told me he was only mythical. Even so, the plant used to distill sleeping tonics was called mohol after him.

Maybe Vehyn is Moholos. Picturing Vehyn bending over beds and breathing on people nearly made me laugh. I would have to ask him about that just to see what he'd say, if I ever decided to speak to him again.

Stop it, I told myself. To Nikha, I said, "I . . . didn't sleep well."

"I can see that. Feel free to claim that as an excuse."

I frowned at her. "Excuse for what?"

"The master of the house has decided to take breakfast with us commoners this morning." Heavy sarcasm underlay her obsequious words. Under normal circumstances, it would have wrung a smile from me, especially since it meant she'd grown comfortable enough around me to mock my fa—*No*, I thought. *Not my father.* "I couldn't imagine you felt like suffering through that, so I thought I'd warn—"

"No," I said vehemently enough to make her raise her eyebrows. "Thank you, Nikha, but it's he who will have to suffer through my presence." With that, I swept out of the room, catching her muttered "Oh boy" as I passed her.

For breakfast, I always had to sit next to the head of the table, where a place had been set for Jidras, in case he felt like showing up and pretending we were something vaguely resembling a family. He usually didn't. It was ironic that he decided to do so right when I'd abandoned any last thought of him as family, but at least it was convenient. He was, for once, the exact person I wanted to see.

He was there at the table when I arrived, a long hardwood affair that was always too big and imposing for just me. I usually asked Nikha to sit with me, which was permissible because of her status as head of the household guard and because she was a woman, so anything untoward was less likely to occur, in Jidras's estimation. But this time, she wisely hung back. Steaming cups of coffee were already laid out, along with plates displaying luscious slices of mango drizzled in coconut cream and speckled with nuts. That dish was normally a favorite, but I ignored it entirely. I didn't pause between entering, dropping into my chair, and opening my mouth to speak—all before Jidras could stiffly bid me good morning.

"The last time I saw my mother, she told me I was to find you," I said, my words as cutting as the knife next to my plate. "She gave me a letter that I wasn't to open until my eighteenth birthday. She wanted me to wait until I was an adult and could judge the contents for myself. I carried it with me from our burning villa." The lie was a ready one. I'd prepared it earlier as I'd tried to mask the circles under my eyes. I needed *some* excuse for the fact that I was reacting to this knowledge only now. "In it, she told me the truth about you."

Jidras's mouth opened in surprise, then in outrage, and then in shock, repeatedly, like a fish's, never once able to form any words. Eventually, he leaned back in his chair and stared at me. He looked as haunted as I had appeared in my vanity mirror. "What truth?" he asked finally, his voice faint.

"You know the one. Do you want me to repeat it in present company?"

He made a show of folding his napkin and setting it carefully next to his plate. "Leave us," he said to the servants lingering along the wall, and to Nikha, standing in the doorway.

Once everyone had departed, some quickly, some reluctantly—with curiosity written all over their faces—Jidras looked at me. "Where is this letter? I would like to see it."

"I burned it."

His face hardened. "Then how do I know—?"

"How else *could* I know that you tricked my mother into getting pregnant just so she would stay with you?" And then, when I realized his true concern, I laughed derisively. "You think only to protect yourself. You're worried I would show it to someone."

"It would be no good for either of us if rumors were to—"

"It's not a rumor!" I said. "You did it, and I know it . . . and that's enough. That should be enough for *you* to be properly ashamed, without the threat of public humiliation hanging over your head. I'm not going to use it against you. I'm not like you, after all. *You're your own person, and I'm my own, separate*," I said,

147

quoting the hurtful words he'd thrown at me the day I'd met him.

His eyes narrowed. "Then what, exactly, do you want?"

I scoffed. "An admission of guilt, perhaps? You can't apologize to my mother, but you can to me, especially given how you've treated me."

"And how have I treated you?" Jidras demanded coldly. "I have fed you, clothed you, put shelter over your head, and more."

I gaped at him. "You've treated me like you had nothing to do with me! Like I wasn't part of your twisted plan to coerce my mother into staying with you! At least take responsibility for that."

"Responsibility?" His jaw went so tight it grew paler at the hinges. "Who should take responsibility? Her work always landed her in trouble, didn't it? Getting so close to people as to make them think you're real, when in fact your heart is false, comes with its risks. First she ended up with you, and now she's dead. I don't know what she finally did to get herself killed, but I can't say I'm surprised."

It took every ounce of restraint to not hurl my plate of mango and coconut across the room. "She was a pleasure artist," I pronounced, hard and cold. "I'm sorry if you wanted to see more in that than there actually was. You were using something other than your brain to assess the situation, and that's *your* fault, not hers. The pleasure she gave wasn't yours to own." His blue eyes widened with icy fury, but before he could interrupt, I leaned forward, my hands gripping the edge of the table. "And if you won't admit the truth, it doesn't matter. Because I know. And you know I know. And *that's* what matters."

His voice was as tight as a fist when he spoke. "I took you in when I didn't have to, and now I will see this through, even though I don't owe it to you, and especially not to Marin."

Apprehension rose in my chest. "What do you mean?"

"I was joining you at breakfast today to tell you we are going to the royal court. Sooner rather than later, I think. There, I will throw you a gala to mark your debut . . . and your eligibility."

My throat went suddenly dry. "Eligibility for what?"

"For marriage, of course. You are now a woman grown, and with your lack of interest in a suitable career path and with our recent . . . differences . . . it has become especially apparent to me that you no longer belong under my roof. All I can hope is that the right man will find you more agreeable, and the sooner I find him, the better." He took a jerky sip of coffee.

"No," I said, my voice faint, "I don't want to marry. I'll do anything else." I couldn't help the pleading in my words. This was worse than anything I thought he would do. "I'll be an accountant, I'll—"

"It's too late for that." There was satisfaction, even relish, in his tone. "Too late for me to trust you to your own whims."

My own whims. In a twisted way, he was inflicting on me what he couldn't on my mother—consigning me to a man who could contain me, *have* me by law.

"You gave me only *weeks* to decide how the rest of my life would unfold! This isn't fair!"

Jidras ignored me. "You will be well matched," he carried on, as if waving away any concern I might have had about my potential husband's social standing—as if that were even close to the nature of my actual concern. "I will give you a respectable dowry, a respectable name, and the chance at a respectable future. Any child of mine will have no less." It sounded more like a requirement than a gift, especially with what he said next. "And in turn, any child of mine will be worthy of no less. Is that clear?"

"Now I'm your child?" It was all I could think to say in the face of such a thing. For a burning second, I wished I *did* have a letter to threaten him with. To show the world.

He didn't bother responding. "I think I've lost my appetite, both for breakfast and this conversation. Make yourself presentable." He stood from the table without another word.

"We're not going to court *now*, are we?" My horror was audible.

"Your gala probably won't be possible without a week's notice, at least. Invitations must be sent to the proper parties, after all, and other arrangements made." He pursed his lips as he looked me over. "But I want the royal clothier to fit you for a new gown, and you need to see a priest of Heshara."

That stopped my breath short. "*What?*"

He arched a cool eyebrow at me. "Don't you know? Anyone and everyone, before they are granted entrance at court, must see one of the royal priests or priestesses."

"Why?" My chest was so tight it was hard to squeeze out more than a word.

"They must vouch you are of sound mind and lacking in murderous intent before allowing you near the king. Even *you*, I think, shouldn't have much of a problem there." He muttered as he left the dining room, "It will be the least of our obstacles."

I sat, staring at the wall in numb shock. How quickly he had turned this situation against me, just like Vehyn had, when all I had wanted was an apology. The only thing either of them had given me was fear. I was too afraid to hate them both as much as I really wanted.

Because there was a problem. *Several* problems for a priest or priestess to discover. Such as the fact that I was a soulwalker and seemed to have no soul to boot. Such as the black door.

Perhaps Jidras wasn't consigning me to a fate worse than death after all. It might only be death.

I had less than an hour to prepare. Less than an hour to change into the most innocent-looking gown I had. Less than an hour to pray to Heshara to spare my life. Less than an hour until I was in the carriage, seated next to Nikha, across from Jidras, as we rode toward the royal palace, all of us silent.

There were many types of silence. Nikha's was born of confusion—I hadn't time to tell her what had happened— Jidras's of anger, mine of fear. I wished I could wrap myself in silence like a cloak, use it as armor. For a second, I missed the fortress behind the black door and its thick, heavy silences. Next to this, it seemed almost like a safe haven.

What does Vehyn think about all this? I wondered. There hadn't been time to even attempt a nap, and he hadn't spoken in my head since last night. He'd said it was difficult when I was awake. Maybe he couldn't now. Maybe he would just have to watch a priest or priestess of Heshara accuse me, condemn me, and then sentence me to death.

I scrunched my nose against the sting in my eyes and stared out the carriage window so the others wouldn't notice.

In the late-morning sun, colorfully tiled roofs burst like blossoms on the sandstone stems of the sheer-faced multistory houses and buildings, winding up the hill toward the bright walls of the palace. Behind them, mountain gullies were emerald green from the recent rain. Women's pale scarves bobbed through the streets like seeds in the wind, out in abundance under the punishing sun. It wouldn't rain every day, only several times a week. Shaded by our covered carriage, I wore my own scarf looped over my head, more to hide from the world than from the sun. But there would be no hiding from Heshara and her priests.

They would find me out.

When we pulled to a stop and our driver opened the carriage door in front of a towering sandstone wall with its narrow, silver-plated gate depicting the phases of the moon, Jidras hopped out immediately. Before I could even gather the courage to follow, Nikha put a hand on my knee. It was such a familiar gesture.

"Are you all right?" she asked, only concern in her voice. "What haven't you told me?"

Everything. The word stuck in my throat. But it was true. I had taken Nikha for granted by not sharing with her. There *was* someone in the waking world who cared for me. She had been easy to disregard so I could feel sorry for myself, but she was here, for me. A companion who'd treated me with respect and consideration, who'd listened to me, who'd never tried to treat me like someone I wasn't, who'd sat through countless awkward meals with me at my request, who'd patiently beaten me in defense training and graciously *been* beaten at Gods and Kings more times than I could count, and who I highly doubted would care that I never wanted to sleep with anyone. So what if she was a little overly protective at times? She'd saved me from Razim, after all.

She was my friend, my only friend, and I'd been a coward in return, too afraid of what she might think of me if she knew the truth. I should have confided in her, because I owed her better.

Instead, I'd lied to her, risked her life, and turned to Vehyn and the black door, and look where that had gotten me.

"I'll tell you, I promise." *If I survive the week.* "I wish we had time now, but . . ."

Jidras cleared his throat loudly outside the carriage. I tucked my scarf tighter around my head and stepped out into the sunlight. Nikha followed, scarfless—I'd still never seen her wear one. She knew something was wrong even if she didn't know what, and she kept close behind me, on her guard.

Standing on the stone cobbles before the silver gate, Jidras eyed her critically. "I don't think we'll be needing you inside, Nikha. You're hardly dressed appropriately, and the palace guards will be more than enough protection. She's only seeing a priest, for Tain's sake. I'm not sure why you're acting like she's going into an ambush."

"But, sir—" Nikha started.

"Wait by the carriage." His tone left no room for argument. He swept toward the gate, which a pair of armed guards, dressed in ceremonial silver-plated armor, opened for him. With a backward look at Nikha, I followed. She grimaced after me.

Each step up the cobbled path felt like I was indeed walking into an ambush, or toward my execution. I barely noticed the meticulously groomed garden around me, or the perfect canals that trickled through them. All I could see was the towering white crescent spires and the black dome of the temple, as alternately sharp and rounded, bright and dark, as the moon itself, Heshara herself. Its lack of color set it apart from the rest of the palace.

Colors were Ranta's domain. Since the king was her ceremonial husband and steward, rainbow hues were in abundance at the palace, not only in the form of bright mosaics and paints I could see from here, but also a riot of flowers. Despite those signs of the earth goddess, and the many sculptures of her wearing dresses made of water or blossoms, her husband had never even seen her, though both she and their marriage were real. I'd admired her parents' protectiveness as a child—Tain and Heshara had taken every precaution for their daughter, recruiting their most devoted and valiant mortal servant, crowning him the first king of Eopia, and binding Ranta to him and the rest of his line in marriage—but now I wondered if the young Ranta'd had any say in the matter.

The queen consort *certainly* hadn't. Never mind that her husband was also married to a goddess; she'd apparently been executed for dallying with Hallan. From what I could tell, marriage didn't favor women.

Jidras and I reached the wide steps of the temple together, which alternated in black and white marble up to the imposing front doors. After touching between his eyes in respect to Heshara, he started up without hesitation. My heart tried to leap into my throat, blood thundered in my ears, and I suddenly felt hot. Dizzy. Maybe I would faint and not have to do this.

No such luck. I only succeeded in standing there, staring like an idiot, until Jidras hissed at me impatiently to follow. All I could do was squeeze fistfuls of my skirt and start up after him. How had my mother managed this? *She* had been at court more times than I could count, which meant she must have gained approval from the clergy. But she'd undoubtedly been the exact type of person they wouldn't have allowed in, who they would have arrested and imprisoned, or pressed into their service . . . or executed. As a soulwalker and courtesan, how had she stayed hidden, survived for so long?

Perhaps if she hadn't kept so many secrets from me . . . As fast as a wave of anger swept through me, shame followed. My mother would have expected more from me, to be able to work through the situation on my own. She'd given me the tools to do so.

Think, think, I told myself, with every step that brought me closer to doom. Jidras was at the temple doors now, nodding to the guards and pointing back at me. No matter how I racked my brain, I couldn't think of anything that would save me.

But there was someone else who might. Some*thing.* The exact creature my mother had never wanted me to turn to, whom I'd just sworn off after making that mistake one too many times already. And yet perhaps he was the only one who could help me now.

Vehyn, I thought. *If you're in there . . . of course you're in there. I'm in trouble, in case you hadn't noticed.*

No response. I reached the high, arching doorways carved with the phases of the moon, where Jidras had already vanished into the cool dimness. The guards nodded at me, gesturing for me to enter. When I did, I could barely make out the cavernous interior, constructed in black and white stone, both because my eyes were still adjusting from the bright light outside and because my focus was entirely elsewhere.

They're going to imprison me, maybe put me to death, if they find out what I am.

Jidras stopped at a short podium near the front of the entry hall to talk in low tones with a young, white-robed priest. The sight of the man spiked fear through me, made my breath come short, my steps stutter to a halt. The incense suffusing the air felt suffocating when it would have otherwise been pleasant. Would they be able to tell I was a soulwalker immediately? Would they denounce me on the spot?

Vehyn, I'm scared, and I thought you didn't want me to fear

155

anything else. The least you can do is make yourself useful. Take my fear away.

". . . and it is indeed Priest Agrir she'll be seeing today, is it not?" Something in Jidras's tone told me whomever I was supposed to see was important.

The priest nodded. "He is expecting her. Right this way."

Not him. I almost gasped in relief at the voice in my head, and then nearly tripped when my foot flushed warm and tingly, twitching underneath me, to my right. *Move, Kamai. This way.*

I didn't mind his bossiness so much now. Without even thinking about how odd I must look, I turned and stumbled away from the podium, from Jidras and the priest, toward a series of doors punctuating the right wall of the temple wing. My eyes downcast, I dodged a line of pale columns in my peripheral vision, the white-and-black-checkered tiles passing in a blur beneath the flicker of my slippered toes.

"Kamai," Jidras called, surprised. "That's not the way."

But it was Vehyn's way, a last resort, and my feet twitched one or two more times until I nearly fetched up against one of the heavy wooden doors. Before I could debate whether to knock or just barge right in, it opened.

I found myself facing a priestess, her night-dark face lined with about as many years as Jidras's, making her somewhere shy of fifty. Her white hood was drawn, but I could see the beginnings of black braids streaked with silver. She was taller than me, her cheekbones sharp in her face. Her eyes widened in a brief flash as they met mine.

Jidras strode up behind me, the young priest trailing. "Kamai, what are you doing?" he hissed, clearly embarrassed. To the priestess, he said, "Apologies, my daughter isn't used to being at court, and this is her first time in—"

156

"I want her," I said. "I want her to conduct my interview."

"Why ever would you?" Jidras lowered his exasperated voice with a sheepish glance around the temple. "It's not as if you know her, and we have an appointment with the king's own holy adviser."

"I . . . I'd be more comfortable with a woman, I think."

That drew them all up short. It was hard to argue against that, though the priest standing at Jidras's shoulder made an attempt: "Priest or priestess, it makes no difference in the eyes of Heshara. We are all her servants—"

"Perhaps this is Heshara's will," the priestess said, speaking up for the first time, her voice deep and smooth, authoritative without being sharp. "I am happy to be of service." Without another word, she ushered me into the chamber she'd just been leaving, shutting out Jidras and the other priest, their eyes wide with bafflement.

This was all well and good, but as soon as she turned to face me, I had no idea what to say.

She did. She took one look at me and said, "You're Kamai Nuala."

Nuala, not *Numa*.

She knew me, even if I didn't know her. And I realized that knowledge might save my life or end it all the sooner.

13

FORMIDABLE FRIENDS

"You're Marin's daughter," the priestess continued, leaving no doubt she knew exactly who I was. She walked past me, moving for the heavy wooden desk at the back of her office, flanked on either side by two long, brown leather couches—one for her, one for whomever's soul she was investigating.

Maybe I'd been wrong and Vehyn did want to get me killed. He'd led me to someone who would already have cause to suspect me. "I don't—"

"Don't worry. Your identity is safe with me. I knew your mother well. We . . . worked together . . . in some capacity." The woman threw back her hood, sat down at the desk, and opened a drawer to pull out a pen—when I'd been expecting a vial of sleeping tonic. "My name is Lenara. She must have told you about me, since you knew to seek me out. And good thing. It isn't safe for you anywhere else here."

"She . . ." I hardly knew where to begin. "She didn't tell me everything. How did you two . . ."

"I know what she was," she said, without preamble. "And I know what you are. I can help you . . . and I think you can help me." Throughout all these jaw-dropping pronouncements, she dipped her pen in ink and began busily writing on a crisp sheet of parchment.

She knew what I was. There would be no trial. No imprisonment. No death sentence. And yet my relief was short-lived. Because if this woman knew of my mother and me through the Twilight Guild—and I could think of no other explanation that made sense—then there was no way I could help her in return.

"My mother wasn't only a courtesan and pleasure artist," I said hesitantly, testing the waters, "or even only . . . what it is that we are." I still wasn't comfortable saying *soulwalker* out loud. My mother had warned me of the danger for so long.

Lenara looked up and met my eyes. Her gaze was warm, heavy. Understanding. "I know. And she wasn't only a member of the Twilight Guild, either. She was something else, on top of all that. And I don't only mean an amazing woman, which she was as well."

"Some—something . . . else?" I stammered. "What else?"

"There are hidden forces at work other than the Twilight Guild. One, in particular, that works in opposition to them."

She went back to writing.

I couldn't help but ask. "Who?"

Lenara didn't look up at me this time, but her words were just as cautious. "Now isn't the best moment."

I didn't know if she meant we didn't have time for discussion, or that she was worried we might be overheard, or that she wasn't sure she could trust me yet. In any case, I was desperate to know more, enough to risk another question. "At least tell me if my mother was a part of . . . this . . . while pretending to be a member of the Twilight Guild."

She met my gaze again and nodded slowly.

"I want to help," I said immediately.

She arched an eyebrow. "You don't even know what it is I do, other than this." She tossed a glance around the room.

"If you're against the Twilighters, that's good enough for me. They killed my mother. Or at least she told me they were responsible for whatever might happen to her, and I believe her."

Lenara nodded again, surprising me. "And I believe the same." She put a few finishing strokes on the parchment before her. "Here, take this, and return to me in several days' time."

"What is it?"

"You were here to get approved for court, were you not? You're making your debut?"

"Yes, but . . ."

"This is your approval. According to this, you lack Heshara's rare gift, and you have only the best intentions for the kingdom. Only one of those is true, but no one has to know that. Am I correct?"

I nodded.

"Good. I fulfilled the same service for Marin twenty years ago." So *that* was how my mother had thrived at court even as a soulwalker. She'd had help. "Do you have a reason to come see a priestess a second time?" Lenara asked.

"I can get to the palace, at least," I said, after considering for a second. "I'm being fitted by the royal tailor in two days. I can say I'm considering Heshara's service—theology, of course, since I lack the ability to become a priestess." Or so the sheet of paper said.

"Perfect. I will be here." She hesitated. "But, Kamai . . ."

"Yes?"

"That misdirection works for now, but that is all it is. Heshara's temple is not where we will need you. I don't think I need to say this, but tell no one what you can do, or what I've told you. Like I said, it's not safe here. Be careful."

"I will," I said, but I was hardly listening after I'd heard *we*. There were more like her. Like my mother. Whoever they were, it was a balm to the ache in my heart. It was a path. It was a purpose. It was a chance at revenge.

I clutched the paper to my chest and went out to meet Jidras, who was looking less baffled and more irate, with a genuine grin on my face. My feet felt like they were floating over the checkered tiles.

The thought that Vehyn had helped me only dampened my excitement a little. It made him even harder to hate, but that didn't mean I wasn't still furious with him.

———

Suddenly, I couldn't wait to be fitted for the dress that would mark my debut in court.

Nikha, however, was making those two days feel very long. I'd vowed to tell her what was going on, but that was *before* a priestess of Heshara had sworn me to secrecy. I still planned on sharing everything I could as soon as possible, but first I had to understand the situation for myself . . . and ask Lenara if I would ever be allowed to tell anyone else. I didn't know what sort of group the priestess represented, but if they valued secrecy half as much as the Twilight Guild, I had to be careful.

For all I knew, Lenara might yet decide to execute me if I betrayed her trust.

"You promised to tell me what was going on," Nikha insisted

161

for the hundredth time by the morning of my fitting. She was pacing my room, dressed in her hardened leather tunic as usual and looking out of place against the frilly pink decor, while I sat before my vanity mirror deciding which bracelets to wear. "Since *when* do you smile so much and practically skip about the house humming? Since when do you look forward to getting outfitted so Jidras can auction you off to the highest bidder?" She froze, aghast. "You don't *already* have a suitor, do you? One you actually *like*? I thought I would have noticed—"

"Gods, no!" I said, horrified at the idea, perhaps even more horrified at the sudden, incongruous flash of Vehyn's smile in my mind. I'd been busily trying to pretend that he hadn't played a role in my good fortune. I hadn't visited him during the past two nights, and he hadn't forced me to. Maybe I could just forget that he existed entirely. "And of course I would never keep something like that from you. There is no such person, not now, and hopefully not ever." I spat out the words as if they were disgusting.

Nikha blinked in surprise at my vehemence, but my reaction seemed to mollify her somewhat. "Still, I wish you would tell me what else it is."

In tandem with our growing familiarity, our relationship had shifted from one of her solely comforting me. She still protected my person, but she now turned to me for reassurance more and more, especially in the mere days since I'd crossed over into adulthood. She was treating me more like an equal.

A friend.

"I will, soon. I just have to . . ."

"What? Get fitted for a gown before you feel like telling me?"

"No, for the gods' sake. I'm not excited to go to the palace for a stupid gown. I'm . . . I've arranged to go back to the Temple of Heshara."

She looked nearly as horrified. "Kamai, you can't let the prospect of marriage scare you into becoming a dried-up old husk collecting dust in some temple archive. You've never shown any interest in theology."

I couldn't help giggling at her unusually vivid description of theologians. "Do you have something against temples, Nikha?" I paused, growing serious. "Or even Heshara?" She'd never worn a scarf, never offered thanks or praise to the goddess of the moon, only the goddess Ranta—infrequently at that, and probably only because she was a follower of the Earthen Arts as a household guard.

Nikha blew out a breath, hard enough to stir a spike of her short hair jutting over her forehead. "No, it's just . . ."

Now I was curious, even though we were getting off topic. "Just what?"

Asking the question was like opening a floodgate in her. "I just don't see what good any of the gods, *especially* Heshara, have offered anyone. She just"—Nikha threw out a hand— "holds back, mysterious, doing nothing, and lets men speak for her, fight her battles. And don't get me started on her allowing her daughter to bind herself to a human king. Ranta could have stood on her own, for one, and for two, now all we humans have is a queen consort, not a real queen with power equal to the king's. No, the 'true' queen is Ranta, who isn't exactly around to exercise her power. Convenient, that. Oh, but if one were to question it, then we're told that's not the king's fault, because that's how the *goddess* wanted it, so we can't complain. Yes, thanks, Heshara, thanks *so* much," she bit off sarcastically.

I stared at Nikha as she stood with her fists clenched, breathing hard, her chest flattened under her armor, her hair short, her face free of makeup, her body adorned with only a sword. It struck me again, suddenly, how little like a traditional woman she seemed most of the time.

Not that I couldn't relate to her frustration, but I believed there was much more to Heshara than that. Much more to a woman like my mother, who had never striven for the exact same things a man would and was yet one of the strongest people I had ever known. Much more to faith and devotion than submission. The argument seemed to be based upon how *Nikha* saw strength and weakness.

"Are you sure Heshara is your problem?" I asked quietly.

Nikha flushed bright red. "Maybe not. Sometimes I think it's all a bunch of gutter wash made up thousands of years ago by a few men so they could forever determine the lives of women. If I don't like Heshara much, it's because of them." Before I could gape at her blasphemy—*no one* doubted the existence of the gods—she turned and stalked out of the room. "Let me know when you're ready to go," she said over her shoulder, shutting the door more forcefully than usual behind her.

I hadn't even gotten a chance to tell her I had no plans to pursue theology within the Lunar Arts. All I had done was prod her into admitting her own painful, personal truths instead of sharing my own. Some friend I was turning out to be.

The royal tailor was able to fit me in only because the king's niece's closest friend had canceled her appointment, and also because Jidras had offered to pay extra on top of what was already an exorbitant amount. Only the best for his daughter—or the best for seeing her married off and gone, leaving his own pristine image intact. He didn't bother accompanying me to the palace this time and sent only Nikha with me as an escort. I wasn't bothered; I didn't even need to give him the excuse I'd prepared to cover meeting with Lenara again.

At my fitting, I requested a black gown. The tailor complained that it was a bit somber, given the occasion . . . but then she mused that it might make a splash by being out of the ordinary and, since black symbolized the freshness of the new moon, it was actually thematically perfect for a debut gala. Besides, it was the wet season, when darker colors were permitted. By the end of the appointment, she imagined she'd thought of it herself.

I'd chosen the color not only because it was my favorite, but because it was probably the exact opposite of what Jidras would have chosen for me. I didn't let myself consider . . . for long . . . that it was also Vehyn's favorite.

Nikha walked me across the palace grounds to the Temple of Heshara afterward, as silent as she had been all morning since she'd stormed out of my room. She hadn't even commented at my fitting, just stood in a corner, arms folded, as taciturn as possible, while the tailor scrunched her nose up at Nikha's attire and then disregarded her as if she weren't there.

It made me even more eager to talk to Lenara, to learn who she was and what I might be getting myself into, and what, if anything, I might be able to tell Nikha. I didn't want this to divide us.

No one stopped us until we arrived at the top of the wide temple stairs, blinding white and gleaming black in the sunlight.

One of the guards raised a hand as we neared. Several pairs of them flanked the doors, silver-plated armor glinting and making Nikha's leathers look plain and well used. I still had the feeling that, if not going to my doom, I was voluntarily entering a sort of prison. I had to remind myself that this was what I had been wanting, *needing*, for years.

"I'm here to see Priestess Lenara," I said, unsure if that would be enough for them to let me enter, never mind Nikha. Jidras hadn't allowed her to come along last time.

But all one of them said was, "She is expecting you. Please leave your weapons outside." I only had the dagger Nikha had given me to unbuckle—I hadn't brought my mother's gift to my fitting—while Nikha had to remove the sword from her hip and two additional daggers from both her belt and her boot. Another pair of guards opened the heavy doors for us and waved us forward.

No one waited at the podium in the entrance hall this time. Our footsteps sounded loud in the cavernous space. Twisting white columns rose high over the black-and-white-checkered floor to support the entry wing's vaulted ceiling, and white walls were shadowed in lightly carved, intricate patterns. Oddly, the style reminded me a little of Vehyn's fortress, except infinitely smaller and brighter. That somehow made it less intimidating, and I peered farther into the temple as we headed for Lenara's door.

Four such wings as the one we traversed, each topped with a white crescent spire outside, were lined in twisting columns and met in the middle under a dome. The dome's huge, curving ceiling, black on the inside as well as out, was seemingly as high as the nighttime sky. Glittering mosaic tiles depicted the phases of the moon, but set in a cross pattern like a compass rose, with the new moon at the center of the dome and four pale full moons against the edges, set above the vaulted opening to each wing. The gibbous, quarter, and crescent phases marked the journey between each outer point and the new moon at the center, either waxing or waning. In the dark slices of night in between, more mosaic tiles sparkled in the form of Heshara's Guardian Constellations.

We arrived at Lenara's weighty wooden door, one of a few spaced widely and evenly along the wing. There was distance between rooms—probably so that unless a priest or priestess was inside with you, no one could intrude upon your soul. It was privacy for both the clergy and their "guests." I knocked softly.

Lenara answered, her eyes and voice as steady as last time. "Come in, Kamai—but, oh, you have a friend," she said with some surprise. "That is fortunate. Can you please remain by the door and inform any visitors that they're not to interrupt?"

No doubt any visitor would already know not to intrude upon a priestess's soulwalking session, but I took the words as a subtle request for Nikha to both wait outside *and* guard the entrance. Nikha did too, judging by the grave nod she gave before she assumed her position.

"A formidable friend, she is," Lenara remarked after closing the door and bolting it. "I assume she doesn't know why you're here?" I couldn't help hearing an edge of warning in her tone.

"No, she doesn't."

"Good." The word stopped short any question of mine about telling Nikha. "The fewer people who know about your business, the better. It's best not to even speak of these things in the waking world." She held up a small, clear vial.

Sleeping tonic. I glanced between it and one of the brown leather couches and took it from her tentatively.

"There is nothing to fear," Lenara said, misreading my apprehension. "I've cleared plenty of time for us to talk, and now, with your friend's help, I'm especially sure no one will come upon us while we sleep."

"It's just . . ." I hesitated. "We can't meet in my soul." Not only was mine inaccessible, but I couldn't even let her near me in the sleeping realm in case she saw the black door and started asking questions I didn't know how to answer. Even if I could confirm that my mother had once trusted her, Marin had warned me to never mention the black door to anyone. Ever. She'd made it sound more forbidden and dangerous than speaking of soulwalking.

If Lenara wouldn't sentence me to imprisonment or death because I was an illegal soulwalker, she very well might do so because of the black door. Not to mention my lack of a soul.

"I understand," Lenara said immediately. "Your mother told me about her protections, but not in detail. They're still in place?"

"Protections?" A chorus of questions rose in my mind, but for once, there was an answer among them. "*She* hid my soul."

"You didn't know?"

"No," I said. Once again, my mother had explained absolutely *nothing* to me. "She said I didn't have a nehym because my soul was so deeply hidden that no one could find it, but I thought . . ." I trailed off, shame and wonder mingling in my voice.

Lenara raised a brow. "That you didn't have a soul? Oh, child. Of course you do."

"I thought she told me that just to make me feel better. Like

168

telling someone they still have a home even if they don't have walls or a roof around them." The words were tight in my throat. Knowing I had a soul, somewhere, even if I couldn't explore it . . . it was like discovering the villa still existed somewhere even though it had burned to ash. That I *did* have a home, however distant. "What can you tell me about it?" I asked, unable to keep the yearning from my voice.

"Not much at all, I'm afraid, only that she sealed it for your protection. I don't know how or why, exactly, but I don't wish to pry into and possibly risk what Marin so dearly wanted to keep safe."

Frustration rose within me, almost as fast as my relief. Even if my mother had done it for my protection, how could she have left me confused over whether or not I had a soul? She'd told me I had one, but in such unclear terms that anyone, let alone a child, would have been uncertain.

But I was getting a hunch as to *why*, at this point. She'd known how potent my curiosity was, so maybe she figured the less I knew the better. That had been her approach to the black door.

Which I'd opened anyway. Perhaps she'd had the right of it.

Searching my face, Lenara said, "A mother's love is powerfully wrought on a young soul, and such a thing is not lightly done or undone, but perhaps you could remove her protections. I might be able to teach you how. Only if you wanted, of course. And even then, it might not be wise. The sleeping realm is a dangerous place, and any protection one has, especially one as strong as yours, is a boon. *You* are still at risk in the sleeping realm, as a spirit, but your soul isn't. A rare gift."

A gift.

"I'll think about it," I said slowly.

"In the meantime, we can meet in my nehym." Lenara's tone became light. "I keep it quite tidy in case I have guests."

I still wasn't at ease—because of the black door, and the chance she might see it. It didn't often bloom right next to me, instead forcing me to hunt for it, but sometimes . . . Maybe Vehyn would lie low. Or maybe that was too much to hope. Either way, I didn't have much choice in the matter. A priestess of Heshara, who knew I was a soulwalker and that my soul was hidden, was looking at me expectantly.

My steps heavy, I approached one of the couches and sat down, playing with the stopper on the vial. Lenara mirrored me on the other couch, putting up her feet without waiting, as if she did this every day in front of other people. She likely did.

She glanced over at me. "You have taken essence of mohol before, right? This isn't a terribly strong draft. It will get you to sleep, but the effects won't linger, and you won't be drowsy when you wake."

"Yes, of course." I had no more excuses. I drew up my feet, unstoppered the vial, and tipped the contents back into my mouth. In my thoughts, I toasted my mother and hoped that somewhere, somehow, she was still looking out for me. I didn't trust Vehyn enough to leave it entirely up to him.

14

SACRED VOWS

I opened my eyes in an airy, beautiful space like a conservatory. The room was octagonal, with a large creamy stone fountain burbling in the center that sent ripples of reflected light dancing on every surface. I'd been so used to Vehyn's fortress that Lenara's soul was nearly blinding in comparison. Through huge floor-to-ceiling windows, hazy light filtered in that kept me from seeing anything beyond. Between the panes of glass, blossoming vines cascaded to the floor like flowing locks of green hair, and a delicate floral scent permeated the air.

With a pang of longing, I remembered how beautiful my mother's soul had been.

Lenara, suddenly appearing before me, gestured around herself. "Welcome."

I spoke around the tightness in my throat. "This is . . . lovely, truly."

"Thank you. You have Marin's nehym to compare it to,

which I know was beautiful, so I'll take it as an especially large compliment. But I didn't bring you here to preen." She took a seat on the edge of the fountain. "Now that I know for an absolute fact we won't be overheard, we must speak in earnest."

That was when the black door appeared in the center of a window behind her like a dark spot of mold on a pale expanse of bread.

I barely kept myself from startling. "Yes, of course." My voice came out higher than I intended, especially since the door began to soundlessly open over her shoulder, a black pit in the bright sunlight. I forced my eyes to hold Lenara's. "I want to know anything you can tell me," I blurted. "My mother . . ."

Lenara folded her hands in her lap. "Your mother, like I am, was a member of a secret society called the Keepers. We have been around even longer than the Twilight Guild. Much longer. And, also unlike the Twilighters, we are almost entirely made up of those with Heshara's gift—soulwalkers, as we are commonly known."

Her words succeeded in drawing my attention. Most of it. The black door stood open, but only darkness, emptiness, was visible in it. No Vehyn. Maybe I could just ignore it, and if I kept Lenara's eyes on me, she wouldn't see it. "But my mother wasn't a priestess," I said.

"Most of us aren't. I am a Keeper first, a priestess second, doing the Keepers' work through my position here in the royal temple."

"Like approving my mother and me for court," I guessed, sidling a step to my right over smooth, opalescent tiles to keep her focus directed even farther away from the black door.

She smiled. "Among other things. It is a useful position to have. But unlike your brave mother, who was a Keeper first and a member of the Twilight Guild second—a spy in a den of spies—I don't see my two roles as conflicting with each other. You see, I am doing Heshara's work through both."

My eyebrows rose, and I managed to forget the black door entirely. "The Keepers are servants of Heshara?"

Lenara nodded. "An ancient order supposedly founded by the goddess herself. She blessed its first members with the ability to walk through the souls of others to discover their deepest truths. Some hypothesize that this is where our gift originated. We are formally known as the Keepers of the Earth, here to maintain order and balance. To protect Ranta, in a sense."

The divinely appointed position sounded familiar. "I thought that was the king's job."

Lenara's mouth quirked. "Yes, well, some would argue that the arrangement with the kings was Tain's idea, and the Keepers were Heshara's. Perhaps the goddess wisely felt a mortal king, however blessed and bound to her daughter, might need help."

That was *quite* interesting, and not only because it was something Nikha might like to hear—if I was ever able to tell her—but because of the other implications. "You don't trust the king?" I asked.

"It's not that we don't trust him. It's that mortals can be weak-willed, especially those without the ability to see the state of their own souls. The kings never have been able to, which has led them to restrict and persecute what they don't understand. Nonetheless, the bond they share with Ranta is real, potent, and vital. The Keepers' mission is to uphold the king's sacred vow to the earth, more than we are here to uphold *him,* shall we say. Although, because of the vow's nature, the distinction is often negligible."

I couldn't help my scowl. "So it doesn't matter that the king punishes unregistered soulwalkers and he might have played a role in my mother's and stepfather's deaths?"

"The king has . . . flaws, shall we say . . . that we must overlook." At my mouth opening in protest, she added, "Let me assure you, the Keepers are most concerned with protecting the land. Protecting the king is simply the means to do that because of Ranta's vow."

"How do you mean? What is the nature of the vow?"

Lenara pursed her lips. "Such things are complex and archaic and not worth delving into at the moment."

"You don't trust me," I said, before I could stop myself.

She arched an eyebrow and a corner of her lips rose with it. "You are much like your mother." With a sigh, she leaned forward on the fountain's edge. "Which makes me want to trust you, perhaps unduly. You are *not* your mother, after all."

I flinched, even though I was sure she hadn't meant it as an insult—but it was something that had plagued me my entire life. I wasn't like my mother. I wasn't brave, wise, alluring, loving.

"I told you," I insisted. "I want to help you. I want to find out who killed my mother."

She held my eyes. "But for whose sake? Heshara's and the stability of the land? Or for your own—for revenge?"

"For my mother's sake," I said, which I hoped was an answer she would accept.

She was silent, considering me. The babbling of the fountain was the only voice rising in the glowing air. My hands started to fidget, so I took up the leaf of a trailing vine, running my fingers over its softness . . . before I realized it was probably rude to touch anything in her soul, even if she was right here with me. Maybe especially if she was. My mother hadn't gotten a chance to teach me the etiquette in these types of situations.

I dropped it with a flush. At the very least, my awkwardness succeeded in unfreezing Lenara's face. Her eyes grew warmer, and she looked as if she was trying not to smile. But she still didn't say anything.

I was too close to the answers I'd been seeking to just stay quiet. "So if the Twilight Guild was behind my mother's death, then they had a reason to kill her. They must be plotting something, right? And maybe my mother discovered it?" I doubted Lenara would want to tell me about such things if she didn't trust my motives, but I couldn't help adding, "Something that could endanger the kingdom?"

"Yes, yes, and yes. That is why we are trying to figure out exactly why your mother died, and why we are working in opposition to the Twilighters."

"Tell me what you know." The demand was out of my mouth before I could recall it.

"Not until you join us," Lenara said. "Become a Keeper, Kamai, like your mother before you. Follow in her footsteps. Serve Heshara with the gift she gave you."

There was no hesitation this time. "I will. I'll join you."

"Are you sure?"

I nodded, my jaw clenched, determination radiating through my body. "Starting now."

"Normally, we would interview you for far longer and walk your soul with you as part of the initiation process. But we can't, because of your mother." She sighed. "But I trusted your mother with my life, and we're running out of time. We need you."

"For what?"

"Repeat after me: 'I hereby swear my body, my spirit, and my soul to Heshara's service.'" She paused for me.

After a pause, I echoed the words.

She continued, "'My purpose is hers and the Keepers' forevermore, to protect her daughter, Ranta, and the earth from evil.'" She paused again, and I repeated the words again. "'If I ever stray from her service, may Heshara take my life and cast my spirit from the warm light of her embrace and out into darkness for all eternity.'"

"Wow, that's . . . a serious vow."

"This is serious business, Kamai, and it's a sacred vow. Say it."

There was nothing else I could do. No other purpose for me. Still, I thought about it, perhaps only for a short while, but it felt like an hour. I had tried to seek answers on my own from the Twilight Guild, and from Vehyn, without success. Besides, this was who my mother had truly been—there was no doubt about that. So I said the vow.

My mother had put me on this path, and I was going to follow it to its end.

I tried not to recall that I'd had the same determined thought after I'd opened the black door and found the trail of roses. It was hard not to, especially with the black door behind Lenara. And especially as Vehyn appeared now in its frame.

He smiled at me, his pale hand raised. Each long, slender finger bowed once, one after the other, in a slow, silent wave.

I widened my eyes at him, my jaw clenched, willing him to be quiet. To go away.

Fortunately, Lenara was looking down at her folded hands. "Your mother died trying to discover a plot involving Hallan Lizier; his son, Razim; and the royal couple," she said.

My attention was instantly back on her. "Razim was involved?"

"They were all tied together somehow, the royal couple as well. Hallan seduced the queen consort as part of it many years ago and had a long-standing affair with her for almost two decades."

"*What?*" My jaw dropped open. "Two *decades?*"

"His affair was for a purpose, and he was careful, as were the Twilighters. Not only were they behind whatever Hallan was up to, but they were behind both his and Marin's deaths . . . and perhaps the queen consort's."

Perhaps he *had* assassinated the queen consort for the Twilight Guild, then. Hallan had never struck me as a killer. "You don't know for sure? How do you know any of this?"

"Through Marin. Yes, I know, we haven't had much to go off since she died, and your mother was never able to give us the complete picture. Indeed, we believe she was killed because she discovered the full scope of it." Lenara frowned into the distance. "In any case, she insisted the Twilighters' plan wasn't as straightforward as a simple assassination plot, either against the queen consort or, Heshara forbid, the king. There was more to it than that." She shrugged. "And yet, in the end, the queen consort died mysteriously, and the king's soldiers sacked your villa and executed Hallan and Marin to bury whatever he'd done."

Now I wasn't focused on what *Hallan* had done. My jaw locked so tight I asked my question through gritted teeth. "So it *was* the king who gave the order?"

Razim had said it was so, but I hadn't wanted to believe him.

"Supposedly, but we have reason to believe the Twilight Guild was manipulating the king, somehow. Blaming him will accomplish nothing. It will not lead to your mother's true killer."

I closed my eyes, trying to exhale my anger. Because she was right; I needed to concentrate on what really mattered. "And how was Razim involved?"

"We don't know for sure. But Marin said he was, and the fact that he wasn't killed along with her and the others is telling . . . and he has just made his appearance in court."

"He *has*?"

"Yes, as a courtier, under a different name and a new title, supplied by the Twilighters, no doubt. Not so different from how your father wishes to disguise and present·you."

"He's not my father," I corrected without thinking. When Lenara blinked at me, I stammered, "I mean, he is, but I don't think of him that way. I want nothing of his, not even his name."

"But his name is protection for the time being. Marin Nuala and Hallan Lizier are names best not remembered right now. Razim is going by Ramir Zareen, a nineteen-year-old lord who appears to have recently inherited minor holdings in the far north that he has no interest in inhabiting. He has come to court to try his hand as a courtier—a musician, specifically."

So that was why, among other reasons, Razim hadn't wanted to show his face when he'd tried to pull me off the street. It wouldn't have looked good for his new reputation as a musician lordling.

I bit my lip, remembering Razim playing his lyre late into the night. "At least some of that is accurate."

Lenara was watching me closely. "Like what?"

"He's a musician, a skilled one. And he is indeed nineteen, almost twenty. Just shy of two years older than me. Sometimes we shared birthday celebrations at the villa." I found myself flustered. Because I *also* remembered how he'd begun staring at me in those later years, and Lenara was giving me a look now as if she knew. I grimaced. "This is strange. I can't believe he's right here, within the palace grounds. He . . . We . . ."

"You have a history, I know."

"Yes, in that he perhaps got my mother killed, and then tried to abduct me as our home burned to the ground."

"And he has been looking for you since. It's a mystery he hasn't managed to find you."

"He did find me," I said, somewhat reluctantly. "But only with my help."

Lenara blinked at me. "Explain."

So I told her, in brief, what had happened in the market with my clumsy attempt to spy on the Twilight Guild.

She rolled her eyes. "That was risky at best, downright foolish at worst. But it does confirm what I've suspected, so at least that's something."

"What?"

"That Razim is obsessed with you." Before I could object, she added, "And that he's been thwarted in finding you. He's only searched through discreet channels, and yet he has access to the best of those through the Twilighters—a network second only to the Keepers', if even."

Her tone was puzzled, but there was a hint in her words, something she obviously wasn't telling me. "Were the Keepers protecting me from him?" I guessed.

"That's a part of it, but not all. We didn't want him to find you before we could talk to you first—though you obviously foiled our intentions there," she muttered. "And we wanted to speak to you only when you were ready. Although we were admittedly about to initiate the conversation on our own, since time is growing short. But we *also* believe the Twilight Guild wasn't forthcoming with Razim about your whereabouts."

Cold fear began gnawing a pit in my stomach. "Why would they hide me from him? I have nothing to do with them! I *hate* them."

Lenara held up her hands in a placating gesture. "I'm not accusing you, Kamai. I believe you. Perhaps they also suspect you might have an influence over Razim, who is obviously a piece in this puzzle, a pawn in their scheme, and they don't want him to tell you what he knows . . . or vice versa."

"You think he might not know the full story himself?" I asked, doubtful.

Lenara shook her head. "We don't know. But he might be a new point of entry, a weakness in the Twilight Guild's plan, and that's what we need you to find out."

My mouth went dry. Vehyn shifted abruptly in my peripheral vision, but I ignored him. "What do you want me to do?"

"Razim trusts you, or at least the Twilighters seem to think so. I honestly believe he might. You grew up together, you share memories and secrets, and he has been avidly seeking you for over two months. You could talk to him, earn his trust if you don't already have it, and discover what he knows."

"How?"

"The Keepers will help you. We'll figure it out together, with regular exchanges of information through meetings like this." In *places* like this that didn't exist in the waking world, she meant. "When we wake, I'll write you a note that will allow you to see me at any time. For now, continue doing what you are doing."

My forehead furrowed. "Which is?"

"Marking your debut in court."

"But I can't marry! And still do this," I added belatedly.

"There are members of the Keepers who are married, who have husbands, wives, or children who don't know what they really are. Your mother was one such, for example. But," she continued, forestalling my objection, "perhaps we can find you a different path, if you wish."

"Anything," I said.

"I'll think on it. In the meantime, carry on with your debut gala, like all is normal. And Kamai . . ." She winked at me. "Make an impression."

"That won't be hard."

It wasn't me who had spoken. Vehyn had. I gasped, my eyes shooting to the black door. He was still leaning against the frame, his arms folded. His smile was wicked.

Lenara spun around on the edge of the fountain to look, and my heart stopped in my chest. But her questions and accusations never came. Instead, she turned back to me with a questioning look. "What startled you?"

"You don't . . .," I began, utterly baffled, looking from her to the black door. To Vehyn.

"Of course she can't see or hear me, Kamai. Only you can."

I wondered if he could control who saw the black door. My mother seemed to have been aware of it. But that was before I had opened it. Maybe now Vehyn had a say in the matter.

Still, it was a secret I needed to keep, for now.

And maybe, I admitted to myself, it—he—was a secret I enjoyed having all to myself. Everybody else had their secrets, their hidden knowledge. I wanted to hold on to mine . . .

I tried to ignore Vehyn as I cleared my throat a bit too loudly. "Strange, I thought I heard a noise, but I think it's just nerves. I'm a little on edge."

"I assure you, we're alone." Lenara stood from the rim of the fountain—oblivious to the yawning door and the person, the creature, standing therein—and put a hand on my arm. "I know this is frightening. But we're here for you."

"Yes, we are," Vehyn echoed, still grinning.

181

15

SILENT LIES

I was now a Keeper. A member of an ancient society of soul-walkers, blessed by Heshara and sworn to protect Ranta and the earth. Like my mother had been. Throughout the next few days, I kept repeating it to myself, like a revelation. It never seemed to sink in, and every time I was left with a newfound amazement.

I was just about the only person I could tell.

After leaving the temple with me and failing to pry anything else out of me about the visit, Nikha settled even deeper into her bad mood, while mine, selfishly, only rose. Just as with the fitting, I couldn't help but embrace the gala, because it no longer signified what it had. It was now a means to an end—a better end. But Nikha didn't see it that way, and I couldn't tell her otherwise.

"Just tell me that you're not planning something horrible," Nikha said suddenly, the day before my gala, lowering her sword.

We were alone, sheltered in the warm, green courtyard of Jidras's town house, practicing self-defense. She was teaching me how to better dodge full-size blades even if I wasn't wielding one myself, which would have helped during the incident in the market. It had rained again, but the moisture didn't help the heat, only worsened the humidity. Sweat poured off us, and we were both breathing hard. "This was the last thing you wanted before, and now you're running for it with a smile on your face. I've heard of soldiers going into hopeless battles like that, or prisoners walking to their execution laughing."

My mouth fell open and I nearly dropped the dagger Nikha had gifted me onto my foot. "You think I'd . . . no! Gods. First you imagine I have a suitor, and now you think I'm going to, what, leap off a bridge or put this dagger through my heart?"

"I wouldn't be teaching you how to use it if I truly thought that, but nothing else makes sense!" Nikha erupted, waving her sword in a way that made me take a cautionary step back. "You still have no intention of marrying, and yet you're *happy* to go through with this gala?"

"Can't I just enjoy the moment for what it is? A party?" I snapped back at her. But this wasn't her fault. It was mine, and yet I could either lie to her or stay silent. The latter had seemed like the better choice, since friends shouldn't lie to friends.

"If you promise me something," Nikha said, wrestling herself under control with visible effort, "I'll stop worrying and leave you be in your apparent lapse of sanity."

"What?" I asked warily.

"When you marry, take me with you, into your household. Promise me, swear to me as a friend, that when you leave your father's home, you'll build a life for yourself into which I can follow you. That way I'll know you're not planning anything desperate or self-destructive and that I'll be able to help you."

I opened my mouth, but for a moment nothing came out. Tears were in my eyes. Nikha would want to leave her respected position in Jidras's household to join mine? It was never something we'd discussed before, and yet it felt right. The sweetness of it was nearly enough to fill the widening hole in my chest, but not quite. Because I didn't even know what the Keepers had planned for me, so I had no idea if Nikha could follow me there. And I was almost certain she couldn't join them. She wasn't a soulwalker.

"I . . . I can't promise you that," I said, my throat tight.

It was as if I'd stabbed her with the dagger, such was the hurt on her face. The look in her eyes felt like a blade right through my own heart.

"Very well," she said, her voice stiff, clipped. Nikha wasn't one to cry over pain, but to grit her teeth and power through it. She nearly powered right through *me* after she sheathed her sword and marched for the house. "Then this lesson is over. Enjoy your party."

"Nikha!" But she was already gone, leaving me standing alone, gasping hard for a different reason, in a courtyard that no longer felt so warm or sheltering.

I was disappointed to find Nikha still dressed in her leathers when Jidras escorted me—neither of us speaking to each other—to my carriage on the night of my gala. All week, she had adamantly resisted my efforts to have a tailor fit her for anything resembling a gown. And now, with a little plummet in my stomach, I realized this was her refusal to attend at all. There would be plenty of the palace guard to protect me and the myriad other guests, and apparently she thought that was enough. She was even playing the footman for the evening. When she held the carriage door open for me, I knew she would be sitting on the bench up top with our driver, forcing me to suffer Jidras's company on my own.

But then Nikha shut the door before even Jidras could join me.

"I'm taking my horse," he said at my puzzled look through the carriage window. "I'll be there to introduce you to society, but I'll want to retire before you young revelers will, especially once the dancing starts." I wasn't shocked; he didn't strike me as much of a dancer. "Nikha will wait for you with the carriage and escort you home afterward."

"But won't I need a chaperone at the gala after you leave?" I asked.

"This is your party, and you're an eligible adult now." His tone as good as said *You're not my problem anymore.* "It's up to you to be responsible and decorous." His eyes drifted down to my gown, disapproval writ all over his face. "And if you're not, at least be practical and marry the man afterward."

I very nearly spat at him, but the reins snapped and the carriage lurched away before I could. I heard both the driver's startled cry and Jidras's yelp as he jumped back—which meant Nikha must have borrowed the reins.

I wished I could thank her, laugh with her to burn off the rest of my anger. But she was out there, and I was obviously, painfully alone in here. And maybe I always would be. I had no family to speak of. I wouldn't marry. I couldn't keep friends.

I blinked rapidly against the nighttime glow of city lights through the window, which wavered like reflections on water due to the tears curtaining my gaze. I couldn't let myself cry, because then everyone in the palace would see the dark smears of kohl down my cheeks. I doubted that was the impression Lenara had wanted me to make. If I couldn't actually enjoy my party, I had to at least convincingly pretend.

By the time Nikha opened the carriage door for me, I was composed. I stepped out onto the sweeping stone path that led to the palace ballroom Jidras had reserved for the occasion. White candles lit the way, floating in black blown-glass globes of water, both dark and light at once. Black, blue, and silver confetti, stamped from thin sheets of tin in the shape of tiny stars, sparkled over the stone like a reverse of the night sky. Evidently, Jidras's decorator had heard the theme was the new moon.

"I'll be here," Nikha said, and that was it. I barely got out a word of thanks before she hopped back up next to the driver and they moved the carriage on.

Fortunately, I didn't have to stand there by myself for long. *Un*fortunately, the person who arrived to escort me was Jidras. It was only fitting, since he was going to formally introduce me to everyone, but at that moment I would have rather touched a pile of horse dung.

I put my arm in his and forced my face into some semblance of a smile. His effort was no better, but at least there was plenty to distract us from each other. The palace rose up before us, walls and towers in intricately carved, creamy coral, stone latticework and alcove windows aglow, bronze domes glinting darkly against the night. Colorful mosaics lined doors that rose to sharp points at the apex, like the black door, except these were bright with light and gold leaf. The gallery lining the outside of the ballroom looked like a gilded cage, balcony columns tiled in beautiful swirls of metal and glass, all of it hung with overflowing baskets of flowers. A massive statue of Tain overlooked the gardens, his body carved in deep brown marble threaded with gold, as if the light of the sun were trying to break out of his very skin.

Indoors and out of danger from the elements, the opulence was in greater evidence. There were endless hammered bronze ceilings, so much gilt painted in patterns over pale stone walls, so many twining carpets in fiery reds, oranges, and yellows, that I wondered if the king had begun to mistake himself for the sun god, despite not having any commemorative statues of himself. This seemed more like a temple than a palace.

Fortunately, the ballroom was subtler and plainer, allowing for decoration. Here, my theme flourished. Black and white globes hung from the ceiling among swaths of sheer black, blue, and white chiffon, moons numbering like the stars among the night clouds. The pale expanse of floor sparkled with the same confetti as outside, and silver candelabras sporting black and blue candles cast shadowy light in every corner. The bright clothes of some of the guests stood out awkwardly against the subtle colors, but I fit right in.

My dark hair tumbled in loose curls over my bare shoulders, restrained only with delicate silvery chains. My dress was practically nonexistent down my back, my skin nearly as pale as the moon goddess's with its dusting of powdered silver, until the black velvet folds dropped as dark and thick as a moonless sky from my waist to whisper along the floor. Only gossamer black threads held up the low-cut bodice in front, lacing around my glittering neck like twining shadows. Heads turned as Jidras steered me to the end of the room, where lines soon formed and introductions began.

That part took forever. So many smiling men. There were older and younger couples too, curious to meet Kamai Numa, Jidras's mysterious daughter, and some flamboyant courtiers and courtesans who clearly had no interest in marrying—and no interest even in women, by some displays—including one handsome young man, a pleasure artist by the name of Zeniri Sarvotha, dressed in a plum silk suit with a voluminous white sash that offset both the darkness of the color and his black skin, who pronounced me the most beautiful, least rotund moon he'd ever seen. At least it gave me a laugh. But the sheer number of single, eligible men was alarming. I nearly didn't have smiles enough for all of them. My cheeks and feet were sore by the end of it, and despite the high, airy ceiling, the press of bodies was making me hot under my folds of black velvet.

Through all of it, I never saw Razim, the one person at the palace I was supposed to find. Eventually, the guests all dispersed to the refreshment tables, where there were burbling fountains of sparkling wine, towering sculptures of shrimp, elaborately carved melons, and all manner of delights, and I was free to excuse myself for a breath of air. I slipped out onto the mosaic-covered gallery outside and leaned against the railing. I'd been lamenting my solitude earlier, and now I was grateful for it.

Until hands caught me from behind, one around my waist, the other over my mouth. I tried to spin around, but the arms were too strong. They dragged me, silently and surely, out of the soft fall of light from inside and pushed me up against a wall between windows. Uneven pieces of the mosaic dug into my bare back.

Razim's dark eyes met mine. For a split second, I wanted to scream, until I remembered why I was here. But the colors of his suit didn't put me at ease—a red brocade so dark it was nearly black, like swirls of blood at night, the silk sash at his waist true black.

"Where have you been?" he hissed.

"I'll be able to answer better if you remove your hand," I murmured, muffled, from behind his fingers. They smelled like the same woody soap he'd always used.

"Still as sardonic as ever, I see." He pulled his hand away slowly, as if ready to put it back at a moment's notice. "Last time I held you, you sicced a demented swordswoman on me, and the time before *that*, you screamed and bit me."

"Maybe you should get the hint," I retorted, lifting my chin. "I seem to recall you tying me up with your belt and gagging me with a handkerchief. I'd say you deserved everything that's followed."

"Where have you been?" he repeated.

"I've been here, in the capital," I said, as if it were common knowledge and I wasn't hiding under Jidras's family name. "You're not a good enough spy to find that out? I'm sure your precious Twilighters knew."

"Kamai, all this time, I would have hidden you, sheltered you," he whispered, leaning closer, his face and voice open and earnest. "You didn't have to go it alone."

I wasn't alone, I thought. *I had Nikha . . . and Vehyn. And now Lenara and the Keepers.* Aloud, I growled through my teeth, "I would rather die than accept shelter from the one responsible for my mother's death."

He drew back as if I'd slapped him. I wished I could have, because he was still uncomfortably close, still pinning me to the wall, his hand ready and waiting to cover my mouth, or touch me, or stab me if he felt like it. "How could you think I would do such a thing? After all we've been through?"

Without realizing what I was doing, I used one of Nikha's defense moves. My knee came up, hard, aiming straight between his legs. He twisted just in time and I kneed him in the thigh.

"That was all a lie," I spat, wrenching against the arm that held me trapped. "You weren't with me back then. You obviously had your own agenda—you still do. The Twilight Guild's. And I don't share it." My anger was real, but I was trying to get him to admit something, anything . . .

"I want the same thing you want."

"Really?" I tossed my head, jerking one of the chains in my hair, but I didn't care. "What's that?"

"Revenge." For a second, Razim's eyes burned into mine, but then he swallowed, glancing away as if he'd said too much.

"Unless it's revenge against the Twilighters, I'm not interested."

"They didn't do it."

"I don't believe that."

"You should. I wouldn't lie to you."

"Then tell me who did."

Razim met my eyes levelly and didn't say anything.

I sneered. "See?"

"I don't trust you not to reveal what I might tell you. Silence isn't lying."

Vehyn had practically said the same damned thing to me. And it was how I'd been treating Nikha. Disgust and anger for myself heated what was already simmering heartily, until I felt like a kettle about to scream. I tried kneeing him between the legs again, knowing he would twist away—right into the tight fist I aimed under the apex of his ribs.

Nikha would have been proud. Razim gasped, and this time it was enough to loosen his hold. I spun away before he could stop me, marching back into the ballroom.

I was too shaken and angry to pause when I should have. But when someone's eyes passed over me and then immediately swung back around, I realized I looked like I'd been doing something *else* in the shadows out on the gallery. I quickly turned away to straighten my gown, smooth my hair, and wipe the edges of my lips in case the color had smeared, ignoring the titter of laughter.

A quick peek over my shoulder revealed no sign of Jidras. So much the better. I didn't need his disapproval or snide insinuations. Before anyone else could notice me, I slipped into the middle of the dancing that was now flowing as strongly as the music and the wine.

The dancing was much less tedious than the introductions, and it didn't take long for my shoulders to relax and for my laughter to return. I still had to fend off about a dozen advances from both men and women, some overtly sexual, since word seemed to have spread like wildfire that I may have been granting favors to lucky suitors out on the gallery. My nerves were still on edge from my encounter with Razim, and I felt ready to break someone's nose.

I thought I might get the chance when a dancing partner passed me into Razim's arms.

I tensed, but he swept me through a few steps by practically lifting me off the ground, my heavy velvet skirts swirling around us. He was even taller and more broad shouldered than I remembered. Apparently, men still grew between nineteen and twenty.

"What are you doing here, Kamai?" he murmured when I finally softened enough to move on my own two feet—only because I didn't want to cause a scene.

"Shouldn't that be my line?" I asked through the fake smile plastered on my face. "This is *my* gala, or haven't you heard?"

"A debut marking your eligibility, yes." He frowned in distaste, looking over my shoulder. "You can't marry one of these people, Kamai. This isn't you."

"Oh? And what is?"

"Adventure. Danger. The night." He leaned forward, his lips coming closer and closer to my ear, and panic shot through me. "You belong in my world."

Based on the stares, we must have looked quite the pair in our midnight blood brocade and black velvet. But I tipped my head back to laugh—away from him. "You don't know me very well at all."

His lips pressed together. "Fine. You want to marry? Then marry me. That's why I'm here. I'm one of your many suitors, after all."

I stopped and nearly made us both stumble. With a smooth apology to the couple next to us, Razim twirled us back into the dance.

I needed to stab this idea before it stood up, as Nikha would have said. "We grew up as brother and sister," I growled, my voice soft and low enough that someone could mistake it for a flirtatious purr.

"You know as well as I how much of a lie that was," Razim said, his dark eyes as hot as coals. He spun me, then pulled me back to him, tighter than before. "And now there's no one left who even remembers the lie. We have different names. Different lives."

"Your life doesn't seem much different to me. You're still working for *them*. You're still living a lie."

"You have no idea what you're talking about."

"Say—or don't—what you want. Silence or pretty words, it all sounds like lies to me." I was being hypocritical, but in this moment, I didn't care.

"You want to know what isn't a lie?" he hissed, his lips coming dangerously close to mine. He pulled me even closer, his hand hot and hard on my bare lower back. But it was all an amorous act, in case anyone was watching. For once, kissing me was the last thing Razim wanted to do. He bent his lips to my ear again, as if whispering a lover's secret.

It was a secret, but not from love. Hatred rasped in his voice, though his whisper made barely a breath of noise. "I lost both my parents that night."

He spun away from me, stalking off the dance floor, leaving my thoughts and my feet in a muddle of confusion. And then the realization hit me, leaving me cold.

Both his parents . . . He didn't mean my mother. Marin and Razim had never been close, or even overly warm to each other, and he'd chafed against the thought of her as a mother figure for our entire childhood.

Another woman had died that night. The queen consort. Hallan had carried on a two-decade affair with her, which had ended a little over two months ago with their deaths. Razim was now almost through his nineteenth year.

Razim was the queen consort's son.

16

IMPOLITE INTRUSIONS

I left the ballroom almost as soon as Razim did, numb with shock. I mumbled excuses that I was feeling ill, ignoring murmurs of sympathy and gallant offers to carry me home on foot. It all rather added to my mysterious air, I realized distantly. Besides, I couldn't be the last one standing at my own gala, nor did I particularly want to be seen leaving with anyone, lest it stoke the fire of more rumors.

If only illness were a mere excuse. I felt like throwing up in the well-manicured flower beds lining the path back to the road, but I held out until I reached Nikha and the carriage.

"Nikha," I said, not knowing what else to say. I couldn't exactly shout, "Razim is the queen consort's son!"

She jumped down from the driver's seat to open the carriage door for me, still grim-faced, until she saw my expression and gripped my silver-dusted shoulders instead. "Kamai, what's wrong? What happened?"

I looked around, probably like a lost child. If I could say anything at all, I certainly couldn't say it on the palace's doorstep.

Nikha understood. "Here, get inside." She flung open the door, shoved me up the folding step, heedless of my thick velvet skirts tangling in my legs, and climbed in after me. All I needed to get her to ride with me was to look like I'd been hit over the head with a club, apparently.

But she wasn't there to hold my hand. "What in all three hells is going on?" she demanded as soon as the carriage jolted into motion. "You look like you've seen a ghost."

The queen consort's ghost, in the face of her son. For a second, I almost wanted to giggle. "I have no clue where to even start."

"Try!" she snapped.

And then I felt like crying. I pressed my palms into my eyes. "Nikha, I can't. I'm mixed up in something big—I have been since I met you—and it's all very dangerous."

"I am a trained swordswoman, Kamai, I think I can handle—"

"A whole troop of soldiers on your own?" I dropped my hands. "Like the ones who killed my mother and stepfather and everyone in our home and then burned it all to the ground?"

"That's what we're dealing with?"

"What *I'm* dealing with, and you have no idea. The king's soldiers aren't the half of it." There were the Twilighters and the Keepers and soulwalking and the black door and . . . Vehyn. It was all a mess, and, somehow, finding out that I'd shared a roof— the one that had been lit on fire—with the queen consort's secret bastard was the ocean wave that made the sandcastle crumble.

How could Hallan have assassinated his son's mother? Nothing made sense anymore.

"Give me a hint, then!" Nikha's voice rose again in frustration.

"Anything I tell you will just put you in danger. I can't do that, Nikha."

She let out a growl, folded her arms, and sat in brooding silence the rest of the way home, the motion of the carriage rocking her hunched shoulders back and forth against the seat.

We arrived in front of the town house, wheels and hooves clattering to a noisy stop over the cobbles. In this neighborhood, the night was especially quiet, everyone long asleep. Nikha jumped down from the carriage and helped me out, her movements stiff with frustration. She waved the carriage off and then led the way to the narrow alley running along the side of the building, toward the back entrance. Unlocking the front door and tromping through the entryway would likely wake everyone.

Too bad Gerresh knew that as well.

The former household guard lunged out of the shadows near the rear door, cracking Nikha over the head with the hilt of his sword. She dropped like a sandbag. Before I could scream, he threw himself on top of me, bringing me to the ground, jarring my head against the cobbles, and trapping my legs with his bulk. His eyes were flat. His hands went straight for my throat, tugging on the gossamer ties of my bodice as he squeezed.

I couldn't breathe, let alone scream. My mouth made a horrible croaking sound. I felt my eyes bulge with unbearable pressure. All I saw of his face was gritted teeth, flared nostrils, and stubble, and then he levered himself higher above me, bearing down on the delicate, crucial point of my neck. The movement freed my hands, but they only scrabbled ineffectually at his, growing weaker by the second. I didn't have Nikha's dagger, or even my mother's knife. The former wouldn't have been allowed in the palace, and my gown was too low-cut to hide the latter.

My vision started to blacken. I was going to die.

Then my hand tingled, flushing warm and strong. It jerked of its own accord, my fingers straightening to form a spade. It lifted.

And punched straight into Gerresh's chest, through his armor and into his heart.

I sucked in a ragged breath with the loosening of his hands. Blood rushed hot over my arm and chest as he collapsed on top of me. He was too heavy to move, or I was too drained. I couldn't even pull my hand out of him, despite what I—what it—had just done. The muscles of his heart spasmed their last beats against my palm, the tissue sticky between my fingers. His body twitched against mine.

My breath was loud in my ears, the only sound I could hear. I gagged.

"Nikha," I tried to wheeze. My voice sounded like the pages of a book rasping against each other.

There was a grumpy-sounding groan, as if she didn't want to be disturbed, and then a gasp as she came fully conscious and realized where she was. "Kamai! Gods, where are you hurt?"

"It's not . . . my blood," I panted.

"I'm so sorry, I shouldn't have—"

A second later, she hauled the body off me . . . but not before she witnessed my hand sliding out of Gerresh's chest with a sickening squelch. It was too dark, and my hand too red, to see if there were any black markings swirling on my skin.

"What . . . ?" she began, and then stopped, her eyes wide, her lips parted in astonishment. Maybe horror.

"I didn't mean . . .," I croaked helplessly from the ground. I didn't know how to continue.

For an interminable moment, she looked back and forth from me to the body, her eyes taking in everything. Memorizing. Gradually, the lines of her face went from slack with shock to hard with determination.

"You *will* tell me what is going on," she breathed, "or when I summon the constable, I'll tell him exactly what I've seen here. Because this is too much for me to take on faith."

I swallowed, wincing at the pain. "Okay, I'll tell you. Everything." There wasn't much else I could do at this point.

That was all Nikha needed. She nodded once, drew her sword, and before I could make a noise of alarm, stabbed Gerresh in the chest where my hand had cut through armor and flesh. She wiggled it back and forth and even violently twisted the blade for good measure. The body, of course, didn't move.

"It has to look like I killed him and not . . ." She didn't finish. She hesitated for only a second before reaching for my hand, but even that slight reluctance made me flinch. "Let's get you cleaned up while I send someone for the constable."

While I took off my blood-soaked, ruined gown and cleaned myself with cloths and a basin of water that Nikha had brought up to my room—after she woke a servant to fetch the constable—she kept trying to apologize. To me. That was the reverse of what our situation should have been, but now, after she'd calmed down, she was more ashamed of dropping her guard and letting Gerresh ambush us than angry at me.

"I was distracting you, Nikha," I tried to assure her.

"That's not an excuse," she muttered. "I shouldn't have

turned my back on you and the real danger. It was a beginner's mistake, letting anger and frustration interfere with my job. I shouldn't have left it up to you to do . . . whatever you did."

"It's okay," I insisted, "because I'm not just your job. I'm your friend." At least, I hoped I still was, after what she'd seen and what I was about to tell her.

There was nothing else for it. I shared what I knew about my mother's murder, the Twilight Guild, and Razim—even that it was him she'd fought in the market. We briefly speculated over whether Gerresh had something to do with any of that, or if he was just a sickly soul who had become further unhinged after Nikha fired him. And then I told her about the Keepers, about *how* I'd known there was something wrong with Gerresh in the first place.

Hearing I was a soulwalker was the hardest for Nikha. She took several quick steps back from me, from where I sat in a clean nightgown on the edge of my pink-swathed bed. She moved in the direction of the door, as if she was ready to run.

Her first question was "Have you walked in my soul?"

I understood; it was the ultimate invasion of privacy, worse than a thief sneaking through your physical house and belongings. I cringed, wishing I could lie. But I couldn't, not to her, not anymore. "Yes, but only once." I hurried on at the horrified look on her face. "I didn't see anything other than its most basic form. I'm sorry."

I didn't mention having opened the black door there, nor anything about Vehyn. I couldn't quite bring myself to give up the last of my secrets.

"What—" She swallowed. "What did it look like?"

Of course, Nikha had never seen—nor would ever see— her soul. She almost sounded like she didn't want to know, but I understood how she felt.

"It's beautiful, Nikha. Big and warm and rich and . . . just beautiful. And I'll never look again. I promise."

"Okay." She swallowed once more, and her feet edged closer to me. "So you're a soulwalker. I've only met soulwalkers who serve in Heshara's temples, and I've never seen a priestess put a fist through a man's chest."

"Yes." I sighed. "That was something else."

"Tell me," she said. "You owe me the *whole* truth, especially since I'm about to go take responsibility for his death."

And so I told her about the black door. The basic story came out easier than I expected, and, oddly, it was easier for her to accept than everything else.

Maybe it was because she didn't have the framework to understand how *wrong* Vehyn and the black fortress were.

Nor did she have much time to mull everything over with me before the constable arrived and she went down to explain why there was a dead man at the back door. I wanted to wait up for her, but I was exhausted. I eased myself gingerly onto my pillows, watching the bedroom door for Nikha's return, but before I knew it, my eyes had closed.

When I opened my eyes, I stood in my clearing. The black door was there, open. Vehyn leaned against the frame, seemingly unconcerned, unmistakably beautiful, just like the last time I had seen him. Except this time, I didn't have a reason to pretend he wasn't there. I still tried anyway, folding my arms and staring off into the indistinct, shadowy trees. What I really wanted to do was scream.

"Kamai, Kamai," he said breezily. "Where have you been? Are you still avoiding me?"

"Avoiding you is difficult when you intrude all over the

place. Like on other people's private conversations, or *in* other people's chests."

"Still vexed over our little argument, are we?"

"No, I'm disturbed. Deeply. You just killed a man."

"I believe that was *your* hand in his chest, Kamai."

"And *you* put it there!"

"Do you want me to apologize this time too? He was trying to hurt you. And worse." His face stilled as his voice dropped. "I thought you were beginning to appreciate my help. I seem to recall you asking for it just a short while ago, in the Temple of Heshara."

"That was different. I just wanted to stay alive. I would never want you to kill someone for me."

"You'd rather I let you die instead?"

"No! But you could have, I don't know, shoved him off me or cracked him over the head instead of spearing his heart!" This was what was bothering me almost as much as the act itself—not only that Vehyn was capable of such a thing, but that it was his *first* inclination. It made the small part of myself still trying to argue he wasn't all that bad grow even smaller, quieter.

"Come now, do you really feel that terrible?"

I opened my mouth. And then I closed it. I wasn't sure if it was because I'd grown inured to the sight of blood after what I'd been through, or if it was because I'd seen the man's disturbed and stunted soul, or if it was because he would have killed me and probably Nikha if he could have, but . . . I *didn't* feel that bad about Gerresh. I was shocked and horrified, but not remorseful. Vehyn was right.

He said, "So now that's out of the way, would you like to come in?" He gestured the way into the black door.

I'd missed the dark fortress, despite myself. Some part of me wondered if I was starting to crave it. I sighed and trekked the short distance across the clearing, kicking up skirts that were once again luxurious black velvet. I was wearing my dress from that evening, the one Nikha had already bundled away in the waking world, soaked in blood. My bare, silver-dusted arms and shoulders glimmered in the faint light.

"You look lovely." Vehyn held out a hand to help me across the threshold, but I ignored it.

Brushing past him, I found myself in a cavernous ballroom. Black, of course. The many spherical lanterns floating in the air cast swirling patterns in deep reds and indigos. Some created the appearance of thorny rose vines twining up the towering walls; some sent a checkerboard pattern twisting atop the floor; some threw what looked like shadows of invisible couples twirling around. None of it was bright enough to be disorienting, beyond giving the darkness a living quality.

"I didn't know you danced," I said, my voice flippant, but really the sight impressed me.

"Would you like to dance?"

I spun to face Vehyn. I couldn't tell if his smile was jesting or not, so I played it safe. "I've had enough dancing for one evening, I think."

"How *was* your evening, by the way? Filled with decadence and delights and . . . suitors?"

I was through giving him what he wanted, telling him what he wanted to hear, simply to please him. "I'm not really in the mood for small talk. And you know everything that happened anyway, so you don't need me to repeat it." Even if he hadn't stated it outright, he'd demonstrated clearly enough that he could see nearly everything I saw. It was better to acknowledge

202

it first and deny him that little power play, even though the thought of it made me shiver.

"But I enjoy hearing it from your mouth." His eyes went to my lips, and I couldn't help pressing them together self-consciously. Suddenly, all I could think about was what kissing him had felt like and if I'd enjoyed it or not.

Fine. He wanted to hear how my evening was? I made my tone nonchalant. "Well, I apparently *do* have a line of suitors to choose from, if I so desire."

Before I knew it, he'd slipped up to me, put one hand on my waist, and taken my own hand in his other. I was so startled, I followed his first few gliding steps without thinking. We were dancing without music, but he moved like air, like breathing, so it didn't matter. We were dancing to darkness and shadows.

"Do you desire?" he asked after a few moments, equally casual.

The question, taken in its broadest sense, was nearly enough to make me flinch. But I chose to assume he meant my suitors. I shrugged, highly conscious of where our skin met: waist, hands, my palm resting against his bicep, bared by the strangely parted sleeve of his black robe, my fingertips grazing the cool silver cuff there. Good thing I had a posture and pattern to follow, or else I wouldn't have known what to do with myself. "Perhaps. Perhaps not. We'll see how well they impress me. I bumped into Razim tonight," I added, like an afterthought.

"Oh?" he said, as if he didn't know. He spun me in a light circle, my skirts twirling.

"Yes," I said as I came back to him. "And it seems I might not have to rely upon you for all my answers. I can glean some from him."

"You don't need to turn to him for anything." Vehyn's casual tone was gone, and his hand tightened infinitesimally on my hip, my skin bare under his fingertips in the low-backed gown. "What he understands couldn't fill a coffee cup. I know things he can't even dream."

If I hadn't known better—and maybe I didn't—I would have thought Vehyn sounded jealous. "Oh?" I said. "Then why don't you tell me? Maybe Razim is the best I can do because you won't give me any answers."

Vehyn's mouth thinned. "The time isn't right."

Now my grip tightened on his arm. "It never is. You have your own agenda, just like everyone else."

"No. Not like everyone else."

"Oh yeah?"

"Yes. Why would I be the same as any mortal? I'm not human." He looked bemused. "Or have you forgotten?"

"How could I? You keep reminding me."

"And yet you so easily treat me like other, *lesser* characters in your life."

"If only because you won't tell me who you really are," I seethed, jerking to a halt and dropping his hand. "Maybe if you did, I would be properly impressed. I wouldn't need to go elsewhere."

"Fine, if you're so keen on fidelity, admit that you're mine," he said, as if it were a simple solution. "Swear to me on your soul, like you swore to Heshara, that you belong to me, and I'll tell you everything . . . the answers to all of your questions."

"Disavow a goddess to treat you like a god?" Hot anger burst in my chest, but I kept it walled in and roofed over, my words as smooth and cool as rain-slicked tiles. He was water, rolling off. "I don't care *what* you are, because that's not happening. Besides, how can I admit something that's not true?"

"Okay, then," Vehyn said, unconcerned once again, "let's play a game."

Why, oh why, in all three hells did I want to play his games? But I did. Something in me always rose to meet his challenge. My will wanted to confront his. And to win.

To follow this through to the end, like the trail of roses.

"If you find out what's going on by yourself," he said, "before events already set into motion come to pass, I'll apologize and admit that I was wrong about you, that you're your own force to be reckoned with, and that you're stronger than I ever could have guessed. I'll cease doing anything you don't like." He smirked, as if that outcome were preposterous.

"Anything?"

"Anything. And if you fail, well . . . *you* admit that you were wrong and that you belong to me. Won't that be fun? I won't even demand an apology."

I gritted my teeth. If this deal meant anything at all, it would be worth the risk on my end to stop what I had started. To stop Vehyn. And if it was meaningless, then it was all just words anyway. "It's a deal."

"Shake?" he said, holding out a pale, long-fingered hand. "Isn't that what you humans do?"

As if I needed yet another reminder I was playing a game with someone inhuman, pitting my will against something I couldn't begin to understand. As if I should be touching him and not recoiling. Still, I took his hand, refusing to let him shake my resolve.

He let his grip linger far longer than necessary. "I look forward to playing with you, Kamai." He leaned forward and whispered in my ear, "A word of warning: you'll find it difficult to make time for the Keepers and, more importantly, for our game, if you're busy considering suitors. But I'm always willing to clear your schedule for you, if need be."

His lips brushed my cheek as fear spiked through me.

Before I could ask if he meant *kill some more people*, I woke up with a jolt and a gasp, sitting upright in bed. He'd just reminded me that he could influence when I slept or awoke. That he already had a certain amount of control over me.

He'd also as good as slammed the black door in my face, like I had in his. And he'd done it with a kiss, not a kick, which was even more insulting.

And so our game had begun.

I realized Nikha was in my room when she flung herself out of a chair only a second after I'd sat up, her sword ringing out of its scabbard in the same moment.

"Are you all right?" she gasped.

My breath was still coming a little fast. "Yes. I think so. It was just . . ." I was going to say *a nightmare*, but then I stopped myself with a swallow.

"Was it . . . *it*? Did you see *him*?"

I didn't have to ask what she meant. *The black door. Vehyn.* I nodded. I couldn't read her expression in the darkness. Part of me was still waiting for her to laugh at me in disbelief.

But she didn't. "Sorry if I startled you," she said, quickly sheathing her sword and moving to light a candle. "I just thought, after tonight, that maybe you shouldn't be left alone."

Gratitude choked me up more than fear had. "Thank you, Nikha."

"I don't deserve thanks, not after nearly letting a lone attacker kill you. Some bodyguard I am. Perhaps it's a good thing I was never allowed to become one."

"Don't say that! You're the best, Nikha, and the truest friend

I've ever had. *I* should be the one still apologizing." I hesitated. "Speaking of which, the constable . . . ?"

"Gerresh was deemed a disgruntled, unstable madman bent on revenge. The constable decided I was right to kill him in your defense, though they'll want to get a look at your neck tomorrow as evidence. Other than that, it's all taken care of, the body removed."

"Sorry. And thank you," I repeated. The words seemed inadequate.

"There's nothing else I can do to help?" Candlelight filled the room with a comforting, soft glow, illuminating Nikha's concerned face as she turned to me. She didn't mean with regard to Gerresh. "Maybe you should go immediately to the Keepers with this—"

"No," I said quickly. "No. There's nothing to be done about the black door right now. The only thing I can do is figure out what's going on with Razim and the Twilight Guild, just like the Keepers want me to. That's the only way to win." If she was surprised by my reference to winning, she didn't show it. I held her eyes. "But I do need to meet with them. I need to tell them about Razim and the queen consort. We need a plan of action, and I need a path that isn't marriage."

Vehyn had been right about that, I would concede that much. But no more.

I sighed, dreading my next words. "And I need to tell them you're in on it."

17

CLANDESTINE MEETINGS

The sun wasn't up yet when Nikha and I departed for the palace, and the heavy, dark sky was pouring rain, but I still looped a scarf over my head to hide the bruising on my neck. We left before Jidras was awake, so I didn't ask permission to go, something I hoped would displease him.

The excuse I left with one of the servants was that my near brush with death had sent me scurrying for the temple to pray to Heshara and seek a blessing. I'd made sure to bring the note Lenara had given me. It was more of a calling card, with her name scrawled in elegant black script.

Dawn was barely silvering the edge of the stormy clouds above the mountains as we entered the rain-soaked temple grounds. When I presented Lenara's card to the guards, they blinked at it sternly, as if wanting to find fault with it, but they couldn't.

The temple was dark and eerily silent when we entered, more like Vehyn's fortress than ever before. Even the hum of rainfall vanished when the front doors closed fully behind us. Only a few scattered candelabras lit the way to Lenara's door, casting narrow pools of light on the black-and-white-checkered tiles, leaving the cavernous expanse shrouded in shadow. I suddenly wondered if she'd be in there, if she was even awake.

I knocked softly. After only a moment the door opened. Lenara's eyes were more anxious than usual, especially when she caught sight of Nikha.

"Is something wrong, Kamai? This is a *remarkably* unusual hour." As in, people might notice, and talk. "You may come in, but your guest—"

"She knows everything, Lenara," I interrupted, my voice barely above a murmur. "We need to talk, but somewhere she can join." Her eyes narrowed; she knew I meant *not in the sleeping realm.* "You can trust her, just like you can trust me." In case that wasn't enough, I added, "Like you trusted my mother."

"Wait here." She closed the door softly, even though I got the sense from her rigid shoulders that she wanted to slam it. She came back thirty seconds later with a folded scrap of paper, torn hastily from another sheet. "Leave now. Go to these quarters in the palace, to this person, and make this introduction."

"Do we need to go unseen?" I asked, unnerved by her urgency. She'd said the temple wasn't safe, and apparently she'd meant it.

"No. Better yet, giggle a little, like you're intoxicated. It's early enough to still be late for some."

Nikha and I exchanged a look. What did *that* mean? "Will you be—?"

209

"Go." She shut the door in our faces.

"Coming?" I finished.

The quarters Lenara had listed were in an especially opulent section of the palace I had never explored. It wasn't until we passed a few stray people in the hallways, obviously still wearing suits and gowns from the night before, that I realized we were in the wing where many courtiers and courtesans took up residence at the palace if they didn't have their own homes in the capital.

It also took me a moment to recognize the name beneath the clipped set of directions. But when the door flew open with a flourish in response to my knock, I had no problem remembering.

"Why, Kamai Numa," Zeniri Sarvotha said, the bright smile falling briefly from his dark face at the sight of me. "You're probably the last person I was expecting." He managed to take any sting out of the words with his jovial tone.

But he was right. He was also the last person *I* was expecting Lenara to send us to. He was a courtier, a pleasure artist no less, and apparently a popular one at that, in the full flower of youthful beauty. He still wore the same clothes from my gala—at least some of them—though my event looked to have been the lightest of his evening entertainments. His plum silk jacket and white sash were gone, his vest and undershirt undone. At least he still had pants on.

Trying to ignore my rising flush, I blurted, "I hope I'm not interrupting anything."

"No, no . . . but what in the name of Ranta's tits can I do for you? Need some tips for your wedding night?"

My blush spread, and my eyes seized on the scrap of paper in my hand, on the other line Lenara had written there. "By the night, I seek the light of your aid."

His smile froze on his face like a mask, and he opened the door all the way without saying anything more. As soon as we were inside, he shut it, locked it, and turned to us. His smile was completely gone. "How do you know that pass-phrase?" he asked, his tone all business, as he crossed to the other end of his lavish sitting room to close the drapes. The space was upholstered in rich oranges and purples, with several closed doors no doubt branching off to a bedchamber and bathroom.

"Because I gave it to her," Lenara said, stepping out of one of those doors—one that *apparently* led only to an oversize, over-flowing closet.

We all jumped, even Zeniri. "Three hells," he said, putting a hand to his chest. "Can you, I don't know, clear your throat before you appear like that?"

I stared at her. "How did you get here?"

"I have my ways of slipping out of the temple and into the palace undetected," she said, straightening her gray, nondescript cloak with exaggerated dignity, "and this room is the safest in the palace. But still, this is a risk. A huge risk."

I blinked at Zeniri, the realization hitting me. "Wait, you're a Keeper?" That meant he was a soulwalker. One who, as a popular courtier specializing in the pleasure arts, routinely slept alongside some of the highest-ranked nobility and officials in the capital.

Zeniri folded his arms and arched a well-manicured eyebrow. "I would be asking you the same thing, but because I *am* a Keeper, I know not to openly *talk about it* . . . and also that

211

Lenara was planning to approach you. Still, I hadn't realized you'd come so far."

"She took the vow a few days ago," Lenara said, and then turned to Nikha. "But *she* didn't, so I'd dearly like to know what all of this is about, Kamai. You are putting my trust to the test."

"You can still trust me, and I promise you can trust her too," I said quickly as a defensive look settled on Nikha's face. "I had to tell her, Lenara. She's been my friend and guardian since I arrived in Jidras's household. She's skilled enough to be a royal bodyguard, besides. The only reason she isn't one is because she's a woman." Lenara's expression remained stony, so I kept going. "She already knows I'm a soulwalker"—I didn't specify for how long—"and she fought off Razim once at the market and saved my life last night, after my gala, from a guard who nearly strangled me. After all of that, I owed her the truth. She's the one person I can trust with my life. I need her."

I was leaving out everything about Vehyn and his influence over me. I hoped it would let Nikha know just how much of the truth I'd trusted her with.

"What of the oath you swore us?" Lenara asked. "The loyalty you owe us?"

I squared my shoulders. "I promised my life and soul to Heshara and the Keepers. I didn't promise my freedom of thought and judgment. If you want to claim my life now, then do it, but I can't unsay what I told Nikha, and I wouldn't if I could."

I felt a hand on my back, supporting me. Nikha's.

Lenara's eyes narrowed at me, as if weighing my resolve. Her gaze found my throat, where my scarf had slipped aside to reveal the bruising. Her expression softened. "What was his name?" she asked finally. "Your attacker's?"

Nikha told her.

"We don't know if he was sent by anyone in particular," I added, "or if he was merely seeking revenge after I walked in his soul and found it . . . wrong . . . and Nikha relieved him from duty."

"I'll look into it. Is that all?"

I suddenly felt silly—perhaps nearly dying and even Nikha knowing about the Keepers weren't big enough excuses to meet like this. But I *did* still have something to share. "I came face-to-face with Razim last night. You're right that he's been looking for me, but he was less than forthcoming about his own plans. Yet—"

"Wait." Lenara held up a hand, cutting me off. "Have you walked in Nikha's soul?"

I flinched. Despite my guilt, I had to be honest, and perhaps honesty would help Lenara trust Nikha. "Yes. And it's beautiful. One of the most beautiful I've seen."

"Good enough. You," she said to Nikha, "don't get to hear another word until you swear yourself to us."

Zeniri coughed. "Um. Is she a soulwalker?"

"No, but she *is* the nearest thing we currently have to a licensed bodyguard, and Kamai needs protection. Keepers haven't always only been soulwalkers. Just usually. Mostly. Perhaps wisely." Each qualifier was like a blow aimed at Nikha.

They might as well have bounced off Nikha's leather tunic for all the damage they did. "You know, what's *wise* is not allowing your sworn members to get abducted from markets or killed in dark allies," she said, her voice low. "I protected her, and I'll continue to do so."

"For Heshara's and the Keepers' sake, no doubt," Lenara said.

Nikha and I exchanged a glance. I well knew how she felt about Heshara.

Lenara read the look and threw up her hands. "Make foolish bargains with your soul at your peril. Goddesses aren't known to be forgiving. But that is the only way we'll proceed here."

And so it was, right there, in the unlikeliest of places, without hesitation, that Nikha swore her life and her soul to Heshara and the Keepers, just like I had done, and for reasons as murky as mine.

Lenara wasn't terribly impressed, more irritable. "Now that that's settled, I'm going to sit down, because I'm not as young as the rest of you." She stalked over to an orange satin couch. "Kamai, you were saying about Razim . . . ?"

And so I told them. About his . . . interest . . . in me, his hints at revenge, and the queen consort being his mother.

I expected Lenara to appear surprised at the very least, but she only nodded, and Zeniri said, "Of course."

"Of course?"

"Your mother knew Razim was the queen consort's son," Lenara said, shooting Zeniri a glare. "She gleaned the secret from Hallan years ago, though it was tightly kept."

I gaped. "And you didn't tell me?"

"Your mother clearly hadn't told you, and an oath, even on your soul, doesn't mean I can entirely trust you." She gave both me and Nikha a look.

I struggled to ignore the sting of *your mother clearly hadn't told you.* "But how could the queen consort hide a pregnancy with a kingdom so desperate for an heir?"

"She had to *precisely* because we're so desperate. A priest or priestess could determine paternity, and the so-called heir would have been uncovered as a bastard. Her affair would have been brought to the attention of the king—as it perhaps was nearly two decades later, and you saw what happened. Anyway, the methods used to hide such a thing aren't all that complex, as long as the mother in question has people she can trust. An illness that keeps her shut away, a lengthy visit to a countryside estate . . . If I recall, the queen consort used both excuses together."

"And afterward, Razim quietly went to live with his father?" I guessed, still stunned.

Lenara nodded, propping her feet on a polished coffee table. As a priestess, she was accustomed to getting comfortable with guests, but it was Zeniri's turn to shoot *her* a disapproving look. "Your mother, pregnant with you, soon joined them. She didn't wish to stay with Jidras Numa after she discovered her situation. She was already a dual member of the Keepers and the Twilight Guild—a fact unbeknownst to the latter, of course—and so the guild facilitated the arrangement as an excuse, encouraging Marin and Hallan to pose as a married couple. It had the added benefit that such a rosily painted picture of a family more easily won over their patrons' trust. It was almost too perfect for us, as well. We would have sheltered and cared for your mother as a Keeper, of course, but this way she was in the home of one of the guild's most suspect members. Hallan's . . . activity . . . with the queen consort had us highly curious."

Lenara knew so much already that I wondered what she might need from me at all. Feeling especially silly to have brought everyone here like this, I couldn't keep my shoulders from sagging. To my surprise, it was Zeniri who patted them.

"You did well. Your connection to the boy is invaluable. That's *quite* the discovery for a first meeting, and without even bedding him! Think what you'll be able to learn once you do."

215

"*What?*" I nearly choked. "You expect me . . . You want me to . . . ?"

"Of course they don't—" Nikha began, stepping closer to me protectively.

Zeniri muttered, "Well, you're certainly not going to charm him with your eloquence."

We all looked to Lenara on the couch. She scratched the corner of her mouth, almost as if she was trying not to smile. "You *did* want an alternative to marriage, Kamai, and we need you here in court. As soon as you shun the more traditional path your father has laid out for you, he'll inevitably disown you. The Keepers are willing to take you in, provide you with shelter and support, but only if it's worth our while." *Only if you earn your keep*, she meant. "Becoming a favored courtesan would be the best possible way for you to find out as much as possible about what's going on. I was planning to apprentice you to Zeniri."

"As a *pleasure artist?*" I tried to keep the raw horror from my voice.

"I thought, with your background, your *mother's* background, and your abhorrence of marriage, this was the most obvious solution."

"And you'd think, as the daughter of Marin Nuala, you wouldn't *need* a tutor in the first place," Zeniri said under his breath again. Lenara shot him another look.

"She's just a girl!" Nikha practically erupted.

"She's an adult," Lenara said. "What do you think of such an arrangement, Kamai?"

Everyone looked at me, waiting. I wanted to flee the room.

18

DEEPEST SELVES

"I . . . I . . ." The first coherent string of words that I was able to spit out was "I can't sleep with Razim." *Or with anyone* was what I really wanted to add.

"Why not?" Zeniri demanded, putting his hands on his hips. "You have a history together, and you also have a duty to us. Besides, he's excessively handsome. But I'm not his type, unfortunately. *You* clearly are. Is it a matter of nerves?"

"Maybe." I still couldn't form the right words. My tongue was heavy, incapable.

"Ah, of course, you're still a maiden. But that's why you now have a tutor." Zeniri spread his arms, presenting himself. His chest, fully revealed under his open vest and undershirt, was well shaped with muscle—but, as usual, that didn't have the same effect upon me that it might upon others. His eyes narrowed. "Wait, what is that face? Don't you find me pleasing?"

Aesthetically, he was quite pleasing. "Yes, but . . ."

"Of course you do. Most everyone does." He took a sudden step closer to me and grazed my cheek with his fingers. "All you need is practice."

He bent his face toward mine. My hand twitched involuntarily, and I shoved him away—almost wondering if it was Vehyn who had done it. But no, it was me. Nikha tensed as if she were about to shove Zeniri herself, but she didn't need to. He stumbled back, his eyes wide.

To my surprise, he didn't look angry. "Lenara, dear, what is the matter with her? Is she only interested in women?"

My eyes shot to Lenara in mortification.

"You don't have to answer, Kamai," Nikha muttered.

I could have hugged her.

Zeniri snorted. "Well, I'm certainly not how she takes her coffee, if you catch my meaning."

"It's nothing to be ashamed of, if you are only interested in women," Lenara said, regarding me curiously from the couch.

The two Keepers stared at me expectantly. I heard Nikha shift in awkwardness. I couldn't bring myself to respond. I didn't even know *what* to say. I wanted to shout *I don't like coffee at all!*

Instead, I threw a hand at Lenara. "What, are *you* going to try to kiss me now to find out?"

Lenara laughed. "Hardly. That's not how I take *my* coffee. And besides, you're young enough to be my daughter."

Something in her and Zeniri's faces suddenly snagged my attention, details that I'd been too distracted to notice before. I blinked at the both of them. "Are you two related?"

"Brother and sister, a generation apart," Zeniri explained. "Same father, different mothers, different names, raised separately so no one suspected the connection." At my confused look, he added, "The clergy knows better than anyone that our gift runs in the blood, so they test family members of their initiates, as well. But that wouldn't have done for me. I mean, can you imagine *me*, a *priest?*" He made a face of distaste.

"Besides, both of us working together under the watchful eyes of the clergy would have left too much evidence that we were up to something other than their business," Lenara said. "This way, the Keepers could place me in the royal temple and Zeniri where they needed him. Our blood relation is a carefully guarded secret." She shot him a glare before settling back to look at me. "This room has especially thick walls that are hard to hear through for a reason. The high priest a few hundred years ago had a favorite courtesan, or so I've been told. The passageway between here and the temple was once used for their clandestine affair, but the Keepers have kept it as our secret since, using it only for our business. Speaking of which . . ."

I'd hoped everyone would forget what we'd been talking about before, but no such luck.

Lenara watched me in that considering, sharp way she had, like a paring knife peeling away the skin of a fruit. "I didn't say there was anything wrong with a difference in age either, among adults, but that's another way I don't take my coffee."

She abruptly stood and moved to a writing desk in the corner. She gathered a pen, inkwell, and a piece of paper. "Zeniri may have asked my opinion for a reason. He's not always a blunt, tactless instrument." She spoke with her back turned, bent over the desk, while the pen scratched on the paper.

Zeniri sputtered. "I assure you, my patrons would argue that I'm *never*—"

"Before you go any further, I don't believe any of us wish to hear about *that* instrument . . . and this will prove it."

Nikha shifted again, but I made no show of noticing. Lenara

had included her in those not interested in Zeniri's *instrument*. Nikha didn't confirm or deny it. And she didn't have to, because everyone's attention was on me and *my* inclinations. Or lack thereof.

It took another painfully stretched moment for Lenara to return to the coffee table with her piece of paper. We gathered around, leaning over a sketched diagram.

I realized I'd seen it before: the repeating, shortened cycle of the moon, one ink-filled circle symbolizing the new moon at the center, with a cross built around it. Each of the four points ended in the full moon, with the lunar phases between new and full stretching out from the center along each arm——crescent, quarter, and gibbous——waxing or waning in opposite directions.

"That's the pattern on the dome's ceiling, in the temple. I was wondering about it."

"You're about to find out one of Heshara's sacred mysteries. This is what's known as a soul chart. We study them as priests and priestesses to better understand souls. Believe it or not, we don't just riffle through everyone's darkest secrets in order to absolve them of sins or accuse them of crimes. Sometimes we actually *help* people sort out their confusion. To come to know themselves better. Find peace with the truth."

She tapped each arm of the diagram. "These are the four branches of your deepest self. For two of them, imagine that the new moon signifies female, and the full moon male——odd, I realize, since we consider Heshara female in all her forms, but that's why this is one of her mysteries. For the other two, imagine that the new moon indicates an absence, and the full moon a presence. Simple enough."

"Uh, okay." Perhaps it was simple, but I wasn't sure I liked where this was headed.

"So for the first branch"——her finger traced one of the moon's half-cycles——"this is how you see yourself. Female to male, with everything (or even neither) in between. Where would you say you fall?"

This was an easy question, but now I *knew* where this was headed, and it definitely wasn't good. "Wouldn't this be Ranta's domain? I mean . . ." I glanced down at myself.

"No. Forget your physical form entirely right now. This"—— Lenara waved at my body, as if sweeping something away——"has nothing to do with who you are and how you feel inside. Only this."

She touched between her eyes, the gesture for the soul, for Heshara, and looked back down at the chart.

"Okay." I pointed at the center, directly at the new moon. "Female."

Her finger traced another line. "This is whom you are drawn to. It doesn't have to be in a sexual or even sensual manner, but it can be." She waited.

I was still safe then, if aesthetic attraction counted. This time, I planted my finger halfway, on the quarter moon. "Men and women, equally."

Zeniri made a noise of doubt.

Lenara ignored him, tracing a third line. "Remember, these last two are an absence or presence, and the scale in between. The first is how much you feel romantic attraction."

"What do you mean, *romantic*?" I asked, trying to stall. "Isn't desire . . . desire?" Everyone but me seemed to think it was. But maybe Lenara was saying something different.

"As your mother should have taught you, there is a difference between sex and love, sex and affection, even sex and sensuality. Just as there is a difference between sexual and romantic attraction."

"Okay . . . so . . . it's how much I want to kiss and hug and fall in love, that sort of thing."

"'That sort of thing'? Oh boy," Zeniri muttered.

"Put simply, yes," Lenara said.

I first set my finger on the gibbous moon . . . and then reluctantly slid it two phases closer to the center of the chart, toward the new moon—toward absence—to rest on the crescent. There had been something there, in Vehyn's kiss, even if it had been small. The sliver of moon looked like a grin etched into the page. Vehyn's.

"Only with certain people," I muttered. *One person.*

"Yes," Lenara said, "people can form various attractions for different reasons, sometimes only after a significant bond has formed. And your position can always change. It's a gray area, not always black and white."

That sounded about right. But that didn't change anything. I couldn't let myself fall in love; it was too dangerous. My mother *had* taught me that much, although maybe not intentionally . . .

Zeniri scratched the stubble on his chin. "Now this is starting to make sense."

Lenara raised her eyebrows at me, ignoring him. "I think you know what the last branch indicates, Kamai."

"Maybe I don't feel like saying," I snapped, mostly to cover the blush already spreading from my cheeks down into my neck. Then again, part of me wanted to shout it to the world and just be done with it.

"You don't have to say, but let me assure you, it's normal to not feel sexually drawn to anyone," Lenara said calmly, even gently. "In that case"—she pointed at the new moon, which I was unwilling to do—"it's called being a 'new soul.'"

"A nice name doesn't make me feel less embarrassed," I said. "But now you all know I am one, so feel free to mock—"

Nikha's finger slammed down on the center, on the new moon, cutting me off. "There. That's where I am too." She looked up at me through her spikes of hair, her gaze as bright and sharp as bared steel. "I'm not embarrassed. And I will let no one mock us."

My mouth fell open as I stared. *Us.* Suddenly, Nikha wavered in my vision, and I had to blink a lot. My throat was too tight to speak. Nikha was a new soul like me. All this time . . . it was yet another thing I could have shared with her.

"I see," Lenara said, without the slightest bit of judgment. "Anything else, Nikha?"

Now it was Nikha's turn to look uncomfortable, but Lenara continued before she had the chance to pull away from the chart.

"We'll go in reverse this time. Romantic attraction?"

Why Lenara was interested, I couldn't imagine. Nor could I imagine that Nikha would deign to respond. And yet . . . her finger twitched, as if some force was compelling her from the inside, against her will, but only as far as the crescent.

Again, like me.

"And who are you drawn to, in whatever capacity: male or female?"

This time, her finger slid in the other direction, back to the new moon. Female only. Not like me.

"And how do you feel *yourself*, Nikha?"

For a long time, her finger didn't budge. But I got the sense—we all must have—that Nikha wasn't finished. And then her finger gradually began to drag, so slowly, so effortfully, like a dagger drawn across a tabletop, past the crescent, the quarter, the gibbous . . . toward the full moon. And then she jerked her hand away as if burned. Her eyes, this time, when she looked at me, were wild and afraid.

She'd had more to hide, more judgment and misunderstanding to fear, than even me. Nikha didn't just dress and seem more like a man at times. Nikha *was* a man.

"This doesn't leave this room," Nikha ground out. "No one call me . . . don't . . ."

"It's okay," I blurted. "I don't care. I mean, I think it's fitting. It's . . . wonderful."

I wasn't sure if my awkward flood of words convinced her,

but she took a deep breath and looked at the other two, her jaw hard.

"So you're a man, then," Zeniri said brightly. Nikha tensed as if ready to attack, but before she could lunge for him, he added, "Like me."

It was difficult to tell if he was mocking her. Nikha's eyes flicked down, in the direction of her chest and maybe lower. "Not quite like you."

"Well, a body is easily seen beyond. I do it all the time, with female patrons."

Nikha gritted her teeth. "I don't want to be *seen*, either beyond or directly, by anyone."

"And remember," Lenara said, adding a voice of reason, "outward appearances don't always reflect matters of the soul. Such a thing is called being 'soul-crossed,' and I assure you, it's also normal."

"Whatever," Nikha snapped. "And whatever you do, *don't* start calling me a man. No one else can know." Her tone was insistent.

She wouldn't meet my eyes. I wanted to reach out, comfort her, but I wasn't sure how. And then I remembered what she'd done for me, and I put a hand on her back. I felt her jump under my touch and she didn't turn, but she might have leaned into me the slightest bit.

"Are you sure that's what you want?" Lenara asked.

I blinked in surprise while Nikha spat, "Of course I'm sure. I've had a long time—my *entire life*—to consider the matter."

"But is that what's best for you . . . or for the Keepers?"

Nikha's eyes narrowed even farther. "Why in Ranta's name would admitting that I'm soul-crossed be good for the Keepers?"

"I dug up any information on you that I could after

225

discovering you and Kamai were close, of course. I already knew you passed the test to become a royal bodyguard."

"Then you already know I was disqualified because of this." Nikha gestured down at herself. "They couldn't see my body because of my armor and helmet during the test, but they found out afterward. I don't know why I hoped my results would speak for themselves. It didn't work for my mother."

Lenara shrugged. "As a priestess, I could help argue your case."

Now it was Nikha's turn to blink. "What?"

"I have the legal means to see and proclaim the truth in your soul. The law is bound to acknowledge those proven to be soul-crossed. With a signed declaration from me, you could be formally recognized as a man and take your place as a royal bodyguard."

Nikha's mouth had fallen open. "But why would you . . . ? Ah."

Understanding hit me at the same time.

Lenara half smiled, almost apologetically. "Yes. If you became a royal bodyguard, you could try to enter the king's service. You would become the only Keeper in such an invaluable position—the only one protecting his person who knows exactly what to guard against."

Nikha began to shake her head. "But then I would have to leave Kamai."

"I wouldn't let her remain unprotected. Besides, she is a Keeper herself, and it is *both* your highest duties now to protect the earth, which regretfully or not means keeping the king alive."

I tried not to flinch at that, but Nikha held everyone's attention anyway. Her words came faster with each shake of her head, her voice rising. "I can't tell everyone what I am. They would think it strange, whatever you insist. I'm not ready. I—"

Surprisingly, it was Zeniri who made a calming motion. "No one will rush you. Right?" He shot a look at Lenara, who grudgingly nodded. "The thought of revealing the truth takes some getting used to. I understand, because I've had to do the same. Despite my particular preference for men being rather accepted—even desired—in my line of work, it was still hard to admit, because of this supposed duty to produce heirs." He snorted and waved the thought away as if it were nothing. "Some of my better-paying female patrons *still* don't know my tastes, though that's more for the sake of their feelings than my own. Anyway, everyone has their secrets, hidden inside." He grinned. "And I mean *everyone*. I make it my business to discover them. Even the king himself, spiritually wed to the earth goddess, Ranta, and physically wed to a queen consort, prefers men as well, which goes far to explain his lack of an heir."

"Executing the queen consort didn't help with that, either," Lenara murmured.

Razim's mother. It was still hard to wrap my mind around it. But this new bit of information on the king made more sense of why the queen consort's sole child had been fathered by Hallan.

Zeniri said, "Yes, well, now that we've all gotten to know each other better, can we get back to the task at hand? Kamai still needs to get close enough to Razim and other people to soulwalk, and she's just nixed the easiest method."

Lenara sighed. "I need a seductress and Heshara sends me a new soul." She glanced at me. "Sorry, dear, I mean no offense, but it is rather inconvenient."

227

I looked down at my hands, which I realized were clenched around each other. "I know. I—"

"Don't apologize," Lenara said, before I could do exactly that. "*Never* apologize for who you are. You are a complete soul, in Heshara's eyes." She gestured at the chart before her. "Now we just need to figure out what to do with you."

Indeed. If they didn't have a use for me, there was no real place for me in the Keepers. Some other apprenticeship would be difficult to arrange at this point, if not impossible, without Jidras's help and with the ruined reputation his disowning me would cause me. So then my last resort would be to keep Jidras's favor and marry, unless I wanted to go penniless and destitute. Both were about equally appealing.

Despite that, I somehow felt lighter than I had in months. *Years.* Maybe ever. For the first time in my life, the people closest to me knew the truth about who I was, and it was *okay*.

Zeniri folded his arms and drummed his fingers on his elbows as he regarded me. "I *could* still teach you all the techniques. I mean, in a lot of ways, it's like acting. It would just be entirely like acting for you."

Lenara raised a brow. "Some new souls can and do and even *want* to have sex for various reasons, it's true."

I wondered, would that be better or worse than marriage? Either way, I would be stuck filling a repulsive role I didn't want, but at least with the Keepers I would have a purpose. Answers. Revenge.

No. It could have been my own horror-tinged thought at the idea, but it was Vehyn's voice, speaking in my mind: *There is another way. Come. I will show you.*

At his words, giddy relief hit me like a beam of sunlight after endless clouds. I needed to lie down, take a sleeping tonic if I had to, and discover what this other path was. But everyone was looking at me, waiting for a response. "I think I have an idea. But I need to consider it some more, and I'll get back to you."

I started for the door. They all blinked in surprise at the abruptness of my departure, and Nikha had to hurry to follow me.

"Kamai," Lenara called, before I opened the door. "You don't have to go back to that hideous man's—excuse me, Jidras Numa's house. We can find quarters for you here and still apprentice you to Zeniri in the meantime, at least by outward appearances."

It was a generous offer, especially since I *couldn't* remain with Jidras for much longer, both because I couldn't stomach it and because he would throw me out as soon as he learned I wasn't planning to marry. But staying here now and waiting for everything to get sorted would take time that I couldn't stand to waste. Not when my future, my purpose, the answers I had been desperately seeking were hanging in the balance.

"I'm pleased and grateful to accept your offer," I said with as much polite decorum as I could muster with my hand on the door latch, "as long as I can go back to Jidras's one more time." I caught Nikha's look. "And as long as Nikha can stay with me when I return."

"That should be no problem, for the moment," Lenara said.

For the moment. As long as I didn't prove to be dead weight. Nikha would be the better Keeper, in that case, at least able to wield a sword. To avoid being useless, I needed to talk to Vehyn as soon as possible.

"Okay. I'll be back in a day or so. I have a few last things to finish up."

Including, of course, saying good-bye to Jidras.

19

SHARED DREAMS

Jidras was out on business by the time Nikha and I returned to the town house. I didn't mind, since it let me escape up to my room after a short visit with the constable, who took one look at my neck, declared that I was lucky to be alive, and congratulated Nikha on a job well done. When I told him I was still feeling weak and needed rest, he immediately waved me off. I had to resist betraying my lie by bounding upstairs.

Nikha didn't abandon the constable to follow me or shoot me worried looks. Because she trusted me.

After everything we'd already shared, I'd thought it would be awkward on the way back home, but as soon as we left Zeniri's chambers, she'd stopped me . . . and hugged me. I was astonished at how nice it was just to receive a hug, without anyone wanting anything in return.

Still, I wanted to give her something back. "I can call you

whatever you wish," I'd whispered. "Even if it's only me who does it."

Nikha smiled but shook her head. "It's enough, for now, that you know."

I smiled back. "Then I'll keep knowing who you really are. I swear it." Even if I didn't call Nikha *he*, not before she was ready, I would remember that her body didn't match her soul. "Was your mother . . . ?"

"No, she wasn't soul-crossed. I got my love of fighting from her, but not that. She taught me the many different things women could be, if they wished. But even being a woman like that didn't fit me right. It never has." She sighed. "Maybe that's another reason why I was uneasy with Lenara's plan for me to become a bodyguard. It's not fair for only me to gain what *both* my mother and I earned, just because . . ." She swallowed. "Because of what I truly am, and not because of skill alone. Women should have the same chances as men."

I better understood, then, why she disliked Heshara and her worship, even if I didn't see the goddess or my faith in the same way. Nikha wasn't resentful only because of what she had been denied personally, but because of what was denied to all women.

She didn't want to be treated better. She wanted everyone to be treated the same. Like her hug, it was the simple desire to share, selflessly, just to be kind.

I had to admit that sharing, at least with Nikha, felt wonderful. Now I had someone who knew almost all my secrets, and I knew theirs. *What a novel concept*, I thought as I prepared to meet Vehyn.

───────

Beyond the black door, he was waiting for me in something like a study, with a black floor, black walls, black desk. From a single floating lamp came a dim red light, casting no intricate shadows this time. His pale face and the shining cuffs on his biceps were the brightest things in the room. He sat in a high-backed black chair behind the desk, regarding me over folded arms. His acute focus nearly made me take a step back.

"Uh, hi."

"How was your little meeting? Learn something about yourself? Chart your inner reaches?"

I raised my chin, refusing to feel ashamed. Nikha's and Lenara's—even Zeniri's—acknowledgment and support had already changed something within me. I felt stronger, lighter . . . brighter. Like a new moon floating in the sky, cloaked in secretive darkness, but with a glowing core. Not empty. Not broken. Whole and wholly myself. "Maybe. Why do you care?"

He stood swiftly. "Because your soul, Kamai, is unchartable. It's useless for them to even try. Only I understand you."

I had to resist rolling my eyes. I needed him to tell me what he knew, and provoking him probably wouldn't help. "That's all very comforting, but sometimes it's nice to relate to . . . I don't know . . . other *human* beings?"

"Can you really, though? If so, why are you here?"

"You told me there was another way to get close enough to people to soulwalk," I said carefully. "Other than . . . you know."

"It sounds to me like you're trying to avoid relating to humans *too* much. I think you know all of that—all of them—are beneath you."

"Thinking of it in those terms *definitely* makes me feel less alone."

Vehyn took a step closer to me across the study without seeming to move. "You're not alone."

I have Nikha, I thought, but I didn't say that aloud. Vehyn was jealous enough of Razim, whom I didn't even like, as it was. The less attention he paid to Nikha, the better. "Yes, because talking to the mysterious being that no one else can see is really helping me feel connected to the world."

He shrugged. "I can leave you to your situation, then, if you prefer. What did Zeniri say? *'It's just like acting'?*"

It was creepy that he overheard so much of what I experienced. I dropped my hands and sighed. "Sometimes I wish I wanted to sleep with people. Not just to feel more normal, whatever that means, but . . . but I don't actually want to," I finished, in case he got any ideas.

He considered me. "Why do you wish you did?"

"Just to share. Feel close to someone. I want that, sometimes." I wasn't sure why I was telling the truth. Maybe because it would be nice to have with Vehyn what I had with Nikha. Honesty.

"This isn't close?" He gestured between us, the floor dark enough that the space could have been bottomless—a chasm.

I snorted.

He took a step closer. "How about now?"

"Vehyn . . . you know I don't mean literal closeness."

"Which is why I'm illustrating the absurdity of tying such sentiment to physical bodies." He looked like he had an idea. "But if it's sharing you want . . ." His black robe swirling, he closed the gap between us entirely, but I flinched away from his hands as he raised them to my face. He froze, his dark eyes serious, searching. "I'm not going to hurt you, Kamai, or try to do anything you won't want."

"I'm a little jumpy," I said with a nervous laugh, my heart stuttering in my chest. "Someone just tried to strangle me to death, after all."

233

"And you saw what I did to him." He hesitated. "May I?"

I couldn't believe he was asking my permission. Because of that, I blinked and said, "You may," even though I didn't know what he would do.

He brushed his fingers along my cheeks and into my hair, tickling my scalp, finally settling his cool palms against my temples.

"What—?" I began.

"Close your eyes," he instructed. And then he did one of the strangest things. He closed his own. I realized I hadn't seen him with his eyes shut for longer than a blink. It made him look almost vulnerable. Almost trusting. His heavy black lashes and something . . . else . . . shadowed his pale lids, something I'd mistaken for kohl, but perhaps it was whatever darkness was beginning to stain my own eyes.

I found myself wanting to stare at his face, map each and every line of his eerie beauty, now that I could look at him without his intense regard in return. Instead, my own eyes slid shut.

Behind my lids, there was only darkness, complete. I had a second realization: I didn't often close my eyes in the sleeping realm, either. I was already asleep, after all. Here, where I wasn't even technically shutting my lids in a real, physical sense, I quickly lost track of any connection to or memory of my body, even the pressure of Vehyn's hands on my face. My spirit was simply floating in the dark. My thoughts began to drift.

And then the darkness began to take shape, passing like rippling black water underneath me. A vague, faint light, a little like moonlight, glinted on the water's surface, and warm wind blew through my hair. I began to feel my surroundings on my skin, such that I *had* skin—distantly, like I was both in and outside of my body. Seeing was like peering through eyes that weren't fully open, and watching from outside myself, at the same time. What I saw and felt was both clear and sharp, blurry and fuzzy.

I was flying through night air over the dark waves, so fast it took my breath away. For a moment, I had lungs to breathe, and then I forgot them, because they weren't necessary.

As a hand took mine, I realized someone else was with me. Vehyn. He was less distinct than I was. A shadow next to me, but I could sense his presence, feel his hand squeeze mine. And then I could feel more than that. His thoughts. A calm assurance blanketed me, and a flash of eagerness pierced me. And then his arms were around me and we were soaring up, up, into the darkness. The bottom dropped out of my stomach, wherever my stomach was, as the water fell away below. We climbed so high that I saw the horizon of a dimmed world far beneath us, with a midnight sky that seemed incomplete, unreal without moon or stars. I laughed in delight; I couldn't help it. Vehyn was still a shadow, but I felt lips brush my cheek.

With his kiss, I felt a rush of . . . something. A warm tingling. A deep, buzzing thrill. I wasn't sure if it came from him or me, but it was strong and heady, like downing a glass of wine.

And then suddenly we were falling. I felt like screaming now, but his strong arms held me tighter, cupped my head to his chest. The dark water flew up to meet us, rising as fast as my fear. When we hit, it didn't hurt, but water was all around me, in my mouth, in my nose. I didn't need to breathe, but still I tried, I struggled, I didn't want to sink into blackness . . . but Vehyn wasn't letting me go.

My eyes flew open. Vehyn's arms were around me, like they had been in the water, but we were standing back in the dark study behind the black door, where he'd first put his hands on my face, the lamplight still red and low. I was gasping, as if I needed air.

"What was that?" I asked, steadying myself against his chest. But I knew the answer to my own question. "Were we dreaming? *Together?*"

Vehyn blinked, as if it was taking him a moment to come back to himself. "I . . . I've never actually done that before. I wasn't entirely sure what would happen, or what I would do." His voice sounded unusually off-balance, dazed. And for a second, that made him look truly young.

"What do you mean?" I pushed away from him, though his arms only slid from my back down to my waist, still holding me close. "You weren't in control?"

When he looked at me again, his eyes were clear, focused, but shadowed. Walls were going up that I hadn't realized were there until I saw them being built. "Not entirely. That seems to be the nature of dreaming, even for me. I was worried I might drop you, but then . . ."

He'd fallen with me, instead. "Could we have gotten hurt?" I demanded.

"I don't think so. No bodily harm, at least. It's a place of pure unconscious thought and emotion, without boundaries. The sleeping realm within the sleeping realm. It's *true* sharing, if you have the ability to go there with someone else. But who's to say what might hurt there, hm?" He shrugged, as if it were of no consequence. His eyes had that ageless quality to them again.

I stepped back so his arms fell entirely away. I was suddenly self-conscious, unsure of what to say. We had shared something dark and deep with each other, a melding of our latent selves, and I wasn't sure how I felt about it . . . or how Vehyn felt. It hadn't seemed planned on his part. I hugged myself, remembering the feeling of his arms around me, of soaring, falling. Good and bad. Had he been able to sense my emotions, like I had his? I both liked the thought and wanted to hide. Maybe this was what people who weren't new souls felt like when they were naked before another person.

"Was that . . . um . . . what you wanted to show me?" I asked, for *something* to say.

Vehyn arched an eyebrow. "No, Kamai, that was my attempt to share something with you without expecting anything in return."

Exactly what I'd wanted, for once. Except this time, I actually needed something else from him. Of course he knew that, so he was trying to make me feel greedy. Even giving me something I wanted, he still managed to try to take from me, to gain leverage.

Manipulative bastard.

I threw up my hands. "Fine, I can just go back to the waking world and——" He caught my hand, stopping me short. I'd guessed he would. He didn't seem to want me sleeping with other people any more than I did.

"What I have to show you is dangerous," Vehyn said. "Very dangerous. I want you to be prepared."

I felt something materialize between our hands, and I pulled away to look at it. It was my mother's knife, which he had taken from me in the sleeping realm the first time we'd met. "*That* dangerous?"

"And worse. So I'm also going to give you this." It wasn't an offer, more of a statement of fact. He kept hold of my wrist, moving his own fingers above it, like he was tying a thread. Shadows moved indistinctly between us. When he let go, there was something dark like a ribbon, but transparent and ghostly, that ran from me to him. "This will help you get back to me."

I tried to brush a finger against the ribbon. It passed right through, but the air felt thicker, warmer there. "Am I, what, wandering into a forest to meet a witch? Is this my trail of breadcrumbs?"

Vehyn gave his end a light tug. I felt the pull all the way into my arm, drawing me to him. "Similar. You're going to wander the ways between souls."

20

SHORT ETERNITIES

*B*etween souls.

I froze, my feet rooted to the floor of Vehyn's study. I barely dared to hope. "There are ways for a spirit to enter a soul through the sleeping realm? Without bodies needing to be close in the waking world?"

Vehyn nodded.

"And you *can't* come with me? Or you *won't* come?" I asked.

Vehyn's eyes narrowed a fraction. "What is that human saying about not inspecting the craftsmanship of a gift?"

"Yes, fine, but where do I go?"

"To whomever's soul you want."'

"I need to get to Razim's."

"He's not asleep right now," Vehyn said. Almost too quickly. He was probably right, but he seemed keen to direct me away from Razim. Maybe because he didn't want me to win our game. That was fine—I would find my way back into Razim's soul sooner or later.

I tried to think of someone else who might be asleep at this hour. *Zeniri*. He'd been up all night and was no doubt sleeping through the morning in preparation for another wakeful evening. This would be the perfect way to present "my idea" of how to soulwalk to the Keepers. "I know someone."

"Good. But before I teach you this, Kamai, you must listen to me very carefully: never try this alone. It might be tempting, knowing you, but without me here to pull you back if you're in danger, you could easily lose yourself forever. Not even I would be able to get you back, if enough time passed. And out there, there are fates worse than death. Much worse."

His warning definitely gave me pause. "But how do I stay out of danger?"

"Much like seeking something within a soul, you must imagine what you wish to find. Focus on that soul, keep moving, and whatever you do, don't stray from your goal."

I lifted my mother's knife, gleaming dully in the dim red light. "When does this come in?"

His lips pursed. "Let's hope it doesn't. But, needless to say, strike first, greet whomever you've stabbed after."

My stomach did a little flip. "Who will be out there? Other soulwalkers?"

Vehyn shook his head. "Not likely. This is too dangerous for most mortals to attempt. Many don't even know of the possibility."

I shuddered to think of what else I might encounter. More creatures like Vehyn . . . or worse? "And it's not too dangerous for me? I *am* still human, you know."

"You have me."

"Not quite." I glanced down at the strange ribbon around my wrist. "I hope this is stronger than it looks."

"You know, sometimes I'm not sure why I bother giving you anything." He said the words in an airy, unconcerned tone as he headed across the study for the black door with me in tow. It was closed now, and when he opened it, my usual clearing didn't lay beyond the threshold. Instead, I saw what looked like a jungle of night and shadow. The sky was black with faint stars overhead, and the trees indistinct smears. A path wandered straight from the door into the darkness.

I hesitated on the threshold. This was definitely the strangest, darkest place I'd seen since I'd ventured into the black door. At least in Vehyn's fortress, there was a sense of order. This looked wild, feral.

"Remember what I said," Vehyn murmured. "Hold your goal in mind at all costs. Don't stray. Don't linger. There aren't only souls to be stumbled upon out there, In Between."

In Between. *Nice.* It sounded like the space between walls or deep cracks or stars. A place for getting lost, filled with cobwebs and dried-out husks and darkness. Small, endless pits and eternities. Nowhere you wanted to find yourself. And I was headed right into it. At least now I knew for sure that marriage or the pleasure arts weren't for me, since I preferred *this* to either of them.

There was nothing else for it. I took a step outside of the black door—wherever this outside place, In Between, may have existed. I glanced back at Vehyn. The study, with only its subtle red light, struck me as much brighter and warmer than it had a second before. It was familiar territory, at least.

"Focus," he reminded me, and so I turned back to the towering, blurry forest. It looked sort of like the distant trees surrounding my clearing, which I could never manage to reach, except now I was *among* them.

"Okay, focus," I muttered. I had never seen Zeniri's soul before, but I didn't think that mattered. I just had to know where I wanted to go, like I'd wanted the truth with Jidras. I hadn't known the specifics of the *particular* truth I'd find; the urge alone had been enough to bring it to the surface in his nehym. In this case, I hoped my will would be enough to bring *me* to Zeniri.

Zeniri, I want to find Zeniri's soul. I held the thought in my mind, repeated it over and over as I readied the pocketknife in my hand. Without warning, the path in front of me shifted slightly, and the surrounding foliage billowed around it like a black curtain in a breeze, flowing into a new shape.

"That's it," Vehyn murmured behind me. "Keep focusing and go. I'll be here, waiting."

Not *watching*, because I would quickly be out of sight of him and the black door. But the shadowy ribbon spooled out behind me as I moved down the path. As nigh invisible and creepy as the link between the two of us was, I was grateful to have it as the trees loomed up around me like a crowd of tall, dark-cloaked strangers, closing me off.

Trail of breadcrumbs, indeed.

Before long, I was utterly alone. The darkness around me was absolutely silent, the only light from the stars above. At least there were stars. Occasionally, I caught a flickering glow between the trees, like candlelight—maybe the door to a nehym—but the trunks would swallow it as soon as I blinked.

Focus on your goal. Don't look at anything else.

But that was difficult, especially when I began to see something wriggling on the path before me. If only it had been a snake, or a river of ants, or a clump of drifting spiderweb, I would have at least known what to do with it. But no, this was more shapeless than that, darker. Whatever it was wavered in a tendril of black mist, right across the path. It looked almost like an octopus tentacle, but made of ink in water.

Focus on Zeniri, I thought as I hopped over it. I could have sworn I'd stepped high enough, and yet the tendril rippled, wavelike, up into my foot. I passed right through it, but I still felt it. It was cold. Ice-cold, leeching the warmth from my entire leg. I gasped, stumbling, and nearly fell.

When I turned back to look at it, another few tentacles had joined the first. They were curling out of the trees, drifting toward me like smoke.

Focus . . .

But fear instantly replaced any focus as the shadow tentacles coiled, then came slithering over the path for me, as fast as snakes. Freezing, I tried to decide what to do, until they all came flying right for my face, deciding for me. I slashed out with my knife and leapt off the path.

Now there was absolute darkness, not only silence. I spun and blinked, trying to get my eyes to adjust, but couldn't see anything. The path was nowhere to be found. And then I felt the cold. Soft whispers of it over my arms, like freezing caresses. Tickling over my cheeks, like chilly fingers.

As my warmth fled, I forgot everything. The icy, invisible fingers beckoned me, and I couldn't think of a reason not to follow. Something tugged sharply on my wrist, but since I was mostly numb, I ignored it.

It didn't take long for me to step out into a clearing, a bit like my clearing. *Wait.* Where was my clearing, again? Wasn't this it? There was a dark ring of trees surrounding an even darker . . . mansion. Stacked with scraggly towers like crooked, blackened teeth, it was darker than the darkest night. There were windows, hundreds, but every single one was empty, sightless. And there was movement. Spreading out through the open doorway, crawling down the steps, squirming across the grass and reaching for me, were black tentacles, made of shadow and cold. Several were already twined around my arms, my legs, my neck.

For a second, it looked wrong, but only because no nehym I'd ever seen from the outside had walls, only a freestanding doorway in my clearing. There were walls on the inside, of course, dividing up each soul according to its particular geography, but the physical body was the *true* vessel containing the soul, unseen on the outside in the sleeping realm. Which meant this house might not belong to a physical body, and I knew that thought should have bothered me. But then I forgot it too.

The tug at my wrist grew more insistent. But the tendrils holding me were even more so. They wanted me to follow them, and so I followed, because this was where I belonged. My steps felt both light and heavy, floating and deadened, as I stumbled over the dim ground toward the sprawling front steps. The massive house remained silent all the while. The doorway stood open, dark as an inkwell. When I put my foot on the first step up to it, I went colder than ever, as if my entire body had been thrown into a mountain spring. And then I could see them.

Faces looked out from the door, gathered as if to welcome me inside. Haunted, cheeks sunken. Eye sockets dark and empty, skin pale as dead flesh. Mouths open in silent screams. Their tongues were black.

I blinked. Warmth suddenly flooded into my hand and up my arm, coming from the tight band of heat around my wrist, and with it came the realization that this was beyond wrong. This was not where I belonged. This was a horror.

I screamed. It was like a spell breaking. I lashed out at the tentacles holding me, turned, and ran back across the clearing. I wasn't sure I would make it far on my own, but the tug on my wrist grew so strong that I was winging through the darkness, like in my dream with Vehyn. Except this was no dream, but a waking nightmare, trees whipping by, branches lashing my face. Suddenly, the black door came flying at me faster than if I were sprinting for it.

It was open, and after what I had just seen, it felt like coming home. I still threw up my hands to cushion my impact and crashed right into Vehyn's chest and the red, warm darkness of his embrace. His arms held me tight against him. I gasped and shivered violently.

"Shh," Vehyn said, stroking my hair. "I have you now. It's all right."

I realized my gasps were sobs. "What . . . was that?"

"Only one of many predators out there: a spirit eater, a hollow shell, really. They lure and swallow the unwary, feeding off them for a short eternity. I warned you," he added, but his voice wasn't harsh or chastising. It was calm, soothing.

I still shuddered. *Short eternity.* "You mean, those other . . . things . . . I saw were lost spirits?"

"Yes, getting slowly devoured."

I couldn't help squeezing my eyes closed, trying to banish the memory of those empty eye sockets and black tongues, burrowing my face in his neck, and enjoying the sturdy feel of his arms around me. Whatever he was, he wasn't anything like a spirit eater. Right now he felt warm and alive and solid.

For a split second after I drew closer, nuzzling him, he seemed to hesitate. Then his arms cinched tighter, and he perched his chin on my head. His vexed sigh was familiar, almost fond, and we were so close it stirred my hair, tickling my scalp. "So that didn't go very well," he said. "The spirit eaters seem to have a particular interest in you—even *they* could recognize your superior nature, unlike yourself." I wondered if their *interest* had to do with Vehyn's influence over me—like calling to like—but I didn't say that. "What am I going to do with you now?"

I shook my head against his chest. "Is there any other way? I don't think I'm strong enough to take that path. And I can't . . ." I couldn't help sniffling, my voice breaking again. "I can't get married or become a pleasure artist or—"

"Shh," Vehyn said again. He inhaled deeply, as if breathing me in. "There is another way."

I blinked, jerked my head up to look at him. "One that's safer than that?"

"Yes." His eyes, for a moment, were inkwells.

His arms suddenly felt a little less warm, and I leaned away. "Then why didn't you tell me before?"

He didn't flinch, or look chagrined, or guilty, or much of anything, really. "Because I didn't know the creatures In Between would react so strongly to your presence, and because I would be giving you strength that you might not want . . . and that *I* might not want to give you."

I had no idea what that meant, but the black marks swirling under my skin came to mind. More shadows, tainting my eyes and making me not look quite right in the mirror anymore— while making me more appealing to monsters like spirit eaters. But if it was a way out of marriage, or the pleasure arts, or the tentacled clutches of a spirit eater . . . and especially if it gave me an advantage Vehyn might not want me to have . . . I was following the path of roses once again, to their end.

"What is it?"

"Hold still." He bent his head, lips slightly parted, as if to kiss me.

I froze. But he didn't kiss me. He *breathed* on me, and with it came darkness, curling out from his mouth. For a terrifying second, I was reminded of the spirit eater's tendrils, but this just drifted and twined around my face like smoke. It wasn't even cold, just . . . cool and peaceful.

His lips quirked. "Breathe, Kamai. It won't hurt you."

I inhaled. It even *smelled* cool and peaceful. Like a deep cave, or well water, or even fresh silken sheets. I looked at him in wonder. "Wait, *are* you Moholos, after all? You know, the mythical folk figure who breathes on people to put them to sleep?"

But I certainly wasn't feeling sleepy.

Vehyn laughed—truly, deeply, throwing back his head. He bit his lip to try to contain it, in a way that made my stomach twist strangely, and I remembered his arms were still around me. "Oh, how you amuse me," he said, still trying not to grin. "But the answer is no. Not quite."

"Who are you, then?" Maybe I could catch him off guard in this more relaxed, delighted state, and he would accidentally answer me.

He smiled, an enigmatic curve to his mouth. But now his eyes were sharp above it, almost displeased. "You'll see. First, we practice."

21

PARTING WORDS

By the time I woke up several hours later, Jidras had returned from whatever business he'd been conducting and sent for me. The timing was perfect, since I now knew exactly how I could serve the Keepers and use my skills to the best of my ability. It involved neither marriage nor the pleasure arts, and yet I would be able to leave this place for the Keepers all the same.

I'd expected to be rebelliously triumphant for this occasion, but when I knocked and entered the office, I only felt nervous and oddly regretful. My steps were hesitant over the plush rug that lay before the large wooden desk, behind which Jidras stood, carefully stacking a pile of papers. Rainy gray light filtered through the tall windows, seeming to shadow more than illuminate him.

I could have had a father, someone who'd appeared in my life right after I'd lost my mother and Hallan, to help fill the hole left by their deaths; instead, our relationship had come to this. Jidras made it worse by looking concerned *now*, of all times. But it was too little, too late.

"I heard what happened with that filthy animal Gerresh," he said by way of greeting, his pale eyes finding my bruised throat, "and I'd like to know why no one woke me."

"I didn't think you'd care," I answered honestly, clasping my hands in front of myself, "and so both Nikha and the constable respected my wishes not to disturb you until morning." Mostly, I'd been too tired to deal with him along with everything else.

And maybe I had been afraid that he would be more irritated than actually worried.

"In that case, both of them deserve a reprimand from their superiors. I am the master of this house, and I should be told *immediately* when my child is nearly strangled and a man, once of my employ, dies on my doorstep."

Of course, this wasn't about me and my safety, but his authority over me and the situation. "Nikha only deserves praise," I said, anger clipping my words. "She saved my life." It hadn't quite happened like that, but it was close enough.

"Commendable as that may be, her judgment was still lacking elsewhere."

"Then it's a good thing you won't be her *superior* for much longer."

He arched a cool eyebrow. "Is she resigning from her position as head of my household guard?"

"In a sense." I took a slow, deep breath. "I'm leaving, and Nikha is coming with me."

He blinked at me in surprise. "Have you accepted a proposal already?"

"No." I squared my shoulders. "And I don't intend to."

Jidras's brow immediately furrowed, his gaze sharpening

249

like a dagger. "Then what in Tain's name do you expect to do with yourself?"

"I've taken an apprenticeship under a man named Zeniri Sarvotha."

"Who—?"

"A renowned pleasure artist, currently in residence at court."

His mouth fell open. And then his expression gradually twisted from shock to ugly rage. "Little whore. Just like your mother."

Even though I'd been anticipating the words, they still cut deeply. I didn't bother explaining that I wasn't ever planning on practicing the pleasure arts, or that he was entirely hypocritical. That was all beside the point.

"And you're just as foul as I always suspected you to be," I hissed, "as my mother *knew* you to be! How could you have ever thought someone as good as her would stay with someone like you?"

"Yes, I know. There's nothing to be expected from a whore that one doesn't pay for, and nothing else owed, afterward." His fist crumpled the top sheet of paper in the nearest stack. "If this is your decision, then get out. You are no longer my daughter, and I never wish to set eyes upon you again."

I had imagined it would come to this: disinheritance. But knowing it would happen didn't change the fact that it stung. I wished tears hadn't sprung to my eyes, but they did—only letting him know how much he could hurt me. He looked on, without a speck of pity in his own chilly blue gaze.

I thought I would be angry, but I only stared back at him. With three fingers, I tapped the crown of my head, my brow between my eyes, and finally my lips in a parting benediction. I kissed my fingertips afterward and then held them out toward him, as if to touch his own lips and complete the blessing. But he was too far away, behind his desk, and neither of us made a move to bridge the gap.

Despite that, his eyes widened, and in them I glimpsed a flash of pain. But before he could say anything else—either spiteful or otherwise—I turned and left.

Zeniri announced that he'd taken me on as his apprentice a week later during a soiree held at the palace, after setting Nikha and me up in a suite of extravagant rooms near his own—paid for by the Keepers, no doubt. As far as everyone else knew, he was investing in me and my potential. Since he was one of the most popular courtiers and pleasure artists in residence at court, it created quite the stir.

The salon we were in was as resplendent as everything else in the palace. Ornate brass lamps ignited the swirls of gilt painted on the walls and lit the air with a golden glow, plush red rugs cushioned my slippered feet, and wine and other refreshments circulated the room on gleaming trays. Too much wine, perhaps. Practically before Zeniri had finished making his announcement, he received inquiries, some discreet and others less so, regarding when, exactly, I would be accepting patron gifts for my art.

Ironically, it was because of Jidras that I'd had anything to wear on such an occasion. I'd left his town house without taking anything, but then a trunk full of my dresses, with no note, had shown up in my suite the next day. He obviously had no need for them, but I'd still figured he wouldn't want me to have anything he'd provided for me. I'd been wrong. Perhaps, at least, he didn't want to throw me out without clothes. So it happened that I wore the midnight-blue spider-webbed gown that he'd given me for my eighteenth birthday, a couple of weeks prior. One of my most alluring dresses, to be used like bait.

"Kamai will not be practicing her art anytime soon. She has much to learn first!" Zeniri declared with a taunting twinkle in his eyes, both for me and the inquirers. They had no idea that I never intended to learn. "In the meantime," he continued, after the chorus of theatrical, disappointed sighs and half-joking offers to help me study, "Kamai might amuse you with a game of Gods and Kings. She has quite the talent. I might even declare it as the basis for another game: whoever bests her first wins the honor of bedding her first."

I had to lock my jaw in a smile to keep it from falling open in horrified shock. It was a good thing looks couldn't kill, because Zeniri would have fallen dead in the middle of the salon. And it was an especially good thing that Nikha had opted not to come tonight. She might have punched Zeniri in the face. He had reason to assume I wouldn't lose, based on my own assertions and demonstrations of what Vehyn had taught me, but I could have done without so much pressure.

And perhaps he knew just whom such a game would inspire. Zeniri had made certain that word of my attendance at this gathering had spread to the right ears. And that was why Nikha hadn't come—she would have been too tempted to punch the person in question, first and foremost. They'd already crossed swords, after all.

Nikha was truly a man, one who was only drawn to women, so was this distaste for Razim of a different nature? Was there an element of competition? A hint of jealousy? I didn't have long to ponder.

Right that very moment, spectators demanded a test of my

skills, and so a small table was set up and two chairs arranged. Before anyone could argue over who got to play me first, Razim—rather, the young lord and courtier Ramir Zareen—materialized from the crowd and took a seat, just as I'd known he would. His face and eyes burned with intensity, as if daring me, or anyone, to contest his challenge.

Giddy whispers rose all around. "Ramir" was even more mysterious and desired in court circles than me, sharing only his music and nothing else with patrons. Rumor had it there was a secret love he had been pining over . . . and now everyone in this room likely suspected who it was.

Zeniri appointed himself the judge and set about shuffling and dealing cards. The four suits were as the name of the game suggested: the three Gods and the King's Court. Heshara's card, her midnight hair bleeding into the black sky and her white arms cradling the full moon, was followed by the seven other phases of the moon in her suit. Tain's card, the sun burning like a halo around his dark face, fire in his eyes, led the seven Guardian Constellations he'd sent to protect Heshara. Their daughter Ranta's card, her soft brown arms proffering a bouquet of roses with a map of Eopia behind her, shared her seven bounties, among them Water, the Harvest, and Iron. The King's card was accompanied by seven members of his court, including the Queen Consort, the Heir Apparent, the Priest, and so on, classically depicted to resemble no one in particular.

There were many ways to win, such as simply having a hand with higher-ranking cards than your opponent. But when it came to the Waning Crescent in Heshara's suit versus the Guardian Constellation Ktema in Tain's, or the Courtesan in the King's suit, or Wood in Ranta's, all with the numerical value of two, who took the hand? That was where the game got interesting—and why a judge was crucial. It was a matter of arguing your case, spinning the best story for the judge's ears. Razim had never been as good as me at Gods and Kings, but perhaps he'd been practicing.

The thought of Razim winning the game spurred me to use Vehyn's gift almost immediately. The look in his eyes had matured with the rest of him over the months, now possessing the deep heat of a well-tended bed of coals. His goal, his desire, was obvious. As he bent over the five cards in his hand, ready to match them one by one against mine, my lips parted and I let out a slow, shallow breath, exactly as Vehyn had taught me. No one would have seen the shadow in the air even if they were looking for it, or have seen Razim breathe it in, his dark eyes clouding almost imperceptibly.

Vehyn might not have been Moholos, but he'd made *me* somewhat like the mythical folk figure. After our exchange, an exhale from me could put people to sleep, or, if used delicately, into a light trance they couldn't even remember falling into afterward. They could still function, but a part of their spirit was slumbering, leaving their soul unguarded and exposed. The gift was a powerful one. *Very.* It didn't surprise me that Vehyn had been reluctant to give it to me.

It also gave me the ability to lapse into my own trance that I could snap out of in an instant. My vision blurring, I pretended to focus on my cards. This wasn't like exploring a soul, walking through the halls of a nehym. It was more like peering through a window from outside, with a curtain billowing across it, and glimpsing only small flashes that overlapped with the waking world. But it was all I needed when I knew exactly what I was looking for and how to call it forward.

That didn't mean it was easy. Not only did I have to keep up the pretense that I was playing cards, but even within my trance, my focus was split. Part of me gleaned which cards Razim held in his hands, while the other concentrated on the question: *What happened the night of the fire?*

The answer floated up like words in a book for me to read through the window into Razim's soul:

I returned from the wine house to find the villa aflame. The Twilighters had given me word, but barely, slipping a piece of parchment under my mug of wine.

Don't try to save him, the note said. He's already dead. But she isn't.

I rode home as fast as I could, whipping my favorite horse to a foaming frenzy. Nyaren followed with a wagon, at a slower but still reckless pace.

The horse would have died for me, just like I would have died for my father. But the Twilighters' messenger was right; my father was already dead . . . and my mother, the queen consort, soon to follow him.

But Kamai wasn't. I had to make sure she was safe and take her away from there.

It told me so much . . . and not enough. I searched with another question: *Were the Twilighters responsible?*

It was more of a feeling than a thought. *No.*

"Play your first cards," Zeniri said, snapping me out of my trance. I had to keep from blinking and gasping, as if surfacing from underwater. I was still getting the trick of it, and what I'd discovered from Razim was so surprising I could barely breathe.

Razim had been telling the truth. He didn't think the Twilight Guild was behind our parents' deaths.

There was no way to signal Zeniri. I would just have to tell him later. He knew what I was doing, even if he didn't understand it. Lenara hadn't, either. My ability frightened them, but I hadn't seen any means of disguising it, other than to imply it was a form of hypnotism I'd always had. There were, of course, street performers and miracle workers who claimed such powers, but the clergy had always denied their existence. Now I was living proof of the ability. Only Nikha knew it had come from Vehyn. · Zeniri and Lenara weren't sure what to make of it, but they *were* cautiously pleased to have me use it in the service of the Keepers.

Razim set down the second-highest card in Tain's suit, with a numerical value of seven: Guardian Constellation Pusha. He was hoping to flush out my highest cards. I played my weakest card: one of Ranta's bounties, Wine, with a value of one.

"Cheers," I said, receiving laughter in response. Zeniri held a hand out to Razim, giving him the point.

The next round, at the same time, Razim threw down Ranta, and I, Heshara. Both goddesses. Both with an equal value of eight . . . technically.

"The daughter is always subservient to the mother," I said, and Razim, like usual, struggled to come up with a suitably clever response. He also looked a little off-balance from the strength of my card, and perhaps the fog of Vehyn's gift. Zeniri gave me the point.

Now, knowing I likely couldn't match such a high card, Razim played the King. It was technically of the same rank as the Gods, but that argument never held up with any judge who didn't wish to anger the gods. A lucky hand, he had. Mine would have to be equally lucky. I needed either Tain to match him, or . . .

I played Darkness next. The card, filled with inky black whorls, didn't belong to any suit. It made the number of cards in the deck thirty-three and was considered both lucky and unlucky. It supposedly didn't bode well for one's game, but it neutralized any card that wasn't a God—*including* the King.

Our audience gasped. What I'd done—killing the King—was considered especially daring and, to say the least, impolite.

Razim's lips thinned and Zeniri gave me the point. Now I was ahead, two to one. While the audience whispered about my strategy and Zeniri let them, waiting to regain their attention before continuing, I took the opportunity to lightly exhale in Razim's direction again.

Who killed our parents?

I didn't see words this time, but a flash of the card that still lay on the table:

The King.

What is your plan?

The words floated up like a message in a bottle: *They told me to finish what my father started and gain revenge for his death at the same time. I must assassinate the king.*

It took all my willpower to keep from falling off my chair. *This* was Razim's revenge? If indeed the king had been responsible for our parents' deaths, I wouldn't have minded killing him, either. But the stability of the land depended on his rule, and just because Razim believed the king was to blame, that didn't mean it was true. Even if the king had given the order, someone may have convinced him to do it . . . such as a Twilighter.

On the other hand, Hallan may very well have been trying to kill the king, rather than the queen consort, for the Twilight Guild, which made sense since my mother had been trying to stop him, as a Keeper. But if so, *why*, and how on earth had everything turned out like it had?

I could have cursed Zeniri when his words once again snapped me back to reality. "Next round."

Razim blinked, looking more muddled, and he played what I knew he would. Between the next two rounds, which I handily won with cards of indisputably higher value, I searched his soul as quickly as possible, like tearing through drawers in a dresser.

Why did the queen consort die?

My father's affair with the queen consort was discovered before he could kill the king, and the king ordered their deaths.

Who betrayed them to the king?

I don't know.

When are you planning to kill the king?

Not until my birthday. I am forbidden. His frustration was clear. *I'm allowed to do it that day and only that day.*

His birthday was soon after mine. I did a quick calculation. He would be twenty in a week.

That was all I could get out of him before everyone was applauding my victory.

Razim was looking around like he wasn't quite sure what had happened.

Before anyone noticed his mild disorientation, I raised my glass to him. "A fair game, sir. I was merely lucky, or perhaps your wine won the game for me." The comment came off as generous, if condescending. More spectators clapped.

Razim glared, his eyes growing sharper now. "A rematch."

I could have agreed and gained more time to search for answers, but I was worried he would face-plant on the table. When I'd practiced on Lenara, Zeniri, and Nikha, eventually they grew tired enough for my gift to put them right to sleep. Maybe I could try getting answers the old way: talking.

"So soon?" I asked, sounding concerned. "While this is a

mere flesh wound, I fear a rematch might cause you to bleed out." More laughter, another glare from Razim. "But I will ease your pain by granting you not my bed, but a few minutes of private conversation out on the balcony." There was a lovely outdoor space, stretching off the salon, with gauzy-curtained doorways and mosaic-studded alcoves to provide privacy. I'd tried my best to sound flirtatious, and it seemed to work.

"Are you going to lick his *particular* wound?" someone asked cheerfully. "Be gentle. It is probably rather swollen."

Gods. Simply pretending I was training in the pleasure arts wasn't enough for me to get a better grip on sexual innuendo. At least this time, my suggestive comment seemed intentional. There were even a few whistles, and someone gave Razim a congratulatory clap on the back. Not that he looked grateful. He knew me well enough to gather we wouldn't be kissing . . . or doing anything else. Rather, he looked careful. Wary.

Maybe I wouldn't be getting many answers. But he still reached for my hand, and I took it across the table. He helped me up from my chair and let me lead him out the nearest pair of double doors, closing them firmly behind us. Both of us ignored the laughter and shouts of encouragement that tried to follow.

"Tain's eye," Razim said as soon as we were alone. "I thought I didn't want you to marry one of them, but this might be worse."

I sighed, looking over the stone banister at the dark palace grounds, lit by the hundreds of glowing windows belonging to the surrounding buildings. It was all night, soft rain, and candle-light swimming in the warm, fragrant air. Colorful tiles, flecks of metal, and slivers of mirror glittered on the mosaic-covered walls and columns around us. Razim leaned out next to me.

Instead of arguing with him, I said softly, "You also lost your mother that night. I didn't know her, but I know exactly how it feels." It was the first time I'd spoken much with anyone about *my* mother's death. Now that I knew he hadn't played a part in her murder, the words came much easier, but I still had to swallow a lump in my throat. "As far as Hallan . . . Just so you know, I loved him like a father." *More than the man who is supposedly my father.*

"He loved you too," Razim said, his own throat tight. I could hear the weight of unshed tears.

A hot, painful knot grew in my chest. But one that hurt in a good way too. "Thank you. That means a lot to me. My mother . . ." I hesitated. I wasn't sure what I wanted to say. Maybe that she'd loved Razim? But it wasn't true.

As if he could read my thoughts, he said darkly, "Your mother hated me."

"She didn't *hate* you," I said, turning to him. "Why would you say that?"

Razim stared at his hands, clasped over the railing. "It took me a while to figure it out. She always seemed to resist my father's orders from the guild, to try to talk him out of it. But she was a member of the Twilighters just the same." Fear caught in my lungs as I waited for him to continue. He couldn't know about the Keepers, could he? "I think it was because she was jealous, because she was in love with my father. Both his assignments and I were constant reminders that his heart was with another woman."

I didn't think that had anything to do with it. Jealousy was powerful, but I remembered the look on my mother's face as she admitted to me that she was in love with Hallan. There was only peace in her expression, despite whomever Hallan himself may have loved.

"Sometimes I wonder if she was the one who . . ." He hesitated.

My fingers tightened against the banister. I knew what he was going to say. He thought *she* might have betrayed Hallan and the queen consort to the king, but I knew she would never have done something like that. I knew it as well as I knew anything.

Maybe because of the hard set of my jaw, Razim seemed to remember he was talking less than generously about my dead mother. "Sorry," he said. "We don't have to discuss this. Tell me about *you*. Where have you been? I've been looking."

"I still find it hard to believe that the Twilighters had no idea."

He glanced at me, his eyebrows flickering a fraction before he smoothed his face, and I didn't need to use my gift to see that he found it odd as well.

"Razim, what are you doing for them?"

"I'll tell you if you tell me what *you're* doing. Because I can't quite figure it out."

"You said you wanted revenge. Maybe I can help, if you tell me how. Because you're right, it's also what I want. I want to find out who killed my mother."

"I know who killed her, because it's the same person who killed *my* mother and father."

He thought it was the king, of course, but there was more to their deaths than the punishment of a discovered affair. There simply had to be, with both the Twilighters and the Keepers involved. Gods, and he wanted to try to kill the king on his birthday? In a *week*?

I understood his desire for revenge, but beyond that I wanted to ask him why he—or rather, the Twilight Guild—was so bent on doing such a thing. Whatever the king's role in this

261

whole affair, he was one of the best rulers in recent history, helping Eopia thrive with his trade deals. And he had no heir, so at the very least his death would plunge the nation into a struggle for succession that could set us back years; at worst, it could perhaps risk the bond with Ranta. But if I betrayed that I knew Razim's intention, that would raise too many questions about *how* I had discovered it, which could lead back to the Keepers and soulwalking. I couldn't risk it.

"Razim, just . . . can you promise me you won't do anything rash? I don't think you have all the answers."

He squinted at me. "Why don't you share some with me, then?"

"I still think the Twilight Guild is behind all of this."

Razim groaned and put his face in his hands. "Would that I could convince you otherwise."

"Then why don't you share your answers with *me*?" I asked, and he couldn't help but laugh.

"Both wanting the same thing, but unable to trust each other." His hands fell away as he looked at me. Something else burned in his eyes now. Candlelight and raindrops gleamed in his dark hair—he was tall enough and leaning far enough out that they'd sprinkled his head and shoulders. He didn't seem to notice, and for some reason, the sight was endearing. Or maybe it was only that my perspective of him was changing. "Kamai, I want you . . . I mean, I want us to trust each other with everything," he amended quickly.

"You could start by telling me everything."

"I *can't*."

"Well then." I smiled. "For the rest, you'd better beat me at Gods and Kings."

I left him standing there alone, staring after me.

22

DARKEST KNOWLEDGE

Nikha and I met with Zeniri and Lenara later. We all gathered in his purple-and-orange sitting room, hunched around the coffee table, whispering by candlelight even though the walls were thick. These were words not to be spoken too loudly, anywhere. I told them of Razim's plan to kill the king—Hallan's original plan, supposedly.

Lenara snorted. "If it was Hallan's intention, he certainly wasn't acting fast. He had ample opportunity during the twenty years he spent with the queen consort. Perhaps he was trying to convince *her* to kill the king for the Twilighters, but he wasn't able to?"

However long it might have taken, Razim now had a week to complete what he thought was Hallan's end goal.

"What would happen if Razim succeeded in assassinating the king?" I asked. "I don't mean politically—"

"Which would be a catastrophe," Zeniri interjected.

"—but to the king's sacred bond with Ranta?"

Both Zeniri and Nikha looked to Lenara, who pursed her lips. This was definitely a question for a priestess, and yet we hadn't talked much about the king's bond, even within this private, secretive group. I got the sense that it was so sacred, so important, that all information about it was carefully guarded among the clergy and maybe even the Keepers.

"If the king dies without an heir, the bond will remain intact," Lenara answered finally, "simply unfulfilled, until an heir is chosen and given the proper rituals and blessings. It won't break. But such a situation is still tenuous and best avoided."

I couldn't help but ask, "What would make it break, and what would happen if it does?"

She held my eyes levelly. "Badness, in answer to both. An extreme violation of the vow would break it, the specifics of which I would rather not go into. That knowledge is kept as secret as possible in case anyone were to get any ideas. As far as what would happen . . . the earth would be unprotected. Without the king shielding Ranta with his bond and without her blessing upon the earth, she, and the land, would be vulnerable to attack."

"From where?" Nikha asked, puzzled. "Across the sea?"

"We're talking about a *goddess* here, Nikha, more the spirit of the earth than the earth itself. There are forces out there, threatening ones, that are difficult for us to comprehend. But," Lenara added, before I could question her further, "we don't have to worry about that. Like I said, even if one king were to be assassinated, the bond would remain. It would simply be waiting for another to take it up again, which the Keepers would ensure happened as quickly as possible. And we would not sit idly by and let the Twilight Guild do such a thing without a fight."

"Still, *why* would the Twilighters want to do this?" I asked, scrubbing a hand over my face. "Without the king, his lack of an heir would mean instability for the entire nation."

"They likely stand to profit off that instability in some way. Perhaps they are working in the well-paid service of someone who has their sights set on the throne. This is no doubt a plan years in the making." Her eyes fell on me again. "I know you don't much care for the king, but we must prevent his assassination at any cost."

"I'll try to talk Razim out of it," I said, "however I can."

"And if you fail?"

I swallowed. "What would you have me do?"

For a moment, Lenara looked hard and cold, and I knew what she was thinking. Then she sighed and rubbed her temples. "If you can't talk him out of it, then it would be best for you to fully enter his soul and try to change his intention there."

"You mean *literally* change it for him?" Nikha asked, aghast. She looked back and forth between me and Lenara.

"That's what I mean," Lenara said.

"Isn't that, I don't know, punishable by death?" Nikha asked.

Lenara smiled, but it didn't reach her eyes. "You're talking to a priestess. I give Kamai my permission. Besides, this is a special circumstance, for a higher purpose—in service of the Keepers, and both Heshara and Ranta. Not to mention the realm."

Again, I had to know. "And what if . . . what if that doesn't work?"

"Then, my dear," Zeniri said, for once without a speck of humor or sarcasm in his tone, as he clasped his hands in front of himself, "we might just need to kill him."

A short while ago, I wouldn't have minded killing Razim

myself. Now my lips went numb. All I could think to say was "Some birthday present that would be."

———

Nikha and I were silent as we returned to our nearby suite later that night. The rooms themselves were a little bright for our mood and my taste, if not quite as garish and lavish as Zeniri's. The furniture and curtains were gaily striped yellow and light gray, with gold and silver lamps lighting the air. But at least we had somewhere comfortable to live, and I'd already asked for a few accent pieces in black to be mixed in. It would add some much-needed gravity to all the levity, so the place would no longer be at risk of floating away.

Or maybe I was growing so accustomed to the darkness behind the black door that a room *without* black seemed strange.

Nikha paused at the door to her small bedchamber, which was meant for a manservant or a lady's maid but which she'd insisted worked equally well for a bodyguard. "Do you think you could do it, if they ask it of you?" *Kill Razim*, she meant.

I sighed, in the process of removing one of my earrings. My eyes looked even darker than before in the vanity mirror, and that, plus the earring's needlessly complex clasp, was filling me with hopeless frustration. Was I following this path, this trail of roses, to its end, or was I being driven toward a cliff, an inevitable fall? I flapped my hand uselessly and ended up tossing the earring halfway across the room. "I'm not sure." I laughed, desperation audible in my voice. "I'm not even sure I know *how*."

The admission brought out a weary half smile in Nikha. "There's always poison, but as for other methods . . . I'll show you. Tomorrow, we'll start practicing death blows with the dagger I gave you." She started for her room again, then stopped. "And Kamai?"

"Yes?"

"If you find you can't do it, for whatever reason . . . I'm here for you, as always."

She wasn't leaving me alone, not even in this—the possibility of committing murder. It was in defense of a goddess and the realm, but that didn't make the burden easier to bear. And here was Nikha, offering to carry it for me. She was so loyal, so kind, so . . . gallant.

The thought made me smile, despite everything. "Nikha, you're the best friend one could ever hope for." My voice threatened to break. "But you've fought Razim once for me already. This is my responsibility."

She shook her head. "Perhaps it should be mine. If I accept Lenara's offer, allow her to declare me soul-crossed, and take up a position in the royal guard, it would be *my* duty to defend the king from Razim—with *my* blade."

"There's not enough time for that now, and you weren't ready." I took a deep breath. "But I am. And I'll do everything in my power to keep it from coming to that."

I didn't even try to enter the black door. As soon as I fell into an exhausted sleep, I was standing before it. I figured Vehyn wished to talk to me, to hear how the evening had gone. To see, first-hand, what the power he'd given me had wrought.

Maybe it was the thought of killing Razim, or the fact that I was learning dark secrets and skills faster than I could have imagined that gave me a sense of wild recklessness, but my tongue was loose with Vehyn when I saw him. "I think I'm going to win our little game," I said, marching right past him and into the long dining room I'd seen before, with its stretching black table and gaping windows that showed only darkness.

"Do you, now?" Vehyn asked, as unconcerned and beautiful as usual. "Need I remind you—"

I spun and leaned against the back of a chair. "Yes, yes, you're not human and you're far more powerful than I. As in, you don't have a body and you live in a vast fortress that doesn't really exist. Some power."

"Oh, it exists. This place is a bridge," he said, gesturing around himself, "connecting your world to mine. A doorway, if you will."

Like the black door. It was strange, eerie, to think of the fortress as a door in and of itself—an opening to somewhere *else*. It was the first time he'd talked about it like that.

I gestured at the windows, still feeling reckless. "So is that it? That's your world? A bunch of nothing?"

"What do you know about darkness, Kamai?"

"Do you mean the dark of night or *the* Darkness?" I asked, my voice still flippant, but something uncomfortable, something disconcerting, was beginning to scratch at the edges of my consciousness. "That great cosmic evil that the gods fought?"

"Yes, that. Tell me about it."

I made myself smile. I'd heard it as a child, over and over, from my mother, but it was a story that was taken very seriously by Marin and the clergy alike. "Ages ago, beyond human comprehension, the gods, Tain and Heshara, sun and moon, fought back the Darkness that had covered everything before time itself. Once they carved out a safe place, they had a child, Ranta, and circled her to keep the Darkness back. Its assault was unrelenting, because the cerebral spirit of Tain and the deep soul of Heshara had combined in Ranta to create a beautiful body that the Darkness desired above all else. Heshara still fights, her strength waxing and waning, while Tain looks over Ranta with his ever-watchful eye. To help Heshara when he couldn't be there, Tain sent his starry guardians to protect her, and so, behind those constellations and the glow of the sun and moon, the Darkness waits, held at bay."

Vehyn nodded. "Nicely told. But you've got it a touch wrong, even within your own limited knowledge." I rolled my eyes at his condescension. "Tain and Heshara never exactly won, nor is it an equally matched battle in the sky between Darkness and the gods' light . . . only the illusion of one."

"What do you mean?" I asked, feeling nervous.

"The light of your world is like a candle in a small room." Vehyn cupped his hands as if around a weak, sputtering flame. "You're able to see so well only for being so close to the candle, in a tiny enough space for its light to fill. But in actuality, Darkness is *everywhere* else, *everything* else, pressing in"—he gestured at the windows, the thick inky blackness beyond—"ready to enter . . . especially now that the door to that room is open."

The door . . . I hoped he didn't mean . . .

I didn't let myself finish the thought. I couldn't. "You sound like it *wants* to come in. Like it's a living thing." I repressed a shiver.

It wants *the door to open.* My mother's words rose to mind once again.

No, I thought. *No, no, no.*

His tone grew hungry. "Oh, it does." He took a breath. "*I* do." His eyes were even hungrier, less of the young man in his face than ever before, and I understood.

"You . . ." I had to swallow to wet my dry throat. "You're saying that . . . ?"

"Yes, Kamai."

For a long moment, I just stood there, while my heart

pounded in my ears with the raging roar of a flooding river. I couldn't even focus on Vehyn or anything but the feeling of my feet against the smooth, black floor. I just had to keep my balance, hold on, or else I would be swept away. Lost.

Hold on, Kamai. Hold on.

My choked voice, when it eventually came, hardly sounded like mine. "*You're* Darkness." The words formed only half a question. Deep down, in the darkness of *my* being, I knew the truth. I just hadn't wanted to admit it. Admit that I'd done something so terrible as open a door for it to the world.

"More of a small manifestation," Vehyn clarified. He sounded as if he were talking about a position he held at court, not the stuff of nightmares. "In your bright world, I am like a shadow, but one that belongs to something much greater, deeper . . . bottomless." The yawning darkness beyond the windows . . . the endlessly plummeting spiral staircase . . . the black pits of Vehyn's eyes as I met them. "I am merely one night of night unending."

It was hard for me to breathe. "Where did you come from?"

His features smoothed, his voice leveled. "From nowhere you could possibly understand." He didn't even sound condescending or arrogant for once.

"What do you want?" I had to work some moisture into my mouth to ask.

"To win our game."

He wanted me to fail to discover what he was plotting until it was too late, so I couldn't stop him. "To what end?"

He only smiled, but feeling seemed to drain from my body all at once, leaving me numb, as if a spirit eater held me in its clutches. It was worse, him telling me something so horrible, and then nothing now. *I often withhold the truth from you, but I rarely speak falsehoods.* The tingles spread down my throat, frosting over my heart. I hadn't known it was possible to be so afraid.

Because he wasn't lying. And what he was keeping from me must have been even worse than this.

"So you're Darkness Incarnate?" My voice came out small, terrified. A whisper.

"Are you happy now, to know the truth? At the very least, you might appreciate what you're up against."

There were only two reasons he would be telling me this now. Either he thought I was doing too well in our game and he wanted to scare me, throw me off-balance, make me think I had no chance of winning . . . or else he truly believed I had no chance of winning.

His hand reached out. Suddenly, he was cupping my face, his thumb caressing my cheekbone, then my bottom lip. He pulled my lip down, parting my mouth, eliciting the little gasp of shock—that mixture of thrill and resistance—that was waiting for him.

Even now, even frozen, blood rose to my cheeks, and I hated myself for it. It was that sudden burst of self-loathing that gave me the strength for what I knew I had to do. I jerked away from him, nearly knocking over a chair as I did, and I fled the room.

I still didn't know what Vehyn was planning, but knowing he had a plan and knowing what he was, there was no question that this was no longer about me or my safety. This was far, far worse—a threat to Ranta, to the entire world.

I'd opened the door to Darkness. It wasn't fair that the door had been placed at my fingertips and no one had told me what was behind it. But I'd done it.

And now I had to undo it. Even if that meant undoing myself.

23

NECESSARY SACRIFICES

I threw myself awake. Dawn was beginning to creep up behind the yellow-and-gray-striped curtains, but we'd stayed up so late the night before, with the soiree and our meeting afterward, that I had only slept for an hour or two.

Tiredness didn't touch me. I could rest when I was dead. And, with any luck, death would come soon. There was nothing else for it. If I was somehow the door to Darkness, I had to close it. I had to cut *myself* off from the waking world, if I couldn't shut out Vehyn.

My mother had always told me that spirits, when untethered from their bodies, would find their way into one of the three gods' presences—or to one of the three hells, but I wanted to think less about that. I always imagined she'd followed Heshara's cool, soothing light into her embrace. I wasn't sure if I could do the same. Those people in the spirit eater's clutches had evidently failed. And, with Vehyn's darkness already weighing me so heavily, would Heshara welcome me into her arms even if I could find her, or would she turn me away?

Whatever might happen, so be it. I had sealed my fate when I'd opened the door.

My mother's knife and Nikha's dagger were both on the bedside table. I chose Nikha's in the end, out of practicality's sake. It was bigger, more recently sharpened. I snatched it up, feeling a wave of resolve, terror, and nausea. The trail of roses did indeed lead to a cliff, but at least I didn't have to drag everyone else down with me.

But I couldn't let Nikha find me . . . afterward. That would be the cruelest possible way to repay her for being my friend. Especially using her dagger. Gods, and this was after she had said she would teach me death blows. The timing was grotesque, but I couldn't do anything about that.

I tugged on a robe over my nightgown and slid into slippers as quietly as possible. I drew aside the curtains, cracked the window in my bedchamber, and looked out. It was no longer raining. Our suite was on the ground level, and the window opened onto a peaceful garden flourishing between several palace wings, interwoven with secluded paths and golden with dew. Wrapping my robe tightly around my waist, I tossed my legs over the sill and lowered myself down into a flower bed. Water immediately soaked through my thin slippers.

Staying on the nearest path for only as long as necessary to reach a silent grove of fruit trees, I ducked and ran, the dagger clutched in my fingers. Once under the cover of trunks and foliage, I stopped, panting, and made sure I was alone. And then I unsheathed the slim, short blade. It glinted in the early-morning light.

Pretend this isn't real. Just do it. You have to.

I touched the sharp point to the inside of my wrist and held my breath. Before I could think twice, I drew it, firmly and quickly, down the path of my veins. Warmth spread through my arm. I gasped.

But instead of blood, blackness blossomed. Spiraling patterns, like miniature bottomless staircases, swirled wherever the blade touched my flesh, refusing to let it break the skin. I tried again with a horrible groan, and again, stabbing viciously at my arm, and then at my heart.

I didn't even get a bruise.

My knees buckled, and I sat down hard on the damp, leaf-covered ground, shaking. The dagger fell from slack fingers. While a part of me was consumed with hopeless desperation, another part of me was giddy with relief.

My relief didn't last long before I tamped it down with a burst of shame. I had to stop this. Stop him. And sacrificing myself to close the door still seemed like the quickest, simplest solution. I couldn't hurt myself, but maybe someone *else* could. Or, at the very least, they could imprison me, and Vehyn as a result, keeping him from affecting the world through me.

I knew one type of person who would gladly help me.

I dragged myself upright, snatched the dagger, and started off through the garden. The white spires and black dome of the temple gleamed in the morning sun through the trees. Even in my sodden slippers, it would be a quick walk across the palace grounds.

Vehyn must have guessed what I was up to. There was the familiar nudge in my head, but I shoved it away. At first, I was almost grateful for it; if he wanted to stop me, it meant I was on the right track. But he was so strong. My eyelids grew heavy, and I stumbled. I forced them back open, kept my legs moving, ignoring waves of dizziness and exhaustion. He tried to seize control of my feet, but I marched right through the attempt.

I had once forced the door closed; maybe I could hold him back. Or maybe he only wanted me to think that. With my thumb, I pressed into my arm again, hard enough to bruise, and saw the black lines curl out from my fingertip, protecting me. His influence over me was still there, hovering just beneath the surface.

And yet, perhaps it was *because* of the power he'd given me that I could now hold him at bay. Hopefully, for long enough to do what I had to do.

Kamai . . . His voice broke into my head, like a gust of wind from an open window, warning in his tone.

I shut out his voice like everything else, slamming the window closed.

Even so, making it up the white and black temple stairs was an act of sheer willpower, with Vehyn fighting me every step of the way. I was moving like someone having a fit by the time I got to the top, gasping and wild-eyed, clutching at my thighs, my head bent. I lifted my gaze enough to find the guards.

One of them, his ceremonial armor blinding with reflected sunlight, looked down at me warily, at the dagger clenched in my fist like a talisman. "Are you all right?"

"I need . . . to see . . . a priest," I panted.

I must have been a sight in my damp and disheveled robe, but even so, he recognized me from my previous visits. "Priestess Lenara?"

"No." I didn't doubt Lenara's commitment to Heshara and the Keepers, but she might not believe me. And if Vehyn regained control of me in her presence, who knew what he might make me do? The thought of my hands hurting Lenara made me sick. "I need to see Priest Agrir. It's a matter of dire urgency."

Jidras had said Agrir was the personal adviser to the king in matters of the soul. If anyone would take this threat seriously, it was him.

The guards heard whatever was in my tone. One of them hurried ahead into the temple, while the other walked me inside to wait in the cool shade of the entrance hall—but not before relieving me of my dagger. It didn't take long for the first guard to reappear and guide me deeper.

The black-and-white-checkered tile passed in a hazy blur beneath my slippers. I couldn't look around, only focus on putting one foot in front of the other. Now it was like Vehyn was pounding on the door in my head. It was hard to think, much less move.

The guard brought me farther into the temple than I had ever been, through the cavernous space underneath the black dome and into another wing, cloaked in heavy shadows. At the very end of the hall, we arrived at a pair of thick double doors covered in intricate scrollwork.

I understood *how* powerful Agrir was when the guard said, "The high priest will see you now."

Agrir was the head of the royal temple. I supposed that made sense, if he was the king's holy adviser. If I'd had the energy to be nervous, I probably would have been. As it was, all I could manage was to hold myself upright as the guard rapped on the doors once and then drew them open.

The room was circular, high-ceilinged, underneath one of the spires that rose at the end of each wing. Silver lamps were spaced at regular intervals around the white walls. A circular black rug, dense and lush, took up most of the white floor, looking like a lunar eclipse. A massive black desk and twin white couches were centered over it. Everything was perfectly polished and gleaming, cool and impressive rather than warm and comfortable.

A man stood before the desk, with a balding head and a long salt-and-pepper beard that dropped starkly from his creased face. He was nearly as pale as Vehyn. His dark eyes were like a bird's—unblinking and utterly focused.

The high priest nodded at the guard. "Leave us."

"But sir, if she's . . . unbalanced . . ." He glanced at me uncertainly.

"There's no need to fear for me. I know her."

I blinked. *He does?*

He smiled slightly. "And besides, I am not yet so old and feeble that I can't hold my own against a young girl."

Little did he know. But the guard bowed his head and backed out of the room, closing the double doors behind him. I turned to the high priest, the words on my tongue, ready to come pouring out, despite Vehyn's resistance.

But Agrir's expression changed as soon as the door closed. His smile fell, and his eyes latched on to mine. "Why have you come? It is risky for you to appear in my presence. We have many eyes in this temple that are not ours."

My mouth fell open, no sound coming out. Lenara had said nearly the same thing to me. Was the high priest a Keeper? I was about to ask when his next words stopped me cold.

"Are you here on our master's business? I'm not sure how much he has shared with you, but let none of Heshara's servants see you here like this. They are not sympathetic to our cause." And then he made a symbol that more than chilled me; my blood turned to ice. He held one hand up, flat as a blade, against his breastbone. It was the signal the Twilighters used to let another member know that you were one of them.

The high priest was a member of the Twilight Guild. And somehow, he thought that I was too, or that I was at least "sympathetic." The only connection between us—aside from my mother, who had never mentioned him—was this "master" we supposedly shared.

"Master?" I said carefully.

His eyes narrowed a fraction. "The dark one who guards the doorway."

I could think of only one person—one *creature*—he could mean.

Vehyn.

"If he's concerned, know that the necessary sacrifices will be made soon," Agrir added, sounding uncertain now. He was looking at me as if trying to read my soul like a book, as I had Razim's. "Does he have a message for me?"

I had no idea what to say. I was gaping at him like an idiot.

So perhaps it was a good thing that my legs chose that moment to give out. The room went black.

———

When I awoke, I was in my own bed in my too-bright suite in the palace, blankets heaped upon me even though I was hot, feverish almost. As soon as my eyes focused, I saw Nikha and Zeniri standing over me in the late-afternoon light, along with a servant, who replaced the damp cloth on my brow with a fresh, cool one.

"Ugh," I said, moistening my tongue. "What happened?"

"We were going to ask you that," Zeniri said, his arms folded.

"You collapsed at the temple," Nikha said, glancing at the servant, who tossed the old cloth into a basin, topped off the glass of water on my bedside table, and left the room. "You must have been going to see Lenara," she clarified when the servant had shut the door. "When she found you, several guards were carrying you down the hall. You don't remember?"

I shook my head. Maybe I should have confessed it all then, but something held my tongue—and it wasn't Vehyn. Not that he would have wanted me to speak.

Horror washed over me. *Vehyn.* He could communicate with people other than me. And he was apparently connected to the Twilight Guild. For how long? My two greatest fears, lurking in the shadows of the sleeping realm and the waking world, had just reached out and joined hands through Agrir. I'd imagined Vehyn to be restricted by the black door, even with it open, but was that true? Could he leave his dark fortress? Would I bump into him, somehow, in the waking world?

And if I did, would I turn and run? Or would I stand and fight? A thrill of anticipation shot through my horror. I knew my answer.

Because Vehyn wasn't only Darkness. It should have been impossible to be anything worse than that, but to me, being connected to the Twilight Guild came close. I needed to confront him. To find out if he was responsible for my mother's death.

In any case, telling the truth right now to Zeniri and Nikha would only cause panic and likely my imprisonment, if Vehyn even allowed me to tell them. I would lose my chance to do anything.

Gods, why did Agrir think that Vehyn was my master too? Did he know I'd opened the door? And how could I tell the Keepers about Agrir? In my muddled state, I couldn't think of an immediate reason for me to know he was a member of the Twilight Guild that wouldn't raise too many questions I couldn't answer. I would have a hard time explaining even to Nikha, who knew about the black door, why I'd been trying to see Agrir in the first place. And for all I knew, the Keepers were already aware of him.

"Lenara made certain all was well with you"—Zeniri's voice dropped—"and that no one else had seen you, and then had you carried back here to get bed rest. Are you sure you don't remember why you went to her?"

I glanced at Nikha. She would understand that my "illness" might have something to do with Vehyn and the black door, but Zeniri wouldn't.

"Sometimes she sleepwalks," Nikha said quickly, covering for me once again. "Especially when she's ill. She would end up out in the courtyard of the town house."

Zeniri's lips pursed. "With a dagger?" He glanced at the bedside table, where Nikha's dagger once again lay.

"I often wake up holding it," I said. "Habit."

Zeniri looked doubtful, but at least he dropped it. "Sleepwalking is a dangerous tendency, especially here. Even *armed*. Anyone could get their hands on you. We'll have to start locking your door from the outside as well as in." I couldn't tell if he was joking. He shot a look at Nikha. "And where were *you*, bodyguard? Isn't this your job? How did you not notice her leaving?"

Maybe because I had sneaked out the window. Nikha obviously hadn't shared that fact with Zeniri.

She flushed. "I was tired. Perhaps I'll sleep in here, on a cot, in case it happens again." She shot me a look herself. She was angry with me. She would be much, much angrier if she knew what I had been about.

Had been? Shouldn't I still be trying to keep Vehyn from the waking world by killing myself? But now that I knew he, Darkness Incarnate, had a connection to the Twilight Guild, which was guiding Razim, who was trying to kill the king out of revenge . . . all this had just become much more complicated and sinister.

Darkness, apparently, wanted the king dead. Razim thought he was avenging his father for the Twilighters, but he was actually obeying the will of the cosmic force that had long sought to destroy the gods and seize our world. I still didn't know quite how he was serving Darkness's purpose, since the sacred bond protecting Ranta would remain intact even if the king died, but even so, all this was so *big* that suddenly I was unsure ending my life would be enough to stop it.

Or that I *could* end my life without Vehyn's assistance. Which I somehow doubted he would give me.

I realized I had a few things I wanted to say to him. As horrifying as his connection to the Twilight Guild was, this new understanding of him somehow made him easier to face. It was an evil, a darkness, I could comprehend.

And maybe attack. At least I knew where to start, in an otherwise complicated, overwhelming, and deeply frightening situation.

"I'm sorry," I said to Nikha and Zeniri, who were still standing expectantly at my bedside while my thoughts galloped far and away. "I won't do it again, if I can help it." That much was true, even if I wasn't referring to sleepwalking. I pulled the covers up to my chin and rolled over. "But right now, I need to sleep."

24

SMALL VICTORIES

Of course, because I actually wanted to see Vehyn, he wasn't standing in the doorway when I popped up in my clearing. He was going to make me look for him.

The black door didn't appear any different as I faced it in the strange half-light. But knowing what it was now—not just a doorway to a dark, strange fortress and a dark, strange being, but a gateway to *the* primordial Darkness—it was more intimidating than it ever had been before. Closed, it had intrigued and frightened me as a child. And since then, somehow, I had grown nearly comfortable with it. But not anymore.

I still didn't entirely understand what the door hid, but now it was more *immeasurable*. Bottomless. An abyss that could rise up and swallow the world.

And I had to head into that abyss.

I reached the threshold and saw that the black door opened

up on the same long hallway as when I'd entered it for the first time.

There was a trail of roses leading into the darkness. This time, they struck me as mocking rather than enticing. Perhaps they should have seemed that way to begin with.

I stepped into the hallway, my footsteps loud in the heavy silence. The door didn't slam behind me. It didn't have to. It knew there was no escape for me. I walked the trail, the lamp-like, floating globes overhead casting no friendly patterns, only enough light to see by. Everything else was cloaked in inky blackness.

Following the roses, I soon came to the great entry hall. Cascading staircases along the length of it arched up to gaping hallways that stared like empty eye sockets. Vehyn and I had explored some of these, but not all—*all* probably would have been impossible. And never the grand spiral staircase that both rose and dropped endlessly through the center of the vast space.

I jumped when I realized Vehyn stood between me and the spiral staircase, in the center of the most wide-open part of the immense hall. He should have been obvious, but he was as dark and unmoving as everything else, his back to me, only his black hair and robe visible, a rose at his feet.

For a split second, I was wildly afraid he would whip around and his beautiful features would be gone, replaced by a skull or simply nothing, a bottomless pit where eyes, nose, and mouth should have been—the true face of the void. But when he turned, it was him. Vehyn.

He was still everything else infuriating and frightening that being Vehyn entailed, but I couldn't help the flare of relief that he hadn't turned into something unfamiliar and horrific.

"How long have you been communicating with people outside?" I demanded.

"Hello to you too, Kamai," he said with a slight smile, almost like he was genuinely happy to see me. Something in my chest twisted painfully. Maybe I was still a hopeful, naive idiot. "Are you jealous?"

"How long?" I repeated. "And *how*, for that matter?"

"Maybe I'll tell you if you're polite. So far, you haven't even said hello."

I made my voice steel. "You're behind the Twilight Guild, aren't you?"

He didn't seem bothered by the accusation in the slightest. "It's more that they *think* I'm behind them, those among them who even know what purpose they're truly serving. Most don't. They're a relatively ignorant, ineffectual bunch when it comes right down to it."

"Are you or aren't you their 'master'?"

He knew where this was headed. "I didn't kill your mother, Kamai, or give the order to do so. In fact . . ." He paused and then didn't say whatever he'd been about to.

"Then *who did*?" My voice rose to a shout, echoing in the cavernous blackness.

"Probably best for you not to know at the moment, because you'd likely do something rash and stupid to endanger yourself, as you already have. You're not allowed to kill or otherwise incapacitate yourself, by the way."

I ignored that. "Did someone in the Twilight Guild give the order to have Marin and Hallan killed?"

He didn't respond, only bent to pick up the rose at his feet. I assumed that meant yes. His feet were bare, pale against the black floor. They always had been, but now the detail seemed out of place. Specific. Alive. *Vehyn has bare feet. Does that mean Darkness has bare feet too, or just him? Are they one and the same? What about his sharp black eyes, that twisty smile?*

I shook my head, bringing my attention back to the matter at hand. "Why guide me to Lenara, when Jidras first brought me to the temple to be tested? It doesn't make sense, not if you're"—I hesitated over the word and then forced myself to say it—"*Darkness*. Not if you're behind the Twilight Guild. You led me straight to her."

He didn't seem to see the conflict, twisting the rose stem in his fingers as he strolled closer until he stood before me, forcing me to look up to meet his eyes. "You asked for help. There were other ways for me to handle the situation, but then you would either be dead or you would have had to marry, and there would be no time for our game."

He only wanted me alive and unbound by a torturous marriage for the sake of his game. I wanted to spit in his eye.

"But why clue in the Keepers?" I asked. "You're *Darkness*, and they are sworn to protect the earth from you. Why not guide me to the Twilighters and Agrir, have them train me?"

He gestured with the rose, as if waving away something minor. "If you won't have the Twilight Guild, it won't have you, and you're too stubborn to ever join. Agrir doesn't know that you're a soulwalker, only that I've claimed you. You'd be a threat to them if they knew the full truth about your abilities, even with my favor, because they can't control you. You need somewhere to be free." He reached out with the rose and brushed my cheek with the fragrant, silky petals. "Beholden only to me."

I batted it away. "I'm doing the Keepers' bidding now, not yours. And our business is *contrary* to yours."

"Is it?" he murmured, the corner of his mouth curving up.

"Of course it is. They want to stop this—you and the Twilighters, whatever it is you're doing."

"But do *you*?"

I didn't dignify that with an answer. "This still doesn't make sense. You've helped me from the beginning. You woke me in the wagon, when Razim and what's-his-name, Nyaren, from the Twilight Guild, abducted me after my mother's death. Why, if Razim is just your tool? He already had me, and if I hadn't come awake at that moment, I might never have escaped."

"And you might have fought so hard the Twilighters decided to put an end to your whining."

That sounded more like him. I snatched the rose out of his hand and hurled it as far as I could. It vanished into the inky shadows. "It seems to me like you have some sort of, I don't know, *immense* influence over them. Agrir called you *master*! Couldn't you have just dropped the hint that you didn't want me killed?"

Vehyn folded his arms, now that he no longer had the rose to play with. "You hadn't opened the door yet, so I couldn't be clear with my intentions. Once you did, giving me access to the rest of the sleeping realm, I could speak directly to Agrir in his dreams. Before that, they wouldn't have killed you, but they may have locked you in a cell for a few years to keep you out of their way. They might still, if you give them no choice, even now that my will is clear." He paused, frowning as if he didn't like what he was admitting. "And also . . ."

Knowing he could communicate in dreams was bad, very bad, but at least I wasn't going to bump into him in the palace hallway. He *did* seem to be contained to the sleeping realm. Not that he couldn't do plenty of damage from here.

"Also?" I prodded.

"He said you were his." I didn't need to guess whom he meant. *Razim*. "And they might have let him have you, back then, when I could only communicate through vague intuitions. But you aren't his. You're mine."

I couldn't help the disbelieving laugh that burbled out of me. "You're insane." Here he was, Darkness Incarnate, a being of incredible power, bound by neither body nor the limitations of a human mind, standing at the center of a place like *this*, and he was bothering to compete with a mortal man. He was willing to go to such great lengths to keep me away from Razim that he had guided me to the Keepers, his opposition. He had given me dark powers to keep me out of the hands of others. We were definitely playing a game . . . and maybe I *was* holding my own, making him take risks with his own cards.

Maybe I could do this. Maybe I could still win, somehow, discover what he was planning and force him to stop. I tried not to let the hope that flared in my chest shine in my face.

Vehyn scoffed. "Insane? Your little mundane terms don't apply to me."

I squinted at him. "More and more, I think they do. You're not only insane, you're jealous. So is *this* your grand purpose? Open a doorway to earth to engage in a pissing contest?"

"Perhaps I *am* getting a taste for all of this," he said. His dark eyes were hard, almost resentful. Maybe he didn't like caring so much about "mundane" things . . . but he couldn't help it. "It's not inconceivable or even unexpected, since I'm both part of the Darkness and part of *this*"—his own fingers caressed my arm—"flesh."

"My body lies asleep in the waking world," I said, brushing away his hand, "so what you see isn't corporeal. Neither are you."

"Yet." The word made my mouth dry, my hope dim. "I plan

on venturing out someday soon. I'd dearly love to meet you in the flesh. Maybe my taste for it will grow even stronger."

Like whenever he was deliberately trying to scare me, I did my best to ignore him, even though my heart stuttered in fear. "Why not just stay here?" I asked, glancing around hopefully.

"Oh, I love it here," he said, taking in the massive space with a fan of his arm, "but it's much too small. I was thinking of finding a home on a grander scale."

I couldn't picture anything grander than this . . . but I knew what he meant. I made my voice light. I couldn't show fear, or he would sense it and pounce. "Like that room with the candle?"

"I simply adore the delicate way you put things. How you cover the truth in softness to make it less sharp. Rose blossoms over thorns."

"You spoke of 'candles' and 'rooms' first."

"So I did. Maybe I adore the way *I* put things, then. In any case, we both now know what we're talking about, so there's no use pretending."

He wanted to enter the world—*Darkness* to enter the world. The king to die. The land, destabilized. At least, that was as much as I could guess, and that was likely not the whole of it. The thought was enough to petrify me, but I couldn't let it. I needed to be moving, acting. Figuring out how to stop him.

"Did your little priestess tell you about another version of the myth?" Vehyn asked casually. "Why the moon hides her face from the sun and goes dark every month? Because Heshara *prefers* the night. She hasn't gone entirely because Tain, knowing Heshara would never leave without her daughter, bound Ranta to a human king. That's what keeps pulling the moon back, according to this version—the one I prefer. It's just so much more fascinating, with so many more questions, don't you think? Who knows whose child Ranta truly is? Whom the earth belongs to? Perhaps not to Tain or any king, but to Darkness."

"And so you've just been *waiting*," I said quickly, angrily, "however long, for someone to open the door?"

"Waiting for you, in particular," he said.

"Why me?"

"I told you, *you* are the door."

"How? I don't understand."

"As I've already indicated, there are many things you don't understand."

"I would if you would just *tell* me!"

"Ah, but then that would spoil the game." His expression grew more serious. "Why did I not show myself to you when you first opened the door? Why did I leave a trail for you to follow, one of soft, sweet-smelling petals and small thorns?" He reached out and took my hand in his, gently pinching the tip of one of my fingers. Then he walked his own fingers up my arm until they reached my collarbone. They slid down the gentle ridge and paused, hovering, right over my heart. "Why do I draw more blood with those thorns only as time goes on?"

My breath came ragged from a heady mix of fear and dread and maybe even the twisted thrill of him touching me. Some absurd part of me couldn't help but be flattered that a cosmic force, albeit an evil one, was so interested in me. Or maybe he was only pretending . . .

"So I won't be too afraid to keep going," I answered. I hated how faint my voice was. I sounded either terrified, or . . . something else.

His grin returned. "Exactly."

He wanted me to follow him to whatever horrible end. He

didn't want only my spirit, or even my body, to make the journey. He wanted my heart with him, as well.

I ripped out of his grasp, smacking his hand away from my chest, just like Nikha had taught me. "I'm not going to follow you," I said, my voice fierce. "I'm going to avenge my mother, save the king, and stop you. I'm going to *beat* you at your game."

Instead of getting angry at my challenge, he laughed. "However you wish to see it."

"And I'm not going to give you . . . give you . . ." I flushed.

His predatory eyes caught the color in my cheeks. "Hm?" he said, slipping up to me. His hand slid along my burning cheek and into my hair, cupping the back of my head. "What won't you give me?"

My heart. "What you want from me," I said instead.

His fingers made slow tiny circles at the nape of my neck. "And what do I want? Tell me."

I swallowed, and he didn't miss the motion of my lips. "I hate you," I whispered.

His smile widened, his eyes still focused on my mouth. "As I said, whatever lies you wish to tell yourself."

I tried not to look at *his* mouth and failed. "I didn't like kissing you, remember?"

Didn't I?

"Didn't you?" Vehyn echoed. He bent his head until his lips were hovering over my own, his breath warm and soft on my face, his dark eyes filling my vision. "I think you're lying again."

"Maybe," I whispered, closing my eyes, unable to resist leaning into him. And with that motion, both he and I knew I'd given him permission. "But not about hating yo—"

He stopped my mouth with his own, his lips parting mine. Before I knew what was happening, both of my arms wound around his back, my fingers dug into his shoulders. As he felt me respond, his kiss deepened, both of his hands threading through my hair to hold me tighter, trapping my face so I couldn't turn or run. Not that I tried to do either.

All I could feel were his lips, his tongue in my mouth. Everything else in my head hummed and buzzed and flew away, leaving me empty. I would have staggered had his hands not been holding me up.

Perhaps I didn't entirely mind kissing. I still had no desire whatsoever to take my clothes off, but it definitely made me reassess my position on the romantic branch of my soul chart, if only with regard to Vehyn. The crescent might now be more like a quarter moon—a widening grin, teeth bared.

When Vehyn finally pulled away, I clung to him, gasping for breath. He tucked my hair behind my ear with a trailing finger and lifted my chin in his other hand, ducking his head to meet my eyes almost playfully. "You were saying? You hate . . . ?"

This is just a game to him, I thought, trying to get my breathing under control. *It isn't real. It's a game to me too. A game, a game.*

So play it. And don't lose. You can't.

If he thought he held my heart in his hand, then, instead, I would have to steal his. He wanted me, so I would give myself to him, to the extent that I could. But I would take from *him* at the same time. Somehow, I needed to own him, whether he knew it or not . . . just as he, however I denied it, maybe owned me.

If his darkness was tainting me, my humanity seemed to be rubbing off on him. He would have more than a taste for it before I was through with him. He would be addicted to it. He would *need* it.

It might be the only way to stop him, whatever he was truly doing.

I steadied myself and took a step back. My hands slipped from his arms . . . only to reach up to his face. I leaned in for another kiss. It would have been worth it for the look on his face alone. His eyes widened with more surprise than I'd yet seen. Had he *ever* been truly surprised?

In any case, he was now. A small victory, but I would take it.

I didn't know how to kiss, but I didn't let that stop me. I pulled his head down to mine, crushing my lips against his. My ferocity took him off guard. He was used to being the predator, and when he found himself in the opposite position, he didn't seem to know what to do. That gave me even more confidence, and I bit his bottom lip, hard, simply because I felt like it, but not enough to break the skin. His fingers flexed into my lower back and a groan escaped him, entirely involuntary by the sounds of it, which made hot elation surge through me. Another point for me.

Wondering if he would like it, if I would like it, I traced the sharp lines of his cheekbones with my thumbs—caressing him. The face of Darkness.

Had he ever been caressed before? Not likely, if this was his first time in spirit form, his first time venturing out of the darkness of his own unfathomable existence. For a split second, pity streaked through me.

My touch had its effect. Even more surprising than his groan, his eyes fluttered closed as if he simply couldn't keep them open, when they were almost always open—always watching, observing, planning. He'd only closed them one other time, when we'd . . .

I brought my hands up along his temples, digging my fingers into his hair. I didn't even know *how* I did it. But I closed my own eyes, and the fortress fell away.

We were elsewhere. Together. Unfettered. Unleashed.

We were flying again, over the rippling darkness, and this time, I took him in my arms first, and we were soaring, my body made of night and wind and freedom. I didn't let fear touch me. Only excitement, and my willingness to experience it all, with him. His eagerness rose to meet mine.

No. More than eagerness. Elation. *Bliss.* With me, careening and dancing through the night, uncontrollable, Vehyn was *happy.* So was I. For a long, long while, I didn't know where I ended and he began. We painted the dark sky with our shared passion.

Passion? Was that what I was feeling? Was what I felt for Vehyn not only hatred but . . . I couldn't think the word. That dangerous, dangerous word. The word that was like opening a black door all its own. It only led to pain, to death. At least it had for my mother. I had to be stronger than that.

This was only a game.

When I finally opened my eyes again, the lamps in the great entry hall had come alive, throwing whirling shadows like clouds floating all around us. Again, they seemed able to respond to our thoughts—maybe only Vehyn's, since he was the master of this place. But for a while, our dreams had been fully intertwined. And we were pressed against each other, arms around each other's backs, fingers clutching for balance.

For a few moments, Vehyn was as unstable and out of breath as I was. As open and vulnerable. "It . . . could be like that with us always . . . Kamai." His eyes were shut, his words distant, almost drunken. I'd never heard him sound more yearning, not even when he was talking about finally reaching into the waking world.

He might be eternal, unending Darkness, but this was his

first time having anything like a physical body. We weren't quite flesh here, but this was as close as one could get in this realm. As close to human, for him. And I highly doubted he'd done anything like make love before. Neither of us had, and maybe this was the way we knew how.

Was that what we'd done? Lenara said that love wasn't sex, after all. As much as I tried to deny it, I'd only felt this way with one person. One *creature*. Those who tied love to sex, or even love to romance, didn't own the emotion itself. I was fully capable of loving. My love for Nikha already proved that.

It was all just variations on a theme. Sometimes sex didn't involve love at all; it hadn't for my mother. It was fine if it did, and fine if it didn't. Loving only as a friend was fine.

Although the love that might have been growing inside me for Vehyn wasn't a friend's.

I had to wonder if *that* was fine, as I took in Vehyn's soft, unguarded expression—because I knew that something harder, sharper, and more frightening lay beneath it.

My mother had always said you couldn't help loving who you loved, even if that person's soul might be dark. Despite being unable to resist, was I *wrong* to feel the way I felt about Vehyn? To thrill at his touch, his black fortress, his sinister dreams? I didn't think so, as long as I knew when to pull away, as if from a fire before it burned me too badly. The question: Was I a good judge of *when* I had reached that point?

All I could do was trust myself. I might get burned. But I also might find heat in the darkness like I'd never felt before—my own strange sort of passion.

And in embracing it, embracing *him*, I might keep *other* people from getting hurt at the same time.

Love didn't mean this wasn't a game, and neither did danger. We were just playing with cards of a higher value. With more to lose. "Remember the terms of our old game?" I murmured.

"Let me guess," Vehyn said, his eyes opening, the sharp, flinty gleam returning to his gaze, "you'd like to go back on them?"

"No," I said, "I'd like to raise the stakes. I want to swear on it. Before, we only shook on our deal, like humans. Now we're going to wager our spirits."

He was silent for a full moment. "Need I remind you, you'd be making an unbreakable vow, entering into a nonreversible contract." He wasn't taunting me; he was deadly serious.

I'd already committed a crime against the gods by opening the black door, so wagering on my spirit with Vehyn wasn't a big deal, as I saw it. If I lost, it wouldn't matter if I had to forswear Heshara and let her cast me into darkness. Because I already would have done the job for her—thrown myself into that bottomless abyss. To Vehyn.

"I know."

His eyes narrowed. "You're still being self-destructive. If you think promising your spirit to me is another way to destroy yourself, you're wrong. I told you, I take care of what's mine."

"I don't think I'll have to worry about that, because *you'll* be *mine*."

He held my eyes for a long time. It was disorienting, after what we'd just shared, to not know what lurked in their depths. "I don't know that I have anything to wager."

"You have something like a soul," I said, glancing around, "just bigger, and you're here, like this, so you must be some kind of a spirit."

He didn't answer.

"Okay, fine, then I'll just get you, whatever you are. You promise to serve me, forever."

He smiled slightly. "Serve you, hm? You know, I don't know that that would be the most terrible fate."

"Good, get used to the idea."

"Not so fast." His smile grew, sharpened. "But, yes, I swear. Do you?"

"I do. I swear."

Vehyn sealed our vow with one soft, relatively brief kiss on my lips.

I couldn't help but think that, in a twisted sort of way—like everything in my life—I had gotten married after all. Only it was to Darkness. To Vehyn.

And only so I could betray him.

25

ROYAL GAMES

I had done as much as I could, for the moment, to gain the same influence over Vehyn that he had over me, but more would take time—which, unfortunately, I didn't have much of. The Twilight Guild had given Razim permission to kill the king on his twentieth birthday. I didn't know why; perhaps it was some curious rite of passage, but in any case, it was soon. Once I woke up the next morning, it was only five days away.

I needed to talk to Razim himself.

He was the Twilight Guild's tool, and by extension Vehyn's, but he seemed necessary to their plan. Through him, perhaps I could stick a spoke in the wheel of whatever they had in motion. What was more, Razim was human, reachable. And Lenara was right that I already had a strong influence over him. It was time to use it. I had to get close to him, to convince him of his folly.

I still had a hard time imagining what would happen if I failed. Even so, early that morning, I accepted two vials from

Zeniri—Lenara wasn't risking being seen anywhere near me again—one of mohol, in case I needed to force Razim to sleep so I could try to change his mind for him, and, failing *that*, one that looked almost identical, except it would send him into a sleep from which he would never awaken.

But when I visited the various salons and courtiers' parlors throughout the palace over the next few days, he was nowhere to be found. All I managed to do was drop as many vague, roundabout hints as possible to Zeniri, behind the thick walls of his suite, that all was not right with the high priest Agrir; spend dark and wondrous nights with Vehyn, as if something terrible weren't heading toward the waking world like a runaway carriage; and play several dozen rounds of Gods and Kings with a dozen different people, all of whom were trying to win their way into my bed. I thoroughly beat every single one of them. Meanwhile, the most useful secrets I learned in three days were that several of my suitors purporting to be single were already married—big surprise—and that a young lord had killed an elderly lady's small, yappy dog and buried it in one of the palace gardens, simply because it had annoyed him.

No one had told me that spying could be so boring.

After a particular game in one of the palace's larger salons, and as soon as my opponent excused himself from the table, yawning sleepily, I had to resist putting my head in my hands. I had just won, after all; I was supposed to look triumphant.

Someone cleared their throat at my shoulder, and I spun around in my chair, thinking—hoping—to find Razim.

I found myself looking up into the eyes of the king. The man whom I'd long heard spoken of with respect bordering on reverence, whom I'd briefly entertained the thought of killing, and whom I was now trying to save. He was tall and broad shouldered, but his gut strained the red royal sash over his black jacket, and his face sagged. His black hair and bearded jowls were streaked with gray, his bronze skin lined. Still, his warm eyes were handsome and reminded me of someone I couldn't quite place. He had a coterie of attendants and a pair of guards trailing after him.

I'd spotted him only from a distance before now, and I hadn't seen his likeness at all, since there were no portraits or statues of the king in public. It took me a moment to recognize him.

I wondered what he would think of me now, openly defying my father to debut as a pleasure artist. Pleasure artists, especially those who were good enough for the palace, were often held in high regard, but as Jidras and his household had proved, there was still a stigma attached—an association with common pleasure workers. I hated the prejudice either way—the stigma against pleasure artists and the hypocritical disdain for pleasure workers.

"Your Majesty," I said, trying not to squeak, especially as a larger audience than usual began to gather around the table.

"May I?" As the king, he didn't have to ask, but it was incredibly polite that he did. "I have heard some rumor of your skill," he said in a calm, cultured voice, "and of your master's wager."

For a horrifying second, my wager with Vehyn came to mind. But then I realized he meant Zeniri's declaration that I would sleep with whoever could beat me at cards.

And then I was horrified yet again. Did that mean the *king* wished to bed me? But Zeniri had said the king was interested only in men. I tamped down my discomfort hurriedly, excitement rising in its place. I could learn more from the king even than from Razim.

"Of course, Your Majesty! I would be delighted." I smiled in what I hoped was a flirtatious manner—but not *too* suggestive—leaning slightly forward to expose some of my cleavage, more for the audience's benefit than the king's. The dress I wore was a deep red with a scooping neckline that served the purpose well. "I have to warn you, I won't go easy on you just because you're the king. My reputation is at stake."

A few people chuckled.

"I wouldn't worry about your reputation," the king said ambiguously. The chuckling turned to nervous murmurs. So he *was* aware of my split with Jidras, and not too polite to hide it. "I am known to be one of the best players in the kingdom," he added with a slight smile, "so if you lose, no one will fault you."

"Ah, but what if you lose to me? I would hate for others to fault *you*."

Silence fell over the gathered crowd. I'd been bold; I hoped not too bold.

The king's eyebrows rose. "No one mentioned your tongue was as sharp as your skill at Gods and Kings."

"I knew that," a vaguely familiar voice said, coming up behind me. I turned and barely kept from letting out a gasp.

Nyaren. I hadn't seen him since he'd hit me over the head and helped Razim bundle me into a covered wagon. I hadn't known where he was from—only that he was a Twilighter.

He was also, apparently, a companion of the king. He strode right up to our table without hesitation or even a bow. Nyaren and the king were obviously on familiar terms. *Very* familiar terms, I guessed, as I caught the look they exchanged, one of frustration and also fondness. Perhaps only pretended fondness, on Nyaren's part.

Gods. Between him and Agrir, the Twilight Guild had the king cornered without him even knowing.

Nyaren's eyes, when they found me, weren't fond. I didn't accuse him of kidnapping me or being a member of the Twilight Guild, and he didn't reveal that my last name hadn't always been Numa, or that I had been raised in the home of the man who'd had an affair with the queen consort. We both had reason to stay silent.

"Are you sure this is worth your time?" he asked, his gaze sliding back to the king.

"Don't be rude, now," the king said mildly. He set the deck of cards on the edge of the table. "Why don't you be our judge?"

Right, he'll be impartial, I thought sarcastically.

As familiar as the two of them were, Nyaren couldn't object to a direct request from the king. His eyes were like arrows nocked and drawn as he picked up the deck and shuffled.

This wasn't going to end well if it came down to the judge's vote. But I still wasn't going to pass up this chance, even if it meant I'd have to make good on Zeniri's promis . . . Gods no. I wouldn't let it come to that.

Except I might not have much choice, I realized, as I received my cards from Nyaren and peeked at them. In the same breath— literally—I peered through the window into the king's soul and saw what he knew. Neither of us had Gods or the King, but he still had two cards higher than any of mine: Waxing Gibbous in Heshara's suit and Water in Ranta's, both worth seven. If I matched my lowest cards against those, a two and a one, the Courtesan and the New Moon, I had the Heir Apparent in the King's suit, which could beat his Stone in Ranta's, five to four. And then, by chance, all our remaining cards were of equal value. Every three in the deck had ended up in our hands. He had the Goat and the Constellation Uma; I had the Waxing Crescent and the Knight.

A victory for me would entirely come down to Nyaren. He would have to judge in my favor not just once, but *twice*. There was slim chance of that.

The king started with one of his sevens to flush out any Gods I might have. I yawned with appropriate daintiness, seemingly unconcerned that it took my Courtesan—confidence that made the crowd chuckle. It also made the king's subsequent yawn, when he inhaled, less strange. Yawns were contagious, after all. Especially mine.

I had to know, now that I understood my odds, if I needed to suddenly faint, or vomit, or . . . anything . . . to get out of this game. *Do you want to sleep with me?*

No. But it's good for appearances to look interested in women and to make Nyaren jealous . . . and you aren't bad to look at, after all, at least for a few minutes, across a table.

I nearly winced at the bluntness. Searching a soul never allowed for politeness, but I felt badly for the king, so seemingly decorous, as I invaded his private, subconscious thoughts. Now I could get on to other, arguably more important questions. Especially the one that had been burning a hole in my mind and heart, like a leftover ember from the fire at the villa, burrowing deeper and deeper into me as time went on.

Did you order the death of Marin Nuala?

Marin Nuala?

He didn't even know who my mother was. Either that, or he simply didn't *remember* who he'd ordered killed. But I knew two names he might recall better.

Did you order the deaths of Hallan Lizier . . . and the queen consort?

Fury answered me—a surprising amount for a man who appeared so outwardly calm and gentle. *Yes.*

302

So the soldiers who'd burned the villa *had* been the king's. Or . . . could someone else have somehow killed my mother? She and Hallan had died separately, after all. But the king wouldn't know the answer to that if he didn't know Marin's name. Still, I had one more crucial question to ask, but I had to wait until the king was looking less bleary-eyed.

"So I hear you are the object of Lord Ramir Zareen's affections," he said, after my Heir Apparent took his Stone in our second round.

I almost choked. The audience tittered at what must have seemed like my obvious infatuation with "Ramir."

"I hear the same thing," I said, my thoughts racing, "but I have yet to witness it firsthand, other than his attempt to beat me at Gods and Kings. From that, I could as easily argue that I am the object of *your* affections." Now that I knew I wasn't, I felt safe teasing him.

"It is merely curious that both you and the young lord have recently come to my attention—sometimes in the same breath." His voice was carefully neutral, but if I'd had to guess, he didn't sound pleased at this.

Why in the three hells did he care about "Ramir"? Did he know, somehow, whose son Razim was? I would have thought that Nyaren, as a confidant of them both *and* the Twilighters, would have tried, along with the rest of the Twilight Guild, to keep that from the king.

Or else the king might not have any clue who Razim was. "Ramir" was one of the most mysterious and desired courtiers, and, judging by Nyaren, the king's tastes ran young. I shuddered, not because of the difference in age, but because Razim would at one time have been, before the king had killed the queen consort, something like his stepson.

The king threw down a three just as I did, still withholding his other seven. This would be our first test. I had known what to expect, so I said, quickly and confidently, "The Knight slays the Goat."

"The Knight needed the Goat to survive," the king shot back. These were familiar refrains, so far.

"So the Knight eats the dead Goat."

"Ah, but as a Knight, he is a brute and didn't cook the meat enough. It makes him sick." Despite revealing his aristocratic biases, that was more creative than I usually heard. But I saw a way to beat him at his own game—a tactic I was using a lot, lately.

"If the Knight is a brute, then he had his way with the Goat before dinner, so I'd say he still got the upper hand."

Surprisingly, a guffaw burst out of the king, and the audience's raucous laughter followed. Not even Nyaren could keep his lips from twitching. I felt especially proud, mostly because I'd made a dirty joke. Those were usually beyond me. The king gestured my way, signaling that the point belonged to me, which Nyaren couldn't argue. The king could afford to be generous, because he threw down his other seven afterward, taking my New Moon.

I had one more shot before the king grew too sleepy—and even that was pushing it—or before the game ended. I now had two questions I was desperate to ask, and I had to choose which came first.

What is your interest in Ramir Zareen, also known as Razim Lizier?

Blank. Nothing. I blinked in surprise. It wasn't that he didn't know; I simply couldn't see into his soul. The window's curtain was drawn. Tentatively, I pushed against the barrier with my spirit, wondering if I could somehow brush it aside. I nearly gasped out loud. It was like running into a wall, even with how lightly I'd tried. It almost seemed to push *back*.

I'd never encountered anything like that before. But then, *I* had protections my mother had placed on my own soul. It was entirely conceivable that the king had a few less-extreme barriers in place too . . . especially with Agrir as his holy adviser.

I tried for the second question before I lost my chance: *Who told you about Hallan and the queen consort's deceit?*

Agrir. As our royal priest, he saw the truth in the queen consort's soul.

The priest had left this information less carefully protected. But the fact that Agrir had discovered Hallan and the queen consort's deceit not because he was a priest, but because he was a Twilighter, was the true secret. Now my own rage rose. I had stood face-to-face with the man who'd planned Hallan's and perhaps even my mother's murder. If I saw him again . . .

I refocused on the task at hand. *What did their deceit involve? What truth was in the queen consort's soul?* I was pushing it.

Nothing. That blank wall answered me.

But I couldn't ask any more questions. The king yawned, blinking, and looked slightly embarrassed. Nyaren's eyes crinkled in concern, and then suspicion as he glanced at me. Good thing the table held no wine or beverages—it was an oversight, really, that in the excitement of the game we hadn't been offered any—or else he might have suspected I'd used drugs.

"Are you all right, Your Majesty?" he asked.

"Fine, fine. Next round. Let us finish this."

We threw down our second pair of threes. Uma was a female Guardian Constellation who wielded a bow to protect Heshara. Before I could argue Uma's subservience to Heshara,

the obvious move, the king spoke first, cutting me off and setting the terms, so to speak. "Uma shoots the Waxing Crescent
from the sky."

It was an argument of weapons, then. No goddess involved.
"But like a curved blade, it rises again, deflecting the arrow and
striking Uma," I countered.

"But she is made of stars and darkness, so the blade passes
through and Uma swallows it," he rejoined easily.

"And yet, inside, the blade pierces her deeply where it can-
not be avoided—her soul. For the Waxing Crescent signifies the
female—Uma's preference. She falls in love with the Crescent
and refuses to fight."

The king's eyes narrowed. He probably hadn't expected me
to go so deeply into both the theological and mythical signifi-
cance, but he wasn't going to give up. "But then the Crescent
betrays her, and nothing can match her wrath. Now the Crescent
is like a shard in her black soul, and she digs it out to crush it to
dust." His own anger was audible.

"The Crescent flees to come back in a month, when Uma's
anger has cooled." I almost said *the king's*. This round had clearly
taken on a personal note. That was the best I could do, without
risking his offense.

"Such anger can never cool."

"And so they fight again, and the same thing happens over
and over."

"Who wears out first—the stars or the moon?" The king
stopped there, on a question, to be answered by the judge. It was
a smart move, considering who the judge was, since the king
couldn't quite argue that Heshara's own protector would best
her, a goddess. He knew I would immediately insist otherwise.

We both looked to Nyaren. I was sure I had lost the round

and thus the game. I hoped the king wouldn't insist on sleeping with me for appearances' sake. I imagined he did all sorts of things, as king, that he didn't necessarily want to do.

Nyaren looked back and forth between us, licking his lips. "A draw?" he suggested, almost meekly.

I felt like an idiot when I realized Nyaren thought I *wished* to lose, so I could hop in bed with the king. It would be quite the debut for a pleasure artist.

Nyaren might not be biased in the king's favor after all. As the king had revealed to me, this was all partially to make him jealous, so it followed that Nyaren would try to thwart my path to the king's bed, if only to play to the king's expectations. And, lovers' quarrel aside, Nyaren more importantly didn't want me gaining any influence over the king. However, he couldn't risk the king's displeasure by declaring me the winner, especially not when the king had, on many fronts, played the stronger game. I had just played the cleverer one.

The king scoffed lightly, leaning back in his chair, some of his anger leaving the set of his shoulders. "A draw? That is the easy way out. I'm tempted to request a tiebreaker round, but perhaps we can let it go at that."

"I am the judge, after all," Nyaren said, over the applause that erupted from the crowd. This would be a game that was discussed for years, no doubt.

"To which even kings are subject, I suppose," the king said with a sigh.

I bowed my head as graciously as possible. "It was a pleasure, Your Majesty. That was the most challenging and enlightening game I've played yet. I'm honored to have been able to learn so much from you."

It had definitely been a learning experience, but perhaps

honored was a stretch. More accurate would be *enraged*, *galvanized*, and *murderous*. I still felt like I was groping around in the dark, searching for answers, but at least I'd discovered something.

I wondered what Razim would think about following the Twilight Guild's orders once he knew Agrir—surely one of their highest-placed operatives—had betrayed Hallan and the queen consort. I planned to tell him as soon as I found him. And now, on top of that, I had all the evidence I needed to tell Lenara that Agrir was the one behind the plot, pulling the king's strings for the Twilighters.

<hr />

I couldn't find Razim, no matter how hard I looked that night and into the next day. Risking gossip and suspicion, I even tried to discover where his living quarters were located in order to approach him there, to no avail. It seemed a closely guarded secret that no one—no one I had access to, at any rate—seemed to know.

I had the terrible hunch that he was lying low before the assassination attempt, and I wouldn't get the chance to talk to him before his birthday. I had only one more day.

I decided that if I couldn't reach Razim first, I would tell Lenara what I had discovered, despite not wanting to draw too much attention by approaching her in the temple. I'd tried to talk to Zeniri the night before, so he could privately send a message to her to arrange a meeting, but the door to his suite had been locked, which usually meant he was occupied with his particular business. Even so, I'd risked both his and his patron's wrath by knocking, only to receive no answer—which wasn't out of the ordinary if he was *especially* busy.

What was unusual was when he didn't answer later the next

morning. He could have been asleep, but not for long with how hard I pounded on his door, drawing irritated glances from others in the hall. A bad feeling began to gnaw on my insides, like a sickness.

I decided to go to the temple. It was worth the risk at this late hour. Razim's birthday was on the morrow.

The short journey passed in a blur of golden palace halls, green gardens, oppressive gray sky, and white and black temple steps. Nikha marched quickly alongside me, tense and alert. Either she felt deep down that something was wrong too, or she was responding to my nervousness.

I handed the temple guards the card that Lenara had given me, permitting me to see her at any time, without excuse. They waved us in after taking Nikha's weapons. I had to give them Nikha's dagger, as well, but not my mother's knife, which I left hidden in the bodice of my dress.

When we reached Lenara's office, I began to relax. I knocked, and the door swung open.

We hadn't seen Agrir because he was already inside, along with half a dozen armed guards. So was Zeniri. Both he and Lenara were on their knees, hands bound behind their backs.

"Kamai," Agrir said, before I could really process what lay before me. "The exact person I wanted to see. You're just in time."

26

MISUSED GIFTS

"What's going on? What are you doing here?" I demanded, before I could think better of it.

Agrir raised gray eyebrows. "I should be asking you the same. And I think I will, once we're finished here." He gestured to Zeniri and Lenara. I realized that Zeniri's handsome face had bruises blooming under his dark skin, as if he'd been hit several times. And not recently; maybe last night. They'd been holding him for a while. He hadn't been answering his door because he hadn't been there. "I've learned enough from them for now. In fact, we've just awoken them, and I've ordered their arrest."

Awoken them? Gods, that meant they hadn't just asked questions using words and fists. That had come first, and then . . . "Arrest?" I said, trying to keep my voice steady. "Why?"

"It appears that Zeniri is an unauthorized, unlicensed soul-walker who has been conducting his business in the palace under the guise of a courtier and pleasure artist. He stole vital information from someone close to the king and threatened to black-mail him with it—"

"*Him?* Let me guess," I snarled. "Nyaren made these accusations."

Agrir's eyes flashed. He knew that *I* knew Nyaren was in the Twilight Guild. "The accuser wishes to remain anonymous for his privacy, but the *pertinent* authorities are aware. Zeniri could have obtained this information only one way, so I thought to recheck him for Heshara's gift. Her *misused* gift, in this case."

The hypocrisy was boggling, coming from him. He was not only misusing Heshara's gift in spying for the Twilight Guild, but in serving Darkness. As *high priest*, no less.

As much as I was tempted to accuse him, that would reveal the Keepers. We were all still playing a game, still pretending, even though our lives were at stake.

Zeniri spat on the rug. His saliva was tinged with red. "You have nothing to prove I have taken any information from anyone. You searched my soul without provocation. I have practiced my art honestly—"

"Shut up, lying bastard." One of the guards cuffed him upside the head. Zeniri's eyes squeezed shut in pain, and my own fists clenched.

"Yes, still making that excuse, are you," Agrir said, staring down at him, "after I discovered you're a soulwalker? Even after I discovered all the places you've walled off in your soul? We'll break into them eventually, you can be sure. It will just take time. And we'll have *plenty* of that while you're locked in a cell."

Walls. Zeniri had protections in his soul too, probably to hide that he was a Keeper. Which meant they probably didn't know yet. The Twilight Guild must have suspected Zeniri was a soulwalker, and now they were using that hunch to move against him. Agrir likely hadn't had any real reason to search his soul—none that he could admit anyway—and he'd only been spurred to fabricate a plausible-sounding excuse by . . .

Me. It had to be. I must have gotten too close to the truth and drawn Agrir's attention. He must have felt me pushing when I had tried to see into the guarded parts of the king's soul, and then he guessed it was me, especially since Nyaren would have told him I was with the king at the time. And now he was using Zeniri and Lenara to get to me.

Agrir was watching me, his eyes curious and predatory. "We also traced this deceit to the source. Zeniri was approved by Priestess Lenara for court. We found the walled-off areas in her own soul, hiding the truth, which necessitates rechecking everyone else she has approved. We can start with you, since you've just arrived at such a *coincidental* moment."

If they searched me and discovered I was a soulwalker, the whole world would know.

Zeniri stared defiantly from his kneeling position on the floor, but I could see the fear in his eyes. His life was about to end. He would be lucky to live out the rest of his days in a dungeon, never mind the inevitable loss of his reputation, his friends, his art . . . And I would follow him.

"No." I backed away and a guard seized my shoulder.

Nikha flew into action before I could blink, smashing one guard in the face, breaking his nose in a burst of blood, and kicking a second's knee into a new, excruciating angle. Even without weapons, she was formidable.

But not invincible. A third guard drew a dagger, ducked under Nikha's scuffle with another two of his comrades, and stabbed her in the thigh. I cried out; she only gasped as her legs buckled and she went down. They soon had her subdued on the ground.

Agrir watched the proceedings without feeling. "Kill her," he said flatly.

"*No!*" I screamed, struggling against the guard who held me, my voice splitting the air. The one who'd stabbed her raised his knife toward her throat. Nikha met my eyes. Hers weren't panicked or at peace or anything I could easily name. They contained so much. Anguish. Stubbornness. Love. Maybe even a good-bye.

"If you do this, I'll want to die, and *he'll* be unhappy with you," I screeched, lunging not toward Nikha, but for Agrir.

The disinterest in his eyes changed instantly to alarm. "Stop," he told the guard.

Lenara's head jerked my way.

"I'm curious what he thinks about much, of late," Agrir murmured, and then turned to the guards holding Nikha. "Throw her in a cell, but make sure she lives."

"*He?*" Lenara asked. The look on her face said enough. It was like I had torn out her heart and offered it to someone else. Zeniri's own gaze was as sharp as daggers through his swollen eyes.

They thought I had connections to someone even higher than Agrir among the Twilighters, that I had been double-crossing the Keepers somehow. And who knew? Maybe I was.

The guards hauled Nikha, bleeding and still struggling, halfway to her feet and dragged her out of the room. I tried to hold her gaze, to show her I would try to make everything right, try to go after her, but my own captors held me in place, and Agrir's voice drew my eyes back to him.

"And now we have an appointment in my office." He nodded at the guard holding me. "But first, search her."

He found the two vials, one of mohol, one of poison, in the hidden pocket in my gown. But they didn't find my mother's pocketknife tucked in my bodice. The thicker fabric, as well as my breasts, masked any sign of it, and the guard didn't get so familiar as to grope overly much there. He was doing a job, if a brutal one, not looking for extra fun. Besides, none of them likely imagined I could do much with a weapon so small as to evade detection.

I doubted I could do much with it, either.

"Hm," Agrir said as he eyed the vials in his hand before pocketing them. "I'm not entirely sure what these are, but they don't reflect well on you. Now bring her, and have the other two locked up as well."

"Kamai!" Lenara shouted, her voice betrayed, afraid, pleading—and still, under all that, concerned for me—but I was yanked out of the room before I could respond.

The trip to Agrir's office was surreal. The temple had become a familiar place, not comfortable or warm, but soothing in its own way. Everything felt wrong now, twisted, as the black dome passed overhead and the checkered tiles flew by beneath my feet, the guard jerking me down the halls in Agrir's wake. Had Heshara turned on me? Was she using Agrir against me, because I had turned on *her* by making promises to Vehyn?

Goddesses aren't known to be forgiving, Lenara had once said.

I felt forsaken by the goddess, by the Keepers, by Razim, by my mother . . . even by Vehyn. Where was he while this was happening? Did he *want* this to happen, despite all we had shared?

Two more temple guards were stationed outside Agrir's

office, and they threw the doors open for us, offering only curious glances. This was their high priest after all. It didn't matter that he was hauling a young girl they probably recognized as a frequent visitor to the temple after him. If he asked them to help kill me, they would. Especially once they all knew I was a soulwalker.

Agrir instructed them to continue standing watch outside the room, keeping just the one guard with us. My captor held me still in the center of the great black rug, while Agrir went behind his imposing desk and removed his own vial of clear liquid. Mohol.

"I suggest you take this voluntarily if you wish to retain your dignity," he said, striding back to me. "Otherwise, we'll hold you down and pour it down your throat."

I snatched the vial from him. Agrir gestured toward one of the long white couches. My knees were wobbly as I walked over to it and sat down. I unstoppered the vial with shaking fingers and looked up at Agrir.

"After you," he said with a nod. He wanted to be sure that I took it and was deeply asleep before he entered the sleeping realm himself, probably so I wouldn't try anything desperate to escape.

Which meant I would reach the sleeping realm before him—and reach Vehyn, who was my last hope. I quickly tipped the contents into my mouth and swallowed. Darkness, in turn, swallowed me.

27

WORST ENEMIES

When I arrived in my clearing, for a heart-stopping moment I didn't see the black door. But then arms encircled me from behind and hauled me back, across the threshold.

Vehyn spun me around, gripping my shoulders.

"I—"

"Be silent, Kamai." But he didn't say it angrily. He seized my hand and dragged me deeper into the study. "You're not supposed to be here. So breathe quietly, if you must breathe."

He situated me in a corner and waved his pale hands before me. Indistinct darkness flowed around me until I was completely covered. And then I was just another deep shadow, one of an endless number in this place.

But why did he need to hide me? No one had been able to enter the dark fortress before, or even see the doorway.

It didn't take long for Agrir to enter the study through the black door. He did so hesitantly, his intense eyes darting about, his steps small. His gaze passed right over me.

Vehyn faced the priest, dark robe swirling, his arms crossed. "You know what I said, last we met. What are you doing here? What do you *think* you're doing with Kamai?"

"My Lord." Agrir bowed deeply, straightened. "It has been so long since we last spoke face-to-face that I thought . . . I wanted to check . . ." He swallowed, quailing under the weight of Vehyn's expression. I really must have gotten used to that dark look, since it no longer had the same effect upon me. "I thought the girl might be here, but perhaps I was wrong."

He had known what to expect, then—this unimaginable place. And Agrir must have known I didn't have a nehym, because he didn't seem surprised by its absence.

"You were wrong," Vehyn said flatly. "As we established long ago, she's not a soulwalker."

"But . . ." He thought better than to argue that point directly. "Something isn't right with her. She's not sympathetic to our cause either, like I thought."

"Are you sure about that?"

"She . . . she's prying where she shouldn't and working with those we suspect stand in opposition to us!" His tone was indignant, defensive. Afraid. Not of whatever I might be doing, but of Vehyn.

"I told you to leave her be."

"I didn't accuse her directly, because I know you're . . . here . . . but she didn't seem to be entirely under your control. I worried she was accessing souls, critical secrets, in ways I didn't expect, and I thought it wise—"

"To test her? To test *me*? Are you certain *that* is wise? I told you *never* to come back here." So Agrir had definitely already been here, behind the black door, at least once.

"I couldn't have even if I'd tried, not since that whore, Marin . . ." He trailed off at the displeased look on Vehyn's face. "Yes, of course. I'll release her, unharmed, if that is your desire."

I wasn't sure what to make of his reference to my mother. Had she somehow forbidden others from entering the black door, not just me? Did it follow Agrir like it did me? Could others besides Agrir see it?

"It is my desire," Vehyn replied. "I will keep her asleep in the meantime. Put her body in a safe place—*not* a cell."

Cell or not, it wasn't good if I was unconscious and unable to act.

Agrir hesitated. "I don't mean to overstep, My Lord, and I know you have a far greater comprehension of the situation than I, but are you sure she isn't risking everything we've been building?"

"I won't explain myself to you. Get out." Vehyn's voice was deadly.

Agrir hurried for the door. Maybe he couldn't quite wake up yet because of the mohol and had to pass time in his nehym until he could. He paused at the door and turned back, glancing around. His tone was obsequious, as if to leave everything on a better note. "She truly has the most remarkable soul I've ever seen. I'm sure you've had much to do with—"

"*Out.*"

Agrir scurried across the threshold, and the black door slammed behind him. As it did, my knees went out from under me, and I collapsed on the floor, gasping. But not because I'd been holding my breath, as Vehyn had suggested. The darkness dissipated from around me, and Vehyn turned to look down at me, his arms still folded. His face was distinctly displeased.

"Why . . .," I rasped, "why does he think this is my soul?"

"Because it is your soul." He smiled, an expression that definitely didn't touch his flat black eyes. "Do you like what I've done with the place? Agrir certainly did."

"Wait . . . no. No, no, no." My breath was only coming faster, until my voice rose in a screech. I launched to my feet with it, my hands in tight fists. "You *stole* my soul?"

Vehyn shrugged, unbothered and unflinching. "I didn't steal it so much as . . . occupy it . . . in your stead. But the door was always there for you, and I'm happy to share. Although, I must admit, I've made some adjustments over the years that are more to my taste."

My volume only rose higher. "You turned it into a godsforsaken fortress of unending darkness!" I waved my hand to encompass it all. "What did it even look like before this?" My voice broke, and unmistakable yearning leaked into the words.

He squinted, as if scrutinizing the place he must have known better than any other. "Why, I can't really remember." Of course, he wouldn't want me to know what my soul had been like before he'd transformed it. "Keep in mind that I never altered it against your own inclinations. I've merely encouraged this place to grow in the direction it wanted. Like a plant toward sunlight . . . or in this case, Darkness. But I didn't change *you*, force you to think or act in any way, despite what you might want to believe. In a way, this was all you."

Now he was being cruel, but his words gave me an odd sort of hope. "So my being a new soul, not desiring anyone like that, wasn't you affecting me?"

His lips twisted in distaste. "Of course not, though as I've said before, the lack of such a desire isn't a bad thing."

I'd learned that on my own already; I just didn't want *him* to be the reason for how I felt, not after everything I'd gone through to make peace with myself. Maybe my soul was tainted and broken, but at least *that* part of me wasn't.

I forced myself to return to the arguably more critical matter at hand, my voice rising once more. "So if you didn't steal my soul, how did you get in? I may have opened the door, but I never put you behind it in the first place."

"Perhaps I'll tell you if you take a deep breath and ask nicely."

I let out a cry of rage and shoved him as hard as I could. He wasn't expecting it, and he actually stumbled back a step.

"All my life, I thought I didn't have a soul, which is bad enough. But this," I shouted, "this is worse! It's *possessed*. *I'm* possessed."

"Possessed? I'm not some common, malignant spirit." He hesitated. "Well, strictly speaking, I might be a spirit, but I'm better than most, and certainly not common."

"*Better?* You're Darkness Incarnate!"

"Is that bad?" He wisely didn't wait for an answer. "My intentions are less petty, and I'm much more civil. A lost spirit would have ransacked the place. Come now"—he gestured around—"is this really so terrible?" Beneath his smirk, I sensed an edge of seriousness to the question.

I wasn't in the mood for sparing his feelings. "Yes."

His face closed off. "It could be much, much worse for you, you know."

"Is that a threat?"

"Of course it is," he snapped. "Don't be deliberately obtuse. It's irritating."

"Oh, is it? Gods forbid I irritate you, the dark monster possessing my soul." My words were riding the line between daring and dangerous.

His hands shot out and seized my arms faster than my eyes could follow. "Want me to act like the 'monster' you accuse me of being?" he asked, his voice low. "Because I can do that."

Fear finally set in, my mouth going dry. I worked my tongue and swallowed, noting that his eyes still went to my lips—so at least he wasn't so angry that he didn't notice those anymore. Or maybe it was worse that he did.

"You said a long time ago that hurting me didn't please you," I murmured. At least, he'd said that the thought of *killing* me didn't please him, but there were many ways he could hurt me besides.

"If you irritate me enough," he said, as deep as a growl, "I may revise my position."

"Let me go."

His fingers loosened as if he wanted to listen, but then he said, "Only if you promise to stop trying me."

"I promise," I said, letting him have his little victory. I still had work to do, even more now.

He couldn't let it drop at that, though, despite letting his hands fall away. "Your mother sealed me off, you know. She found the darkness in your soul the first night of your life. She shut me—and your soul—away behind a lovely black door."

For a moment, I was struck utterly speechless. Then: "*She* made the black door? *She* left my soul to you?"

All those times, she'd said my soul was safe, hidden from what was behind the black door, and what she'd really done was hide *me* from my dark, poisoned soul. I should have realized it as soon as I'd discovered this place. I should have known because of what Lenara had said about my mother's protections, or how much Vehyn could affect me, or how the door followed me from soul to soul.

"How did she do it?" I asked.

"Only for a few days of life is a soul easily affected on this scale, because it isn't fully inhabited by its owner yet. That's how I did what I did and how your mother, in turn, did what she did. After much longer, neither of us would have been able to exert our influence here without changing *you*, damaging both you and your soul beyond repair. Still, ironic, isn't it, that you opened the door and ruined all her hard work? You're your own worst enemy—your mother's worst enemy— not me."

Here were my answers now, delivered when they would most hurt me. My mouth worked, but nothing came out.

Vehyn, on the other hand, wasn't quite finished. "I told you, you're mine. I embraced you before your mother did. My lips touched your brow before hers. I protected you from the world first."

Fury tore through me. "What do you mean? You possessed me, you didn't protect me!"

"Agrir was the one who forged the link between you and me. The night of your birth, he was the priest that blessed you— all arranged by the Twilight Guild, of course, to open the way of Darkness into your soul. Darkness needed a human agent on earth, not only a manifestation in this realm. *I* was created specifically to inhabit someone like *you*." He smiled. "Really, we're the same age, born together, even though I came into this world like this." He gestured down at himself. "Fully grown, as you humans count things, and with a deep understanding of my purpose, but only a vague understanding of the world—distant memories from a time long gone." His voice sounded equally distant. "I learned it all, through your eyes."

I was shocked beyond anger, despite myself. "If my mother locked you away, you were here, all alone, until I opened the door. Only seeing what I saw." I blinked and looked up at him. "No wonder you're insane. How is it that you don't *hate* me?"

He regarded me for a moment. "Sometimes I did. But this was my purpose—to inhabit you—and I couldn't hate that. I built myself a place I could tolerate from the bones of your soul, and after you opened the door, I couldn't hate *you*. I knew you too well. As well as I knew myself." His eyes glinted with shadowed mirth. "Though I will admit your singing lessons were torture. I'm eternally grateful you gave those up."

He was right—I couldn't sing. I'd been eight years old when I'd quit. He had seen absolutely *everything*. Maybe he could tune me out, but I had to assume he'd witnessed my entire life: every joy, every embarrassment, every horror. I was truly a part of him. What I didn't know was how much *he* was a part of *me*. And yet if my soul was any indication . . . this strange piece of Darkness and I were very much intertwined.

"What *are* you?" I breathed. I had asked before, so many times, and I still didn't truly know the answer.

Vehyn shrugged, as if it didn't much matter, but something in his eyes betrayed him. "Until I came about, Darkness had only been able to influence chosen ones like Agrir with vague intuitions—what I was once again limited to after your mother sealed the door. But before that, I could speak to him as you and I are speaking now. He let me into your newly formed soul with a ritual he spent half of his puny life learning, expecting my arrival here, as I was expecting to meet him. But neither of us were expecting you. We didn't know you would be a soulwalker, because we hadn't known Marin was one. And Agrir still doesn't know about you, because I found you first and hid you from sight then, as I did just now."

"Why?" I shook my head, baffled. "Why did you, back then?"

He hesitated, as if truly considering his answer. "You surprised me. Your presence, the possibility of company here, intrigued me, even though at the time your spirit was only a tiny thing small enough to fit in my hands." He held up his palms, as if remembering. His look was curiously vague. Almost soft. He shrugged, the look dropping away, the moment broken. "Agrir would have tried to control you if he knew you were a soulwalker, and it's thanks to *me* that he doesn't."

That was why he hadn't wanted Agrir to come back to my soul, even before Agrir wasn't able to. "Only because *you* wanted to control me," I snapped.

"True, I wanted you all for myself. But then your *mother* took you from me, building a wall between your spirit and your soul, between here and the rest of the sleeping realm. At the time, no one had any idea she wasn't a true member of the guild, or that she was a soulwalker. And after she foiled the ritual by sealing away your soul, she kept up her act so successfully the Twilighters didn't suspect what she'd done. Agrir assumed the ritual failed somehow, that your soul, irreparably damaged in the process, had collapsed, closing the way into the world for me. But on the slight chance that even a part of me had survived inside you somewhere, he ordered you protected."

"You want to take credit for that too?" I scoffed. "Some protection. He tried to kill me at the villa."

"Agrir gave the soldiers orders *not* to kill you, but the soldiers didn't realize you were inside when they started the fire. Agrir even tipped off Razim to ensure your safety, but that fool nearly didn't get to you in time. This is why I don't trust anyone but myself with your safekeeping."

"Still, any safety I have was carved out by my mother first."

"Your mother's influence is *nothing* compared to mine." Vehyn's lips snarled. "I didn't see you face-to-face again until you were nearly grown. But I watched over you, shaped you from the shadows. You're my child, my bride, my soul. You are mine, forever." His voice dropped. "And forever, Kamai, is a very long time."

I shoved him violently. It hardly budged him. He narrowed his eyes.

"*Why?*" I screeched. "Why did you do this to me?"

"I told you. Darkness needed a vessel, and among the Twilighters, your mother was conveniently about to deliver one. It's as simple as that. She was merely a tool to be used, and you and I came together through chance alone." He smiled. "Or perhaps it was fated, since we go together *so well*."

"What do you intend to do with me?" I ground out, ignoring that last part. "You owe me answers at the very least, after borrowing my soul for so long."

"I owe you nothing, because this place is as much mine as yours now, if not more so." He paused, as though reflecting. "And yet, in spite of that, I'll tell you what you've always wanted to know. I'll tell you who killed your mother: Agrir did."

He'd been responsible for the queen consort's and Hallan's deaths, so I'd already guessed as much. That was probably the only reason Vehyn was telling me now, other than to upset me. Hearing it confirmed made my eyes close and my teeth grind. "He ordered Marin's death specifically, not just Hallan's and the queen consort's?"

Vehyn nodded. "Not on my command. I would have spared

your mother's life, for you. But I was locked behind the black door, unable to make my will known, and Agrir made a . . . hasty . . . decision."

My eyes were still closed, my voice nearly a whisper. Pained. "Why?"

"He discovered that Marin knew too much."

I opened my eyes. "The plot to murder the king."

"Something like that."

I shook my head. "But against Razim's wishes and *on* Agrir's orders, the king is still alive. My mother's discovery of the assassination plot couldn't have been the only reason she was killed, if that was it at all. I don't suppose you'll tell me what else she discovered?"

"No. But don't be vexed, dear Kamai—I am nothing if not generous. Soon, I'll give you all of your answers and more." He paused, the silence heavy. "I'll give you the world."

The offer was obviously meant to impress, but I stared at him in horror. "If the world will be anything like my soul once you're done with it, I'd rather have no world."

"I'm sure that could be arranged, if that's what you really want."

It was too much: his talking about my mother's death and threatening to destroy the world so casually, as if all life on earth were a card in a match of Gods and Kings to use against me. I couldn't pretend this was only a game anymore.

I slapped him as hard as I could.

For a second, he looked as surprised as when I'd kissed him. That alone made him appear younger, more human than I'd ever seen him. But then his eyes sank a shade darker than usual, more like a skull's than ever, and his face went as deathly still as a

326

corpse's. His expression was an ugly, angry bruise, even if his cheek wasn't.

Bruise. Something occurred to me that should have ages ago, a thought that fit like a missing piece into this grisly puzzle. "How was Gerresh able to bruise me, if I can't even bruise myself?"

Vehyn blinked at the abrupt change in topic, but then his expression went even more flat, if that were possible. "You needed bruises, so I let him bruise you," he said, his voice chilly. Before I could gape at that, he added, "It was for your protection. Gerresh—that was his name?—needed to die, but I couldn't let anything look too suspicious."

"Oh, so the *hand* through his heart was subtle?"

Vehyn shrugged. "I assumed you would figure something out. You convinced that great, lumbering woman to cover for you. She's about as smart as she looks."

"She *is* smart, she *isn't* a woman, and she *saved* me, as much as you want to take all the credit and make me feel like I owe you." I wasn't betraying Nikha's secret because Vehyn already knew what we'd discussed over the soul chart. But there was more to this, and I carried on before he could argue any other point. "Was Gerresh a Twilighter?"

This time, he didn't answer.

"He was, wasn't he?" I demanded. "He was in Jidras's household as a spy, because the guild must have known I would seek shelter there." I held his eyes. "Did *you* order him to come back to try to kill me?"

Again, Vehyn didn't answer.

"You sacrificed him. You wanted me in danger just so you could rescue me, wrap me more around your finger . . . or, better yet, wrap your fingers around my *neck*. For all I know, you arranged this little scene with Agrir yourself, to make me think you cared enough to hide me."

"I didn't."

At least there was that. But it wasn't much to weigh in his favor; it wasn't close to enough. "Still, with Gerresh, you may as well have put those bruises on my throat yourself."

"I told you, I'm the only one who can hurt you."

I returned his stare for a long moment. Neither of us moved or blinked, the silence like a held breath between us. And then I shook my head, once. "You disgust me."

My word had even more of an effect than the slap. "Get out, Kamai." His voice was low—worse than a growl.

Fear began to chill the fire of my anger, but not before I shouted, "This is *my* soul! I'm not leaving."

"Since I'm not going to let you wake up for at least another two days, you actually *can't*. I mean get out of my sight, if you know what is good for you." His voice grew softer, but that made me shiver—in an entirely bad way, this time.

I could tell when my life was in danger. I fled the study. I wished there were a door to slam, but there was only a long hall. I ran down it, and countless hallways after. The dark maze passed in a blur, maybe from the tears flooding my eyes.

This. This was my nehym. Endless warrens and cavernous halls and pits of darkness. I'd wanted to find my soul all my life, and now that I had, I was horrified and trapped here until my friends' lives fell apart and something terrible happened in the waking world.

But what, exactly? It had to do with the king's assassination, I knew that, but why? And what else?

Eventually, somewhere, I stopped, sagging against a wall,

and slid down it. I looked around. It was all black, of course, with hallways shooting in all directions. For a flaring moment—a first—I hated everything about this place. I didn't know where I was going, there was hardly any light to see by, only faceless walls . . .

Before my eyes, the hallways began to shift, leaning, collapsing into one another, combining, until there was only one way stretching forward. The lamplight brightened, to the extent that it could, and cast a pattern on every dark surface that hadn't been there before, floral on the walls and checkers on the floor.

It had listened to me. It had always seemed to respond to me in slight ways, and now I knew why. This was my soul too, not just Vehyn's dwelling.

And so maybe it could help me. Maybe it remembered.

28

BURIED SECRETS

Souls could speak, in a sense, at least through memories, like Jidras's nehym and quite a few others' had to me. Perhaps I could search my own soul for a message.

But not from myself. From my mother. She had sealed my soul, after all. She'd been here at least once before and obviously knew how to affect a soul to a great degree. I figured that, as a soulwalker and a Keeper, she would have hidden her deepest secrets not in the waking world, but in the sleeping realm.

Is there something my mother left me? I thought at the dark walls surrounding me. The single hallway before me shifted, curving in a slightly different direction than it had before.

I leapt up from where I'd been sitting on the floor and took off down the passageway at a run. The walls seemed to fight me at times, and I had to keep focusing, like I'd done In Between, as Vehyn had taught me. It probably took far more winding passages and stairs than it could have, but eventually I ended up in

330

a small, deep room, not unlike a cellar. At first glance, it was empty.

But then I heard a scraping sound, and one of the black stones in the floor didn't seem to be sitting quite evenly anymore. I dropped to my knees next to the stone and wedged my fingernails around the edges. It shifted, and I was able to lift it.

Underneath was a creamy white letter, the brightest thing I had yet seen in this place, with my name written in my mother's handwriting on the front. The image blurred in my vision. Impatiently, I dashed away my tears and broke the wax seal.

You are only just born now, but I don't know how old you will be when you finally read this. If you ever read this. I hope you never do, because that would mean the door remained closed. But in case it hasn't, and I haven't already told you all of this face-to-face, I leave you this letter that you might someday find it.

You may or may not have heard about what your father did, but, Kamai, I have never regretted you. That didn't mean I could let him get away with deceiving me, trying to use my body, and you, to get me to stay with him. I left him, carrying you inside of me.

You might know already that I am a member of the Twilight Guild. That is not all that I am, but I fear to put more in here, so that will have to do.

She explained, in brief, what I already knew: how the Twilight Guild had sheltered her in her pregnancy, sending her to live with Hallan and baby Razim—whom she knew to be the queen consort's child as well—where she was to pose as Hallan's wife, so the birth of her child would be less scandalous . . . supposedly. But in reality, the Twilight Guild had plans for me.

Once again, Kamai, men have used the both of us for their own dark purposes. The day you were born, you were taken from me to be washed ... and you didn't come back. I became distressed, knowing you needed to be fed. Eventually, you were returned to me with the excuse that you'd received your birth blessing. And yet, as I fell asleep with you at my breast, I knew immediately something had been done to you.

Your soul is ... wrong. It is dark and much too big for an infant. Much too big for anyone. There are strange pathways to young Razim's soul that should not be here, and there is someone else here too. I whisked your spirit away from ... him ... when he wasn't quite aware, and as I prepare this letter, I plan to trap him inside your soul. He isn't human, and I fear he comes from a place antithetical to our own.

I also fear the Twilight Guild is darker than their name suggests. That they are merely the prequel for something else, the darkest chapter in the history of our entire world. If I haven't already told you, Kamai, never ever trust them. Know also: wherever you or I might be now as you read this, I did my best to try to stop them.

If I discover anything else, I will leave my findings hidden in Razim's soul. I have easy proximity to it, living with Hallan, and I believe he is as important to the guild as you are, with the disturbing connection between you two. Hallan and I are less so, and even if I am no longer here, I want my words to reach you.

I love you.

Razim's soul. I'd only been in it once, long enough to see the black door and sob against it, just after my mother had died. I hadn't been back since, only catching glimpses of its hidden knowledge during our game of Gods and Kings.

I needed to get there immediately, even if it meant trying to travel the path In Between.

But perhaps I didn't have to go that route. My mother had said there was a "disturbing connection" between Razim and me. All this went far in explaining how wary she'd been of him for all our lives, how cool she had been toward him. And yet . . . she'd blamed a child who had been used as a pawn as much as either of us, and not Hallan?

I supposed love could make you forgive an incredible amount. I certainly wasn't one to talk.

Never open the black door. Never fall in love. Those were the lessons I'd learned from her, and I'd failed at both, I now knew. Because while I hated Vehyn . . . I also loved him.

I loved Darkness Incarnate. I didn't know if I loved him for *him*, or if it was because we shared a soul, but I didn't dwell on the thought for long. There wasn't time.

I hesitated before stuffing the letter back under the stone, wishing I could destroy it so Vehyn could never find it . . . and then it turned to ash in my fingers, just like that. My soul was still listening to me.

Take me to Razim's soul, I thought.

The black door, as quick as a wink, appeared in the dark cellar. I barely dared to hope it could be so easy as I drew it open. Gray stone walls, torches burning in sconces, and sumptuous rugs and tapestries greeted me on the other side. I'd glimpsed it only once, but I recognized it. Razim's soul.

"Huh," I said, more bemused than anything. Perhaps I was in shock. "That wasn't so hard."

I tentatively stepped inside, feeling the thick rug under my slippers. It was a handsome nehym, despite being a little imposing and windowless. The stones were clean and smooth, the rugs a rich burgundy, and the air warm and glowing from the torches. Razim's fresh woody scent permeated everything. As I looked closer, details on the wall tapestries seemed to come alive, deepening and spreading. There were horses, hunting scenes, a father and son fishing that made my heart twist, thinking of Hallan . . . and some that would have made me blush in less dire circumstances, with young men and women kissing, offering gifts of flowers and ribbons, and even entwined in more suggestive ways.

His soul seemed to be revealing itself to me more readily than others. I didn't know if it was that I had grown more skilled at soulwalking, or if it was because of his feelings for me, or something *else*, whatever my mother had meant about "strange pathways" in her letter.

I strode into the center of the room. *What lies between your soul and mine?*

The walls changed around me. Darkness rippled and flowed out of cracks in the stone like liquid, pooling in specific shapes. I spun in a circle, my mouth falling open in horror.

Every surface was lined with black doors. Riddled with them, like a sickness. Our souls weren't simply connected. Razim's was *infested*, burrowed into, by Darkness, ready to be opened.

But all the doors save the one I had come through were still closed. Darkness hadn't entered. Yet.

Urgency overrode my horror. *Did my mother leave me anything here?*

A drawer creaked in a gleaming wooden buffet table set against one wall. I dashed over and yanked it open. The drawer was empty, but I understood the hidden nature of these messages now, and so I groped around until my finger poked through a hole in the wood in the far back. Hooking it, I pulled up a false bottom.

A leather-bound journal lay beneath. Words, in my mother's writing, filled the pages, the dated entries going back to when I was a baby and reaching to roughly two and a half months ago, to the days right before she died. Years whipped by with the flip of pages. I skimmed as quickly as possible.

> *The darkness was meant for Razim, I know that now. But something Hallan did kept Razim from it, and that was why they needed me, and you, my darling. The guild offered you up instead, and even though they think the ritual failed, the evil inside of your soul built a bridge to Razim's. It hasn't come through, yet ... It seems to be waiting.*
>
> *...*
>
> *Hallan is growing more anxious. He still visits the queen consort, but it is not love they make between them. Every time he returns, he is angry, because she is angry. And it has to do with their son.*
>
> *...*
>
> *Hallan and I ... we made love for the first time. After all these years, I think I'm falling for him ...*

I skipped quickly over that part, flipping to the last pages.

> *Gods. Oh, holy Heshara. Hallan finally told me the truth. Finally, I understand. Just as I am not his wife, but he loves me anyway, Razim ... isn't Hallan's.*
>
> *Razim isn't a bastard. He is the heir.*
>
> *The guild placed Hallan close to the queen consort so he could gain her trust, influence both her and the eventual heir, not father a bastard. And he succeeded. As heir, Razim was supposed to have*

that strange darkness filling him from the day of his birth instead of you, Kamai. Hallan didn't know what they had planned for the child—he still doesn't know, since he can't walk within souls—but he knew the babe would become a pawn.

(Nor did he have any idea what would happen to you, Kamai. He doesn't know the guild has any interest in you at all. He bought their false reasoning for our arrangement, just like I did.)

Back then, Hallan had fallen in love with the queen consort and decided he couldn't hurt her by using her child so. Pregnant, she was already in seclusion to avoid public scandal in case a priest determined the child was a bastard. Everyone knew of the king's taste for men, not women. But then Hallan arranged for her to vanish to a different location that the guild hadn't expected, around the time of the child's birth. The guild didn't have their own priest at hand, ready to work whatever dark rite. Not that Hallan suspected this—he simply wanted a priest whom he had chosen. This new priest quietly confirmed—lied—that the child was Hallan's, a bastard, without actually checking whose it was, so the babe would be of no use to the guild.

And so Razim went to live with Hallan, safe—or so Hallan thought—from the guild's plots for the heir. His soul formed on its own, growing strong, so by the time the guild discovered Hallan's deceit, it was too late for the rite.

The sound of clapping made me spin around, interrupting the flow of written words. Vehyn was leaning in the open door.

29

BRIGHT BLADES

"Well done," Vehyn said. The cluster of doors around him reminded me of a spider's multitudinous eyes, but still only the one stood open, and Vehyn was careful not to step through. "I see you've been up to no good." He gestured at the journal in my hands. "Would you like to finish?"

I doubted he would let me, and sure enough, he said, "But why don't I tell you the rest of the story, since I know where you left off, after all?" He tapped the side of his head, reminding me that he knew what I knew—what was in my soul. I already held the truth in my hand, so he didn't mind revealing it now. And he wanted me to hear it from *him*, not my mother. "Hallan presumed he would somehow escape punishment from the guild, not realizing he had stalled a plan that was years, decades, *centuries* in the making. He actually thought the guild would be content with him supposedly fathering a bastard on the queen consort, pleased that he could at least use the child to keep her under his influence."

"So of course you had to kill him for his presumption," I whispered, my throat dry.

"No, remember, the *king* had him killed." Vehyn smiled, as if this were an inside joke we shared—a secret. "Besides, Agrir wasn't too angry with him, since having a secret heir stashed away for future use, especially when Agrir thought the ritual had failed, was better than nothing. And he still hoped we might someday use Razim for his original purpose." He gestured at me, careful not to let his hand cross the threshold. "Through you. And his hope wasn't unfounded."

"Lucky me."

Vehyn didn't seem to appreciate my sarcasm. As if I *should* feel lucky to be a part of this. "In the meantime, the queen consort grew to hate Hallan, did you know that?" He shrugged, as if all this were trivial. "But she was unable to expose what he had done for fear of retribution from the guild or the king."

"I don't blame her for being angry," I said, making my voice hard. "Despite everything, her child still became a card in a game of Gods and Kings."

"And she didn't even know how he would come into play." He swept his hand to include the *many* black doors in the walls. "I suppose this is a fitting way to repay her ingratitude toward Hallan, despite his trying to save her child."

"Don't pretend you actually care about any injustice, perceived or otherwise, against Hallan," I spat, unable to help myself.

"I won't, especially since he more thoroughly vexed the guild when he told Marin about Razim's true parentage. And she, knowing the ritual hadn't failed but was merely postponed, started poking her nose where it didn't belong. See how well that turned out?" He nodded at the journal. "Truly, go ahead and read it."

I couldn't help myself, even though I knew it would hurt. I wanted to scrape up my mother's words like they were the last remnants from a dish. I skimmed to where she finally discovered the Twilighters' plan:

The guild will arrange the king's death somehow and position Razim on the throne. Having a king as one of their members will serve them far better than a secret heir. And yet, because of the darkness linked to his soul through yours, I fear such an outcome would be worse than anyone could imagine. But I can't tell anyone, not even those I truly serve, because they might kill you for the danger your soul poses. I am even afraid you would want to end your own life, practical, kind, clever girl that you are, and so I have yet to burden you with this knowledge. There must be another way—I have to believe that. Despite the very real danger, the black door inside you remains closed.

And so maybe you, with your fortitude, and Hallan, with the goodness of his heart, can stop this. After some discussion with him, the queen consort has claimed she will finally tell the truth to the world and beg her husband's clemency. Hallan, out of his love for Razim, won't stop her, even if she risks the king's wrath. The kingdom will keep its king and yet finally have its heir, one who knows the guild is only trying to use him. And you, Hallan, and I will hide somewhere far away and finally become the family we have only seemed for so long. I hope, and I pray to Heshara, that between us all, this will be enough to keep the lurking evil at bay.

It ended there. I knew what had happened after. Their affair had been outed by Agrir before anyone could beg for clemency or escape into hiding, and Hallan, the queen consort, and my mother had died. My mother's prayers, Hallan's goodness, the queen consort's determination, and my supposed fortitude obviously hadn't been enough. My mother had been right about one thing, though—I would have killed myself. If only I had known the truth then.

But now that I'd opened the black door, I couldn't, and Razim was going to kill the king anyway . . . and unintentionally become king himself. And then Darkness was going to finally make its move. I still wasn't sure what that would entail, but I had a hunch, based on all the black doors ringing me.

And Vehyn was trying to tell me there wasn't anything I could do to stop it.

"I know the truth," I whispered, backing away from him, my heart climbing my throat in fear. "So that means I win our game. You have to halt what you're doing, by your own vow."

He raised his eyebrows in mock surprise. "I do? But how have you won? What truth might you have discovered that I didn't tell you myself?"

All I could do was stand in the center of the room. There was nowhere to run. "Razim will kill the king and become king himself. He's the heir."

Vehyn *technically* hadn't told me the latter part.

"That's not the full truth, but yes, you are correct."

"The king's sacred bond with Ranta will break." Vehyn was Darkness, after all, and the bond was what protected the earth from him.

"Yes, but that was just a guess. You don't know *how*."

"The truth is the truth!" I shouted.

"And yet, even so, you haven't found all of it. You haven't won."

Gods, if only Lenara had told me everything about Ranta's bond with the king. The darkest creature in any realm already knew the details; I couldn't do much worse with the knowledge than him. But it wasn't Lenara's fault. I hadn't told her the truth about my situation, either. The fear and mistrust went both ways.

I tried to guess the other parts of his plan, but I could feel my victory slipping away. "So, you'll possess Razim first, instead. Jump from me to him." Lenara had said simply assassinating the king wouldn't break the bond, but perhaps if the Darkness itself were controlling the hand that wielded the knife . . . ?

"No, you're missing a few steps. It's not that simple. I can't just possess a fully formed soul, and through that, a body, like I have yours. Your soul was built around me—we built it together." He waved at the room I stood in, still careful not to let even a fingertip cross the threshold. "If I barged in here now, even with all of the doorways that I've carefully constructed over time, I might destroy him inside *and* out before I could make myself at home anywhere, body or soul."

I gritted my teeth in frustration. I was still guessing, and he was proving it. "You'll kill him, then."

"Wrong. What good would killing him do?"

Never mind that theory, then. I wanted to scream.

No, I wanted to move. I needed to get the answers that Vehyn couldn't give me, and I knew who had them. And even how to get to her. Not that she'd necessarily want to talk to me.

At the thought, my mother's knife appeared in my hand.

Vehyn smirked. "Are you going to fight me?" He shook his head, surety in his eyes. "You won't."

He was right. I backed away from him.

"You think you can hide in Razim's soul? Suit yourself—time will pass all the same in there. It's already deepest night in the waking world. Everything will happen tomorrow, and I'll be able to join you sooner rather than later."

Perfect. It was night. I edged past all the black doors, staying out of arm's reach, until I found the door I was looking for. The door that wasn't black. The one that belonged to Razim and led outside of his soul.

"You can't go that way, Kamai," Vehyn called suddenly, realizing where I was headed. There was a different, urgent note to his voice. "You can't wake up."

"I'm not trying to wake up." I wrenched open the door and leapt through it.

To In Between.

The starry sky expanded far overhead, the dark path unwinding before me through the suddenly looming trees. I ran as fast as I could away from Razim's soul and out into the strange night, thinking all the while, *Lenara, Lenara. Take me to Lenara's soul.*

But then I felt the tug on my hand. For a second, I was terrified it was a spirit eater, but then I looked back and saw that Razim's door had vanished. In its place was the black door, Vehyn standing in the threshold, silhouetted by faint red light. The shadowy ribbon ran from my wrist to his grip, and he gave it another jerk.

"Kamai, stop!" he shouted.

I swung my knife around, the blade glinting brightly in the darkness, and slashed at the binding. It parted, and Vehyn's outline staggered. I didn't wait to see more, stumbling back into a run, his shouts fading behind me. I tried to ignore the fear in his voice. My link to Vehyn had saved my life last time, and I'd just severed it.

Lenara, Lenara, Lenara.

I kept chanting her name in my head, and then I realized I was saying it out loud. I kept repeating it, even after I leapt over a dark tentacle that flowed across the path. Even after it sprang at me and I slashed it with the knife. Even when a dozen of them wriggled out through the trees and surrounded me, forcing me to stop.

"Lenara, I'm coming. Lenara," I said. With the words, I exhaled.

I hadn't possessed Vehyn's gift last time I'd tried walking In Between. It was worth a shot, even if it only slowed the spirit eater's tentacles.

They recoiled, whipping and lashing in the dark night, slithering back to whatever monstrosity they'd ventured from. I blinked in shock, before quickly resuming my chant. Even spirit eaters were afraid of Darkness, despite being drawn to it. Whatever they were, they existed here, in Heshara's realm, not the unimaginable place Vehyn had come from. Which meant that not even a spirit eater was as bad as what dwelt in my soul.

I shivered and looked up at the stars, wondering if Heshara would turn on me after I'd used Vehyn's gift in her realm. But the sky and trees were still and silent. Maybe she was waiting to see what I would do.

Lenara, Lenara. I continued moving.

The path veered, cutting into the trees, and opened into a space that reminded me of my clearing. Perhaps in the sleeping realm, such glades surrounded the entrances to souls.

My mother's protections must have extended to my clearing. All my life it had seemed safe, limited, even boring, until the black door had begun to appear there. In actuality, she had fenced off that space somehow from In Between.

In this particular clearing, a lone door stood without walls, made of many shimmering glass panes—the same glass I'd seen in the windows of Lenara's soul.

I gripped the door's faceted knob and turned. It didn't budge.

"Lenara!" I shouted. "Let me in! It's Kamai!" I didn't want to stay out here any longer than I had to, and not *only* because the entire kingdom was at stake. I couldn't help my rising terror now that I'd traversed In Between. It was like feeling the sting only after the cut.

But she wasn't answering. Perhaps her spirit was awake. Either it wasn't late enough in the waking world, like Vehyn had claimed, or she simply wasn't able to sleep. Or perhaps, even asleep, she could block who tried to enter her soul—a wise skill to hone, if it was possible—or . . .

The door opened a crack and Lenara peered out, looking shocked to see me—and then intensely distrustful. "What are you doing here? *How* are you here, Kamai?"

"Just let me in! I know this is strange, but I just risked my life to reach you. I'm trying to fix everything, I promise!"

The earnestness in my words, the desperation, must have touched her, because she opened the door wider and let me step past her.

"Thank you."

"Don't thank me yet." She gestured the way forward, through a glowing entryway and into the central room with the fountain, ringed by windows and lush greenery. Like last time, her nehym struck me as almost painfully bright and beautiful . . . especially now that I knew what my own soul looked like. I took the lead. I guessed she didn't want me behind her—a realization that struck deep and sharp in my chest. She came around me to sit on the edge of the fountain, keeping me in her sight.

"Are you all right?" I asked, my fear switching targets now that I was no longer in immediate danger. "How are you and Zeniri . . . and Nikha?" My breath caught on her name.

"I haven't seen Nikha since you last did, and Zeniri and I are imprisoned in the royal dungeons," she said, businesslike. "Now tell me how you got here, and who it is you serve."

"I came In Between, from my own soul, and—"

"No one travels In Between," she interrupted. "The way is too dangerous, especially of late."

"This was a special occasion," I snapped. If she was going to question every word I said, this would take too much time. "And, in case you were wondering, I serve the Keepers and the earth, and right now, the safety of everyone depends on you giving me some answers." I bent forward and took her hands. She tried to pull away, but I held tight. "I swear on my mother's spirit, on mine, I am telling you the truth."

Lenara opened her mouth and then hesitated. "All right," she said eventually. "Don't make me regret this, or I swear on my spirit, my body, and my soul that *you* will regret it." Her eyes were hard.

I swallowed and straightened. "Fair enough."

"What do you want to know?"

"If a spirit wants to possess an already strong soul without destroying it or killing the person it belongs to, how would they manage it?"

Her eyes narrowed a fraction, her gaze growing even more intense. She clearly didn't like the nature of my question. "There are ways to surrender your soul, or to lose it."

"How?" I pressed.

"By killing, among other things. It damages a soul without destroying it. Weakens it. It would take a powerful soulwalker, or—"

"Is killing a particular person worse for a soul?" I asked, interrupting. "Say, a son killing a father?"

"Yes, definitely."

I took a deep breath. "Razim is the king's son. He's the heir. That's what my mother discovered. Before she could tell you or the Keepers, the Twilighters had her killed."

Lenara's mouth fell open. She stared at me for a long moment, the light of her intellect practically whirling behind her eyes. A shadow seemed to fall across her face then, as she realized. "And you're concerned about Razim's soul? Far, *far* worse things would befall us if the heir kills the king."

"The bond with Ranta will break?" I guessed. She nodded, and I was unable to restrain myself. "But you said that even if the king dies, it would remain intact! Because Razim is the king's son, it's a different story?"

"Of course! The heir killing his father to take by force what should have been rightfully granted would most *definitely* destroy the sacredness of the bond! Ranta would turn her back on humanity, and leave herself open to attack, rather than honor such a vow."

"But how is she open to attack?"

"Tain made a guardian of the first human king of Eopia—the first king in all the world—a status that remains with each new king so long as he's married to Ranta. With the king filling such a role, there's too much light and strength between humanity and the earth for Darkness to get between them—the same purpose the Guardian Constellations serve for Heshara."

Tain's fiery, exacting gaze flashed in my mind's eye, along with Heshara's mysterious smile. "Right. I've heard that Heshara might have *left* Tain if not for those guardians."

"Who told you that?" Lenara asked, suspicion ringing in her tone. "That's not a widely acknowledged—"

"It doesn't matter," I interrupted. I wasn't about to tell her it was Vehyn. "So, what if the situation I was asking about earlier, about a spirit possessing another's soul, is actually *Darkness* wanting to enter Razim after he kills his father and becomes king?"

Lenara's eyes shot wider than ever, but her voice was curiously quiet. "Darkness would inherit the earth. Consume the land. Cover the sky. Cut off Ranta entirely from her parents' light."

"Yes, well, that's the Twilight Guild's plan." My jaw locked, not wanting to say what had to come next. I forced the words through my teeth. "And they let Darkness into my soul the day I was born, so he's been biding his time inside of me—his name is Vehyn—behind the protections my mother built, waiting until Razim kills the king."

Lenara went absolutely still, staring into the distance. "Vehyn," she murmured. "It means *face*, sometimes *mask*, in the old tongue." Her eyes snapped back to me. "Your mother's protections? Are they still in place?"

"She never told me about any of this, and I don't think even she fully understood what was wrong with me, but all I knew was that this black door followed me around, and I opened it when I was seventeen." The truth spilled out of me in a torrent. Maybe if I said it fast enough, admitting everything wouldn't be so terrible. "Now there are all of these black doors in Razim's soul, ready to open, and—"

Before I could blink, Lenara launched into motion. A gleaming sword, shining brightly in the light of her soul, was in her hand. I didn't try to raise my knife to block her. I didn't want to, and besides, I didn't have time before she struck. She stabbed the blade right into my heart.

Or in the direction of it. The sword didn't strike true, because the tip bounced off my breastbone in a burst of black swirls. I staggered back, more from the shock than the blow, and fell against the wall.

If a soulwalker died in the sleeping realm, they died in the waking world too. Lenara had just tried to kill me. Understandably, perhaps. But it didn't make it any easier to face.

"I tried that already," I said, my voice shaking, one hand braced on the wall for balance. With the other, I rubbed my chest reflexively, even though it didn't hurt.

Lenara stood panting, sword in hand, staring at me with wild eyes. She finally lowered the blade. "Then we must try something else. Kamai, this is bigger than anything the world has ever seen. More important than your life or mine. This is why the Keepers exist, to prevent this."

"I know, and I'm going to try to stop it. I promise. And you've helped. You've given me the answers I need to"—I couldn't tell her about my "game" with Vehyn; she would probably try to stab me again—"to get the upper hand."

"Are you going to cut off this *Vehyn's* power, inside of you?"

I blinked. "Can I?"

"It has to come from somewhere. It doesn't exist in your soul. You are—"

"A doorway," I interrupted. Even Vehyn had admitted as much. "You're right."

And suddenly I knew where I needed to go.

But before I could summon the black door, or sneak into my own soul by another path to avoid Vehyn, it appeared under my hand on the wall. The door was open. I lost my balance and toppled inside.

Right into Vehyn's arms.

30

DEEP WOUNDS

Vehyn wasn't gentle as he dragged me fully inside the black door. He waved his hand and the door slammed, shutting out Lenara, her horrified expression, and the light of her soul, leaving me in the darkness of my own. *With* Darkness.

"The door won't be opening again, not even for you," Vehyn said, his voice low and deadly. "I can't believe you did something so idiotic. I could have lost you In Between."

"Why do you care?" I gasped as he hauled me into the great entry hall. The lamps were bright red, no patterns or cool indigo to soften them, like glaring, angry eyes against the blackness of the cavernous space. Probably reflecting Vehyn's mood.

He stopped, whipping me around to face him. For the first time in a long while, I felt his strength and how it could be used against me. I was like a rag doll in his grip. "Why do I care? Are you being deliberately obtuse again?"

Of course he would care. If my spirit was lost, my body

would die, and if my body died, so would my soul. His lovely fortress. All his plans. I realized I probably should have fed myself to the spirit eater . . . but then I remembered it would have taken a "short eternity" for my spirit to die. My body might eventually waste away, collapsing my soul, but there could still be plenty of time for Vehyn to jump safely into Razim, his plans fulfilled—kings killed, bonds broken, candles snuffed.

So perhaps he cared for a different reason. But I couldn't allow myself to think about that. "Let me go."

With another brief shake, he did. He was obviously trying to get his anger under control. The redness of the lamps dimmed around us. The cold fury in his black eyes faded too, until they were merely sharp. Fondly irritated. Worriedly frustrated.

Why did he have to look at me like that, now of all times? His anger would have been easier.

"I know the truth," I whispered. And I told him about the nature of Ranta's bond, the precise way it would break, and the exact way he would overtake Razim's soul. "And you'll become king," I finished.

He stared at me for a long moment. His gaze was definitely, absolutely no longer fond. "So what happens if *I* become king and the bond is broken?"

He knew I didn't want to say it, and so he was forcing me to. To lose something, even as I won our game. It was the dark truth I had been afraid of ever since he'd told me who he was, and what Lenara had just confirmed. The full consequence of what I had done in opening the black door.

"You would snuff out the candle," I whispered. "The world's light."

"Don't look so horrified. We share the same dreams, Kamai. You've been there with me, in a world consumed by darkness, and you felt *bliss* at my side." He briefly closed his eyes on the word, as if savoring the memory. His eyes snapped open. "You know, I think this worked out for the better. I would have preferred sharing a soul with you over Razim, given the choice, and now I'll never have to put up with him. When the time comes, I'll simply take everything from him. I'll pick up the pieces of his shattered soul, remake it as mine, and then force his spirit out of his body. He won't be able to fight back, without a soul." He dusted his hands against each other. "No more Razim."

I didn't want to hear this, because it wasn't going to happen. "You won't, because I wo—"

He cut me off. "The bond with Ranta will be broken and eternal night will cover the earth, but *you* and I will be forever bound, with all of those black doors stitching your soul to mine, an unbreakable thread. You'll be my dark queen, in place of Ranta." He raised his hand to cup my cheek, but I shied away. "We will be the new gods, Kamai. The earth will be ours."

I shook my head, taking a step back into the vast hall. "You can't do this."

Vehyn followed me. "You belong with me, in my world."

"I don't."

"You always have. You just won't admit the truth."

"Will admitting it get you to stop?"

"If you truly believe it, why would you *want* me to stop?"

"Because I'm not a selfish bastard like you are."

His smile, this time, was less confident, less cocky. "Whatever lies you wish to tell yourself."

I halted, realizing I'd been retreating during our exchange, with him pursuing me—a slow chase, like the one we'd been on my entire life. It was time to stop running. From him. From the truth.

"You're right," I said.

His smile grew—more genuine, more confident. "Say it."

"I belong with you." And I meant it. "We share the same soul, the same dreams. If you become king, I will be your queen. I'm yours."

He stepped right up to me, lifting my chin with a gentle hand. I let him, tipping my head back to receive his kiss.

At the last second, I turned my face aside, clutched him hard around the neck with one hand, and whispered in his ear, "But you're also mine, because I win. And you're not going to be king."

And then I stabbed him with my mother's knife, thrusting it as hard as I could up under his ribs, pulling him into it at the same time. The blade bit deep for its size. Nikha had taught me well. It was a death blow, not that I assumed anything could be strong enough to actually kill Vehyn. Not even this knife, which seemed to be able to cut Darkness when nothing else could.

With a cry, he staggered backward, his hands clutched to his breast. I didn't feel like I'd won as I looked at him. It wasn't red liquid that seeped between his fingers, but black shadow.

His eyes were pained as they rose from the wound and focused on me, his breath coming in short gasps. "You . . . would betray me . . . like this? Did you ever really feel . . . for me . . . what it seemed?"

He knew I had, since he'd felt it as we'd dreamed together. Still . . . "It's all a game, remember? You did the same to me. Made me believe you felt something, just to manipulate me."

"Was that all it was?" he growled, in anger and pain. "Were my feelings only false? I've told you . . . I rarely speak falsehoods."

I needed to start moving, but my feet were rooted. I was furious at him for everything he'd done, even more so because he was breaking my heart. "You wear this mask and give me roses, when this isn't you!" I shouted, my voice cracking. "The real you is *Darkness*. The real you is the one who stole my soul, and Razim's family, and now wishes to take over the world with trickery and murder. *You're* false." I jerked my hand at him violently, tears overflowing onto my cheeks. "*This* is a lie!"

Maybe if it was, this would be easier.

"Perhaps," Vehyn gasped. "But how I feel about you isn't."

"Why not? If this is all just a game to you, you shouldn't feel anything for me."

"I can't . . . I can't help it." His words were small in the dark. *He* seemed small in the vast space, his shoulders hunched, arms clutching himself.

"You've been in this form for too long," I said. "Eighteen years. You're as old as I am, really. This mask, this card played by Darkness, made to look human, to act human—it's more than a mask or an act now. This is more than a game for you."

"I . . . I've never felt like this before," he said, looking down at his shadow-bloodied hands. "I've never *felt* at all, until now."

"So don't do this," I said, my voice pleading. "Help me."

He looked back up at me. "I can't, Kamai."

"You can!"

I saw a flash of fear in his eyes for what had to be the first time. "If I act abnormally . . . then I might . . . *it* might . . . take me back. Reclaim me. I would be lost in the greater night. Gone."

"Then leave the Darkness. Break away. Let the mask be your true self." I laughed desperately, fighting tears. "You could truly be Moholos, helping Heshara, sometimes getting up to mischief . . . but nothing worse. Nothing like this."

"And give up the source of my power? If I sever this part of me, I would be no more than a shell of my former self. A hand without an arm or body." He shook his head, wincing, but it seemed the idea pained him more than his wound. "Never."

"Why don't I help you do it, then?" My words were quiet, and I took another step back.

"You can't. You won't," he said, trying to reclaim some of his old authority, his surety. "You belong to—"

"You serve me now," I said, my voice commanding. "I won our game. Stay here."

Vehyn shuddered. He looked down at his legs, which seemed rooted to the ground . . . but then he took a slow, lurching step toward me. "I can't. If you try to control me, Darkness will—"

"Stay here," I repeated, my words ruthless, even though my voice broke.

Black spirals shot out over his pale skin, like I had seen on my own so many times. The power of Darkness, to counteract the strength of our binding oath. Vehyn threw back his head and screamed. It was pain and fear . . . and rage. His eyes were completely black when he looked at me.

"Run, Kamai," he hissed. He was still in there, somewhere, if he was warning me. And he didn't need to tell me twice.

"It's down the stairs, isn't it?" I asked, breathless, backing away.

His head jerked, as if he wanted to nod, but something was preventing him. He stumbled toward me. Despite his unsteadiness, he was still faster than I expected. His hand latched on to my wrist as I tried to dance away, the strength of his fingers grinding into my bones.

I stabbed him again, in the arm. At the give of his flesh against the blade, and his scream, I felt a stab of a different sort, deep in my chest, up under my own ribs. My heart cracking in two. But I ignored the pain as his grip came loose. He knocked the knife out of my hand, sending it spinning into the shadows, but I didn't go after it. I turned and ran.

Vehyn's ragged voice followed me, echoing off the impossibly high walls, his cry rising to the darkness above, to the ceiling I couldn't see, if there even was one. But I was headed for the endless darkness below.

"Kamai!"

I ignored him. I reached the wide spiral staircase in the center of the great hall, both rising and dropping into oblivion. The deepest of wounds, piercing straight through my soul. I hesitated only for a second, fetching up against the banister, before I shoved my terror away and started down the stairs as fast as my feet could carry me. I didn't turn, but I could hear Vehyn's footsteps behind me. They were slower, labored, but they were still coming.

The darkness thickened the deeper I went. There were no lamps down here.

"Kamai, stop!" His voice was different, harsh. Darkness had control of him. And yet not completely. My own command still had an effect upon him, or else he would have been fast enough to catch me already. A cosmic force was waging war against the strength of our promise, and Vehyn's spirit was both the battleground and the spoils.

But hopefully not for long. I would free him from Darkness. I would free the both of us.

Soon, I couldn't see at all. Only blackness surrounded me. I slipped on a slick step, careening into the banister that I was using as a guide, but I didn't let that stop me, turning my sliding fall back into a mad dash. I just couldn't let myself tip over the side. Both the drop and the winding stairs themselves were supposedly bottomless, the place where the Darkness had burrowed deepest, affecting my soul the most drastically, and yet . . . this was still my soul. Maybe I could change it, make these steps lead me to where I needed to go.

Take me to the Darkness. Take me to its doorway.

"Kamai, wait!" Vehyn's tone changed in the inky air as I thundered down the stairs, becoming more pleading. I wondered if this was more *him*, or a trick. "If you cut off the Darkness, you'll lose her!"

Her? My footsteps faltered for a second.

"I saved her for you, Kamai! Her spirit, after she died, drifted near . . . I took it, kept it. It was a surprise. A present for you."

No, no, no, no, I thought in time with the pounding of my feet, of my heart. Horror filled me; it was a tangible, consuming presence. He couldn't mean . . .

"The Darkness is all that's keeping her here. Your mother will be gone if you close the door!"

My mother . . . I slipped again, fell hard, jarring my bones.

"I will give her to you." His voice was getting closer. "She'll be with you here, forever, even after I have my own soul."

Forever. A spirit trapped in a dark house for a short eternity. That sounded sickeningly familiar. If he thought such a vision would turn me from my goal, he was wrong. If my mother was here, that meant she was a prisoner, held in my soul by Darkness. Like a spirit inside a spirit eater.

I hauled myself to my feet, but then Vehyn was upon me. I couldn't see him; I felt his hand seize my shoulder. I threw myself sideways, twisting out of his grasp. I slammed up against the banister. The blackness was all around me. Maybe I could pretend I was near the bottom. There was no way I would outrun him now anyway.

I tipped myself up and over the edge. I felt Vehyn's fingers claw at my dress, but it tore, and then I was falling. Down the center shaft.

"Kamai, no!" he screamed after me. His *true* voice, fraught with distress.

I was falling fast. Far. Deep. I clearly hadn't been near the bottom. Perhaps it *was* bottomless.

I wondered if I would fall forever. For a short eternity.

The words reminded me: *my mother.* I had to reach her. *Take me to my mother.* The command burned in me, its own sort of light in the darkness. It filled my chest, becoming the shape of my breath, my lungs, my beating heart. The shape of my soul.

The walls caught me. At first, I feared I'd drifted in my fall and hit the banister, and would then bounce horrifically against the stairwell until my spirit shattered into a thousand pieces. But no. The surface that cradled me was perfectly smooth, like warm glass, slowing my descent with the steepest of slopes and then gradually leveling out. The silk of my gown slid over it like a whisper, carrying me, gliding, through the darkness. It was like I was flying instead of falling.

And then I saw a light up ahead. Warm, golden, faint. Approaching fast—*very* fast. My chute was working all too well, and even after it became perfectly level, it sent me tumbling over the smooth black floor to finally skid to a stop.

Vehyn's cries echoed distantly behind me. Far, far distant. I had some time. Battered, torn, my hair in my face, I rose to my aching hands and knees and looked up. Even if the light was weak, it blinded me, and I had to squint to focus.

It was my mother—Vehyn hadn't been lying.

My mother. She was the light in the darkness, her flesh seemingly made of it now that she was wholly a spirit. But dark, whorling patterns etched her bare skin like the bars of a cage, and heavy, thick links chained her ankle to the floor. Our eyes met, and I thought my heart would burst.

But then I saw what was behind her. *It.* The other black door, the one that made my soul a gateway to the waking world from somewhere else. *From nowhere you could possibly understand,* Vehyn had once said.

The doorway was open, revealing a gasping, sucking void. Darkness swirled in and out of it like a screaming breath. It blew around me, tossing my hair wildly, feeling like both a caress and death on my skin. Looking into the depths, I froze, forgetting my mother.

Kamai . . .

It saw me. It recognized me. It spoke my name in that night-dark whisper that I'd heard when I was twelve. The voice that *wasn't* Vehyn's.

Vehyn had a voice like coffee. And he had bare feet. Sharp eyes. An arrogant smile. A deep laugh. Hands that held me. A spirit that flew with me on the wind.

This . . . this was nothingness made real. It terrified me to my bones, down to the depths of my soul—which was deep, as it turned out—leaving me colder than the spirit eater had. I couldn't look at anything else.

"Kamai." It was a different voice. A familiar, warm one, if only a whisper. It wrenched at my heart, tore my eyes away from the door, forcing me to come back to myself.

My mother smiled at me, repeated my name. I took a shuddering breath. My lungs felt frozen. *I* was frozen. I didn't know what to do.

"Kamai, my sweet, close the door," she murmured. She said it like we were back in the villa, as if she were talking about a normal wooden door I'd left open. It brought me jarringly back to where I was. My soul. At the bottom of a bottomless pit. At the gateway to Darkness. I lurched forward, clawing my way up, stumbling toward the door.

"Be careful," my mother called. Or tried to. Her voice seemed to crack apart, like the desiccated wings of a moth, turning to dust in the air.

I soon understood her warning. At first it was hard to get close, the exhalations of the void blasting me back like a gale. But then, as I drew nearer, I felt the pull. My mother was at the midpoint, in between, but I had to move beyond her. And suddenly I was bracing myself, trying not to step too quickly, the wind at my back now. Trying not to go tumbling and flailing into Darkness.

Kamai, it whispered. *Come.*

My slippers started sliding over the smooth ground. I wobbled desperately, my arms windmilling. Disoriented, dizzy, I didn't know if I was looking into the doorway or *down* into a vast sea of endless nothing.

Something caught my ankle, steadying me, drawing my eyes. My mother was stretched out along the floor, at the very end of her length of chain, her hand barely able to reach me. I felt her strength, her warmth, her light, flooding me.

I turned back to the door, gripped its heavy black edges, and pulled as hard as I could. At first it didn't move, but I strained until I thought something inside of me might break.

"This. Is. My. Soul!" I cried, willing it to be so, every word punctuated by a ragged gasp.

And then it began to shift, bit by excruciating bit, toward me. Toward closing.

The Darkness screamed, fighting me, pulling against me, but I only screamed back and tugged harder, feeling my mother's hand squeeze my ankle, bracing me. And there was also the tug of the void. Once I reached the halfway point, it did the rest of the job for me. Its sucking darkness caught the door, ripped it out of my hands, and slammed it closed.

The scream cut off abruptly. The wind died. Off-balance, I collapsed to my hands and knees. Just breathing.

I wasn't sure what to expect, but if I'd thought everything would magically change, that the darkness of my soul would be swept away instantly, I was wrong. At least as far as the section of floor I was staring at. It still gleamed like a piece of polished night.

I felt a hand on my shoulder, one on my cheek. They were so bright and warm. I turned my head to see my mother crouched next to me. At least one thing had changed. Her brilliant spirit was free of cages and chains.

"Kamai . . .," she said. So much love in her voice, it was practically glowing too.

Tears flooded my eyes, and I threw myself into her arms. She held me tight, letting me cry. But not for as long as I would have liked. I would have accepted a short eternity in her embrace.

She pushed me back, but only to hold my damp face in her hands, kissing my forehead with her lovely lips. "I don't have much time, but I have so much I want to say. Forgive me, for doing what I did and not telling you. I didn't want him to affect you like he has this place. I wanted you to grow up without his influence, until I could figure out how to get rid of it . . . or until we could, together. Perhaps that was a mistake."

I shook my head. "It's not you who needs forgiveness, it's me. You told me not to open the black door."

She sighed. "It was inevitable. This is your soul. Perhaps it's

Heshara's will that someone so strong, so brave would bear such a burden."

"I'm not strong or brave!" I cried. I felt weak. Tainted. Fractured. Like only she was holding me together, and yet she'd said she didn't have long here. Not long before she left me for Heshara's embrace, depriving me of her own. But I wanted her to have peace more than anyone. More than I wanted it for myself.

"You are the strongest, bravest person I know, and I am so proud of you." A little shake of her hands emphasized each word, and her face crumpled, tears like liquid light in her eyes. "Even though you have made your own path, so different from mine, I am proud. And I know you have it in you to make it the rest of the way."

In that moment, I knew she saw *me* and knew everything about me that I'd once been ashamed to tell her. Now we *both* knew the truth, and it was good.

And yet I hadn't gotten this far alone.

"But it *wasn't* my strength, all along," I insisted. "It was Nikha's and Lenara's and . . ." I didn't say *Vehyn's*, or let myself think about all the strange ways he'd helped me even as he'd hurt me. "And your knife." I choked on something that was halfway between a laugh and a sob.

She smoothed my hair back from my face. "It was more than just a knife. It has a spirit of its own, because I fashioned it from part of mine to protect you. A mother's love made tangible."

That was why it had always been here in the sleeping realm—waiting for me. Why it could hurt Darkness when nothing else could. Why Vehyn had taken it away from me . . . and then given it back. And now I would lose it for good when I lost her. She had done so much to protect me, and yet I would have to continue alone. Without Nikha, Lenara, my mother's knife . . . or my mother.

As if she knew what I was thinking, she said, "But you don't need me anymore. I once told you that you didn't have a nehym, but you had a soul. I was telling the truth. Your spirit might belong here, but these halls aren't fully yours so long as they are still his too. Reclaim this place, Kamai. I know you have the strength on your own now."

I didn't quite know what she meant—I'd already closed the door, hadn't I?—but before I could ask, her head cocked, as if she heard something I couldn't.

"Heshara is waiting for me. I must go." She wavered in my vision, through my sheen of tears. Her hands felt less solid on my face, and so did her lips when she kissed my forehead one last time. Her spirit was departing, but she was smiling radiantly as it did, and it was the most beautiful thing I'd ever seen. "Perhaps I will see Hallan again. And you, someday." Her words grew more rushed. "Please tell Razim that none of this was his fault, Lenara that I miss her, your father that I forgive him, and Kamai . . . know that I love you more than life itself."

"Mama," I sobbed as she faded. "I love you too."

Her beautiful smile was the last I saw of her. Her voice lingered in my ears. "Go, Kamai. Be strong. Be brave. You already are."

Go, Kamai.

I realized, with the gateway shut and Vehyn's power diminished, I *could* go now. And I was out of time. Razim would still kill his father. Still break the bond protecting Ranta. Vehyn could still invade his soul, perhaps open another door to Darkness, and take over the world. If I didn't act fast.

I threw myself awake.

31

HONEST DISGUISES

I didn't know where I was for a moment after I awoke. And then I recognized the white walls, the brown leather couch I was lying upon: Lenara's office, in the temple of Heshara. Lenara wasn't using it, after all, while imprisoned in the royal dungeons. Agrir must have left me here, not in a cell, on Vehyn's orders. The door couldn't be locked from the outside, but that obviously hadn't concerned Agrir overly much. He likely didn't imagine I would wake until it was too late.

There was an armoire against one wall. I stood stiffly—I must have been lying without stirring for nearly a day, judging by the late-morning sun outside. It was Razim's birthday. I moved as quickly and quietly as my limbs would allow.

Go, Kamai. My mother's words echoed in my ears, urging me on. I couldn't let myself think about the rest of what had happened, with her, or with Vehyn, or else I might crumple to the ground and never get up again. I had to be strong. Brave. For her. For the realm.

I threw open the armoire and tugged out Lenara's long, nondescript gray cloak. I'd seen other priests and priestesses wearing them when they ventured out. At any other time, I would have been hesitant to take the guise of a priestess for fear of angering Heshara, but I was more her servant now than I had ever been. I tossed the cloak over my shoulders, fastened the clasp, and drew up the deep hood.

I paused before opening the door that led out of the office and into the temple proper. Part of me wanted to find Nikha, no matter the consequences, make sure she was all right . . . but if I didn't do what I had to do, *none* of us would be all right, let alone her. The best thing I could do for her now, I tried to tell myself, would be to leave her, wherever she was.

I took a deep breath, my heart aching, and eased open the door.

It would have been too much to hope that I'd been left entirely unguarded. A woman in silver armor stood watch out front. She came alert at the creak of a hinge, shooting upright from where she'd been leaning against a white pillar, her eyes meeting mine.

"You're not supposed to be awake yet," she said, coming quickly toward me. I retreated just as quickly into the office. I worried she would stay outside and shut the door, trap me, but instead, she followed me in. "The high priest said that if you woke up, I was to give you—"

She only got as far as the rug, which was fortunate for her skull. I exhaled heavily in her direction, hoping against hope that I still had the power, even though the gateway was closed. Black fog curled over her face, and her eyes rolled up in her head. She collapsed. The thick rug also muffled the sound of her clattering armor. Maybe, somehow, Heshara was looking out for me.

And I still had Vehyn's gift. My soul had enough darkness remaining in it, I supposed, to be saturated like a sponge. But that meant Vehyn would still have some power too, for a time. He hadn't tried to stop me yet, but that didn't mean he wouldn't soon.

I leapt over the fallen guard, pausing only for a moment in the doorway to make sure no one was running toward me at the commotion I'd caused. The hall was clear. I closed the door quietly behind me, hiding the unconscious woman, and started down the wide wing, deeper into the temple, sticking to the shadows.

Lenara had told me the secret passage to Zeniri's suite was behind a statue of Heshara, in an alcove with wood paneling, rather than stone. I had only been in two of the four temple wings, and I hadn't seen anything matching that description. When I reached the black dome, where the four wings branched from the center like the points of the soul chart depicted on the ceiling, I had to decide which of the other two wings to search.

And fast. Voices echoed behind me, coming from the direction of the temple entrance. I skirted the edge of the black dome, passing a priest and priestess who either didn't notice me or weren't interested, and then I dashed into the nearest unfamiliar wing. Chance had decided for me, but this wing was the closest to the palace, most convenient for any underground tunnel, and it also looked to be the dimmest, which boded well for the "secret" part of secret passageway.

Unfortunately, it was filled with statues. Cursing under my breath, I hurried down the length of it, head whipping side to side. I had to force down my rising desperation when I realized they were *all* sculptures of Heshara. Her hair-shadowed face and its mysterious smile seemed to chase me down the hall.

A shout rose behind me. Someone must have noticed there was no longer a guard stationed outside Lenara's door and gone inside. The shouts spread, and so did the pounding of boots. My skin prickled and sweat broke out under my cloak. I ran faster.

Wood paneling. I needed to find wood paneling.

The footsteps were getting louder behind me.

And then I saw it. It looked more like an altar, with an unusual statue of Heshara holding the babe Ranta, kneeling atop a wooden base. Wood paneling, almost like a screen in an altarpiece, made up the back of the alcove behind it. This was the only depiction of Ranta I'd seen in Heshara's temple, and since the Keepers were Ranta's protectors in Heshara's service . . .

I ducked behind it. Just in time. I held my breath as the echoing footsteps drew closer . . . and then passed by. But it wouldn't take them long to begin checking behind the statuary.

I faced the panel, trying to figure out the trick of it, if indeed I was in the right spot.

The phases of the moon were carved into the panel in the form of a soul chart. The new moon was a deep indentation at the center, with a clearly defined outline. Almost like it was an inset. I pressed it, and it sank deeper. The entire panel swung inward an inch, on silent hinges.

Thank you, Heshara.

It was only after I'd slipped behind the panel, shutting it carefully behind me, that I realized I had no light. The tunnel was pitch-black. But after the training my mother had given me in maneuvering through rooms at night, never mind what I'd gone through on the spiral staircase, this was child's play. Following the rough-hewn wall with my hands, I made my way in the darkness down a set of stone steps and through a tunnel.

Even the passageway didn't feel terribly long after the halls and tunnels I had traversed in my own soul. I was moving so fast I tripped when I hit the stairs, too eager to mind my stubbed toe. I hoisted my skirts with one hand, kept my other on the wall, and made my way up the steps as quickly as I dared, until I reached what felt like another smooth, wooden panel. I felt around for the inevitable latch and tripped it. It opened just as quietly as the way in—but with some difficulty. Something soft hindered it. Feeling my way forward, I realized they were clothes. *So many* clothes. A slash of light from under a door opposite me helped my eyes adjust quickly, confirming where I was. Zeniri's closet.

I had no idea if Zeniri's suite would be guarded. But since he was imprisoned and no one knew about the passageway, I hazarded a guess it would be abandoned. I still eased open the closet door cautiously.

His rooms were a wreck. The orange and purple chair cushions had been slashed, the coffee table upturned, curtains thrown to the floor. Stuffing and papers littered every surface. They'd obviously been searching for what Zeniri's soul hadn't revealed. He might not have done whatever they'd accused him of, but they knew he was hiding something.

Zeniri, I thought with a pang. But, just like Nikha, I could only help him or Lenara by carrying on.

Go, Kamai.

I left the closet, making sure the panel to the passageway was closed behind me. Before I moved for the door, I exchanged Lenara's gray cloak for a deep blue velvet one of Zeniri's. It was a touch gaudy and too long, but it would be less noticeable than plain priestess's garb in *this* part of the palace. I wouldn't have far to go, because the wing reserved for courtiers and courtesans was near the king's quarters. And hopefully no one would be looking for me, besides. Because of my shortcut, I could safely assume I had outpaced news of my escape. But it probably wouldn't be far behind me, and delivered to very specific ears.

There hadn't been the slightest hint of Vehyn's presence. Not a whisper of his voice in my head or a flicker of his power in my flesh. I hoped he wasn't waiting, saving his strength. All I could do was keep moving.

I cracked the door. No one was in the hall outside. I slipped out, keeping my cloak held tight. The gold and red of the palace blurred by me, my feet carrying me like a shadow. I soon passed others—courtiers, nobles—but no one paid me any mind. With my hood up, I was just another person returning from a discreet visit to someone's private quarters.

I made it all the way to the gilded double doors to the king's apartments. But there was no avoiding the pair of guards in equally gilded armor standing on either side.

Not knowing what else to do, I walked right up to them. "I need to see the king. It's an emergency."

One of them scoffed at me, but the other said more seriously, "The king left orders that he is not to be disturbed at any cost. He has sensitive business he is attending to. Whatever yours is, you'll have to wait, make a formal petition for an audience—"

My breath hitched. "Is his business with Ramir Zareen?"

The man, caught off guard, nodded. "It is, but that isn't your concern."

It was already starting. I had to get inside, now.

I exhaled what I hoped was the right amount of fogging

darkness. Their eyes clouded. The one closest teetered slightly but didn't fall. I peered through the window into their souls and pushed my own thoughts inside.

There's no one here. No one at this door. No one entering.

I had no idea if it would work. They both merely blinked, staring down the hall, past me. I slipped between them and put my hand on the golden doorknob, expecting at any moment for one of them to shout, or grab me. But they didn't. It was as if I wasn't there. Part of me hoped I hadn't permanently fixed such a notion in their subconscious minds, or they could never be guards again. But even so, it would be a necessary sacrifice.

I opened the door . . . and walked right in on Agrir and Nyaren in an ornately gilded sitting room. They stood, their stances tense, before another pair of doors that undoubtedly led to an inner, more private meeting chamber. Razim and the king were nowhere to be seen, which meant they were likely alone inside, together.

The noise of my entrance caused Agrir and Nyaren to spin around. I shut the door quickly, before the guards could come to their senses and follow me inside.

"What? How—?" Agrir sputtered. "Did *he* permit you to be here? Razim has just gone in, you can't—"

I had no idea how they had managed to arrange a private audience between Razim and the king, but there was no more time for questions.

I wished desperately that Nikha were with me, but I only had myself. One breath took out Nyaren, dropping him like a bag of stones, but Vehyn's gift . . . it was weakening. Either I was exhausting the power I had, or Vehyn was choking it, or Agrir had some sort of resistance to it, because his eyes only half closed before he shook off the effect. He dove for the doors to the hall to alert the guards, moving faster than I thought a man of his age could. He didn't shout, at least, probably because he didn't want the king to think something was amiss and interrupt whatever was happening between him and Razim.

Which gave me time to swipe a golden candlestick off an end table. It was the first thing I could reach. I threw myself at Agrir, hammering him savagely over the head. He joined Nyaren on the floor, groaning.

Nikha's strength, and her training, had been behind the blow. She was here with me in spirit. I dropped the candlestick and tore open the doors to the inner room to see Razim, with a long, wicked knife unsheathed and held ready behind his back; the king, sitting in a plush chair behind a wide desk; and the walls, splattered with as much golden opulence as one would expect a king's office to have. It looked like they had only finished introductions, Razim straightening as if from a bow, and yet he was already prepared for a killing blow. So much for pleasantries. I should have kept the candlestick to bash Razim upside the head.

Razim didn't even turn to see who was at the doors, though the king's gaze jerked to me in surprise. Maybe Razim had been waiting for an intrusion, a distraction, which one of the others was supposed to have caused.

I stepped into the room just in time for him to lunge at the king, dagger outstretched.

32

BIRTHDAY PRESENTS

"*No!*" I screamed, lunging for Razim just as he had for the king. By the time I caught him, Razim was already halfway across the king's massive wooden desk, scattering papers. I seized hold of his jacket, yanking, trying to hold him back.

Razim's arm swept out. The dagger slashed the air. The king gasped.

I hauled on Razim hard enough that we both tumbled back, careening off a high-backed leather chair and landing in a heap on the plush carpet. I cried out, shoving him off me with one hand and pinning him down with the other. He didn't resist, oddly. We both looked to the king.

The king's eyes were wide. They were Razim's eyes, I now realized. The king's hand was at his throat.

"No," I whispered.

But then he pulled his fingers away, revealing only a small gash in his neck and a trickle of blood, not the cascade of red that I'd feared. I fell back with a sigh of relief, still holding Razim down with a hand on his chest.

"What is the meaning of this, Razim?" the king asked, his voice shocked.

For a second, I was surprised he wasn't shouting for the guards, but then what he'd said dawned on me, surprising me even more. Both Razim and I blinked from the floor. "*Razim?*" I said. "You know his true name?"

"Of course I do," the king spat at me, anger coloring his voice now. "He's my son."

My mouth fell open. "You know?"

Razim gaped back and forth between the both of us, clearly with no idea of what was going on.

"Of course I know!" the king snapped. "Why do you think I've invited him here, on his twentieth birthday? I've just signed the official decree declaring him the heir apparent." He gestured at the scattered papers, half hanging off the desk, some on the floor. "What I *don't* know is why you just tried to kill me, *my son.*"

"I didn't know," Razim said, sounding dazed.

"But—but," I stammered at the king. "How did *you* know?"

He blinked at me from behind his desk, as if surprised to find me still there, asking questions, never mind that I had just saved his life. "This is none of your concern. Why are you even—"

"Why didn't you tell me sooner?" Razim interrupted, in that same distant voice.

Maybe it was because Razim asked, or because the king seemed a little dazed himself, but he answered. "The truth about you was brought to my attention only recently. My holy adviser discovered the queen consort's deceit. She had hidden you, our child, the kingdom's *heir*, preventing me from fulfilling my sacred duty to pass on . . ." He blinked, shook his head, perhaps realizing he shouldn't be talking about something as important as Ranta's bond in front of me. "I had the criminals executed."

"Your *wife*, you mean," I snarled, "and she was going to tell you the truth! You also killed Marin Nuala, my mother, but you probably don't remember her. And Hallan Lizier—"

"Hallan!" the king cried, his lips looking pale in his reddened face, his breath coming faster. "He was the greatest deceiver of all. We treated him like family, my wife and I, but . . ." He glanced to the side, unable to meet my eyes.

And then I understood. The king had never been in the dark about their affair. He had been a part of it. Hallan had played the role of what was sometimes referred to as a "marriage aid," especially in arranged or royal marriages, wherein one of the partners wasn't so . . . interested . . . in the other. Perhaps *both* the king and the queen consort had loved Hallan, for a time. Until they found out what he had been doing when he wasn't in their bed.

An affair seemed a harsh reason for an execution, which was why I'd thought it had been done in a fit of rage and then quietly buried. But that hadn't made as much sense after I'd met the king and found him to be calm and stable, even while angry. Now I knew—it wasn't the affair he had discovered, but Razim.

"He stole my child from me," the king continued, still breathing hard, even though his anger seemed to have cooled as he looked to Razim, "and kept you hidden for all these years."

Razim's voice rose. "Mere days could have made a difference. I wouldn't have done this, if only I had known!" He didn't seem to care that he was nearly shouting at the king.

Neither did the king, oddly. "I wasn't sure how Hallan might have poisoned you against me, my son, so after his execution, I allowed you, with Agrir's help, to come to court with a different name, so I could observe you."

That was why the king had been so curious as to Razim's obsession with me, Jidras's scandalous courtesan daughter. He was looking after his *son*—a fact that Agrir had taken care to hide in his soul.

"But . . .," Razim stammered. "But Agrir said . . ."

The king scrubbed at his face. He was sweating. "You probably didn't know I was the one behind your new title and lands to the north. Agrir provided you with some other excuse for your new fortune, did he not?"

Agrir had tricked both of them, giving Razim an "excuse" the king would never have anticipated: that the Twilight Guild was helping him avenge his father.

"I determined you were of sharp intellect and sound character, aside from your strange interest in *her*," the king added, glancing at me. "But now . . ." He refocused on Razim, who stared back at him in growing horror. The king blinked, his eyes looking suddenly hazy.

Alarm bells started ringing in my head. The king's lips were too pale, his breathing too labored. The knife had merely nicked him, but . . .

"Razim," I cried, reaching for the dagger, "what was on that blade?"

He yanked it out of my reach, looking at me with wide, wild eyes. "Poison," he said. "A fatal amount." That was why he hadn't bothered striking again after he'd only barely touched the king. "I thought I was avenging my father. I didn't think . . ."

"That you would become king?" a voice said behind us. Razim and I both spun on our knees. The king only glanced to the entrance, his head wobbling unsteadily. Agrir stood in the doorway, holding a hand to his own head, which was covered with blood, thanks to me. His other hand held a knife. "Prepare yourself, Razim. It is your destiny."

"No," Razim said, coming to his feet shakily. "I didn't want this. I never would have done this if—"

"You'd known?" Agrir finished, coming farther into the room. He took his hand from his bleeding scalp to pick up one of the sheets of paper, covered in flowing script, with a sweeping signature at the bottom, along with a red wax seal that looked like a splatter of blood from this vantage. It might as well have been the king's blood. "That was why we didn't tell you and fought hard to keep others from telling you. And now here you are." He lifted the document. "It says right here, signed and sealed by the king, witnessed by the high priest—me, of course. You're the heir apparent, to be crowned king at the time of your father's death." He glanced at the king. "Which might come sooner rather than later. How do you like your birthday present?"

Razim was shaking his head, over and over again. The king wasn't doing much of anything, only staring, but then he coughed, spasming, and spittle dripped from his lips. It was tinged red.

"He did this, Razim," I said, gasping in fear. "Agrir arranged everything. He convinced the king to kill Hallan, my mother, your mother, to keep the truth from you and to make you a pawn. The guild tricked you. *He* deceived you. Don't be fooled by him any longer."

But maybe it didn't matter anymore, I realized, as the king coughed violently. I could hear the truth. He was going to die by Razim's hand, and the bond with Ranta would break. There was nothing I could do to stop it. And then Vehyn . . . I didn't know if Vehyn was watching all this, waiting for Razim's soul to tear, but I had a strong premonition that he was. Vehyn, Darkness, would rule the land wearing Razim's body.

Maybe I could stop *that*, at least. And maybe, somehow, the bond wouldn't break if the heir died first. I glanced around wildly, seeking anything that I could use to help me. I looked up at Razim, and he down at me. As if reading my thoughts, he glanced at the poisoned dagger on the carpet.

Both Agrir and I followed his gaze. I dove for the dagger first, snatching it up. But Agrir was already coming at me, his own knife raised.

Razim stepped between us, planting a fist in the high priest's stomach, doubling him over. He swept Agrir's knife from his loosened grip and in the same fluid motion buried it in the high priest's spine.

Agrir collapsed on the ground, limp and staring. Razim didn't turn, only stood, broad shoulders rising and falling, looking down at the body. His back was exposed. The poisoned dagger was in my hand. The king slumped onto his desk and began sliding, inexorably, toward the floor.

It was now or never. I raised the dagger.

Razim spun and his hand caught mine. Except—it wasn't his hand. His fingers were whorled in black. With a cry, I looked at his face. His eyes too were dark as night.

"Don't, Kamai." Razim's voice grated. But it was with Vehyn's inflection.

Had he already moved into Razim's soul? But that would mean the king . . . I glanced in his direction. He still had breath, but it was rasping, wet, in his chest.

Razim winced, buckling as if in pain. "What's happening?" he gasped—his own voice, this time.

His soul hadn't entirely surrendered yet. But as the king slowly died, it was beginning to do so.

"Fight it, Razim!" I shouted, but then he twisted my hand until the knife dropped from my nerveless fingers.

"He can't fight me, Kamai," Vehyn hissed through Razim's lips. As he spoke, the room began to darken, and I realized it was the sunlight outside, through the windows of the study, beginning to dim. "And neither can you. You can't win."

He shoved me away, probably in case he lost control of Razim's body again and I tried to retrieve the knife. I hit the king's desk hard, and both the dying man and I fell onto the carpet. His eyes were already open, unseeing. His breath was a whispered rattle. It was so pained, so horrible, I almost wished I could end it for him sooner.

The realization hit me: *I could end it sooner.* My mother's knife—I'd only lost it in the sleeping realm. Its manifestation might have faded with her spirit, but here it was still made of solid wood and metal, the same as when she'd gifted it to me for my tenth birthday, for my protection in the waking realm. I yanked it out of my bodice, springing the small blade free from its wooden handle.

Vehyn suddenly realized what I was doing. "Wait, Kamai."

I didn't. I slit the king's throat and then stabbed him as many times as I could, in the chest, blood spattering me, before hands tore me away.

"What are you doing?" Vehyn shouted. He ripped the red-stained knife from my grip and threw me aside, turning to the king. Perhaps he thought to make one last strike. The final death blow.

"What I should have done a long time ago," I said, and closed my eyes.

I reopened them in my soul. *My* soul. My *soul*. It was dark, but it was mine. I knew it, and I loved it. I felt all the open doors to Razim's nehym like drafts in a house, and I brought them together in a line before me, along one side of the great entry hall, summoning them as simply and quickly as a thought. Vehyn appeared in one of them. His eyes were wild. "Kamai!"

He came charging toward me, into my beautiful, dark fortress. That was when I closed all the doors. Every single one. But I didn't *just* close them; I made them vanish, until only smooth wall remained. There was one door left—the black door, the one that led out of my soul—but nothing led to Razim's anymore. Vehyn was trapped in here, with me. I had broken the connection.

Because I had the power. This place was mine. I had reclaimed it, as my mother had urged me to.

"No!" Vehyn screamed.

"I told you," I said, my tone merciless, "and you made the promise yourself. You serve me. So guard my soul for me. You are bound to it. It is your duty. Your prison."

His voice, his face, was desperate. Pleading. "Wait, Kamai! It will be different without the Darkness. *I'll* be different. I can already feel it leaving me. I'll be better, I promise—"

"You have to keep your old promises before I can trust you with more. Good-bye, Vehyn."

He let loose a wordless cry and lunged for me. I stepped back, through the final black door, the one that had haunted me from my birth. I closed it on him.

The door shuddered. But it didn't open. After all, I was the only one who could open it now.

Eventually the pounding fell silent.

───

When I next opened my eyes, I was staring at a molded bronze ceiling. The light had returned to normal, bright and golden through the windowpanes. Razim was leaning over me, stroking my hair, my face. Tears were in his eyes.

Only tears. No darkness. He was only Razim again, the young man. My fake ex-stepbrother.

And soon he would be king. I turned my head to find the staring eyes, the unmoving, bloody chest of the king. He was dead. I had killed him. And in so doing, I'd kept Razim from killing him. Kept his soul from surrendering. Kept the king's sacred bond with Ranta intact. Kept the world from falling to Darkness. *Kept.*

Maybe I was a Keeper. The thought, for the moment, didn't taste like victory, but like blood. Or maybe that was actually what was on my lips. I was covered in blood—the king's. Razim had actually been wiping it off my mouth with his sleeve. Of course, it was poisoned. He hadn't wanted me to swallow any of it.

For the moment, I didn't really care if I died.

"Kamai," Razim gasped, bending over me and touching his forehead to mine. "I felt it. What was entering me. What was going to happen to me. It's gone. You stopped it. Oh, gods, it's gone." He was shaking, terrified. But he wasn't so beside himself that he didn't ask, "What do you need? Are you hurt? What can I get you?"

I opened my mouth, my tongue dry. "Nikha. I want Nikha." Soon after, I asked him to free Lenara and Zeniri from the royal dungeons, but right then, all I could think of was her.

She found me in the king's sitting room. Razim had moved me there, after guards and advisers began flooding the inner meeting room in an uproar. Razim was with them, answering what I imagined were tens of thousands of questions. I knew I would have to answer some soon myself. But at the moment, I was incapable.

I was shivering badly, teeth chattering, despite the blanket Razim had wrapped around me, and I couldn't stop crying. The king. He had been far from perfect and had even been involved with my mother's death, but he hadn't been an evil man. And now all I could see were his sweat-sheened, pale lips and staring eyes as I cut his throat. Feel the give of his flesh as I stabbed him in the chest. His hot blood on my hands.

And Vehyn. Vehyn's expression as I shut the door on him. Locked him away in my soul.

I felt that too, like a wound. Vehyn *was* evil, but I loved him anyway.

At least the tears, and the cloth Razim had given me, had cleaned most of the blood off my face by the time Nikha found me. She came limping through the doorway, a thick white bandage around her thigh, in her usual leather tunic and wrinkled undershirt, which no doubt needed washing, her hair mussed and spiky.

She was the most beautiful person I'd ever seen. Like a prince come to rescue me—never mind that I had already rescued myself *and* a prince, no less. But I didn't feel saved. I felt lost, and Nikha was finding me.

I started sobbing uncontrollably at the sight of her. She rushed to the couch and threw herself down, her arms around me. She held me while I quaked and cried, rocking me back and forth against her chest.

"Shh," she said into my hair. "Shh, it's going to be all right."

There was no way she could even know what had happened. But for some ridiculous reason, I believed her.

33

SOFT TRUTHS

I was reading aloud to Nikha when a knock sent me sitting up in my chair.

Nikha was sprawled across the foot of my bed, much in the careless way of a young man—legs spread wide, arms folded behind her head, staring at the ceiling, lost in the words. She'd tried to read to me at first, when I was either refusing to sleep or to get up, but she'd never learned to read very well, and I grew impatient and ended up taking the book from her. I supposed that might have been her intention. She rather enjoyed being read to.

But at the sound of a fist on the door, she shot upright in an instant. A familiar surge of apprehension swept through me. The last few weeks had been reverberating with the sound of knocking.

Although only on the door to Nikha's and my suite. The other door, my black door, had been silent.

It was only Zeniri, who slipped into the room without waiting for one of us to invite him in.

"What's wrong?" Nikha demanded. We weren't under arrest, exactly, but if we didn't wander about the palace much, everyone was more relaxed. Even *I* preferred it that way. I'd kept the curtains drawn in our usually too-bright suite. Nikha, for her part, had ended up *actually* dragging a cot into my room like she'd threatened, to the horror of the palace servants, so she could be right there when I woke up screaming at night. She even climbed in bed with me a few times, holding me until I fell asleep. Neither of us really wanted company in this state, but it was unavoidable.

Zeniri, Lenara, and Razim were our most frequent visitors, but I'd also seen dozens of others with dozens upon dozens of questions, accusations, threats . . . Only reading aloud, playing Gods and Kings, and listening Razim's music, which he occasionally played for me, had made it bearable.

Not that Razim had an excess of spare time. In the few weeks that I hadn't left my room, Razim had been busier than he'd ever been in his life. While I was remembering how to feel again, he was learning how to rule a kingdom.

Not only that, he was actively dismantling the Twilight Guild with what knowledge he had of their members and their dealings. He couldn't weed out all of it, and much of it likely went to ground, but he did what he could. These were the people who had once been his comrades, whom his adoptive father had once worked alongside, but now that Razim understood their true purpose, he punished them without mercy. He even sent Nyaren, his friend, to the dungeons.

"*What's wrong?*" Zeniri threw Nikha's words back at her. "Look at her! Is she never going to wear something remotely presentable again?" He arched an eyebrow at Nikha. "Though I shouldn't expect you to be much help. Good thing you both have me."

Rather, it was a good thing—probably—that I cared about his insults. Feeling anything at all felt nice, even if it was the sting of indignation.

Zeniri noticed it in my expression. "Feeling less numb, are we? That's not the only thing that's receding. Your eyes look better, though they're the only part of you that does."

Less shadowed, he meant. Indeed, the darkness under my eyes had faded, if not the shadow over my heart.

"At least you can no longer cheat at Gods and Kings," he said, changing the subject, no doubt sensing my clouding mood. Zeniri hadn't been a good spy purely because he was a soulwalker—the man was as sharp as a honed dagger. I was glad he was on my side. Most of the time.

"She doesn't need to cheat to win," Nikha muttered, flopping back down on the bed. "She destroyed me earlier. And yesterday, and the day before that."

"Another indication she's feeling better."

I narrowed my eyes at him. "Better enough for what?"

He grinned. "The ceremony, of course."

"*What* ceremony?"

"Razim didn't tell you?" His voice was all too innocent.

"No, he didn't," I said, "and I'm not going anywhere."

"That's probably why he didn't tell you. And now with me here, you can't run away." He waved his arms at me. "Go, get out of those rags. The servants are already drawing a bath in the other room. In the meantime, I'll pick out something properly humble and penitent."

Which meant he would pick something out that was precisely the opposite.

"Zeniri, I'm a regicide. No one cares if I'm sorry. And no one wants me at any ceremony."

"Even if it's *your* ceremony?"

My mouth fell open. "You can't be serious."

"Of course! Our lovely lad—excuse me, *king*—needs to put a less official but no less important stamp on your pardon with a celebration. It's only fitting."

Razim had pardoned everyone who'd tried to thwart the Twilight Guild—including Lenara, Zeniri, Nikha, and me. Especially me. Several of his advisers called for my punishment, even execution, never mind what else I might have done. I had killed the king, just like Razim's and my fated game of Gods and Kings had once foreshadowed. An unforgivable sin. And I had also meddled in souls.

But I had done it in service of the land, and saved Razim's life, his soul, and the realm while I was at it. So, since he was the new king, he had some say in the matter. He pardoned me without condition.

Likewise, Zeniri could walk around the palace freely because "unauthorized" soulwalkers such as my mother and he had played a large part in helping me. Razim looked upon the old problem of their existence in a fresh light and established a new guild, monitored by the priests and priestesses of Heshara, for soulwalkers who didn't wish to be trapped in a temple and robes. There was no longer only a choice between the clergy or imprisonment and death. Razim made Zeniri the head of it, since everyone agreed he couldn't simply go back to the pleasure arts. I became the first signed member, after him, of the Soulwalkers Guild. It was also excellent recruiting grounds for the Keepers, though that fact was kept quiet, of course.

Not that there weren't still murmurs against me, the Soulwalkers Guild, and Razim himself.

"Zeniri—" I said, already feeling tired and overwhelmed.

"Ah!" He cut me off with a raised finger. "No arguments!"

I let him hustle me into the bathroom, where the servants undertook the unpleasant task of scrubbing hair that hadn't been washed in far too long. At least the steaming water felt nice. I sat there in silence, submerged up to my chin, contemplating how difficult an escape out the window would be.

It was only when the hands in my hair stilled and the room fell silent that I looked up. Lenara stood next to the bathtub, and the servants were quietly letting themselves out.

"Here to congratulate me on being a regicide, as well?" When she didn't answer, I asked, "How do those new robes feel?"

Shortly after Agrir's death, Lenara had been named the new high priestess in his place, due partially to her role in exposing and defeating his plan, which had been the greatest of blasphemies, and partially to *other* loyalties of hers within the clergy. Razim had no part in this decision, which made her support of him all the more convincing.

After her rise, both she and several other well-respected priests and priestesses of Heshara—members of the Keepers, she'd told me after—had sworn on their power that Razim hadn't had any ill intent toward his father and had never himself been a member of the Twilight Guild, and that the murder plot had been entirely Agrir's. It was a total fabrication, of course, but necessary, Lenara argued, for the stability of the kingdom. The new high priestess also supported the formation of the Soulwalkers Guild, and since she was the one ceding her own clergy's absolute control over soulwalking, no one could argue.

Lenara glanced down at her robes—those of a high priestess. "They don't feel entirely settled yet," she admitted grudgingly. "There are those among the king's advisory council and the nobility who still question everything, but none dare openly defy both the new king *and* the high priestess. Sooner or later, Razim will have to deal with those dissenters and their plotting and backstabbing that will make his rule less than smooth. But for now, everyone will put on a smile, even if they don't want to."

Even me.

"So I have to go to a party?" I muttered into the suds.

"Razim insists. As do I. People need to see your face—that it belongs to a young girl, not . . ."

"A killer?" I finished for her.

"I was going to say a traitor to the throne."

I winced.

Her hand found my shoulder, and her voice was soft. "Kamai, I'm sorry. For everything. For doubting you, for what you had to do. You're not a killer or a traitor. You're one of the bravest people I know. Your mother would be so, so proud of you."

"I saw my mother," I blurted. "Before I closed off the source of Darkness. She was there, her spirit, at least, held captive, but then I freed her. Before she left, she . . . she told me to tell you that she misses you."

Lenara's fingers flexed on my shoulder. "Thank—" It took a moment before she could get her voice under control. "Thank you for telling me. It means more than I can say, even if I can barely fathom it. I would like to discuss this more with you later, but for now I won't let you use it as an excuse to get out of the ceremony." She paused. "I'm asking you to be brave once again and put on whatever horror of a dress Zeniri chooses for you."

If I agreed, my first official outing from my rooms—other than my discreet walks at night in the gardens with Nikha—would be to go into a ballroom where everyone's eyes would be on me. Razim had insisted likely just to pry me out of my bed.

I ducked my head under the bathwater, wishing I could hide, but when I resurfaced, Lenara was still there.

"Fine," I said. I would have to face all this sooner or later.

She smiled at me, her expression radiant. But then it fell. "Before I go, I just want to check . . ."

I knew what she was going to ask. "It's closed, Lenara."

"You're sure—?"

"Yes, and I don't want to talk about it again."

Lenara left me in peace after that.

In front of a large audience in one of the palace's grand halls, Razim awarded me Ranta's Heart, granted for an act of supreme service to the kingdom. The ceremony involved his glowing speech, my acceptance of a beautiful bronze pendant, cast in a heart shape—which only reminded me of the hearts I'd stabbed or broken, my own included—and an excess of applause that sounded too loud to be entirely genuine. I mostly tried to imagine I was elsewhere. My off-the-shoulder, wine-colored silk gown didn't help—it was far too attention-grabbing, and I cursed Zeniri under my breath the whole time. So much for looking "penitent."

Jidras was in attendance. When he caught my eye, he gave me a tentative nod, which from him was like an embrace. Still, I knew it wasn't for me. Since I had saved the realm, I was now a Person of Importance. Only now was I worth acknowledging.

But if my mother could forgive him, so could I. I walked

over to him afterward, his eyes widening at my approach. He probably hadn't expected, nor wanted, me to find him.

"I saw Mother," I said. "Marin's spirit, in the sleeping realm." I didn't elaborate how, but by now everyone knew I had at least worked *some* sort of strange magic there. His eyes shot even wider. "She couldn't stay long before she . . . passed on . . . but she told me to tell you that she forgives you."

I gave him the same benediction as I had when I'd left his household, touching the crown of my head, the spot between my eyes, and my lips with three fingers. This time, I reached out and touched his lips.

I walked away soon after that, but not before I saw Jidras's face crumple.

My steps took me out onto an adjoining mosaic-speckled gallery, to look for fresh air. There were too many bodies around. For once, however, Nikha was enjoying herself with other people, drinking rather a lot of punch and laughing with a group of palace guards. I didn't want her to stop on my account, so I tried to escape her notice, sitting on a bench in a quiet corner.

Eventually, Razim sat down next to me, surprising me. His deep green brocade jacket painted the perfect picture with my wine-colored gown, and I wondered if it had been planned that way. He put his hand on mine before I could do more than shift on the bench, let alone say anything.

"You know, you would do me a great honor by becoming my queen consort." I looked at him in shock, and he grimaced. "No, that came out wrong. I would vastly prefer ruling this kingdom if I had you to help me do it."

I shook my head. "But . . . you don't even feel that way about me anymore."

It was true. Ever since I'd severed the connection between

our souls, the look in his eyes had been different. Softer, calmer. He still cared for me, but the possessive fire that had burned there was gone. I knew now it must have come from Vehyn's influence over him.

He sighed. "I know you better than anyone, and you know me better. You saved my life, despite . . ." Despite nearly killing him. "Despite everything. You saved my soul too, and *my* supposed kingdom . . . whereas I would have destroyed them both."

"Not you," I said. "That wasn't you. And the things you did by your own hand . . . Razim, you didn't know. My mother told me to tell you too: this wasn't your fault. Those were some of her last words, so listen to them." He blinked at the news. "You were just trying to seek revenge, like I was. And hey," I said, and laughed weakly, "you killed your father's killer, like you wanted—Agrir."

"My father . . . Hallan wasn't . . ." He choked slightly, cleared his throat.

"Hallan *was* your father," I said vehemently. "He loved you, so much that in the end he died for it. Just because the king was your blood, that doesn't mean he was your father."

This I knew all too well.

Razim sat quietly for a moment. "All of this aside, I can't think of anyone else I would rather have rule with me."

"You'll find someone." I tucked his hair behind his ear, and he leaned into my hand. "In the meantime, you have Lenara to help you. And you'll always have me as a friend. I'll be here whenever you need me, I promise."

Which was no small thing, as Nikha had proven, time and again.

He smiled ruefully. "It doesn't sound like you'll be *here* much, at least not for a while."

389

That was true. Nikha and I were soon going to travel, to spread the word about the Soulwalkers Guild and try to bring others like me out of hiding. That wasn't the only purpose of our adventure—Lenara had strongly hinted that it would be good for me to leave the city for a while, royal pardon aside, to let the murmurs die down. At least I would get to explore the land I had so long dreamed of seeing.

I tried not to think about my other dreams.

I focused, also, upon Nikha fulfilling her dreams. *His* dreams, soon. Before we were to travel, Lenara would declare Nikha soul-crossed, so she could finally accept the title of royal body-guard, even though she would only be guarding me, for the time being. More important, she would begin living as a man. She was ready now to do this for herself. *Himself.* Sometime later, when it felt comfortable, Nikha would take the name *Kihan*— different, masculine, but built with the letters of the old name, to honor it.

I wished I could rebuild myself from the pieces that were left. But I wasn't truly broken, I knew. Only time would heal my wounds. The least I could do, in the meantime, was honor myself, as I was.

Lenara didn't have to worry, as least not that the black door was sealed. I checked on it more often than I should have. So I knew precisely when the rose petals started to appear from under the crack at the bottom. Kihan—no longer Nikha, at least with me—and I were on the road, in a small town a few days out from the capital, roughly a month after I had killed the king.

I tried to ignore the petals at first, but they piled up in heaps that never withered or blew away. One day, I couldn't ignore them any longer. I swept them aside and wrote a note, on a small scrap of paper, thin enough to slide under the black door.

I can't think of a better use for my soul than to keep you from the world . . . nor can I think of a better keeper of it. The last part was my own rose petal. Soft and sweet, masking the sharper truth that came before.

The paper came back with black, angular print that looked like thorns but didn't prick . . . except for my heart. There, the words lodged.

I want to say something pithy here, but I find myself uninspired. The truth is: I love you, as much as I am capable of it. I wish I didn't, more powerfully than I've ever wished for anything, but there it is. The irrational, bitter, impotent truth.

Only he could make something so romantic sound unromantic. Or was it something so unromantic, romantic? I could have laughed if tears weren't building in my throat instead.

My feelings exactly, I wrote back.

Then why not open the door and join me? This night is lonely now, without you. And then: *I have changed. I'll be good. I promise.*

Had he truly changed? My mother had always taught me that men like that rarely did. Evil, abusive people were rotten in their souls, and nothing you could do would fix them. Vehyn's feelings for me didn't make him a better person, or more human. He'd probably loved me, in his own twisted way, from the very beginning, even as he'd hated me. But Vehyn's soul was my soul, and while *I* couldn't change him, perhaps the Darkness leaving him had.

Besides, he wasn't quite a man. Not only because he wasn't human, but because he was really only eighteen years old. That was when he had come into existence, and he'd been living with Darkness since then. Now, without it, perhaps he could truly grow. Become something new and different and . . . good.

But he would have to do that on his own, first, without me.

That didn't mean I didn't love him.

I'd learned another of my mother's teachings for myself: you couldn't help loving whom you loved. Or *how* you loved. I loved Vehyn, despite who he was, despite the dark power over me that he shouldn't have had. Maybe I even loved certain shades of *that*. That didn't make me evil, or wrong. But I also knew I needed to pull away before I got hurt too badly. Or when I needed to heal.

And now I trusted myself to know exactly when that was.

I leaned against the black door. The strange, living warmth touched me through my gown, and I could almost feel Vehyn's breath against my neck, his smile. I wrote two words on the paper—rose petals, perhaps.

Maybe someday.

I slid the paper back underneath, and I looked up at the shiny black globe of the doorknob, the stars of my clearing twinkling above it. Did it look like darkness against the sky, or a new moon?

Without deciding, I stood and walked away from the door, back to Kihan and the waking world.

Acknowledgments

Thank you to everyone who believed in this book. I wrote it for teen-me who never saw myself on the page and who thought, because of that, something was wrong with me and not what was getting published. After writing the book, I still found myself wondering if I was the only one who would want to read it, but luckily the enthusiasm of others helped carry me through those times.

Thanks especially to my editor John Morgan, publisher Erin Stein, and the whole team at Imprint for not only publishing this book, but publishing it proudly. John loved the parts that were dearest to me when I thought they would have to be cut, and even encouraged me to dive deeper, to say it louder. Thanks to Kirsten Carleton, for championing this book from my first pitch to pitching it to editors, and for finding it such a perfect home.

Finally, thank you so much to my earliest readers who suffered through the roughest drafts: Lukas Strickland, Michael Miller, and Deanna Birdsall. You guys are my pillars. Many thanks also to my unflagging, amazing critique partner, Chelsea Pitcher, and to beta readers, Katherine Locke, Tyler Murphy, Rosiee Thor, and especially Terran Williams, for giving me such thoughtful feedback. And finally, thank you to those future readers who have been so enthusiastic without having read it yet because you suspect you might see yourself in these pages. It means more to me than I can say to share this with you.

About the Author

A.M. Strickland was a bibliophile who wanted to be an author before she knew what either of those words meant. She shares a home base in Alaska with her husband, her pugs, and her piles and piles of books. She loves traveling, dancing, tattoos, and every shade of teal in existence, but especially the darker ones. Find her on Twitter @AdriAnneMS.